"I'm sorry. I didn't mean to frighten you." Duane's voice was soft, comforting.

Destiny glanced up at him. Her chest was heaving, and moisture shimmered in her eyes.

Curving an arm around her shoulders, he pulled her close and cradled her head to his chest. He was surprised when she wrapped her arms around him. Her breasts trembled above her rib cage; her chest fell and rose rapidly beneath her shirt. His protective instincts kicked in, and he knew his cry had little to do with it. Something else had scared her. He pulled her closer, feeling a strong need to protect the vulnerable woman in his arms.

Expelling a deep breath, he tried not to think about how she felt just like he had dreamed. Her lush body pressed against his felt so good; he had almost forgotten how wonderful it felt to hold a woman. Holding her, he felt the heat from Destiny's body seep into his, the sensation too vibrant to ignore. What was it about this beautiful young woman that affected him in a way that no woman had in a long time?

He continued to ponder that question until the runaway beat of her heart slowed. Her arms fell away, but she didn't move.

"Are you okay?" he whispered against her hair.

Raising her chin, she stared up at him. She read concern and trustworthiness in his dark gaze. His hold was protective. Could she trust Duane? she wondered. It was too soon to tell.

Destiny forced a smile she did not feel and fumbled for a lie to divert him from prying. "I'm fine. Just a little shaken up, but I'll be all right. How about I make us some more eggs?"

She nibbled on her lower lip and rendered Duane momentarily speechless. All he could do was stare at her mouth, taking in her perfectly white teeth and sexy lips, and wonder how they'd taste beneath his.

"Duane?" he heard her call.

Shaking the thought away, he focused on her puzzled look before allowing his eyes to travel down past her neck. What he noticed was far more tempting than her nibbling nervously on her lip.

DESTINY IN DISGUISE

ANGIE DANIELS

ARABESQUE

BET★ BOOKS

BET Publications, LLC
http://www.bet.com
http://www.arabesquebooks.com

ARABESQUE BOOKS are published by

BET Publications, LLC
c/o BET BOOKS
One BET Plaza
1900 W Place NE
Washington, DC 20018-1211

All Kensington Titles, Imprints, and Distributed Lines are available at special quantity discounts for bulk purchases for sales promotions, premiums, fund-raising, and educational or institutional use. Special book excerpts or customized printings can also be created to fit specific needs. For details, write or phone the office of the Kensington special sales manager: Kensington Publishing Corp., 850 Third Avenue, New York, NY 10022, attn: Special Sales Department, Phone: 1-800-221-2647.

BET Books is a trademark of Black Entertainment Television, Inc. ARABESQUE, the ARABESQUE logo, and the BET BOOKS logo are trademarks and registered trademarks.

First Printing: December 2005

10 9 8 7 6 5 4 3 2 1

Printed in the United States of America

This book is dedicated to my children
Mark, Ashlie, and Evan. Mama loves you!

ACKNOWLEDGMENTS

Thanks to all my readers, as I could not have made it this far without your words of encouragement.

It's wonderful to have a network of authors that I call my friends. Shouts out to Michele "Toni" Sudler, Doreen Rainey, and Toni Staton Harris. Thanks for all the love and support.

To my dogs, Nikki and Champion, Mama loves you both so much that I can't stop writing about you!

To my family, words can't begin to express how much you all mean to me. Thanks for your continued love and encouragement.

Prologue

Desiree Davidson parked her Buick between two late-model vehicles and shut off the engine. She then flipped the visor down and peered at her reflection in the small mirror. Peering through dorky glasses with clear plastic lenses that had no corrective power at all, she resembled Steve Urkel.

There's nothing you can do about that now.

Reaching up, she pushed a strand of her long, cinnamon-colored hair safely beneath a Cardinals' baseball cap. Her hands were shaking and for a very good reason. As she took several deep, calming breaths, she reminded herself that as long as she wore the disguise, it would be virtually impossible for anyone to recognize her.

Stepping out of the car, Desiree quickly shut the door and scrambled from beneath the glaring streetlights onto the sidewalk. She walked rapidly, glancing nervously over her shoulder every three or four steps.

Cleveland pear trees along the street bore the bright stamp of spring; they were green with bouquets of lovely white blossoms, which released a floral fragrance that floated through the air. But Desiree didn't have time to appreciate the beauty of the neighborhood. She had to get out of sight as quickly as possible. With her sharp-eyed gaze, alert for trouble, she scanned the area in front of her as she drew closer to her destination.

While still looking furtively over her shoulders, she turned at the corner. From there, it was an easy hike through an alley for the next two hundred yards. She felt her heart pumping rapidly against her chest, yet didn't realize she was running until she stepped on a soda bottle and almost lost her balance.

Desiree reached a four-foot chain-link fence and scaled it with very little difficulty. Once she had reached the top, she climbed over effortlessly and landed on a thick green lawn in back of a house. Staying low, she moved toward the corner of the house, where she carefully opened a small basement window and climbed through.

I made it.

After exhaling a sigh of relief, she couldn't resist a smile as she lowered the window and snapped the lock firmly back in place.

The things I'll do for Denzel.

In fact, she loved the award-winning actor so much, there was no way she would not have been in attendance at the sneak preview showing of his new movie that night. The action-packed thriller was worth all the trouble she had gone through to be there.

Would it have been worth it if someone had recognized you?

The smile vanished from her face as she suddenly realized that she wasn't in the clear quite yet. She still had to make it up to her room unnoticed.

Removing her glasses, she laid them and the baseball cap on top of a box of books beneath the window, then moved toward the other end of the basement.

Desiree ascended the stairs, then slowly opened the door, expecting to find Jarvis sitting at the small kitchen table, waiting. Instead, the kitchen was just as she had left it. The chicken she had fried earlier was still sitting on a plate on top of the stove. The homemade buttermilk biscuits also looked untouched. She frowned. Jarvis loved her cooking so much, there were rarely ever any leftovers. Also, he would have already eaten by now. Glancing down at her wristwatch, she frowned again. Jarvis always had the television on, especially at ten o'clock on Wednesdays. For as long as they'd been together, he had never missed an episode of *Law & Order,* even if he was working. The thought made the hairs on the back of her neck prickle.

Where the heck is he?

The house was completely still, except for the chirping of an annoying smoke detector. Her eyes traveled to the ceiling, where she watched a red light blink. Just yesterday she had threatened Jarvis with bodily harm if he didn't get a ladder and change the battery in the detector. With a hearty laugh, he promised to replace it the next day. Only he hadn't. If the ceiling wasn't nine feet high, she would have changed it herself. Either that or taken a rock and knocked the device from its mount on the ceiling.

She remembered that when she had made the comment about the rock, Jarvis had scolded her as if she were a child, then reminded her that the house wasn't theirs to destroy. The rental property belonged to a doctor on sabbatical in Australia.

"Jarvis?" Desiree called as she stepped out into the

foyer. Except for the moonlight streaming in through the floor-to-ceiling windows, the living room was relatively dark and silent. Shifting slightly, she stared up at the top of the winding staircase. His room was the first one on the right. Surely, he had heard her calling his name, she thought to herself.

Maybe he's asleep.

With an exasperated sigh, Desiree climbed the stairs, then took the hallway to the right, where there were six bedrooms. While Jarvis's was at the front, she occupied the one on the very end. She stopped in front of the first door. Discovering it shut, Desiree tapped lightly on it with her knuckles.

"Jarvis?"

Silence.

"Jarvis!"

Still silence.

Her mind began playing tricks on her. And for the first time since she had crawled in through the window, she remembered why she was living in this house. Then that all too familiar ache of dread reminded her that her life was in danger.

Desiree now had the strongest impulse to bolt out the front door and run as far and fast as she could manage. Had Lucas Blake's goons found her?

No, that couldn't be. Officer Jarvis Jackson had assured her that her whereabouts were a secret.

Desiree willed herself to remain calm despite the shiver snaking up her spine. "Jarvis," she called again. Her voice had grown weak and unsteady.

There was still no answer. With her ear to Jarvis's door, the only thing she could hear was her own heartbeat thundering in her ears. Taking a deep breath, she drummed up enough courage to reach for the knob. Her hand shook uncontrollably, but she managed to turn the knob and push his bedroom door open.

At first glance she found the heavy blue drapes drawn and the room pitch-black. Running her palm along the wall to her left, she located the light switch and turned it on.

Desiree gasped when she spotted Jarvis lying on the floor beside the queen-size bed. One hand clutched his side, where blood oozed between his fingers.

"Jarvis!" she cried as she rushed into the room and sank to her knees beside him. Quickly, Desiree yanked the blanket off the bed and pressed it to his wound, hoping to slow the flow of blood. Her eyes darted quickly around the room as she made certain she was alone with Jarvis and also looked for anything out of the ordinary. Other than an overturned chair, nothing—except for Jarvis—appeared to be out of place.

Glancing back down at the old man, who had become a dear friend in just a few short weeks, she saw that his eyes were closed and the color had drained from his olive face.

"Hold on, Jarvis, please," she pleaded. "I'm gonna call for help." With one hand, she continued to apply pressure to the wound while with the other, she reached as far as she could and grabbed the phone cord. Yanking the phone off the nightstand, she then dragged it over to her and placed the receiver to her ear. But before she could dial 911, Jarvis's hand came up to grasp her arm, his fingers cold and clammy against her skin.

"Get . . . out," his words were garbled but clear enough for her to understand. A fit of coughing took over, and blood bubbled at the corners of his mouth. "Trust . . . no one," he said with one deep final breath.

Desiree watched helplessly as his eyes flickered before his body went limp and his head dangled to the side.

"Officer Jackson is dead."

"And the girl?" asked a man with a strong Hispanic accent.

The question was greeted by prolonged silence.

"What about the girl?" he repeated impatiently.

"S-she got away."

"You stupid fool! I should have taken care of this myself," the man with the accent growled through the phone.

"I'll handle it."

"You'd better. There is no way she can go to court and testify!" he snapped before slamming down the phone.

Chapter 1

Duane Urban strode up the sidewalk to the dilapidated house and shook his head. The wooden trim had begun to rot, and thick weeds choked the path that led to a dangerously sagging porch. The property looked as if it had been abandoned for years, when in reality, it had been vacant less than two years.

The house had belonged to Benjamin Barton, a kind old gentleman from Baton Rouge, who had shared countless tales of the time he had served in World War II. Almost two years prior, he had lost his battle with lung cancer. The ramshackle house had not been occupied since.

As he stepped over dead branches, lying where they had fallen from a large oak tree in front of the house, Duane remembered Benny, as they all had called him, telling him about his only next of kin, an older sister, who was too old to travel. It seemed that she had finally decided to come, despite her age and weariness. Then again, depending on her health, she may have sent someone on her behalf.

He stepped onto the rickety porch that stretched

across the front of the house. The place was quiet and still, other than the creaking sound of rotting wood under his feet.

It was mid-May and the weather was mild, yet all the windows were shut and the shades drawn. In fact, if it hadn't been for the light shining from the living room window, or the phone message Duane had found on his answering machine when he returned home that evening, he would have assumed the house was still vacant.

Raising his hand, he put his finger on the doorbell and pressed firmly. He didn't hear the chime. However, instead of ringing it again, he decided to wait and give the woman inside an opportunity to get to the door.

He had received a call from a Ms. Destiny Davis, asking if he would be interested in doing some minor repairs in and around the property. He had laughed at the message. With one quick glance at the house, anyone could honestly say there was nothing *minor* about what it needed. Luckily for her, he had some spare time until the end of the month.

Last summer he had formed Urban Designs & Improvements, and in doing so, had resigned from his position with one of the largest contracting firms in the state of Delaware. At one time, he had questioned his decision, but it wasn't long before he realized there was nothing like being his own boss. Thanks to the numerous referrals that had come his way, he had established a steady client base and had enough projects to keep him busy for the rest of the year.

Certain he had given Ms. Davis plenty of time to respond, he reached up, turned a handle, and opened a beat-up screen door. The steel door behind it had a stained glass window, preventing him from seeing if anyone was inside.

As Duane knocked on the pane, he had to admit that he was curious to meet the woman who had left the message. Her deep, sultry voice had immediately invoked images of a petite woman with lush curves and large bedroom eyes. He scowled at the silly idea. He knew she couldn't be Benny's eighty-something-year-old sister. However, the mystery woman was probably approaching her sixties, even though her voice was quite misleading.

Realizing what he was doing, Duane scowled again. His imagination was a result of being too long without a woman. Nevertheless, after several failed relationships, Duane was beginning to think that being single was probably the smartest decision he had ever made.

Glancing down at his watch, he noticed it was almost eight o'clock. *Maybe she's already gone to bed.* He decided to ring the doorbell one more time. He pressed the button again, then dropped his hand. He waited several seconds and was about to turn and leave when he heard movement inside. Then, with the chain lock still firmly in place, she cracked the door open slightly.

Duane's breath caught in his throat. The woman who stood before him was certainly no sixty-year-old. With short, dark brown hair framing a small face and revealing a long neck and slim, sexy shoulders, she had to be around thirty.

Staring into those arresting eyes of hers, he felt as if he had been hit over the head. They were the color of a polished new penny, large and lushly lashed, with unexpected depths. He forced himself to speak. "Destiny?"

"Who are you?" she asked, eyeing him warily. Apparently, she wasn't too pleased to find him standing inside her screen door.

He smiled at her as he spoke. "Duane Urban. You asked me to drop by."

She continued to stare at him suspiciously. "You got some ID?"

He reached into his back pocket, removed his wallet, and held his driver's license close enough for her to view. His eyes clung to her, analyzing her reaction. After Destiny gave his license a thorough once over, he watched her shoulders sag with relief and her expression softened.

A flush swept over her cheeks as she raised her eyes to find him watching her. "You can never be too careful," she replied, as if apologizing for her reaction.

Her voice was softer in person. Even so, the sound shot a new wave of pleasure through him.

Pulling himself together, Duane nodded. "I have a sister, so I completely understand." He was protective of his younger sister and fully understood that in this day and age, one could never be too careful.

She smiled, yet her eyes were distant and still full of distrust. Destiny closed the door long enough to unfasten the lock; then she stepped aside so he could enter.

Duane paused inside the door frame. "Let's try this again . . . Duane Urban."

He watched the corners of her lips twitch in amusement. "Nice to meet you. I'm Destiny Davis." Her long, slender fingers disappeared as his large hand closed around them. At contact, the softness of her skin ignited a searing heat that burned the moisture from his mouth. Using his tongue, he quickly wet his lips and pried them apart.

"The pleasure is all mine," he finally said. *A sexy name for a sexy woman.* Just the sound alone said intimacy.

After releasing her hand, Duane entered the narrow foyer. The smell of potpourri was prominent in the air. Stepping into the small living room to his left, he noticed that the flooring changed from wood to brown shag carpeting. Benny's familiar living room brought back memories. In the middle was a large, worn-out green couch, where Duane had sat many evenings watching the news with his good friend.

After Benny's funeral, the house had gone under estate management, and the furniture had been covered. The sheets had since been removed, and the rooms looked clean and more alive than ever before.

Glancing over his shoulder at his hostess, Duane noticed that Destiny was still standing near the door with her lips pressed firmly together. His gaze lingered on her face. And what an exquisite face it was: delicately carved, mouth full, nose short and charming. He forced himself not to gawk at perfection, even though he was stunned by the beauty of the woman before him.

Snap out of it. You're going to scare the lady.

He cleared his throat. "It looks like you're getting settled in."

Destiny blinked her eyes as if clearing her thoughts. Then her expression changed from leery to relaxed so quickly, Duane thought he had imagined it.

A smile tipped the corners of her lips as she spoke. "Not quite. I'm trying to liven up the place. Everything in here is either too old or too dark and dreary. But I thought I would focus on one room at a time."

The glow of her smile warmed him from across the room. "Smart move. Why don't you show me what you want me to work on first?"

Nodding, Destiny brushed passed him, leaving behind the sweet scent of freshly cut flowers.

Duane followed her down the hall toward the kitchen while silently admiring how shapely her backside looked in a pair of black Capri pants. Her waist was small; her hips were round. He wasn't sure which view he liked better, the front or the back. Both looked sensational.

Destiny stopped at a large hole in the floor of the kitchen. Duane halted before running smack into her.

"What happened here?" he asked, glad for somewhere else to focus his attention.

Destiny stepped around the hole and turned around so she was facing him, then shrugged a slender shoulder. "The floor must be rotten. All I did was use a chair to change that lightbulb." She pointed to a light socket directly over the hole. "I had barely applied any weight when one of the legs of the chair fell through."

His eyes traveled down to the bottom of her pants, which stopped right below her calves. There he got a glimpse of her shapely, nut brown legs. "Did you get hurt?" he asked. His voice was filled with genuine concern.

He towered over her by more than a foot. The top of her head barely reached his shoulder. Tilting her head, she said, with a significant lifting of her eyebrows, "Thank goodness, no. The chair tipped over, but I managed to land safely on my feet."

He nodded, surprised by his need to ensure her safety. He barely knew her, and already he was concerned.

Duane removed the measuring tape from his utility belt. "How did you know to call me?"

"I found one of your business cards on the refrigerator and another one in the bedroom. So I figured that you and my great-uncle were friends, or that you had done work for him in the past."

He glanced up at the water-stained ceiling, then down at the linoleum, which was cracked and peeling. "If this kitchen is any indication of the work in store for me, I'm in trouble," he teased.

Destiny raised a hand to her mouth, trying unsuccessfully to stifle her laughter. When she lowered her arm, Duane felt the jolt of that gorgeous smile deep in the pit of him, like the heat that warmed his chest after taking a shot of good cognac. He tried to shake it off and focused his attention on the size of the hole. Something was happening between them, and he wasn't too sure how he felt about the emotions stirring within.

"If you don't mind, I need to go down in the basement and check the underside of this subflooring."

"Sure, the stairs are right there." She pointed to a door in the corner of the kitchen, near the hallway.

Rising to his feet, Duane opened the door and descended the stairs. At the bottom, he pulled a chain and switched on the light.

Alone at last, he was thankful for a few minutes away from the intriguing young woman. So that was Benny's niece, he thought. *Very interesting.* His attraction to her was like nothing he had ever experienced. There was something about her that evoked bursts of desire and challenged his grasp on his self-control. He would just have to find a way to contain himself.

Taking a deep breath, he found the small concrete room dry and musty. It was a good sign. He maneuvered around a room full of old furniture to the area where a hole as big as his fist had worn clear through. For the next few minutes he focused on the damage, temporarily suppressing the realization that he was more than attracted to Ms. Destiny Davis.

After taking several quick measurements, he calculated that the subfloor was three-fourths of an inch thick. It would be a simple job to complete.

Returning his measuring tape to his belt, he looked up again. Big, bright eyes stared down at him through the hole. Destiny was kneeling on the floor beside the hole.

"What do you think?" she asked.

I think you're beautiful. "I wanted to make sure the rotting wasn't a result of a plumbing leak."

"Is it?" She continued to gaze at him, eyes wide with curiosity.

Duane had a strong desire to hold her in his arms and reassure her that everything was going to be just fine. "No. Discolored areas on the floor usually indicate a plumbing leak. Luckily for you, that's not the case. The structure of this floor is strong. However, the rotting is right where two boards meet a joist." He paused, realizing he was probably talking way over her head. "Do you understand anything about flooring?"

"Some."

"Well . . . subfloors are typically constructed from three-by-four sheets of lumber and are laid diagonally across joists. This here is a joist." He pointed to the large two-by-four beam that was visible through the hole in the floor. They are the primary support. What I'll need to do is replace a considerable area." He quoted her a drastically reduced rate.

She nodded. "Whatever you think is best." She gave him a warm and trusting look before she rose and moved away from the hole.

As soon as she was gone, Duane forced himself to breathe again. When he felt his emotions had been contained, he moved back upstairs. However, as soon as he saw Destiny leaning against the kitchen counter, looking expectantly at him, with her arms folded beneath her generous breasts, his control vanished.

"Where are you from?" he asked, with nothing better to say. He had to do whatever he could to stay focused.

"Uh . . . south."

The uneasiness of her voice drew his complete attention. "Oh, yeah, what part?"

"I'm from San Antonio," she answered with a bit more confidence.

He furrowed his brow. "You don't sound like a Southerner."

She tilted his head slightly. "That's because I grew up in the Midwest."

Duane nodded, then crouched down and reached for his measuring tape again. He made a show of extending it across the length of the hole. He had already measured the damage below but desperately needed a distraction. If he didn't do something with his hands, he might have found himself pulling her body against his.

"What brings you to Dover?" he asked, continuing with his questioning and not bothering to look at her.

He heard a soft sigh. "I needed a change of scenery while I'm working on my Master's thesis."

He made another mental note of the measurements, then hit the button and retracted the tape. "What are you studying?" This time he looked at her, and their eyes collided.

Pausing for several seconds, she finally said, "English."

"Ouch! I was never any good at conjugating verbs."

She smiled, and her eyes crinkled attractively. "According to my instructor, neither am I."

Duane chuckled as he rose again to his full height. He knew everything he needed to know in order to repair the floor, but suddenly he found he wasn't in any rush to leave. "So tell me a little bit about life in Texas."

She shrugged, then turned and walked toward the refrigerator. "What else is there to tell besides Texas being very hot and sticky?" She gave an odd laugh. "Would you like something to drink?"

He lifted his brow, looking at her profile uncertainly. Why did he feel like she was changing the subject?

"Sure. That would be great." He let the subject drop, although what he wanted was to discuss Destiny Davis. For some unknown reason, he wanted to know everything there was to know about her.

Destiny removed a liter of orange soda from the fridge, then gestured to him to have a seat at the small table.

Tearing his eyes away, for the first time he noticed that the kitchen was clean and fresh. Gone was the clutter on the counters. Benny had had a horrible habit of saving everything.

"I haven't had a chance to do any major shopping; otherwise, I would offer you some cookies or something," she said apologetically as she reached into the cabinet, removed two glasses, and carried them over to the table.

"That's okay. I stopped and picked up a couple of burgers on the way home."

She nodded as she reached for a pitcher. "I spent most of the day lining the cabinets with paper and cleaning this kitchen."

"I was going to say that I've never seen the kitchen this clean."

She smiled knowingly. "My uncle wasn't much of a housekeeper, was he?"

"No, he wasn't," he said with a laugh.

She poured him a large glass, then handed it to him. Duane thanked her, then took a long, thirsty sip. "Ahh, that's just what I needed."

A slight smile parted her curvy lips as she glanced casually at him, causing an electrical charge to run through him. "How long have you been here?" he asked.

She took the seat opposite him and rested her forearms on the table. "I arrived on Tuesday."

It was Thursday, so she had already been in Dover, Delaware three days.

"I'm surprised I didn't see you before today."

She shifted her gaze out the window. "I've been inside most of the time."

He watched her nibble on her bottom lip for several seconds before he realized he was staring and tore his eyes away. Needing a diversion, he allowed his eyes to travel around the room again before returning to her. "I tried for years to get Benny to let me do some work around here."

She gazed at him with a perfectly arched eyebrow, and once again he found himself trapped in the intensity.

"Benny?"

He offered her a warm smile. "Yeah, that's what he was called. Actually, that's the only name anyone around here knew him by. He was a great guy . . . just stuck in the past."

Resting her chin in her hand, Destiny stared passed him. "My grandmother used to talk about my uncle quite a bit. I met him when I was young, but that was so long ago, I don't remember. However, before he died, he and I talked on the phone quite a bit."

Watching her kind expression, Duane wondered why Benny had never mentioned having such a beautiful niece. Remembering how often Benny had misplaced his keys, Duane suspected there were quite a few things his dear friend had forgotten to mention. "Maybe sometime over coffee I can tell you about him."

Her eyelids lowered slightly, concealing her deepset eyes. "I'd like that," she said softly.

Although innocent, the gesture was sensual enough to cause his breath to catch in his throat. A smile tilted her lips, and Duane wondered idly if they were as soft and inviting as they appeared. Just thinking about kissing her sent a tremor of excitement quivering low in his belly. "When would you like for me to replace the floor?"

"The sooner the better. I would then like to do something about the porch before working on the bathroom. I tried to run a bath, and the water was rusty."

"Try running it for thirty seconds. It should clear

up." He raised his glass to his lips and finished his drink. "I can begin working on the floor early tomorrow morning; then I can start on the porch next week."

"That would be wonderful." She rose and he followed. "I hope I'm not taking you away from anything."

Duane fought a war of emotions. He wanted to work with Destiny, but he also knew that if he undertook the projects, it meant interacting with her. Her presence reminded him of what he had been lacking. The stirring of desire brought back a yearning for intimacy, which he had missed for more than six months. If he stuck around long enough, just looking at her wouldn't be enough. He would need to touch her, to hold her, and before he had a chance to realize it, kissing would no longer satisfy his hunger.

He didn't know what it was, but he couldn't keep his eyes off of her. Her smooth skin looked soft and touchable, and her hair was a perfect complement for her startling, copper brown eyes. He had to put his hands in his pockets to keep from reaching out to touch her.

Being the gentleman that he was, he didn't have the heart to tell her no. Nor did he have the desire to do so. He would just have to keep his guard up.

"No, not at all. I just finished remodeling a kitchen for a couple. I have a few minor jobs scheduled before I begin a major project in a couple of weeks. Otherwise, I am at your service."

When her eyes slid up to search his face, Duane couldn't help looking at her for the longest time without saying anything. The air between them seemed to dance with tiny electric sparks that made him tingle. He tried to ignore the fluttering in his stomach.

Why was his heart racing wildly? The sensation moved through him, an excitement he didn't understand. Then there, in the middle of the quiet room, he wondered what it would be like to hold her, skim his hands over that soft flesh, and make love to her. He was startled to realize that Destiny Davis was the first woman he'd ever met that made him want more with one single glance.

She tensed as if she also had made the shocking discovery. Duane stepped back from the intensity and tried to push the emotion aside so he could think clearly.

"Well, I better get home," he said unevenly, then added, "I have an appointment early in the morning." He turned, and they both headed toward the front door.

"Thank you so much," she said with a bright smile.

He winked at her. "No problem, and let me be the first to welcome you to the neighborhood."

Her eyes widened. "Oh, do you live around here?"

He paused in the doorway long enough to say in parting, "I live right across the street."

Across the street!

Destiny stared at his retreating back as he strolled down the sidewalk. He hadn't exaggerated, Destiny thought, as she watched him cross the street and enter the house directly facing hers.

She pushed the door shut and automatically snapped both locks in place, then took extra care to turn the new dead bolt. Turning around, she leaned against the door and breathed heavily. She was disturbed by a desire too strong to ignore.

Duane was nothing like she had envisioned. Since he was a friend of her great-uncle, she had expected a visit from a middle-aged man. Instead, he was younger and more handsome than any man had a right to be. On her doorstep had been a sable-colored brotha with thick, sensual lips and a voice that made her body hum. His close-cropped hair was the only indication that he was older than her, as it was sprinkled with flecks of gray. However, the gray only intensified his masculine appearance.

When his fingers had clasped around hers in greeting, the pressure of his hand had spread warmth to the depths of her body. His intimate study of her had sent a strange sensation racing down her spine. Those cocoa-colored eyes of his had taken in everything about her, from her lips, down to her throat, and then even lower. His slow, appraising look had unnerved her. A wave of sensation seemed to flow from him, curling around her, taking her breath away. From the way he had stared at her, she suspected the attraction was mutual.

She inhaled, bracing herself. She wouldn't let her emotions intimidate her. Duane Urban was exactly what she didn't need. Not now. She didn't need any more complications in her life. Quickly, she reminded herself why she was in Delaware and shook off the lingering thoughts. She had to keep her focus. Her future depended on it.

Stepping away from the door, she moved to a large window in the living room and adjusted the heavy, dark beige drapes, ensuring there was no way anyone could peep through the glass and see inside. Momentarily satisfied, she strolled into the kitchen, where she poured herself a cup of decaf coffee, then returned to the living room. Curling up at the end of the couch, she tried to make sense of everything that was going through her mind.

The lies had already begun.

Before she had fled from Missouri, she had been attending classes at Saint Louis University working on an MBA. While reading a three-day-old newspaper, she had discovered that evening Master's courses were offered at Wilmington College. Posing as a graduate student would be the perfect cover.

Destiny settled back against the cushions, disappointed. She wished she could participate in their program. Taking classes would help pass the time. However, enrolling meant registering, and registering meant requesting transcripts, which meant revealing her true identity. She couldn't afford to take the risk.

Breathing in the coffee's aroma, she stared out into the hallway, trying again to make some sense of it all. Instead, she felt a painful tinge of despair.

After Jarvis was murdered, she had stuck around long enough to grab her laptop; a suitcase full of money, which she was thankful she had kept hidden in the attic; and Jarvis's gun. Then she retraced her steps, hopped into her car, and drove as far away from Chicago as she could get. She had done everything she could to cover her tracks.

At least I hope so.

The clatter of the cup on the saucer caused her to shiver. She lowered them to the end table, then scrubbed her face with her hand, which came away shaky and damp with tears. Tears had become as familiar to her as breathing.

Before Jarvis, the only person she had watched die was her grandmother. Unlike Jarvis, Nana had died of natural causes. In the short time that they had been cooped up in that rented house together, she had grown quite fond of Jarvis. He had reminded her of her grandfather who had died of a massive stroke when she was barely ten.

Holding his hand and watching Jarvis struggle for his last breath would be forever embedded in her brain. Terrible regret assailed her. If Jarvis hadn't been assigned to protect her, the burly old man would still be alive today.

Destiny dried her hands off on her pants, then reached for her cup again. Taking a large swallow, she tried unsuccessfully to alleviate the lump of despair in her throat.

After she had made certain there was nothing else she could do for Jarvis, she had left the house and called for help. While sitting in her car a couple of blocks away from the house, she had watched the sirens race past her. Tears had streamed down her cheeks. For the first time she had realized she was alone and had no place else to go.

Her mother had walked away from her when she was just a little girl. Her father, she had never known. If it hadn't been for Nana, she would have been an orphan.

After her grandmother had passed, she had been all alone. That is . . . until Lucas came into her life.

"Don't go there," she warned herself firmly. But it was too late. Her mind had already begun to drift. Closing her eyes, she relived the painful memories.

She was at a mall, signing copies of her latest best-selling novel, *Intrigue,* when he stopped at her table. She had raised her eyes to find the prettiest man she had ever had the opportunity of meeting. Lucas Blake was six feet two inches tall with a warm, tawny brown complexion and the lightest brown eyes she had even seen. His hair was coal black, straight, and long enough to brush his shoulders.

He had told her she was his sister's favorite author, and since she had been unable to attend, he had volunteered to appear on her behalf. By the time Destiny had autographed a copy for his sister, Lucas had given her his business card and had asked her to dinner.

After six months of dating, Destiny had thought she had found her prince. Their time together had been the happiest period of her life. Surrounded by his family and friends, for once she had felt part of a family. And she looked forward to having her own someday with him.

How wrong she had been.

She took another sip of her coffee and scowled when she discovered it was cold. Rising, she returned to the kitchen for a fresh cup. As she stepped over the hole in the floor, Duane's face came to mind again. He had eyes that seemed to read deep inside one's soul. The distinct scent of his aftershave still lingered in the air. Despite everything that was happening in her life, she was looking forward to seeing him tomorrow.

She refilled her cup, then moved over near the window and stared out while she sipped. Night had fallen. Stars were shining bright. The neighborhood was located in an historical section of Dover and had a great number of row houses, mansions, and mom-and-pop stores. From what she could tell, this particular street had been preserved. That is, everything but her uncle's house, she thought with a chuckle. It looked like something out of a fifties movie. The television was so old, the cable guy had laughed at her when he had tried that morning to install cable. He was quick to inform her that the twenty-four-inch black and white, with its turn dial and rabbit ears, was not going to work. She was going to have to buy one that had been designed in the latter half of the twentieth century.

She had to agree, the house could use numerous upgrades—its radiator heating, rattling plumbing, and old furniture covered in plastic needed attention. She had her hands full. But with everything happening in her life, she was actually glad for something else to do. She had plenty of time to work on the house when she wasn't writing. She was going to be in Delaware for at least six weeks. She might as well make herself at home.

Glancing down at the warped floor, she instantly thought of Duane again. He was definitely eye candy. From the first moment she had seen him, her female hormones had shifted into overdrive. As she continued to drink her coffee, she realized it wasn't just his smooth, dark skin that had instantly attracted her. It was the dimpled smile and those hard, muscular thighs, which were encased in his jeans.

Duane had filled the air with his presence and had reminded her of everything she was missing. She didn't know why, but the virile man made her feel comfortable. Sighing, she wrapped her arms around her midsection and for just a moment allowed herself the luxury of imagining what it would be like to be held by his strong arms. She sensed that he was a man who knew about passion.

Destiny snapped her eyes open, recognizing that she was indulging in a silly game. Those days were long gone. There would be no men for her. Not now. Maybe never again.

Moving over to the sink, she poured the last of her coffee down the drain, then walked to the doorway and turned out the light. She strolled into the living room and reached up to the key pad and punched in the security code. After turning out the rest of the lights, she headed up the first flight of stairs to the second floor and made her way to the last room on the left. She had set up a small table in the corner of the room for her laptop. With a groan, she took a seat and decided to try writing until she was ready for bed.

Nightfall was always the worst time of day. Except for the wind whispering outside her window, silence crashed around her. Being alone reminded her of her fears. It had been a week since Jarvis's death, and it still weighed heavily on her mind. She wanted to forget the murder. She wanted to forget who murdered him. All she wanted was to return to her life as it once was. She was tired of hiding and just wasn't sure how much more she could endure.

She reached up and rubbed her forehead with the palm of her hand, as if by doing so, she could wipe away the painful memories. But she knew it couldn't possibly be that easy. Pulling her legs to her chest, she wrapped her arms around them and rested her chin on top of her knees. What she needed was a good night's sleep and the strength to stay strong.

As moonlight spilled into the room, she felt the weight of her sadness. All she wanted to do was curl up in a ball and cry. She was all alone with nowhere to turn and no one she could trust. In her despair, she had always turned to her grandmother for comfort. But Nana was no longer with her. She had been gone for over three years. Nevertheless, ever since she had gone into hiding, Destiny found herself grieving for the sweet old lady again.

She blinked, feeling light-headed. Fatigue had begun to get the better of her. However, rest was the least of her worries. She needed to be alert. She had to stay strong.

The only way to turn her life around was to stay hidden until it was time to testify in court. As long as she stayed on the East Coast and remembered her name was no longer Desiree Davidson, she was confident she would be okay.

However, as she remembered the cold hatred radiating from Lucas's eyes when the police raided his home and took him away in handcuffs, her determination to hold on just a little while longer wavered slightly.

"Please, Lord. Don't let Lucas find me," she whispered as she wiped a lone tear from her eye. She had been hiding from him for months. First Chicago, now Delaware. If he found her before she returned to St. Louis, then she would never return home alive.

Chapter 2

Duane drove away from the lumberyard, flooded with anticipation. He took several deep breaths, trying to return his heart rate to normal before he arrived at Destiny's place.

Reaching for a rag on the passenger's seat, he mopped his forehead. Three weeks before Memorial Day, the day already proved to be hot and sticky. Or was it memories of Benny's sexy niece that had hiked up his body temperature to a scorching degree? He just couldn't understand why his body was reacting this way.

Yeah, right. He knew why his stomach felt the way it did—even though it had been quite a long time since he had allowed himself to feel like this for any woman. Destiny excited his senses in such a way that he had little to no control over his body's reactions.

Last night she had invaded his dreams. He had kissed her lips and several other areas of her body. They had lain in his bed, naked and locked in an intimate embrace. His fingers tingled with the imaginary pleasure of stroking her body, caressing her short curls. And in his dreams, her sultry voice had cried out in pleasure as he'd taken complete and total possession of her body.

Crazy, Duane thought as he manually rolled down his window, immediately thankful for the warm breeze. Yet when was the last time a woman had invaded his dreams? He shook his head in disbelief. In light of his casual attitude toward women since his last breakup, he was puzzled by his attraction to his lovely new neighbor. He tried to dismiss the thoughts from his mind. But there was something so intriguing about her, he couldn't think of anything or anyone else.

Inhaling deeply, he could still smell the seductive scent of her perfume. The captivating fragrance demanded a man's attention. And that is exactly what it got. He breathed quietly, leaning back in his seat, stunned by the physical need that had lain dormant for several months. He was anxious to see her smiling face, the curve of her full, lush lips, and the laughter in her sparkling, copper brown eyes.

Duane ran a hand over his hair, shocked by the depth of his need, and tried once again to calm his pulse. However, turning onto his street only made it speed up another notch. There was no mistaking it, he was extremely attracted to the beautiful, intriguing woman, and his behavior was that of a starstruck teenager.

As he pulled in front of the house and brought the truck to a complete stop, he remembered their brief conversation the night before. When he had asked her where she was from, she had hesitated a moment too long. Was Destiny hiding something? What, he wondered? *Duane, you think too much.*

Maybe she didn't feel that her past was any of your business.

Or maybe she is hiding something.

In a moment of déjà vu, Veronica Valentino came to his mind. She, too, had been hiding something. Unfortunately, it wasn't until Duane had received a threatening visit from her husband that he discovered what that *something* was. He hadn't noticed a ring on Destiny's finger, but then Veronica hadn't been wearing one, either.

They had met at a nightclub. From Hispanic descendents, the bronze beauty with sun-kissed hair and a long, willowy body had swept him off his feet. They had dated off and on for almost two years before Mr. Valentino had caught wind of what was going on and had confronted him. All Duane could do was apologize and promise the guy it would never happen again. Unfortunately, it had taken two more weeks before he was able to convince Veronica that their relationship was over. She just couldn't see what the big deal was. The big deal was that he had fallen in love with a married woman. Since then he had vowed to never be that naïve again.

Duane glanced down at his watch. It was barely nine o'clock. He had done more before eight o'clock than most people do all day. Last night he had had a bad case of insomnia thanks to Destiny, so by five he had headed to Brandywine Park and had run a mile along the trail. After a shower and a quick trip to Dunkin Donuts, he had arrived at Ms. Henry's to fix her dripping faucet. The appointment had begun at seven and had ended shortly before eight.

The seventy-year-old widow had been his first customer and had been loyal ever since. In fact, she was better than any public relations firm. She had spread the word of his reasonable rates and friendly service throughout her congregation, as well as to members of her bridge club and several senior citizens' groups. As a result, his clientele consisted mainly of retirees, and he was fine with that. It had provided him an opportunity to bid on a very important job.

He was now responsible for the restoration of a small soul food restaurant located in the heart of downtown. Murphy's had been around since before World War II. The restaurant had served as a meeting place for blacks during the sixties and seventies. Sometime in the late nineties, the kitchen had caught fire, and the restaurant's owner had perished in the blaze. The building stood empty for a long time while the family battled with one another over the estate. Finally, after seven years, the restaurant had a new owner and was scheduled to reopen in the fall. Every contractor in town had submitted a bid. Duane had bid low. Even though he knew he would barely break even on materials, the opportunity would open a lot of doors for him. Just as he had hoped, his smart thinking had won him the contract.

Duane climbed out of his truck. Walking around to the back, he reached down and grabbed his saw and tool box. Destiny's rotting floor would take the rest of the morning.

The work required cutting out a portion of the floor big enough to reach from one joist to the next. Then he would replace it with two pieces of thick plywood he had purchased. The linoleum would also need to be replaced. He had brought along several samples for Destiny to choose from. He would suggest that she replace the entire kitchen floor, which would save him from having to deal

with seams. That job would take two additional after-
noons to complete.

Crossing the street and walking up the sidewalk,
he felt a knot tighten in his stomach. *Get yourself together, Urban. She's just a woman.* As he moved up the
porch stairs, he admitted to himself that Destiny
had an appeal that wasn't going to be easy to resist.
Yep. Something told him she was in a class all her
own. He wasn't quite sure what it was about her that
attracted him to her. But he knew he wouldn't rest
until he had found out.

Duane knocked. Out the corner of his eye, he
spotted her peering through a window; then seconds later he heard a lock turn and the front door
opened.

"Good morning," Destiny greeted him with a wide,
brilliant smile.

He held her eyes within his depths before moving
over her slowly, beginning at her face and ending at
her feet, which were clad in slippers. She was wearing a pink top and a pair of knit shorts that showed
off perfectly slender legs. He closed his eyes. She
looked even better than he remembered. And he
would have been willing to bet that wasn't possible.

The sight tempted him to slide his fingers down
across her firm thighs and curvy calves. The incredible heat of desire consumed and shocked him. He
tried to quell the hot sensations that shot through
his body, playing havoc with his mind, but he could
still see the soft curves as clearly as he had before.
He forced himself to breathe.

"Duane?"

His eyelids snapped open to find her eyes sparked
with curiosity.

"Is something wrong?" she asked.

Shaking off the distracting thoughts, he smiled. "No, I'm fine. I got up pretty early this morning and just realized how early."

"You look fatigued. Would you rather come back later? If you do, I'll understand."

Her concern caused his lips to curl upward. "No. I'm fine, really."

She didn't look convinced. Nevertheless, she stepped aside and allowed him access to her home.

He followed her down the narrow hallway, dropping his toolbox and circular saw on the floor in the kitchen. The room smelled of fresh brewed coffee.

Standing in front of the refrigerator, she smiled sweetly. "I was just making myself some breakfast. Would you like something to eat?"

Duane knew he was in way over his head from the minute she had answered the door. She was wearing that floral fragrance again, and the captivating scent was driving his hormones insane.

He took a deep breath, forcing his mind and body to get it together, and focused on the pending question. "Um . . . no, thank you. As soon as I clear the area, I'll take a quick break and run across the street and grab a bite."

She shrugged one shoulder. "Nonsense. I have to cook something for myself. Making a little extra will be no trouble at all."

He wasn't one to pass up a home-cooked meal. "If it's not too much trouble."

"It isn't, really. Besides, it's the least I can do." She shot him a smile that sent his pulse racing, and he felt himself caught up in the woman and the moment. He knew he should keep things strictly professional between them, but damn, she was making that task impossible. He studied her, trying to deter-mine what elusive quality had so tilted his world.

Destiny stepped around the hole in the floor and made her way over to the stove, where she was frying bacon. With her back to him, Duane ad-mired her shapely behind. Forcing his eyes to the floor, he strode over to the hole and began peel-ing the linoleum away.

"I'll wait until after breakfast before I start send-ing sawdust flying around the room. Have you de-cided if you want the same type of linoleum or something else?" he asked, trying to keep his thoughts focused. "I did bring a couple of sample squares for you to look at."

Destiny turned away from the stove and faced him, holding a spatula in her hand. "I was think-ing about laying a ceramic floor."

Duane raised a quizzical brow as he gazed at her, wondering if she realized how much ceramic cost. "Ceramic floors are low maintenance, but they are quite expensive." He gave her a ballpark figure that he expected would make a poor graduate student flinch. Destiny didn't even blink an eye.

"I know ceramic is expensive, but I think a mosaic design will look very nice in here. It will also add value to the house when I put it up for sale."

She turned back toward the stove, while Duane pressed his lips firmly together. It was strange hear-ing her talk about selling Benny's house. He hadn't even considered the possibility of having a new family living across the street. "If you want ceramic, then when I'm done, I'll lay cement backerboards on top of the linoleum. They come in sheets and are a moisture-resistant material that won't curl or loosen the tiles." He shrugged. "It will take me a little longer to do ceramic, but I'm sure I can work it into my schedule."

She glanced over her shoulder. "Oh no, I plan on doing it myself."

He arched a questioning eyebrow. "Excuse me?"

Her eyes crinkled with a smile. "You heard me."

His curving eyebrows met in amusement.

She crossed her arms underneath her breasts. "What's so funny? You don't believe a woman is capable of doing just as good of a job as a man?"

He put his hands up at the same time he shook his head. "I didn't say anything chauvinistic like that. I'm just surprised, that's all. You don't look the type."

He watched her temper flare. "And what type is that?"

"The type to get grout under her fingernails," he countered with a kind chuckle.

Destiny tapped her temple and winked. "I'm smarter than I look. I've always been fascinated with renovations. I've taken several classes at Home Depot and have laid ceramic tiles in a small bathroom before. So I thought laying tiles in here would be a whole lot of fun." Without warning, the smile returned to her face.

"And hard work," he said. He saw the animated glimmer in her eyes and had to admit that he was clearly impressed. Brains, brawn, and good looks, what more could a man ask for? A wonderful combination and a lot more than he could say about most of the women he knew.

A flicker of excitement lit up her eyes. "Yes, it is, but it's going to look good," she said confidently. "Besides, I have nothing but time on my hands."

Duane gave her a quick glance. "I thought you were concentrating on your thesis?"

"Uh . . . yes, I am, but I can't write all day long."

Her gaze scurried away from his. What was she hiding?

He quickly forgot the question as his eyes strolled down to her chest. Her perfect, firm breasts were thrust up against her shirt. It was obvious she wasn't wearing a bra. The outline of her nipples was visible to the eye.

Destiny looked up and caught him staring. Embarrassment flamed his cheeks and warmed his stomach. He tried to think of something to say, anything to play it off. Unfortunately, nothing came to mind.

Forcing his gaze away, he looked down at the floor, then up at her face again. "How about I screw down the boards for you and then help you move appliances or anything else you might need?"

"You've got yourself a deal." She removed the bacon from the pan and laid it on a plate covered with a paper towel to drain the grease. "How do you like your eggs?"

"Scrambled is just fine."

"All right. Three eggs coming right up. Help yourself to the coffee."

"Thanks." Rising from the floor, he moved to the sink to wash his hands. Destiny stood beside him, cracking eggs in a bowl. He tried to focus on lathering his hands and not the scent of her, which wafted beneath his nose.

Get a grip, Urban!

Moving away from her, he reached in a cupboard at the end of the counter and removed a large, green mug. He noticed the bottom of the shelves had been nicely covered with floral contact paper.

Just like her perfume.

He shook the thought away and moved over to

a small utility table that held a microwave and the coffeemaker. He reached for the pot and filled the large, green mug.

"I know for a fact, Benny never owned a microwave."

Destiny chuckled. "You're right. I bought it at the store two days ago. Who in the world doesn't have a microwave?"

He shared in the laughter. "You're right. Without mine I wouldn't have any way to fix my frozen dinners."

She directed the power of her copper eyes toward him. "You could use your stove."

He pressed two fingers to his eyes. His hands fell away as a chuckle slid free. "Yes, but I have never been any good at using one."

She smiled in agreement, then returned her attention to the eggs.

He moved to the kitchen table, took a seat, then reached for the sugar bowl and dumped a generous helping into his mug. While he sipped the perfect-tasting blend, he watched Destiny scramble the eggs.

Duane found himself wondering about the man in her life. Surely, there had to be someone. She was too beautiful to be alone. Although, deep down, he selfishly hoped she was single. Suddenly, he felt like they were a married couple just waking up from a night of mad, passionate love and sharing breakfast.

Where in the world did that thought come from?

A jolt shot through him, causing him to jerk and spill hot coffee down his shirt. "Damn!"

Destiny jumped at the sound. She swung around, dropping the skillet of eggs on the floor.

Duane stared at her startled gaze. She reminded

him of a deer frozen by an automobile's headlights. She was breathing hard, and her eyes were
large with horror. Something had frightened her,
and it was something far worse than him.

"Are you okay?" he asked. In one swift motion, he
stood and walked over to where she was standing.

"You shouldn't have scared me like that!" she
spat, placing a hand over her heart. "L-Look at
what you made me do," she said, referring to the
eggs, which were now decorating the floor. With
one hand pressed gently at her heart, she reached
down with the other for the skillet.

"Here, let me get that." Before she could reach
it, Duane picked up the skillet. He sat it in the sink,
turned off the fire, and reached out and gently
touched her arm.

"I don't know what's wrong with me." There was
a sob in her voice.

"I'm sorry. I didn't mean to frighten you." His
voice was soft, comforting.

She glanced up at him. Her chest was heaving,
and moisture shimmered in her eyes.

Curving an arm around her shoulders, he pulled
her close and cradled her head to his chest. He was
surprised when she wrapped her arms around him.
Her breasts trembled above her rib cage; her chest
fell and rose rapidly beneath her shirt. His protective instincts kicked in. She was frightened, and he
knew his cry had little to do with it. Something else
had scared her. He pulled her closer, feeling a strong
need to protect the vulnerable woman in his arms.

Expelling a deep breath, he tried not to think
about how she felt just like he had dreamed. Her
lush body pressed against his felt so good; he had
almost forgotten how wonderful it felt to hold a

woman. Holding her, he felt the heat from Destiny's body seep into his, the sensation too vibrant to ignore. What was it about this beautiful young woman that affected him in a way that no woman had in a long time?

He continued to ponder that question until the runaway beat of her heart slowed. Her arms fell away, but she didn't move.

"Are you okay?" he whispered against her hair.

Raising her chin, she stared up at him. She read concern and trustworthiness in his dark gaze. His hold was protective. Could she trust Duane? she wondered. It was too soon to tell.

Destiny forced a smile she did not feel and fumbled for a lie to divert him from prying. "I'm fine. Just a little shaken up, but I'll be all right. How about I make us some more eggs?"

She nibbled on her lower lip and rendered Duane monetarily speechless. All he could do was stare at her mouth, taking in her perfectly white teeth and sexy lips, and wonder how they'd taste beneath his.

"Duane?" he heard her call.

Shaking the thought away, he focused on her puzzled look before allowing his eyes to travel down past her neck. What he noticed was far more tempting than her nibbling nervously on her lip.

Trying to ignore the heat generating down low, he cleared his throat. "How about *I* make some more eggs while you go and change your shirt before that coffee stain sets in?"

Destiny followed his gaze. While she was in his embrace, the wet coffee on his shirt had transferred to hers. Already braless, the moisture outlined the full, rounded mounds of her breasts, leaving her nipples erect and visible.

She was too stunned to do anything more than nod. Without another word, she turned on her heels and walked away.

Once safely in her bedroom, Destiny closed the door behind her and allowed the tears to flow freely. She had just made a fool of herself, she chided herself. Now how was she supposed to face Duane?

She didn't know what had gotten into her. She had never been that easily frightened before. But when she had heard him curse, her brain had reverted back to the night she had witnessed Chief Cook's murder. It had been his last words before he was shot. *Damn you, Lucas.* Because of him, she was a bundle of nerves. Brushing the tears away from her cheeks, she rose from the bed. Before this was all over, she was going to lose her mind. She was frightened and had every reason to be. Knowing Lucas the way she did, she knew he was looking for her.

Reaching up, she massaged her temple; then she forced her thoughts away from what she couldn't control and back to the problem at hand.

Luckily, she had withdrawn enough money from her account before leaving St. Louis that she could stay hidden for the next year. No one knew her whereabouts. And she wanted it to stay that way. Therefore, she could not afford to be sidetracked. She couldn't risk Duane asking too many questions about her. She couldn't allow herself to get too close, which was why she needed to resist the attraction.

She reached in her duffel bag and removed a white lace bra and a light blue T-shirt. Quickly slipping both on, she then turned to the mirror and examined the damage crying had done to her face.

Staring at her reflection, she knew she wasn't immune to Duane. The power of his body, his presence, was without question. However, she had no intention of permitting herself to fall under his spell. She had come to Delaware to hide, not to become involved in an affair with her neighbor.

Remembering the way it had felt being held in his comforting, warm embrace, she released a deep breath. It wasn't going to be easy. When Duane had taken her in his arms, she had wished she could stay in his protective embrace until her world returned to the way it had once been.

How did he know that comfort was exactly what she had needed? During the few minutes that she was pressed tightly against his solid chest, breathing in his masculine scent, she had felt safe and protected, without a worry in the world.

The air had whispered chills over her skin where he had touched her. Craving the closeness of human warmth, she had indulged deeply in his embrace and had taken the strength she needed to draw from him.

She sighed as she moved down the hall to the bathroom to wash her face. If only things could remain that way. Safe. Protected. But she knew that was impossible unless Lucas was safely behind bars.

Destiny returned to the kitchen just as Duane was sliding mounds of fluffy, yellow scrambled eggs onto their plates. He carried them over to the table along with the bacon she had fried.

"Feeling better?" he asked.

She lowered herself into a chair, then reached for a slice of buttered toast and nodded.

"I really didn't mean to frighten you. I hope you believe that."

His smile was so dazzling, she hated to have to lie to him. She shook her head. "It wasn't your fault. I've been like that all my life."

His jaw twitched in amusement. "Why? Did you have a big brother who used to tease you all the time?"

Destiny giggled as she shook her head. "No, nothing as tormenting as that, although that would have explained it. I asked my grandmother about it once, and she said my mother was the same way."

Duane took the seat across from her. "Do you have any brothers or sisters?"

She shook her head as she toyed with her scrambled eggs. Despite years of yearning for a sister, siblings were something she never had. As far as she knew, neither of her parents ever had any more children. She had often wondered what it would have been like if she'd had someone in her life other than Nana.

Sitting up straighter, she met his direct stare. "No. What about you?"

Duane shoveled a forkful of eggs into his mouth. "More than I care to claim. I'm the oldest. Then I have one sister, Chelsea, who's married with a daughter. And my brothers, Garrett and Reyn."

"Are they married, too?"

His brow shot up and laughter curled his lips. "My brothers? No way. Reyn's married to his job. He works for a security firm. Garrett's a comedian and isn't ready to answer to anyone. They both prefer coming and going as they please while breaking hearts along the way." What he didn't tell her was that both of his brothers had experienced the darker side of relationships and now didn't want emotional ties of any kind.

A slight frown made furrows on her smooth forehead. "And what about you, Duane? How do you feel about marriage?"

His chewing slowed as he glanced at her. What would she think if he told her that before he met her, commitment was the last thing on his mind? *She'll probably think you're some kind of stalker.*

"I believe marriage is sacred and shouldn't be taken lightly. If and when I find the right person, I intend to commit my heart to her, and hopefully, she'll love me enough to want the same."

Destiny felt the heat of his gaze as he watched her reaction intently as he spoke. Was he testing her? Struggling to maintain her composure, she reached for another strip of bacon and brought it to her lips.

"What about you? Do you want a family?" he asked.

She lowered her gaze. She would probably scare him if she told him she wanted a house full of hyperactive children and a husband with enough love to wrap them all up within it.

She ran her finger around the rim of her coffee mug. "Someday. I love children. But I don't want to do it alone. I'll just have to wait until I've found a husband first."

In that instant, Duane realized he liked Destiny Davis. He found her poised and beautiful. But he also knew she had brains and a personality. And she would make a fabulous mother. Suddenly, images of her round with his seed danced before his eyes. He was falling fast and hard.

After draining her mug, Destiny rose from the table and reached for the coffeepot. Returning to the table, she refilled his mug and then her own. When she reached across him, she lightly brushed his arm, sending a jolt of energy surging through his veins. He was tempted to encircle her waist, lower her soft body across his lap, and kiss her senseless. Instead, he concentrated on eating his food.

After returning the coffeepot to its holder, she slid back onto her chair. Duane waited until Destiny had taken a swallow of coffee before he asked, "Are you thinking about staying here permanently?"

She met his questioning eyes but waited until she took another cautious sip before she spoke. "I don't think so," she answered honestly. "I have a job, and all my friends are back at home."

He lifted a thick, black eyebrow. "What kind of work do you do?"

Resting an elbow on the table, she leaned forward. "I edit manuscripts for a literary agency in the area." It wasn't a complete lie. She did on occasion work part time with John Harmon, a good friend who was a literary agent and had an office in St. Louis County.

"That sounds fascinating."

She nodded her head, grateful that they had found a safe subject to discuss. "It is an interesting field."

Duane's eyes narrowed as he nibbled on a strip of bacon. "I have never been much of a reader. I buy a paper every Sunday and try to keep up on current events, but reading just for leisure has never been big on my list of interests. I guess I just haven't found the time."

Destiny looked stunned by his confession that he rarely read. "You have to find the time. There is nothing better in the morning than a cup of coffee and a good book. I read a lot for school, but I always find time for reading for pleasure, even if it means leaving a book on the side of the tub."

Duane swallowed a piece of bacon that had suddenly gotten caught in his throat. Thinking about her lying in a bubble bath was not a smart move.

He gave her a lingering look. "How long are you planning to be in Delaware?"

"At least two months. I figure it will take me that long to finish my thesis and get this house ready to go on the market."

Why did the idea of her leaving bother him so much? he wondered. Brushing the issue aside, he tried again to concentrate on his food. They were both relatively quiet as they finished their breakfast. After they were done, Destiny stacked the dishes in the sink for later.

While Duane worked in the kitchen, clearing the rotted wood, Destiny passed the time doing housework. One thing she had discovered about her uncle was that he was a pack rat. He kept just about everything.

The old house was long and narrow with three floors and a basement. A small living room, dining room, and kitchen were situated on one side of the main level, while a staircase occupied the other side. At the top of the first flight of stairs was a bathroom, and to the left of the railing were two bedrooms. After filling twelve trash bags full of worthless junk and old newspapers, she had cleared away everything in the bedroom that she had decided to use as an office. With her laptop computer already set up, all she needed to do now was run out and buy supplies.

The other bedroom she planned to use as her bedroom. The day before she had removed the twin bed from the room by sliding the mattress and box spring out into the hallway. She had then dismantled the small bed frame and also removed it from the room. As soon as she got a chance, she would haul them down to the basement. In the far corner was a treadmill, which she had found buried beneath a stack of blankets. After a quick examination, she had discovered that the exercise equipment had barely been used.

For the past five years, she had made it a habit to jog every morning before breakfast. This invigorating form of exercise was something she thoroughly enjoyed. Since she had gone into hiding, exercise was something she had gotten very little of. Now that she was unable to leave the house for extended periods of time, she would definitely put the treadmill to good use.

Moving down the narrow hallway, she climbed another flight of steps, which led to the third floor, where there was a large master bedroom and a sitting room that had belonged to Uncle Benjamin. She could smell the scent of his cigars as soon as she reached the top step. She stopped and took several deep breaths. Forty-two steps were quite a workout.

The master bedroom hadn't been used in two years, but it looked as if it were waiting for someone to return. A homemade quilt was spread neatly across a full-size bed. Toiletries still lined the top dresser drawer, and a tattered wallet lay on a small round table beside the bed. Even though she had been too young to remember him, being in her uncle's room among his things made her feel close to him.

When she had first arrived at her uncle's house, Destiny thought she would be afraid to be in the same place where he, a man she had never really known, had died in his sleep. Instead, for the first time in her life, she felt as if she were home. She thought it was strange that she had never felt that way in her condo. She found that her uncle's home reminded her so much of her grandmother's house: the photographs, the old furniture, and even the smells were so familiar.

As she reached for a wastebasket and began filling it with the useless items on his dresser, Destiny again wished she'd taken the time to know her uncle. She would have attended the funeral, but Uncle Benjamin had already been buried by the time his lawyer had contacted her. For days she had blamed herself for not taking the time to visit him sooner.

She had considered it on several occasions after the success of her books. Then her tour schedule became so hectic that she barely had time to write. However, she did call him on holidays and wrote to him on occasion, but she knew it wasn't enough. Nevertheless, she did nothing about it, and then it was too late. That bothered her because Uncle Benjamin had been the only family she had left after Nana had passed. Now all she had was the memories and the stories that her grandmother had shared.

Although she felt guilty, Destiny had convinced herself it was a good thing that she had never visited, that Lucas knew nothing about her uncle. As far as he knew, her grandmother had been her last living relative, which was why Delaware was the perfect hiding place. Had Lucas known about her uncle, she would have had no other place to go.

Preferring not to think about how he had ruined her life, she quickly pushed the disturbing thought away and lowered herself onto the corner of her uncle's bed. Destiny reached for a picture of her great-uncle in his military uniform, embracing a beautiful, light-skinned young woman. They were a striking couple, with his milk chocolate complexion and brilliant smile. She remembered Nana telling her that his lovely wife had died young. Uncle Benjamin had never remarried.

After her uncle's death, she had hired a property management company to close up the house and keep an eye on it. On arrival, she was relieved to discover that it had not been vandalized. Not even a broken window. In the neighborhood where she had grown up, if someone moved and left a house unoccupied for too long, they ran the risk of drug dealers moving in and taking over the property.

She returned the picture to the table, removed the alarm clock from the corner of his dresser, and carried it down to her bedroom. As soon as she got settled in, she was going to gather his clothing and donate everything that wasn't of sentimental value to a local charity.

Hearing the sound of a circular saw, her mind drifted. She imagined that by now Duane was covered in sawdust. The mere image made her insides tremor. What she wouldn't give to wipe the shavings away from his face! He was such a fascinating man. As she stepped into her bedroom, she found herself wondering if he was involved. She wouldn't be surprised if he was. Rarely was a man that good-looking single. Any woman with any sense would have snatched him up a long time ago.

Yesterday she had noticed a white Chrysler in his driveway. It could either be the vehicle he used when he wasn't working or the car that belonged to his wife.

What difference does it make?

She told herself it didn't matter because she wasn't looking for any kind of involvement outside of working on the house. However, she could not help but to be curious.

Reaching down, she plugged the clock in the wall. She was setting the time when she heard the doorbell. Destiny flinched in terror. Had Lucas found her already?

Chapter 3

As Destiny slowly descended the stairs, she tried to calm her racing heart and prayed it wasn't so. By the time she had reached the bottom step, the doorbell had rung again. The hairs at the back of her neck prickled as she moved to the window and peered out the corner. The days of throwing her door open without checking first were long gone.

It took several seconds before she realized it was a delivery truck from a neighborhood furniture store. She placed a palm to her chest and took a deep breath. "Thank you, Lord." Taking one final deep breath, she opened the door.

"I bet you've got my new bedroom set," she replied as a greeting.

The short, carrot-topped man tipped his hat and smiled. "You've bet right."

He handed her a clipboard with several forms to sign. Fifteen minutes later, he and another worker had hauled up a mattress, box spring, headboard, footboard, and a dresser to her bedroom on the second floor. Tonight she wouldn't have to sleep on her uncle's lumpy mattress. For the first time in days, she hoped to have a good night's sleep. She smiled with anticipation.

When they were done, she walked them to the door, turned the lock, and returned to her bedroom.

She was so busy reading the furniture assembly instructions that she was not aware of Duane's approach, but suddenly he was right beside her. Their bodies weren't touching, but she was acutely aware of him. The smell of him filled her nostrils— a hint of soap and the sweat-induced scent of his masculine essence. She took a deep breath and felt a tingly response. *This is a bad idea*, she thought.

"You need some help?" he asked. His mouth was so very close to her ear that his breath was fanning over its sensitive outer rim.

She shook it off, turned, and smiled at his kindness. "No, the delivery guys did the hard part."

"Oscar's," he replied, reading the name on the side of the box. "You made a good choice. They're a family business that has been around for a long time. They stand by their money-back guarantee." Attractive lines fanned over around his dark eyes as he spoke.

He was standing so close, Destiny had to take several deep breaths to restore her heart rate to normal. "Good. I'm glad to hear that."

Duane stepped away to look inside the box, and Destiny's shoulders sagged with relief.

"This is a nice set."

She nodded, quite pleased with her choice. Yesterday she had bought a heavy carved walnut bed and a matching dresser. It had caught her eye and drawn her out of her car into the Amish furniture store.

Smiling up at him, Destiny noticed his eyes traveling slowly around the room.

"What's wrong?"

Duane looked down at her. "This used to be Mannie's room."

"Who's Mannie?"

His expression suddenly became serious. "A good kid. Benny used to be his foster grandparent. He was ten years old and loved being here. Mannie's from a broken home with a mother who was in and out of rehab so much that Mannie spent a lot of time in foster care. Benny wanted to keep him but was too old. However, a couple of years ago the Department of Services for Children, Youth & Their Families started a program for foster grandparents for kids like Mannie. Benny enjoyed having Mannie around as much Mannie loved to be here."

Destiny was fascinated by the information. "Do you know what happened to the little boy?"

He shook his head. "The last time I saw him was at the funeral, and he was so upset he left early. I tried contacting him at the agency, and he visited me once or twice, but after that he returned to live with his mother, and I never saw him again."

She sighed. "How sad."

Nodding, Duane continued. "Your uncle was the best thing to have ever happened to that kid. I watched him change from a frightened little boy to a child with hopes and dreams. When Benny died, Mannie reverted to that scared little boy again."

Destiny was quiet as she thought about what he had said. She knew first hand what it was like to feel frightened and alone.

"The more you talk about my great-uncle, the more I regret that I never got the chance to truly get to know him," she began in a soft, distant voice. "He sounds so much like his sister. My grandmother was something extra special."

"So was Benny."

For several seconds they both stood lost in their own thoughts.

Destiny then turned and reached for a utility knife off of the windowsill. "Maybe I'll try to find him."

"Who?" Duane asked.

She looked over at him again. "Mannie."

When he nodded, she began to open the box with her new dresser.

"Here, let me give you a hand." Duane ignored her protest and tore open the box with her dresser inside. Then together they moved the dresser to the perfect spot in the corner.

Now she would have somewhere to put her things and could finally get them out of her duffel bag. Not that she had much. Whatever she had, she had picked up on the road during her trip east. Everything else had been left in her condo. She felt a tinge of sadness that she had been forced to leave the city she loved so much. Someday soon she would be able to return. *God willing*.

"What's wrong?"

"N-nothing," she said, then forced a silly smile. "Except you, of course. You're filthy."

His lifted brow said he was amused. "Yeah, it's a dirty job, but somebody's got to do it."

Duane stepped out into the hallway and, without asking, tucked the twin mattress, box spring, and bed frame under each arm and carried them down to the basement.

While he was gone, Destiny tried not to think about how good it felt to have a man around. She barely had time to erase the thoughts from her mind when he returned.

"Thanks," she said.

"No problem."

With the utility knife, she sliced open the box with the bed frame inside. "How about I make lunch while you clean up?"

He immediately shook his head. "Oh, no. I don't want to impose. Breakfast was more than enough. I can run home and—"

"And do what?" she interrupted. "Warm up a TV dinner?" She stopped any further protest with a wave of the hand. "No way."

Duane couldn't help the chuckle that escaped his lips. "Okay. I never pass up a home-cooked meal."

Her jaw twitched. "Who said anything about homemade? Nothing fancy. I bought some cold cuts and cheese at the deli. I'll fix a couple of sandwiches and open a can of chicken soup."

"Sounds good to me." His smile changed into a boyish grin that made her heart do a somersault. Casting her eyes downward, she ignored the feeling and began to assemble the bed.

Duane helped her snap the bed frame in place; then he screwed on the headboard while she worked on the footboard. Lastly, they lowered the box spring and mattress on top.

After all of the boxes had been tossed down the stairs for disposal, the two of them stood at the center of the room, staring down at the bed. Without warning, they both raised their eyes and locked on each other. Destiny found herself imagining the two of them breaking in her new mattress together.

"Are you involved with anyone?" she heard Duane say.

Destiny lowered her lashes, attempting to hide her surprise. He was attracted to her. A short silence stretched between them as she pondered her answer; then she lifted her gaze to meet his. "No, not anymore."

A tiny smile tilted his lips. "Good."

"What about you?" she boldly asked.

"Not in a long time," he whispered

He stood close enough for her to feel the moist whisper on her forehead. Her breasts trembled above her rib cage. He reached up and ran a finger-tip around her earlobe. Destiny shivered as a sensu-ous current ran through her. His eyes glittered, taking in her face, her neck and inch by inch follow-ing her throat down to her breasts. A flush of heat caused her nipples to harden. The feeling of intimacy was a clear indication that being in her bedroom was not the place for them to be. Time stood still as they shared an intense physical awareness of each other. She met his smothering gaze, feeling the heated intensity. They stood less than a foot apart, their chests rising and falling in unison.

She wanted so badly to step closer. To lose herself in his comforting embrace and feel his arms slide around her again. She wanted to rest her cheek against his solid chest and listen to his steady heart-beat. Because she wanted it so badly, she folded her arms behind her back and fought the attraction.

She looked up at him, taking in his hair. Wavy and begging for a woman to smooth it. Droplets of per-spiration clung to his forehead. Traveling farther, she stared at his mouth, finding it firm and sensual.

She wondered if Duane knew what he was doing to her. Did he know he was sexy enough to be in one of those male calendars? The look in his eyes told her he was well aware of the effect he had over her. On the one hand, she was flattered; on the other, she didn't want to be attracted to him, because she couldn't afford the distraction.

It had only been three months since her relationship with Lucas had ended, and even now the connection was a long ways from over. The unresolved issue of his trial reminded her of her assumed identity and the painful truth. A man was something she did not need.

Lucas was out looking for her, and if she allowed her guard to slip for even a second, he would find her. She couldn't be careless. She couldn't afford to take chances, and that was why a relationship was something she had to stay clear of.

Blinking her eyes several times, she suddenly realized Duane was looking at her expectantly, as if waiting for her to make the first move.

Clearing her throat, she pretended not to notice. "Let me get you a towel so you can wash up before lunch."

He also blinked several times, as if coming out of a trance. "Sounds like a good idea."

Destiny led the way down the hall to the bathroom. Duane followed, and she couldn't help but notice how close he was again. The mutual attraction still sizzled between them. When she gave him a set of towels and brushed past him so she could head down to the kitchen, the contact sent sparks flying all the way down to her toes.

She needed time to regroup. Quickly, she descended the stairs. When she reached the kitchen, she flopped down in a chair and reached for a napkin on the table. It had suddenly gotten very hot in here, she thought as she mopped the napkin across her forehead.

Duane lathered the washcloth, rubbed it across his face and neck, then rinsed with cool water. The rumbling of the pipes alerted him that he needed to put plumbing near the top of his list. With the amount of work the house required, he would be hanging around for quite some time. The possibility brought a corny grin to his face.

He was quite pleased because he wanted to stick around long enough to discover exactly what it was that had drawn him to Destiny Davis. She was beautiful and sexy, but it wasn't just a physical need. There was something else about her that drew him to her, and he was determined to find out what that thing was.

He silently cursed himself for not kissing her. He had been provided with the perfect opportunity to sample the sweet contours of her mouth.

"Next time," he murmured. And there would be a next time. That he promised.

Later that evening, Duane was inside his garage sharpening his tools. What typically took twenty minutes had turned into an hour. He wasn't sure which tools he had already done and which he still needed to do, so he ended up starting over twice. One thing was for sure, he couldn't seem to get Destiny out of his mind.

He had spent most of the day repairing the floor, yet even while he was cutting and measuring, he hungered for her. He wasn't sure how he had man-

aged to sit across from her first at breakfast and then
at lunch. Food had been the farthest thing from his
mind. He would rather have feasted on her beauty.

Duane, man, you're slipping.

It was so unlike him to want a woman as much as
he wanted her. Yet for the first time since high
school, his hormones were in overdrive.

After lunch, he had spent the entire rest of the
afternoon working across the street. To hell with the
work he planned to do around her house. He
would much rather have spent the time breaking
in her new bed.

His mind was filled with images of satin sheets
and naked flesh. He could almost feel her skin
beneath his. Taking a moment, he imagined her
lying on her back with the hardness of him inside
of her, while she cried out in pleasure and repeat-
edly screamed his name. But he knew that wasn't
possible. Even though he had been doing odd jobs
on the side for years, he still had a fairly new business that he had to foster. He needed to stay focused. He didn't need another distraction.

However, while running a saw across the blade he
thought about the way Destiny had looked in shorts,
about her long, slim legs and generous curves
both above and below the waist. He imagined his
hands sliding up her thighs. He knew they would
be silky smooth.

It had been a long time since he'd really looked
forward to spending time with a woman. Maybe if
he spent enough time in her company, the attraction he felt for her would die a natural death.

Inexplicably tense, he turned off the blade and
headed toward the door. He was stepping out of his

garage when he spotted Destiny coming out of the house. At least he thought that was her.

She had changed into an oversized sweat suit and a pair of running shoes, which didn't faze him in the slightest, even though it was well over seventy degrees outside. What did were her base-ball cap and dark shades. He frowned. Where was she going in that getup, he wondered as he watched her race down the steps and into her car in rapid time. Curiosity got the better of him, and he headed down the driveway, but before he could reach her car, she sped out of the parking space and down the street.

Duane stood there for the longest time with his hands planted firmly on his hips. Something strange was definitely going on. And he planned to find out what it was.

Thirty miles on the other side of Baltimore, Des-tiny studied her rearview mirror, making certain she wasn't being followed. As soon as she was confident the coast was clear, she pulled her car into a gas sta-tion parking lot and got out.

Reaching into her purse she removed a calling card, then strolled over to a pay phone at the far left side of the building and dialed a number. It wasn't long before a soothing voice came across the line.

"Julia Joyce Agency."

"Julia."

"Desiree!" Julia screeched. "Is that you?"

"Yes, it's me." It felt so good to hear a familiar voice.

"What happened? Where have you been? I've

been so worried," she whispered from the other end of the line.

Destiny couldn't do anything but sigh. Was she all right? Yes, but for how long? Only time would tell.

"Desiree!" Julia said, agitated after a prolonged silence. "What's going on?"

"It's a long story, but first I need to know if you have caller ID."

She snorted. "Everyone has caller ID."

"Can you tell me what showed up when I called?"

"You're kidding, right?"

Julia just didn't know how badly she wished it was a joke. "No. I'm serious."

"Okay, hold on." Shortly after, she came back on the line. "It says you're calling from a pay phone with a 708 area code." She then rattled off the number.

Destiny released a sigh of relief. Two days ago while at the store, only minutes after buying the sixty-minute calling card, she had placed a call to her uncle's house so that she could check the ID on the answering machine when she returned. The ID message had been identical. The calling card was from a service in Chicago.

"Thank God."

"Desiree, what's going on? You are really starting to scare me. I've been trying to reach you at home and on your cell for weeks and have come up empty."

Destiny quickly turned around in the phone booth, making sure no one was listening. "I-I've been in protective custody."

"Protective custody . . . for what?"

She hesitated. "I witnessed Chief Cook's murder."

A gasp came through the phone. "Oh my God! That murder was all over the news. The media said it was drug-related."

"It was. Lucas killed him." She choked on the words.

There was a noticeable pause. "Y-your Lucas?"

The question brought tears to her eyes. For almost two years he had been her Lucas. She had thought he was her prince and she his princess. She had looked forward to a life of happiness and lots of babies. But her perfect world shattered when she began to suspect that Lucas's commercial shipping and receiving business was a high-class drug operation.

Taking a deep breath, she shared with her good friend, in confidence, everything that had happened in the past several months.

Lucas Blake owned L&B Distributions, which shipped goods overseas to textile corporations. The brief visits to his plush corporate office left Desiree feeling proud and quite impressed with her man's brilliant mind. She noticed that people flocked to him. He had friends that were in law enforcement and political office, including the mayor.

It wasn't until she decided to use the business as a setting for an upcoming romance novel that she first became suspicious. According to their annual report, L&B Distributions barely grossed one million dollars the previous year. Desiree found that quite strange considering the three-million-dollar home Lucas lived in, as well as the private jet, the flashy cars, and the large staff he employed at both his office and at home.

Her suspicions that Lucas was involved in illegal activities had been aroused when she picked up the phone to place a call and overheard tidbits of an illicit transaction being conducted over the phone. From that point on, she realized that her head had been in the clouds for so long that she had ignored the obvious. Her fiancé was a drug dealer. The frequent trips to Mexico. The thirty-second phone calls in the middle of the night. His home office, which he kept locked. All those things and more began to add up. However, because she had such an emotional investment in their relationship, she did not want to believe it. That is, until she had come home after a book tour in Dallas a day early.

After a week of soul-searching, she had come to the decision to return to her condo, which she had been using as an office since ever she had moved in with Lucas a year after they first began dating. She didn't expect him to be happy about her decision. However, she hoped he would understand she needed space and time to think about the man she had agreed to spend the rest of her life with.

One day she had pulled her Mercedes SLK into the circular driveway, then entered the house in search of Lucas. Unable to find him, she had headed down toward his office in the basement, where she heard voices. Standing outside the door, she heard a familiar voice. She paused and heard a man threaten to expose Lucas's operation if he didn't pay his bribes in full. Lucas had laughed at the warning. Feeling uneasy, Desiree had turned and was heading back up the stairs when she heard four gunshots. Startled, she stumbled on the steps. Hearing the noise, Casper, one of Lucas's hired hands, came out of the office and spotted her trying to run away. He snatched her by her hair and dragged her into the room while she demanded he let her go. There, lying on the floor, was the chief of police in a puddle of blood.

In his usual charming tone, Lucas threatened to

kill her if she ever breathed a word of it. Scared out of her mind, she had no choice but to agree. From that day on, Lucas watched her like a hawk. On one or two occasions she thought about trying to call the police. However, since the chief had been on Lucas's payroll, she wasn't sure whom she could trust.

And then she remembered Chuck.

He was a lawyer whom she had consulted about several of her literary contracts, and through the years, he had become a good friend. She knew she would only have one shot at getting word to him, so she bided her time and waited for the right opportunity.

As a prisoner in Lucas's home for over three months, she played it cool. When she was asked to speak on a panel at St. Louis University, she jumped at the chance. As usual, whenever she needed to leave the house, Lucas sent one of his goons to escort her. While everyone was crowding her on the stage after the presentation, she managed to get lost in the crowd and sneak out to a coffee shop a couple of blocks away. She contacted Chuck, and he immediately came and picked her up. Within hours he had taken her directly to the top of the chain, and she was placed under FBI protection. According to the FBI, they had been watching Lucas for some time. However, with her information, he was arrested and was soon standing trial for murder for the police chief's death. Other than his hired men, who would never dream of testifying against their boss, Desiree was the only witness.

It had only taken three weeks for Lucas's thugs to discover the safe house where she was staying with Jarvis. A pain squeezed her heart as she thought of him. Quiet and worried, she wondered how long it would be before they found her in Delaware.

Julia, who had been quiet during her entire story, shrieked the moment Destiny finished. "Oh my God! Why didn't you go back to the FBI for help?"

She closed her eyes tightly, as if squeezing them shut would turn off the memories for just a moment. But she knew that was virtually impossible.

"Because I—" her voice broke miserably. "I don't know who I can trust. Like I said, if the chief of police was in cahoots with Lucas, there is no telling how many others are. I thought I would be a lot safer if I left the state. So I bought a used car under an assumed named and left for—"

"Don't tell me," Julia interrupted. "As long as I don't know where you are, I don't have to risk slipping and saying the wrong thing. Who knows, my phones might even be tapped."

Destiny's chuckle lacked humor. "I think you've been reading too many of my mystery novels." Gripping the receiver, she released a long sigh as she watched the flow of traffic. "But you're right. The less people who know about my whereabouts, the better." Her statement was followed by a prolonged silence.

"Is there anything I can do for you?"

Brushing her fears aside, Destiny regained her usual merry tone. "Actually, there is. I was calling about my latest manuscript."

"What!" Julia gasped. "How can you think about writing at a time like this?"

Destiny snorted. "I need something to keep my mind occupied." It was impossible to pretend that everything in her life was the way it should be . . . when nothing was. But if she didn't try, she was certain to go insane. "Writing is my life. It takes me away from my problem by allowing me to be whoever and wherever I want to be. If I couldn't write, I would have gone crazy right about now."

"All right, then business it is. The editor loved the proposal. How soon can you have the first novel of the series ready?"

She couldn't help but smirk at her friend's immediate transition from personal matters to business. Julia was a trooper and a strong believer that despite everything, the show must go on. "How about August first? That should give me plenty of time."

"That sounds wonderful. I'll let Warner know." There was something in her tone, an edge of excitement, that caught Destiny's attention. Her agent believed in her work as much as she did, and that was what separated her from all of the others. "I can't wait."

Glancing over her shoulder, Destiny spotted two cars pulling into the gas station. With a feeling of uneasiness, she decided it was time to return to her sanctuary. "I guess I better go."

"Okay. Be safe," Julia replied, her voice tight with worry.

"I will."

"I love you," she added.

A lone tear eased down Destiny's face. Julia was the only family she had left. "I love you, too."

Destiny lowered herself into the tub. It was so short and narrow that she didn't know why she even bothered. But like the expression went, beggars can't be choosers, and right now she was definitely down on her luck. Besides, she needed to unwind, and taking a bath was the only way she knew how. She could have stayed at any hotel in the world; however, the first place Lucas would have looked for her was at a five-star hotel. She had to live outside of the box if she didn't want to risk being discovered.

It wasn't until a week ago that she had come to understand that she had been lonely for so long and had wanted happiness so badly that it had clouded her judgment. She had been living a fairy-tale life and had thought Lucas was her prince. She wanted to live happily ever after, and because of it, she had refused to see what was right in front of her. She didn't want to believe that he wasn't the man she thought him to be.

Leaning back in the tub, she released a long sigh as the heat enveloped her. The ride back from Maryland had been during the hustle and bustle of rush hour. She could have saved herself a lot of time and energy if she had driven over to Philadelphia instead, but she thought she had a much better chance of hiding her whereabouts by taking the extra hour-long drive. One thing she knew, Lucas was no dummy. Wilmington, Delaware, and Philadelphia were too close for comfort.

Closing her eyes, she pushed Lucas and her worries away from her mind for a moment and decided to think about something uplifting. The only thing that came to mind was Duane. She propped her hands on her stomach as she thought about him. The power of his presence was without question. He was handsome and intriguing, and he was going to be difficult to resist. Despite her interest, the last thing she should do was to invite a man into her life. She was living a lie and was too considerate a person to mislead him. Her life was in danger, and she couldn't risk getting anyone else mixed up in her mess. Besides, she couldn't afford the distraction. If

Lucas found her, she needed to be alert and ready to run at a moment's notice.

Destiny drew in a ragged breath and willed her heart to slow as she sunk deeper into the tub. No matter how captivated she was by him, she had to do whatever was in her power to keep Duane at a distance.

Chapter 4

Duane rose early as usual. With a fresh cup of coffee, he stepped out onto his deck in time to watch the sun rise. Taking a seat, he tipped his chair back and propped his feet up on the railing. He took a sip of the hot, black liquid, allowing the heat to flow through his chest as he enjoyed the view before him.

Most of the homes in the area had a view of a concrete slab, or even worse, the alley, but on his block there was nothing in view but a thickly forested area and the horizon. Glancing up, he noticed that daybreak had painted blue, mauve, and pink streaks across the sky.

A cool breeze tickled his cheek, and he closed his eyes in appreciation. Instantly, Destiny's image came to mind.

She had returned home well past dinnertime and had quickly dashed back into the house. He knew because he had watched her house from the window. And not like a father waiting for his daughter to come home, but like a jealous boyfriend. He had then spent the rest of the night wondering where she had gone, or even worse, whom had she gone to see. He didn't know why, but the thought of her spending time with another man bothered him.

After lifting weights, followed by a long, hot shower, he had hoped to find sleep easily. Instead, he spent the night desiring a woman he barely knew. He didn't know what it was, but somehow Destiny had cast a spell over him. As a result, he had done nothing but lie there and think about her. She haunted his every thought. She had maneuvered her way into his dreams and filled his thoughts until he couldn't even take a deep breath without it being filled with her sweet fragrance. By one o'clock in the morning he had finally fallen asleep, only to awaken four hours later from an erotic dream that left him hard and throbbing. He had imagined making love to her in every room of her house. Even now, just thinking about it was enough to heat up his bloodstream again.

However, what bothered him the most was that long after his body temperature had returned to normal, he lay there awake experiencing feelings of loneliness. He didn't confuse loneliness with sex, because he'd never had a problem in the sexual department. He'd gone out with numerous women and had shared several of their beds. But no real bond had ever developed. Thus even after he left their beds and returned to his own, he had never felt such emptiness.

He had spent the last year building his business and didn't have time to think about relationships or the possibility of spending the rest of his life alone. It wasn't until after spending less than twelve hours around Destiny that he had begun to rethink his future. How was that possible?

Shaking his head, he took another sip of his coffee. He had definitely been too long without a woman if a single encounter could make his mind start playing tricks on him.

Duane sighed and faced reality. He was going to have to keep their relationship strictly professional. Or at least try. He had a strong feeling that he was fighting a losing battle, that it was already too late to retreat.

The phone rang, interrupting any further deliberation. He rose from the chair and stepped into the kitchen, grabbing the phone on the wall near the door.

Glancing down at the caller ID, he smirked. There was only one person who had the audacity to disturb his early morning tranquility.

"Good morning, Mom."

His mother's husky laughter came through the earpiece. "Good morning, sweetheart. And how is your day starting?"

"Wonderful."

Mrs. Urban snorted. "Obviously not wonderful enough if you're answering the phone. I guess you still haven't found anyone to share your life with."

Duane covered the mouthpiece long enough to release a frustrated grunt. His mother was never going to leave well enough alone.

Removing his hand from the mouthpiece, he cradled the phone beneath his chin, frowning. "Mom, I hope you didn't call me this early in the morning to discuss my love life."

"No, I called because six o'clock seems to be the only time I can reach you."

"How's Dad?" he asked.

"He's fine, and don't you dare change the subject."

He groaned, and this time he didn't even bother to cover the phone.

His mother didn't appear to notice. "I can expect you for Memorial Day, right?"

"I . . . uh . . . sure."

"Good, because Maureen is in town, and I'm planning on inviting her to our family barbecue. You know she has just started her own catering business. That girl makes the best jerk chicken on this side of the state. The two of you have quite a bit in common with both of you being entrepreneurs and all."

Oh no. Donna Urban was up to her matchmaking again.

He made a strangled sound. "Mom, I really wish you wouldn't."

"I'm only inviting her and her parents over. No big deal."

He knew his mom well enough to know that she made any event a big deal.

"Duane, you're getting older."

"I'm not even forty yet."

"And I want grandchildren before I'm too old to enjoy them."

"Mom, Chelsea has an adorable baby girl," he replied, referring to his baby sister. She had been married for almost five years. She and her husband didn't think they could have children, but then on her twenty-fifth birthday, she had discovered she was pregnant with Cherie, who had just turned one.

"I know, and I love my granddaughter. However, one is not enough. At the rate you and your brothers are going, I'll be dead and six feet under before there's another Urban to carry the family name."

He couldn't resist a chuckle. Donna took turns calling each of her sons weekly to remind them of her impending demise. What he couldn't seem to get his mother to understand was that he was happy by himself. Nevertheless, if he found the right woman—not that he was looking—he would consider settling down. His brothers, on the other hand, preferred the privileges of being confirmed bachelors.

"I'll tell you what . . . don't invite Maureen, and I promise to bring a date," he said before he realized what he was saying.

She gasped. "Does that mean you are dating?"

Duane hadn't missed the note of excitement in her voice. "That means I have been seeing someone." *Although it has been strictly business.*

"What's her name?" his mother asked.

"Uh, her name is . . . Destiny."

"That's a pretty name. Is she someone special?"

Duane wanted to tell his mother that what he felt for Destiny ran deeper than an initial attraction. What he wanted was to be around her every day. He wanted to pull her in his arms and inhale her feminine fragrance. He wanted to claim her as his. After just one day, he wanted all that and so much more. "We just met," he said instead.

"What does she do?"

"Mom," he groaned, "You're ruining the surprise."

"All right. I'll look forward to meeting her. You know my heart can't take too many more disappointments."

Duane frowned. Since his mother was a part-time aerobics instructor, her heart was in better shape than his own. He knew the disappointment she was referring to was his failed relationship with Veronica.

"I won't disappoint you. Well, I got to go. So I'll talk to you this weekend."

He hung up the phone before she could pump him for additional information about his mystery woman.

Only minutes ago, he had decided to keep their relationship strictly professional; then what had he gone and done? He had promised to bring Destiny to a family gathering.

Now what had be gotten himself into?

Destiny pumped a small mound of mousse into the palm of her hand, then combed the rich foam into her freshly washed hair. Using her fingertips, she lifted the strands on the top, then teased the rest of her short crop away from her face.

Satisfied with her hair, she reached for her concealer to fix the dark circles beneath her eyes. Last night, despite her new bed, she'd had another restless night. After tossing and turning for hours, she had finally climbed out of bed shortly after midnight and spent the rest of the night in front of her computer. She had barely typed two pages before her head had hit the keyboard. She had awakened to find sunlight streaming through the window.

While taking a shower, she had thought long and hard. For weeks she had been living in fear, wondering when she was going to be found. When was it all going to come to an end? And because of it, her work had been affected. She always spent an average of five hours a day working on a manuscript, sometimes even longer, depending on how involved she was with the story. But it had been months since she'd written for that many hours in a day. She had come to the realization she was letting Lucas win. If she crawled farther into a shell, hid away from the rest of the world, and allowed her fear to affect her level of productivity, then Lucas would win.

By seven o'clock, Destiny had convinced herself she was safe hundreds of miles of away with no record of her whereabouts. Now the thing to do was to go on with her life as if nothing was wrong. To surrender was to give in to her fears, and she wasn't about to do that. She had fought for her life and had managed to stay alive thus far. She had given up her home, her friends, public appearances, and her life as an author when she had made the decision to report Lucas to the police. She had made the choice to testify. Now she needed to find a way to survive until then and make her temporary life as normal as humanly possible.

She glanced down at a pair of torn gray sweats and a T-shirt she had found in her uncle's dresser. Today she was planning to do some cleaning, and she needed to be dressed for the occasion.

Slipping on socks and shoes, she went down to the kitchen to make breakfast. She had just removed a pan of bacon from the fire when she heard the doorbell ring. Uneasiness skittered across her spine as she headed to the door, but without hesitation she glanced through the peephole to make sure it was who she was expecting.

"Good morning," Duane said immediately after she opened the door.

Destiny returned his smile as he stood before her and felt a change come over her body—her skin tingled beneath her shirt, the tips of her breasts hardened. "Morning." Somehow she found the strength to squeeze that one word out of her tight throat.

He strolled past her, carrying his toolbox, a power drill, and another tool she didn't recognize.

"Would you like some breakfast?" she asked.

He swung around. "No. I've already eaten."

"Then how about a cup of coffee? I made a fresh pot just for you."

Duane looked stunned yet pleased. "You didn't have to."

"I know . . . but I did it, anyway." She couldn't resist the grin.

Duane returned her smile with one that said "thank you," then headed toward the kitchen.

As she followed, Destiny couldn't help admiring how good he looked in a pair of black jeans. His shoulders strained against a T-shirt that was slightly yellow and thin with age. The fabric looked ready to give at any moment. The thought of seeing what lay beneath sent her heart rate up a couple of notches.

Taking a deep breath, she strolled over to the coffeepot, determined to keep her hormones under control.

Destiny usually spent hours online e-mailing other authors who were also networking to get new information. The African American literary market had grown so much in the last five years. At one time, finding black fiction was a rare experience. But after Terry McMillan came on the scene, doors opened for so many others.

During her travels, Destiny had met several authors and had formed lasting relationships. She met Tina Tate on a tour, and in less than two hours the two clicked and had been fast friends ever since. They had spent many hours on the phone, bouncing ideas off of one another or just gossiping. It had been four months since they had last spoken. She wanted so badly to call her friend. But she couldn't pick up the phone and call anyone because she didn't want to take the chance of the call being traced.

She wrapped her arms around her body in a protective manner and closed her eyes. She had taken a big enough risk contacting Julia, and she didn't want to press her luck. Carelessness would get her killed. All she had to do was lay low for six more weeks, and then she could return to St. Louis and testify in court. After Lucas was locked away, she could return to life as she had known it.

Remember, you promised to stay strong.

Rising from her chair, she pushed her fears aside. She had made a pledge not to allow Lucas to destroy her life, and she was going to try to do everything in her power to make sure that didn't happen.

Duane laid another cement backerboard over the faded linoleum, then reached for the box of screws and drilled one in each corner. So far he had covered half the kitchen floor with the ten-by-twenty sheets. By noon the floor would be ready to be prepped for the ceramic tile squares.

Shutting off the drill, he reached for another screw and heard soft humming coming from the other room. A small smile curved the corners of his mouth. A singer was something Destiny Davis was not. The off-key sound was almost as bad as fingernails on a chalkboard.

He chuckled at the comparison. Luckily, Destiny had several gifts that made up for her lack of musical talent. One of them was her ability in the kitchen. Unconsciously he realized he had purposely eaten his usual meal of frosted shredded wheat to avoid having breakfast with her that morning. He knew he needed to avoid contact with her as much as possible, or risk falling under her spell again today.

However, she had offered breakfast again after she had made two of the lightest and tastiest meat lover's omelets he had ever encountered. He found he was unable to resist. The taste of sausage and bacon sautéed with mushroom, onions, and green peppers was out of this world.

Not only was she a fabulous cook, he enjoyed her company at the table. As he reached for another backerboard, he thought about how much he had enjoyed sitting across from her. Watching the way she lightly patted her mouth with her napkin between bites was quite a joy. She had a natural way of puckering her lips that sent heat shooting straight to his loins. When he wasn't intrigued by her gestures, he had talked to her about the burning desire he had had to branch out on his own before he founded Urban Designs. She listened with genuine interest, as though hanging on his every word. Unlike some of the women in his past, Destiny didn't appear bored, nor did she cut in rudely in an attempt to change the subject.

Reaching for his drill and a handful of screws, he began securing the board to the floor. By the time he had finished, he realized, to his disappointment, that she hadn't revealed much about her past. Duane was intrigued by her and wanted to learn everything he could. So far she came across as a very private person who didn't easily trust others. Both could be good things, but by the same token, they could also be red flags.

He told himself it was a good thing she was holding back because then he couldn't run the risk of getting involved with her. He had made the decision just this morning to keep their relationship on a professional level.

So why did you tell your mom you were bringing her to the holiday barbecue?

He had screwed up. Now he had to find a way to fix it.

After ensuring the backerboard was secure, Duane rose from the kitchen floor and stretched his legs. Even while wearing knee pads, he could feel the pressure against his kneecaps when he worked on his knees. As a habit he tried to take a brief break every couple of hours, just long enough to stretch.

Hearing the humming again, he unsnapped the knee pads and allowed them to fall to the floor, then wandered into the hallway.

Destiny was standing on a step stool in front of the main door with a bottle in one hand, stretching up to reach the top hinges. He stopped in his tracks long enough to admire her from behind. It was amazing to him, but even in sweatpants and an old T-shirt, Destiny managed to look fabulous. There wasn't a lick of make-up on her face, yet her skin looked fresh and had a natural glow of its own that reminded him of a newborn baby's skin.

"What are you doing?"

She stopped humming and glanced over her shoulder. "Oiling these hinges," she replied. "Just about every door in this place squeaks, and it's driving me crazy."

"I thought you were working on your thesis?" he asked as he moved closer to the door.

She squirted oil in between the hinges as she spoke. "I was, but I went into the bathroom and the door squeaked so badly, I knew I wouldn't be able to concentrate until I got this done."

He couldn't blame her. He had found the same thing to be true of the doors he had opened.

Destiny came down off the stool, and he walked over to stand beside her. "How many have you done so far?"

"All of the ones on this floor, except for the kitchen. I thought I would slowly work my way up to the top."

Duane reached out and took the bottle from her. "Why don't I finish this floor while I rest my knees?"

She looked up at him with her brow lifted. "Really?"

"Really. But only if you do me a favor."

She looked at him, eyes twinkling with curiosity. He felt the overwhelming urge to reach out and pull her body flush against his, then kiss her.

"What kind of favor?"

"That you stay up in your room and work on your paper and let me worry about the work around here."

Her whole face lit up. "You've got yourself a deal." And she dashed up the stairs without another word.

He oiled the kitchen door, then went up to the second floor and worked his way from room to room. The last door to tackle was the door to her office. Just as he prepared to knock, she pulled it open from the other side and bolted through.

She ran smack into his chest, catching them both off guard. Automatically, he reached out and caught her by the arm. Destiny jumped as if he had burned her.

Duane stepped back. "Where are you rushing off to?"

Destiny stared up at him and licked her lips. "Um, to the kitchen," she murmured.

"Slow down before you hurt yourself." He smiled at her, trying not to stare at her beautifully curved mouth as she nervously moistened her lips again. With a nod of the head, she turned and hurried down to the kitchen.

Duane watched her leave, all the while feeling the same sting of awareness he felt with each encounter. He found her petite body and tantalizing fragrance both distracting and tempting. It baffled him that he was physically aware of everything about that woman. Although he knew it would be to his advantage to keep from reacting to her, the attraction was too compelling to resist.

The rapid intensity of his desire was beginning to bother him, and he wasn't quite sure what to do about it.

I'm not going to fall for Duane.

Destiny retrieved glass cleaner from the kitchen and then made her way up to the second-floor bathroom. She sprayed the small bathroom window with glass cleaner and wiped it with a clean cloth.

He was too kind, and her attraction to him too overpowering to put into words. Something intense flared through Destiny when Duane showed a slow appreciation of her features. If he smiled at her one more time and spoke to her in that deep, husky voice, she might just have to grab him by the hand and lead him into her bedroom, where she would be forced to make love to him until this ridiculous attraction was zapped from her system.

Are you nuts?

After a hectic last couple of weeks, she was running out of steam, which would probably explain why her thoughts had a tendency to fly off to areas better left unexplored.

Satisfied with the small window, she moved over to the medicine cabinet and sprayed glass cleaner on the small, round section of glass. Reaching for a clean rag, she had to spray, then wipe several times before the cloth came away clean. Focusing on housework temporarily suppressed the realization that she was more than attracted to Duane. She just didn't want to dwell on how he made her feel every time she was in his presence.

She was not going to fall for him. Although Duane was approachable and charming, at thirty, she'd had enough relationships to know that the way she was feeling was common after the first couple of interactions. She had felt the same way when she had first met Lucas and several men prior to him.

Only once had the feelings developed into an all-consuming love that was both powerful and undeniable. Maybe that was why she was curious even though she refused to have her heart broken again. She was probably unconsciously looking for that kind of feeling again. Yet the timing was all wrong. And a relationship with Duane wouldn't work because they lived worlds apart in different parts of the country.

Moving over to the tub, she slipped her shoes and socks off and stepped inside. Her grandmother had taught her the only way to really clean a tub was to get down and dirty with it. With the cleaner in hand, she sprayed the tub, then scrubbed it with a small bathroom brush.

"Now what are you doing?"

Her arms swung in the air, and the hand holding the wet brush sloshed a long, dripping streak across the bathroom floor. Turning in the direction of the masculine voice, she saw the object of her thoughts standing in the doorway.

Her breath hitched. Duane had removed his shirt. His chest was as hard and chiseled as she'd imagined, and he glistened with sweat. She tried to ignore how good he looked, and it took every ounce of willpower she had not to go to him and allow her fingertips to glide across his bare flesh. "You've got a bad habit of scaring me."

"Sorry. I thought I made quite a bit of noise. What are you doing now?"

She rose. "Cleaning the bathroom." *Isn't that obvious?*

Duane was frowning. "You shouldn't be doing that."

Destiny planted her hands firmly at her waist, then lifted her chin. "Why not?"

She then noticed his gaze had strayed from her face to her body, and when he swallowed, she realized her defiant stance had thrust her breasts forward in a way that made them stand out and be noticed. The look in his eyes was definitely hunger. It elicited a shiver of arousal, and she had to catch her breath. She was not falling for him, she reminded herself as she quickly crossed her arms.

She watched as he forced his eyes back to her face, then searched for the question she had posed before he had become distracted. Swallowing slowly, he answered, "I, uh, this place is pretty big, and at the rate you're going, you'll never finish your thesis in time. I know a lady who cleans houses for a living.

I'm sure she'd be delighted to come in and give you a hand."

Destiny lifted a shoulder in a self-conscious shrug. "I like doing this."

His brow rose as he studied her. The look told her he knew very few women who admitted they actually enjoyed cleaning. "I thought you came up here to work on your paper?"

"I can't work every minute," she told him as she dropped the brush into a small bucket. "Creativity just doesn't work like that. Doing housework allows me a chance to mentally outline the next section of my paper." It was true.

An irresistibly devastating smile tugged at the corners of his mouth and scrambled every brain cell she had. Before she could regroup, he stepped into the bathroom, clasped her hands to his, and assisted her out of the tub.

The bathroom was barely big enough for two. However, his presence wouldn't have been so unnerving if he hadn't stood so close. He didn't move away. He didn't release her hand. Instead, Duane's eyes captured hers, trapping her gaze.

His touch made her skin tingle and sent sparks flying all the way down to her toes. Under his intense appraisal, she felt breathless, as if he had somehow zapped all the oxygen from the room. *So much for thinking you could keep your hormones in check.* Every muscle in her body was on edge. With one last attempt at sanity, she shifted her gaze. Swallowing, she realized that act had been a big mistake. Duane was standing so close, she could have counted all of the hairs sprinkled across his chest. The musky male scent of him and the gleam of his sweat-dampened skin made her swallow hard.

Destiny took a deep, cleansing breath while she collected her thoughts. She reminded herself that this was not the time to get lost in the spell he weaved. Wiggling her hand free, she reached for the cleaning supplies. "I . . . um . . . guess I better get back to work." She didn't dare look at him again as she carefully moved around him and headed down the stairs.

An hour later, Destiny stood near the living room window and watched Duane disappear inside his house. Once again she hated to see him go, because his departure meant she was alone again. She liked having him around and wanted him to stay but knew she couldn't ask that of him.

She put her headset on and set the timer on the treadmill. Pacing herself at a slow jog for twenty minutes, she moved to the beat of the music. At home she jogged around the park with the wind blowing through her hair. A treadmill wasn't the same, but under the circumstances, it would have to do.

She tried to think of pleasant things, but her mind kept shifting back to Jarvis. Squeezing her eyes tightly, she tried to shut out the fearful expression on his face when he had said, "trust no one." Those last words would be forever embedded in her brain. It had been his way of reminding her that her life was in danger. Not that she hadn't already known that.

Feeling slightly off balance, Destiny opened her eyes and reached for the handrails for support. After fifteen seconds she began to feel in control again.

All she had to do was keep her whereabouts unknown for the next several weeks, and then she could return home and resume her regular life as De-

siree Davidson, *New York Times* Best-selling Author.
She missed her pastel-painted bedroom, her large,
round garden tub, and her king-size bed.

But those are material things.

What was important was making sure someone
paid for what they had done to Jarvis. She owed it
to him. And to do that, she had to make sure she
stayed alive long enough to put Lucas away for the
rest of his life.

Taking a deep breath, she concentrated on the
music, singing along with Outkast, drowning out
her thoughts until the timer went off.

She turned off the treadmill, then went downstairs for a bottle of water. Stepping into the kitchen,
she paused. Now that the backerboards covered the
entire floor, the room looked much larger. While
nibbling nervously on her lip, she realized that
she had her work cut out for her. Tiling a small
bathroom was one thing; tiling a large kitchen was
another thing altogether.

You asked for it.

Yes, I did.

Brushing her apprehensions aside, she looked on
the bright side. Between writing and home improvements, the time should speed by quickly, she
thought as she moved to the refrigerator.

Opening the refrigerator door, she found the
shelves practically bare. She was out of eggs, there
was barely any bacon left, and she was down to
her last stick of margarine. As much as she dreaded
the idea, she had no choice but to go to the grocery store.

She grabbed a bottle of water from the door, shut
the fridge, and headed down the hall toward the
stairs. She traveled up to her bedroom, then glanced

down at her watch. It was almost four o'clock. As she got dressed, she considered waiting until sundown, when she would be less noticeable, but after giving the idea considerable thought, she decided against it. She had a better chance of not being spotted in a crowded store. Besides, there was less chance of someone trying to hurt her if there were other people around.

She had considered ordering her groceries, but the idea was ridiculous. She believed in bargain shopping and couldn't see anyone else trying to do that for her. Normally, she stuck to her list, but if she saw something on sale or if the produce looked extremely fresh, she had no problem tossing the additional items in her cart. A personal shopper wouldn't know to do that.

By the time she had taken a seat on the end of her bed, she changed her mind. She would shop tomorrow. Today she would just have to order a pizza.

"Who's the man?" Reyn cried after he weaved around his older brother and, like a point guard, soared through the air and slammed the basketball through the hoop. Grabbing the ball, he stuck out his chest like a WWF wrestler and growled.

Duane gave him a dismissive wave. "Man, you cheated," he managed between breaths.

"What? What? Quit hating," Reyn cackled as he dribbled the ball to the other end of the court, where Duane was standing. "You just can't stand to lose."

"I don't mind losing; it's cheating I can't stand. You fouled me twice."

"Ahh, no, he didn't say I fouled him!" Reyn

chuckled some more, then passed the ball to his brother as they both moved to the bench for their water bottles.

"I think I'll wait until Garrett gets back before I play you again."

Reyn reached for his towel and mopped his bald head before commenting. "Go ahead. I'm still gonna win. Cause this brotha's got skills."

Trying to catch his breath, Duane took a seat on the bench. "Yeah, whatever, man." He removed the cap on his bottle and took several long, thirsty swallows. His eyes traveled around the court. It was well past sundown. The neighborhood park was relatively quiet except for a couple of men sitting on a bench in the far right hand corner, sharing a forty-ounce beer.

Stanley Lake Park was a great place for kids to hang out. It had a large pond for fishing, a track to run around, swings for the little kids, and a court to shoot hoops. It was in rather good condition. The city was committed to beautifying the grounds and keeping on top of trash collection. Park equipment was also repaired as needed.

Reyn draped his towel around his neck and lowered himself on the bench beside Duane. "All right, I'll give you the benefit of the doubt. I know I got skills, but your performance was less impressive than usual this evening. Whatzup with you?"

Duane took another drink, then shrugged. "I'm not sure."

"You got some honey on your mind?"

The question caused Duane to smirk. "Yeah, I guess you could say it's something like that." With both elbows resting on his knees, he told his younger brother about the woman who had moved in across the street.

"Damn, she sounds phat."

"She is," he replied in a distant voice.

"So what's the problem?" Reyn asked.

"I don't know. Something about her ain't right. I mean . . . I feel like she's hiding something."

"How you figure that? You just met her. Maybe she needs to get to know you first."

"Nah, I think it's something else. I just haven't figured it out yet."

"Then stay clear of her," he suggested.

Duane turned and gave his brother a look that said, "you've got to be kidding." It would be virtually impossible to remain detached and impersonal now that he had gotten to know just a little bit about her.

Reyn shrugged. "Then I suggest you tread lightly."

"Oh, yeah. No doubt." He knew his brother would suggest that he be careful. Reyn had been aware of his feelings for Veronica. In fact, he had been with Duane when he had gone and purchased an engagement ring for her. Reyn had seen the pain that he had gone through after he had discovered she was married. He had witnessed how long it had taken him to get over her and return his life to normal.

Duane took another drink from the bottle, finishing it. Reyn was right. The best thing he could do was to watch his step. Otherwise, he ran the risk of getting emotionally involved once more. Once had been bad enough; he wasn't sure if he could handle that kind of rejection again.

Chapter 5

Destiny was awakened by the screeching sound of a garbage truck pulling in front of her house. The sun had barely risen, and it had been a relatively cool night, yet her sheets were saturated with moisture.

She moaned in frustration. The vehicle had ruined a perfectly intimate moment in her dream. She had spent the better part of the night dreaming about Duane making love to her on every floor of her house.

Rolling onto her back, she stared up at the ceiling while she waited for the sexual feelings to subside. She hated to see them leave. Six months without sex was much too long a time.

A smile tipped the corners of her lips. *Who are you trying to fool?* She had gone without sex before for an even longer time. In fact, toward the end of her relationship with Lucas, their sexual relationship had become less fulfilling because subconsciously she had known something wasn't right about him.

The feelings and the dreams she'd had were attributable to one man. It wasn't just because Duane was handsome and sexy rolled up in one. There was more to it than that. The outside was the initial attraction. What mattered most was the man on the inside. Duane was kind, warmhearted, and very smart.

He also lives here in Delaware.

She dismissed the thought and rose from the bed, then strolled over to the window and glanced out. The trash truck had already moved down the street, leaving her empty trash cans on the curb.

She wasn't going to fool herself. Her reason for not wanting to become involved had little to do with their living miles part. Although long-distance relationships were hard to maintain, she was confident that if two people truly loved one another and really worked at it, all things were possible.

What was stopping her from crossing over the line was perfectly clear. She was carrying excess baggage.

A breeze sailed through the room and kissed her on the cheek. It was going to be another beautiful day. She smiled. It was also a perfect day to write. Allowing her eyes to stray across the street, she noticed that Duane wasn't home. It was barely seven o'clock, and already he had started his day.

Nothing like the present.

Throwing caution to the wind, she decided to go shopping for food. She turned and danced over to her dresser. She removed fresh underwear, then moved to the bathroom. Within seconds she was beneath the spray of water. When her nipples hardened, she thought of Duane again.

As much as she liked him, she knew sleeping with him would be a big mistake. When it was time for her to return home, she wanted to leave free and clear, without looking back.

That's easier said than done.

She knew she was lying to herself. In the few short

days they had spent together, she had grown quite fond of him. Even if she didn't give in to the attraction, walking away would be anything but easy.

She could not afford to think about Duane. Not the gentleness of his touch, nor his alluring smile, nor the twinkle in his eyes. Nevertheless, she could not deny that she wanted him more than she had wanted her fiancé. It didn't matter that she barely knew him; she still wanted him.

The water cooled her, and she had a strong feeling she would be taking a lot of showers in the next couple of weeks. Wrapping herself in a towel, she returned to her room and dried off, then slipped into a new outfit.

Destiny stood in front of the mirror, dressed in seventies garb—a purple-and-yellow tie-dyed shirt and bell-bottom jeans with painted daisies—she had found at a store in Maryland.

Looking at her reflection, she was pleased with the result. The outfit was something Desiree wouldn't have dreamed of wearing. Her taste, although expensive, had always been plain and simple, nothing to draw unwanted attention. However, since she had become Destiny, she had tried things she had always dreamed of trying. Especially when it came to her hair.

Making a quick trip to the bathroom, she rubbed styling gel through her hair and picked it, giving it a spiked look. She smiled. Despite all of the changes she'd experienced in the past several months, she could honestly say she liked her new hairstyle.

She had always prided herself on her long, thick, cinnamon mane. When she was ten, she had chopped off her ponytail. It was the only time she remembered ever seeing Nana cry. That day she made a promise to never cut it again, and it wasn't until her grandmother had passed that she considered cutting her hair a second time. But Lucas had talked her out of it. Now as she shifted her profile from side to side, she could honestly say she didn't miss the weekly three-hour appointments she had to fit into her schedule just to patronize a local beauty salon. Instead her current routine was simply wash and wear.

Feeling slightly more comfortable, she headed back to her bedroom, where she retrieved her purse and dark shades before walking to the door. Five minutes later, Destiny was in her car, heading west on Route 13.

According to a sales ad she had received in the mail the day before, there was a strip mall not too far from the house. Sure enough, as she turned right at the next light, she spotted the strip mall's crowded parking lot. Luckily for her, an elderly couple parked near the grocery store, was pulling out. Before another car could beat her to it, Destiny swerved into the vacant space.

Once she climbed out, she quickly crossed the parking lot and entered the grocery store. After reaching for a shopping cart, she traveled down one aisle after another. The last stop was the frozen food section. She was dying for strawberry shortcake ice cream bars. She spotted them in the center aisle and dropped three boxes into her cart.

"It's nice to know I'm not the only one addicted to those."

Destiny glanced to her left to find a young, petite woman with laughter in her eyes.

"I've been addicted to these since I was a kid," Destiny admitted.

"So have I. The ice cream truck stopped in front of my house every evening because the ice cream man knew I was going to be waiting for him."

Destiny threw her head back with laughter. "Ours did the same thing."

The woman also grabbed three boxes of ice cream bars off the shelf; then the two chatted all the way to the checkout lane.

Destiny was still smiling as she pushed her grocery bags out to her car. The shopping trip had been better than she had anticipated.

See, all that worrying for nothing.

As she loaded her bags into the trunk, she found herself starting to believe that everything was going to be all right because no one knew she was in Delaware.

She pulled out of her parking spot and coasted over several speed bumps while checking out all of the shops in the strip mall. There was a clothing store, which she vowed to patronize when time allowed, a shoe store, and a music store. However, the store that interested her most was at the very end. It was a small bookstore name Aisha's.

The store had to be African American, she thought as she noticed the display of books in the window. Curiosity got the better of her, and the next thing she knew, she was pulling into another parking space. Getting out of her car, she trotted across the lot into the store. Sure enough, African American books dominated the floor space.

It was a quaint little store with a small coffee shop to the left, near several couches and small tables. Destiny glanced around, spotting the names of dozens of authors whose numbers she had saved on her speed dial at home, as well as several new authors. As soon as she stepped around the corner, she found an end cap that displayed her latest book, *On the Run. How ironic,* she thought as she picked up the hardcover edition. She never grew tired of holding her own books.

"Can I help you with something?"

She glanced up to see a young, toffee-colored teenager standing beside her. She shook her head and said politely, "No, I'm just looking."

The salesclerk glanced down at her hand. "That's a wonderful book!"

"It is?" Destiny asked innocently. It was always a pleasure to discover she had a new fan.

"Oh yes, that is probably one of Desiree's best books."

She purposely kept her head tilted to the floor, not wanting to take a chance of the woman recognizing her. "I'll have to keep that in mind."

"Rumor has it, she's missing."

Her head snapped up. "Missing?"

The girl nodded and appeared happy to share a bit of gossip. "My book club leader told me that someone told her Desiree hasn't been seen in months. Some say she might be dead."

"Dead?" she croaked.

"Yep. Can you imagine how valuable her books will be if she is. I went out and bought every copy."

Suddenly feeling light-headed, Destiny returned the book and, ignoring the salesclerk, headed back out to her car.

Dead! If she were dead, her books would be priceless. The thought made her sick to her stomach.

Squeezing the steering wheel, she closed her eyes and waited for the feeling to subside. It was followed by a wave a disappointment. She had been having such a good day and had ruined it by going into the bookstore. She should have just gone home. Remembering she had ice cream in the trunk, she opened her eyes, then reached for her keys.

As she drove away, she couldn't help thinking about what the salesclerk had said about her supposed death. By the time she was a couple of blocks away from home, her confidence had returned. There was no way she was going to allow that to happen.

She stopped at a light, glanced into the rearview mirror, and noticed that the same blue car that had been behind her when she had first pulled out of the parking lot was still behind her. Panic struck, and at the next corner she made a left instead of a right. Glancing in the mirror, she almost came unglued when she found the car was still trailing her.

Don't panic.

Despite the words, she pressed her foot down on the gas and sped through the next yellow light. The blue car did, too. Eyes darting nervously back and forth, she almost ran into the back of a silver Cadillac. Quickly, Destiny swerved into the left lane and turned the corner. Once there, she pulled her car over to the side and waited.

Chest heaving, heart pounding, she was terrified but refused to live the rest of her life in fear. If someone was following her, she wanted to know who it was.

She waited and waited some more while she listened to the pounding of her heart. She waited for what felt like an eternity but, according to the clock on her dashboard, it was only two minutes. Releasing a sigh of relief, she put the car in drive and headed home. On the way there, she found herself thinking that maybe hiring a personal shopper wasn't such a bad idea after all.

"How about we break for lunch?"

"All right, boss," a young, olive-colored man agreed. After lowering the roller back into the pan of paint, the young man eagerly left the house and headed to his car. By the time Duane told Mrs. Jackson he was leaving for lunch and made it out to his truck, his assistant was long gone.

Percy Taylor was a tall, slim man with a hearty appetite. Duane could bet that he had rushed home for some of his Mama's fabulous fried chicken. He couldn't blame him. The couple of times Duane had accompanied Percy to his home, the meal was like Percy always said, "Slap-yo-mama-good."

A woman from the old school, Ms. Taylor didn't take kindly to her son using those exact words, so Percy shared them when she wasn't listening.

Duane drove his truck to the Concord Pike, where there were numerous restaurants to choose from. He quickly decided on a restaurant famous for its crab cakes. Lunch was usually an hour; however, it was a rather warm day, and he wanted to get back before the paint brushes dried. Service was prompt as usual. While he ate, Duane thought about how proud he was of his assistant.

He had met Percy a year ago, while replacing the windows on a row house in the heart of the city. The nineteen-year-old had sat on the porch across the street and watched for almost an hour before he found the nerve to come over and ask Duane for a job. When Duane had asked him to grab a rake and clean the trash from the yard, the young man ran home at once, retrieved a rake, and worked in silence until the job was complete. What impressed Duane the most was that he didn't have to tell Percy to bag it up and carry it out to the curb. It had already been done.

Without references, he had hired him on the spot. It wasn't until weeks later that Percy confessed that he had a juvenile record for stealing. Duane had thanked him for his honesty, and not once had he regretted his decision. Percy was dependable and hardworking, and to reward him for his dedication, Duane intended to give him several additional responsibilities. In fact, while he worked on the renovations at Murphy's, he planned to turn a great deal of the work over to Perry. With a baby soon on the way, he was certain Percy would be eager for the added duties and income.

Duane finished his food, left a sizable tip, and returned to his truck. He was heading back to the house when something that had been at the back of his mind for the past several days pushed to the surface. At the next corner he turned right and headed farther into the city. At a corner liquor store he hung a left onto a one-way street, then slowly drove through housing projects, looking for one unit in particular. Men sat on the curbs laughing; others stood around a car with forty-ounce bottles of beer in their hands. There was a woman pushing a shopping cart down the sidewalk, picking up things that appeared valuable to her and tossing them in under an old, grimy blanket. Trash flooded the sidewalk and what was once considered grass. Clothes hung from clotheslines in back of the houses, while cars that probably hadn't moved in years took up space on the street in front.

At the end of the block, Duane recognized an old, yellow Nova in front of a unit that hadn't seen a screen door in years. Certain he had the right place, he backed into a tight parking spot and climbed out. Stepping over broken bottles, he made his way to the door and knocked.

A young woman in her early twenties appeared, balancing a small toddler on her hip.

"Yeah, can I help you?"

"Sorry to bother you, but does Shaunda or Mannie Kelly live here?"

She shook her head of shoulder-length corn-rows. "Nah, not anymore. They got evicted a couple of months ago."

Duane pressed his lips together in disappointment. "You wouldn't by chance know where they went?'

"Nope. All I know is that she hadn't paid her rent in six months, and they got evicted." She rolled her eyes and sucked her teeth. "Rumor has it, she's a crackhead, but I ain't one to gossip so I don't know how true that rumor really is."

"Thanks for your time." Ignoring the woman's appreciative stare, Duane turned on his heels and returned to his car.

Destiny didn't know why, but suddenly she had a strong sensation that something bad was about to happen. When or to whom she had no idea; all she knew was that her instincts told her to be extra careful.

She stopped typing and leaned back in her chair, thinking of different possibilities. Her feelings probably had a lot to do with what had happened during her trip to the store that morning. Although, since her return, she had convinced herself it had just been her imagination. So then what else could it be?

Was there any chance that she had left something in her condo that would reveal her whereabouts to Lucas? She nibbled on her bottom lip and went down the list. She had burned the statements from the property management agency. When she had first become suspicious of Lucas, she rented a safety-deposit box and filled it with anything that connected her to her past, including her grandmother's letters, pictures, etc. The only things she had left in her condo were furniture and clothes. Nothing in it connected her to Destiny, or even Desiree. The phone had been disconnected. She had even terminated her Internet and cell phone service. She had cut up all of her credit cards. Bills were being paid automatically out of her checking account, which she hadn't accessed since she had left the state. Everything she had obtained in the last several months, including her dependable car, had been purchased with cash.

A wave of uneasiness told her that no matter what she did, she still wasn't safe.

Rising from her chair, she moved over to the window and raised it, allowing in a stream of fresh air. It was the first time she had opened the window in her makeshift office since she had arrived. Last night she had opened the window in her bedroom long enough to cool it off, only to lower it again before she had gone off to sleep. The only other window she opened was the one in the kitchen, and that was because Duane was working in there, and she didn't want him to get overheated. She shut it immediately after he left.

She breathed deeply, then told herself it was okay. She was on the second floor. The only way a person could get to her was if they scaled the side of the house.

Destiny sat back down at her desk, lowered her forehead in her hands, and took a deep breath. She tried to convince herself it was all in her mind. Everything was going to be okay. However, no matter how much she tried to convince herself otherwise or to put her mind at ease, she could not shake her feeling of foreboding. Her experience that morning had only made matters worse.

Raising her head, she brushed the tears from the corners of her eyes. She had to stay tough. She was not going to let Lucas kill her spirit.

That is easier said than done.

She heard Duane's truck pull into his driveway. Rising from the chair, she went to the window again. He climbed out, removed another backerboard from the back, then headed toward her house.

The instant she saw him, all the tension melted from her body. With a loud sigh of relief, Destiny raced to the mirror to look at her appearance. Quickly, she ran a comb through her hair, then made it down the stairs just as he rang the doorbell.

"Hey," he said with a grin when she answered the door.

Despite the fact that he and his clothes were speckled with paint, her heart banged uncontrollably. "Come on in."

"I didn't mean to disturb your writing. I wanted to get this last board down. Then I'll get out of your hair as quickly as possible."

"You're not in my way." She liked having him around. Just him being there made her feel safe.

She followed him into the kitchen. "Tomorrow I'll take care of the plumbing and replace the screen door for you," he told her.

She hesitated, contemplating her next question, which would likely draw suspicion. Then she decided to risk it. "Would you be able to put bars on the first-floor windows?"

Duane raised his brow. "We don't have a lot of break-ins in this area of town."

She wasn't surprised by his answer. Since her arrival, she had reviewed the crime statistics in the area and found the crime rate to be quite low. However, her reason for asking had nothing to do with what was currently happening in the area. Her reasoning had to do with what might occur if she wasn't careful. She needed to do whatever she had to do in order to feel safe. "Maybe so, but I would feel a lot safer."

Duane's eyes never left hers, and she could feel them burning inside her as if he were trying to read her mind. The intensity was so strong, she almost felt the need to squirm.

"All right," he finally said.

With a sigh of relief, she nodded. Turning, she poured herself a glass of lemonade, then retreated back up to her office.

Duane stared after her, more curious than ever about what was going on in her life. She had walked away looking painfully vulnerable and fragile. The only message he had gotten from her request was that she was afraid. Why else would someone want ugly iron bars on their windows when they already had an alarm system? The area even had its own neighborhood watch in place, and if all else failed, there were several busybodies between the ages of fifty-five and eighty who spent the majority of their day peeping out their windows. But as Duane laid the backerboard onto the floor, he had a strong feeling that none of those things would make a difference.

Just leave it alone.

Unfortunately, ignoring the warning wasn't an option. As long as he could remember, he had never been one to look the other way. At least not since the last time.

He reached for his drill and within seconds secured the board with his first screw. While screwing in several more, he allowed his thoughts to travel back in time.

Duane remembered that when he was in college, there had been a beautiful young woman named Layla Lewis who used to miss class quite a bit. When she did come to class, she always looked tired and sad. He had made it a habit of copying two sets of notes so that whenever she came to class, she could always catch up on what she missed. He remembered one time seeing the glimmer of tears in her eyes at his kind gestures. Feeling that it was none of his business, and not wanting to come across as nosy, he didn't ask questions. A couple of weeks later her face flashed across the television screen during the ten o'clock news. According to the report, her body had been found in a dumpster a couple of blocks away from campus. Weeks later her ex-boyfriend was arrested for her murder. Apparently, he had been stalking her for some time, and she'd had no one to turn to for help.

Duane swallowed the lump that had risen in his

throat as he thought about how guilty he had felt. He had blamed himself for weeks, thinking that if he had asked questions and showed concern for her tears, maybe things would have turned out differently. Maybe Layla would still be alive today. He had attended her funeral with the determination to never look away again.

While sweeping the dust in a neat pile, Duane's thoughts shifted to Destiny again. Something was going on with her. He could feel it in his gut. There was something warm and vulnerable in her eyes that made him want to protect her. And because of it, he had a strong urge to drop the broom and dash up the stairs. He would then scoop Destiny into his arms and hold her in a tight, comforting embrace. He told himself the impulse had nothing to do with his sexual attraction to her. It had nothing to do with feeling an obligation to her uncle. He merely wanted to ease her mind by letting her know that everything was going to be all right, especially as long as she had him as her neighbor. Or so he tried to convince himself that that was the only reason.

He contemplated going upstairs and asking her what was she afraid of. Why did he care so much to know what she was hiding? As far as she was concerned, she didn't owe him an explanation and probably might even go as far as to tell him so. Besides, it really wasn't any of his business. If she told him off, it would be well deserved. Nevertheless, he would stay alert and keep his eyes and ears open.

Duane's mind raced, and by the time he had cleaned up the last pile of his mess and discarded it in an industrial garbage bag, he decided he

wanted to do something for her, anything to erase
the faraway look in her eyes and make her smile.

He carried the bag through the house and across
the street and dropped it on the side of his house,
beside his trash can. There was no reason why she
had to lug it out to the curb on trash day when it
was his mess. By the time he had crossed the street
again, he realized what Destiny needed—a night of
dancing, drinks, and casual conversations. His
mouth curved into an unconscious smile. That
was exactly what she needed.

Reaching down to his tool belt, he unhooked a
Phillips screwdriver. When he reached the screen
door, he swung it open and began removing the
screws that held it firmly in place. He would pick
up another one while he was at the home improvement store tomorrow. While he was at it, he would
look for the bars Destiny asked him to install. In the
meantime, as soon as he finished removing the
door and loading it in the back of his truck, he was
going to ask Destiny to spend the evening with
him. He removed the last screw while ignoring
the voice inside his head that told him she was a
woman he should stay away from.

Destiny was supposed to be writing a love scene for
her novel, and she was so embarrassed because all
she could think about was what it would feel like to
be made love to by Duane. Writing about passion and
intimacy left her breathless and panting for him.

Duane was the perfect model for the hero in her
new novel, Destiny thought as she put the finishing touches on her character sketch. Her character, Stan Lee, was a police officer investigating the

murder of Tina Calvin's sister. As the two joined forces, they fell in love.

Shaking the traitorous thoughts, she pushed her chair back from the computer, wishing she could make the chair swivel. At home she had a big, old executive chair that she called Aler. She and Aler had been together ten years. She had written her very first book sitting in him. When she had gotten *the call*, she had been sitting in Aler with her legs curled beneath her.

She chuckled inwardly. She was thousands of miles away from home, yearning for a chair. *Talk about pathetic.* She would just have to go out and find a substitute. In the meantime, the chair she sat in, which belonged to a card table in the corner, would just have to do.

Before she had fled from St. Louis, she had already completed one third of *The Last Mile.* Since then she had done a chapter here and there. Today, however, she had barely finished two pages. If she kept up that pace, she wouldn't even have the first rough draft completed before her return home.

Home?

A flicker of uneasiness coursed through her. Did she even know what that word meant anymore? She clenched her hand until her nails dug into her palm. It seemed as if she was still searching for the meaning behind the word.

"Destiny?"

She was barely able to control her gasp of surprise. Turning, she found Duane standing in the doorway.

She blinked, then forced a smile. "I'm sorry. I was deep in thought and didn't hear you."

His lips curled into a slow smile. "It appears I am always apologizing for startling you."

"May I suggest tying a cowbell around your neck?" she said in a teasing manner.

"I think my grandpa might still have one."

She giggled as he stepped into the room, stopping just inside the doorway. "I'm finished for today. I'll get started early tomorrow. As soon as you are ready, we can go shopping for tile."

"Sounds good," she said, her voice slightly husky. She stared up at him for what felt like forever before he spoke again.

"What do you have planned for the evening?"

She broke eye contact and pointed to her computer screen. "I'm going to sit here and work on my thesis."

"How about a little fun?"

She gazed up, and amusement flicked in the depths of the eyes that met her. There were so many meanings behind those simple words. The room was full of new, fragile feelings, feelings such as she'd never experienced before.

Destiny looked down for a moment at her keyboard as the world seemed to tilt off its axis. When she returned her gaze, she noticed he had stepped a little farther into her office.

She cleared her throat. "What do you have in mind?"

"How about ten-cent wings and a fish bowl of draft beer?"

She glimpsed childlike amusement flickering in his eyes. "You're kidding, right?"

He shook his head. "No, I'm not. There's this little joint I go to that plays oldies from the seventies and eighties and serves the best wings in town, any way you like them."

"You mean I can get ten wings for one dollar?" Her eyes held a wistful yearning.

"Yep."

She stared at him. He was staring at her in a way that drew a quiver from deep in her abdomen. There was no way she could accept his invitation. Adjusting to life in Delaware was going to be enough of a challenge without adding to the complications. She planned to be strong but knew better than to risk trying to be anything more than friends.

She had decided it was safer not to go out again unless she had to, in the hope of remaining undiscovered. But it was the evening, and she had been cooped up for so long. It would be nice to go out for once and have some fun.

"What time?" she asked before she could change her mind.

Duane grinned as he spoke in a low voice. "How about seven?"

She nodded. "Seven is perfect."

Duane tried to suppress a rush of pleasure at the chance to see her again that day, but an eager smiled curled his lips. "Good. I'll be back to pick you up later."

Her voice was very soft. "I'll be waiting."

Duane came to her, reached down in a silent gesture, and grabbed for her hand, pulling her to her feet. "Walk me to the door."

Her heart contracted briefly as his thumb slipped into the cup of her palm. Holding her hand was innocent enough. However, even when he released it and walked beside her, brushing against his clothing was enough to send her pulse hurtling.

She followed him downstairs and locked the door behind him. It was quite a while later that she realized that he had long since gone into his house and she was still standing at the window watching.

Destiny turned off the treadmill and stepped off. While walking toward the bathroom, she removed the towel around her neck and mopped her forehead. Part of her knew she shouldn't go out that evening, but the other part of her was tired. Tired of Lucas dictating her life. Tired of living in fear. She had a right to be happy, and doggone it, she was going to be just that. Starting tonight.

Moving into the bathroom, she turned on the shower, then removed her clothes and stepped in under the stream of hot water. Closing her eyes, she wet her hair, then reached for her shampoo and poured a dab in her palm. As she lathered her hair, she felt her lips curl upward. She was looking forward to an evening out on the town with Duane.

She liked him, even if she wasn't ready to admit just how much. Duane was sensitive, considerate, not to mention handsome. There was something so infectious about his smile; she couldn't help returning it with one of her own. He was a wonderful distraction from her problems.

She showered quickly, reached for a towel, and wrapped it around her body, then walked down the hall to her bedroom.

Plopping down on the end of the bed, she reached for her favorite scented lotion and spread it generously on her body. Tonight she looked forward to an evening without a worry in the world.

Duane hadn't been exaggerating about the wings. There were twenty-five types to choose from. She ordered ten honey barbecue wings, ten teriyaki wings, and an apple martini.

"How do they taste?" Duane raised his voice to be heard over the music coming through the speakers on opposite sides of the room.

While licking the sauce from her fingers, Destiny glanced across the table and grinned. "Fabulous," she answered.

Freddy's was a moderate-size bar and grill with a trio of pool tables to the far right. There were dozens of tables, all of them occupied and positioned close to the walls, allowing for a large dance floor at the center of the room. As Duane had promised, the deejay was playing tunes from the seventies and eighties. The song playing at that moment sounded so familiar, yet Destiny couldn't place her finger on it.

"Ready for the World," Duane said as if he had read her mind.

She nodded her head rapidly. "Ooh, I used to love them!"

"We all did," he said, grinning with fond memories. "Back in the day, I pulled more women on that song than I could count."

Destiny playfully rolled her eyes at the comment, then calculated quickly. "I think I was in the second or third grade."

"I remember I was a senior in high school," he said, before taking a sip of his fish bowl of beer.

She turned slightly, her brow wrinkled with curiosity. "Senior . . . how old are you?"

"I'll be forty on my next birthday." When her eyes grew large, he asked, "Why? Does age matter?"

She simply shrugged. "Why would it matter? You just don't look that old."

Duane managed to look thoroughly insulted. "Oh, so now I'm old?"

She playfully jabbed him in the arm. "You know what I mean."

He chuckled, and her frown dissolved into laughter. Duane found that he liked the sound of her laughter. It was warm and seductive. It was a far cry from her nervous, far-off look, not to mention the tears. Suddenly, he wanted to kiss her lush mouth and discover if it was as soft as the skin on her radiant face. He was amazed that he wanted her with as much intensity as he had wanted the success of his own business. "Have you ever dated an older man before?"

She looked startled by his question. "Who says we're dating?"

Lowering his chin, he studied her features intensely under the dim lighting overhead. Her cheekbones seemed more pronounced with her hair swept away from her face. He wanted to touch her, put his mouth on places that would make those copper brown eyes close. "What would you call it?"

"Two neighbors enjoying a night out," she answered smoothly as she sipped her martini.

Duane sat back comfortably in his chair. "Believe me, I could have found a better way to spend my evening."

She inhaled sharply and quickly glanced at him. "Then why didn't you?" she asked, her chin tipped defiantly.

"Because I would rather spend my evening in the company of my beautiful, intriguing neighbor." He leaned forward, then added, "I'm anxious to learn all I can about her."

Destiny took a deep breath as her heart hammered heavily in her chest. Finding Duane watching her intensely, she turned her head and brought her glass to her lips. The drink was generously laced with vodka, and she welcomed the warm feeling spreading through her chest.

She lowered her glass and tilted her head so she could see him. The lighting overhead made Duane's eyes appear large and vivid. For the second time that evening, her mouth went dry. The first time had been when he had picked her up.

When she had opened the front door, she couldn't help but stare. He was dressed handsomely in a pair of freshly pressed black jeans that fit his waist and hips with precision. The gray short-sleeved, button-down shirt outlined his broad shoulders. As if he knew she was watching, he shifted and she watched his biceps flex at his forearms. To say he had a nice body was an understatement.

Everything about the man spelled S-E-X-Y. The way he shoveled food in his mouth, the way he waited until he had completely swallowed it before taking a sip from his glass. However, nothing was more sensual than the way dimples appeared on either side of his jaw when he gave her his signature smile. Seeing his sparkling pearly whites did *things* to her insides.

To be this attracted to a man she'd just met couldn't be natural. And to make matters worse, she couldn't remember a time when Lucas made her feel uneasy to the point that her stomach quivered. As far as she was concerned, no man she had ever dated made her feel the intensity she felt right now with Duane.

Hey, who says you're dating?

"Would you like another drink?" he asked, noticing her glass was almost empty.

She shook her head free of her meandering. "Sure, why not."

He raised his hand and captured the waitress's attention.

For the last hour she had enjoyed his company and the best wings she'd ever tasted. The spicy sauce contributed to her desire for another martini.

Duane gave their drink orders, then returned his attention to his date. "So tell me about San Antonio, Texas."

She reached for another wing and bit into it. "There isn't much to tell."

A slight frown created furrows in Duane's forehead. "I beg to differ. There's the Alamo, the River Walk."

"You just named everything, so there really isn't much more to talk about."

Her gaze scurried away from his. What was she hiding?

"What do you usually do for fun?" he asked, his gaze fixed on her profile.

She mopped her mouth with a napkin, then looked at him again. "Movies, dinner, shopping, reading a good book." At the mention of recreational activities, she realized it had been a long time since she'd spent time with friends. They used to go clubbing once a month. "My girlfriends and I have so much fun together."

"I hope to make you fall in love with Delaware," he replied, white teeth flashing against his sable skin.

Again, Destiny felt the familiar quivering in her

stomach. "I'm leaving in a couple of weeks," she reminded.

"Maybe." There was a gleam of determination in his eyes as he bit into a wing.

She ticked her head to the side and crinkled her nose. "There's no maybe about it."

Duane stared at her, his dark gaze burning her face with intensity. "What would it take to change your mind?"

She observed the way his tongue darted out the corner of his mouth every now and then to capture a bit of barbecue sauce. Nervous excitement bubbled inside her. "I haven't thought about it. I have a job, and all my friends back home."

Duane gazed at her over the rim of his glass. Watching the flutter at her throat, he wondered if maybe he was acting too quickly. He had vowed to take things slow, but Destiny nearly took his breath away. Today was the first time he had seen her looking both beautiful and sexy. He was shocked by his uncontrollable urge to touch her. He stared at the natural glow of her face beneath the lighting. Except for a hint of pink on her lush, full mouth, her skin was free and clear. He gave her a half-smile, his gaze shifting from her lips down to her orange blouse with a round neckline, which revealed a hint of the swell of her full breasts. A short, white miniskirt showed off her bare, toned legs. The strength of her calves was quite noticeable in her pair of matching high-heeled orange mules.

Their waitress returned with their drinks and another dozen spicy wings. When she departed, Destiny shifted on her seat, drawing his attention, and said, "Listen . . . Delaware will be my home for as long as it takes to finish my thesis and put my uncle's house on the market."

He leaned forward, staring at her. "Then what happens?"

Heat rose to her face under his penetrating eyes. Her heart beat rapidly. "Then it's time for me to return home."

Duane paused briefly, a smile tilting the corners of his mouth. "What if I don't want you to leave?"

There was so much passion in his question that Destiny found it difficult to breathe. What was he trying to say? Could he possibly be just as intrigued by her as she was by him? She tried to push that possibility aside. She also refused to think about returning to St. Louis. Returning meant sitting directly across from Lucas in a courtroom. "I have to. It's my home."

"What about the rest of your family? Where are they?"

She shrugged a slender shoulder, pleased he had allowed the subject to drop. "There is no one else. Just me."

He stopped eating and slowly lowered his chicken wing to the Styrofoam container. "I'm so sorry." He clasped her hand.

"No need to be sorry. It's not your fault." She gave him a sad smile. "Nana said my father stopped coming around after he discovered my mother was pregnant. Not that I blame him. He was only seventeen and my mother a year younger. Nana said she was wild as all get out." She paused to give a laugh that lacked humor. "I was barely a month old when she walked out on me. Then she dropped in and out of my life for six years before she stopped coming around all together." While growing up, Destiny had often thought about the woman who had given birth to her. Grace Davidson was a woman she never expected to cross paths with again. "I used to think that it was something that I did, that maybe I had been a bad girl, and that's why my mother stopped coming around, but Nana wouldn't have it. She taught me that it was Grace's loss, not mine."

He squeezed her wrist. "Your grandmother sounds like a very smart woman."

"Yes, she was." Destiny closed her eyes briefly, with her lips curved in a faint smile of remembrance. The memories of her grandmother would be embedded in her heart forever. Opening her eyes, she found Duane staring at her with a concerned expression.

"You okay?" he asked.

Quickly, she looked away and reached for another wing. "Yes, I'm fine. Are your grandparents still around?"

Nodding his head, he reached for a clean napkin, then said, "My paternal grandfather had a fatal heart attack before I was even born, and my grandmother has lived with us ever since. She's a feisty little lady who loves water aerobics. My mother's parents live in Philadelphia when they aren't spending time at their home in Fort Lauderdale."

Destiny listened as he talked about his grandparents and realized she envied him. He had so much more than she would ever have. He and his siblings used to take turns spending the summer in Florida. The four of them had been too much of a handful for his grandparents to handle at one time. Destiny quickly forgot about her loss as she listened to several animated tales of sibling rivalry.

"I was locked in that chest two hours before my grandma found me," Duane concluded.

Destiny's gentle laughter rippled through the air. "That's what you get, *Houdini*."

"Believe me, I never tried that magic trick again. My grandfather made sure of that." He rubbed his butt to emphasize his meaning. Destiny threw her head back with laughter; the sexy sound vibrated up from her throat.

They music changed, and the room was filled with a song that was slow and sensual. Destiny watched as several couples moved out onto the dance floor.

Duane took one last swig of his beer, then sat the fishbowl down and rose. "Come, let's dance." He rounded the table and, extending his hand, waited for Destiny to place her hand in his.

She shook her head. "I can't dance."

"Everyone can dance," he insisted.

Her eyes grew large and round. "Not me. I have two left feet."

He noticed the indecision in her gaze. "All you have to do is follow my lead."

Before she could protest further, he grasped her hand and gently pulled her to her feet. Curving an arm around her, he led her out onto the dance floor, where they were quickly swallowed up by a lively crowd.

"All you have to do is wrap your arms around my waist and move with me," he whispered close to her ear.

Destiny wished she had as much confidence as he had. Still, she wrapped her arms around him as he pulled her tightly in his embrace. Resting her cheek against his chest, she closed her eyes and followed the sway of his body. She started out with her body stiff and uneasy, but as she became more and more comfortable with his movements, her body began to relax one degree at a time. As they moved to the beat of the music, their bodies molded together, and she inhaled the mild scent of his cologne and the essence of the man himself. The combination engulfed her body, assaulting her senses. At such close range, she was getting the full potent effect of it.

She was where she wanted to be. Close, so close their thighs were touching and her breasts were pressed snugly against him. His warm breath was in her hair, causing a heat that had nothing to do with the temperature of the room.

"I thought you said you couldn't dance?" he asked.

She giggled softly, then pulled back slightly and stared up at him. "I can't."

The soft sound of her laughter vibrated against his nose. "You sure had me fooled."

She shuddered as a spell weaved itself around them as she continued to meet his penetrating stare. Heat began to radiate throughout her body, making her blood flow heavily through her veins.

Duane tightened his grip on her waist, pulling her closer. "You're gorgeous."

There was something very masculine in his tone, which made everything feminine in her stir. "You're not bad yourself," she said, deliberately flirting with him.

"Thank you."

The burning look in Duane's eyes made her think of another rhythm, that of bodies locked, moving together at an even pace. She rested her cheek on his chest again and closed her eyes as the song changed to an old Babyface favorite of hers. She had last heard the song during couple's night at the roller rink. It was one of the last places she and Lucas had gone together. "Do you roller-skate?" she heard herself ask.

"No," Duane whispered against her hair.

"Then it's time you learn. Next time the evening's on me."

He pulled away until he could see her face. "So you plan on seeing me again?"

"I . . ." Destiny's voice trailed off as she realized she had extended an invitation to see him again.

"Well, do you?" He continued to stare down at her, waiting for an answer.

She closed her eyes briefly and smiled. "Of course."

When she stared up at him, his chin tilted slightly downward. The gleam in his eyes beckoned to her as time stood still.

When the song ended, the deejay decided to speed the music up a notch. Sliding his arm around her shoulder, Duane led her off the dance floor.

"I'm going to run to the ladies' room."

"I'll see you back at the table," he replied with an irresistible smirk.

Destiny stepped into the restroom. Catching her reflection in the mirror, she found herself smiling. She was indeed enjoying the atmosphere and the company.

On the way back to the table, she spotted a pay phone. Pulling her calling card from her purse, she dialed her lawyer's office. While the phone rang, she glanced down at her watch, knowing Chuck never left the office before nine. It was almost eight in St. Louis.

The phone was answered on the third ring. "Chuck," Destiny said, relieved that his secretary, Marlene, hadn't answered.

"Desiree, where the hell are you?" She couldn't miss the agitation in his voice.

"I can't tell you that."

He groaned through the receiver. "The FBI has been breathing down my back trying to find you."

"Well, they can keep on looking! I don't trust them. They assured me I was safe in protective custody and look what happened. Somebody on the inside leaked my whereabouts. How else was Jarvis murdered?"

"Yes, I have to agree." He paused as if choosing his next words carefully. "So far there isn't any evidence to pin that murder on Lucas Blake or his men. The bullet that killed Officer Jarvis Jackson was from a gun that was involved in a liquor store robbery a year ago."

"Great! Just great!"

"That's not all." He hesitated again. "I hate to tell you this, but Lucas was released on bail."

Her voice dropped in volume. "I thought the judge denied him bail?"

"His lawyer had it overturned."

Fear and anger twisted inside her. "Oh no." Closing her eyes, she swallowed a dry taste of fear from her throat as her stomach started to cave in. This wasn't happening.

"The police are watching him like a hawk. However, Hector has skipped town."

Her eyelids snapped open. "What do you mean skipped?"

"I mean, it appears he has left the city, the state, the country, who knows. All I know is that he isn't here."

Since she had first gone into protective custody, the feds had kept up around-the-clock surveillance on Lucas's goons. Hector, who had always been the one to call the shots, was second in command. Now that Lucas was unable to leave the state, Hector was probably running things.

Chuck interrupted her thoughts. "Desiree, I'm worried he might be out looking for you. When are you coming home?"

Destiny closed her eyes again. She wished she could forget her given name and all the problems she had left behind. Desiree's life was a big mess. She wanted so much just to be the character from her first romantic novel—Destiny Davis.

She felt a surge of confusion merging with feelings of distrust. At the moment she wasn't sure who she was anymore.

"I'll be home a few days before the trial begins," she finally said.

"It probably is a good idea that you stay out of sight as long as possible. Be safe and please keep in touch."

"I will." She hung up the phone, then said a silent prayer. *Lord, please don't let them find me.*

Duane looked up from his seat as she approached him. He immediately sensed something was wrong. "Is everything okay?"

Destiny gave a smile that didn't quite reach her eyes. "Yes, everything is fine."

They danced to a couple of more songs, but Duane noticed that ever since she had returned from the restroom, her mood had changed. Silence and tension surrounded them.

"You sure you're okay?" he asked after they danced to another slow number.

Destiny hated having to lie to him again, but what other choice did she have, considering her life was once again in danger. "I'm kind of tired. Can we head back home?"

Although her lips curved in a smile, the burning, faraway look had returned to her eyes. Instinctively, Duane knew she wasn't telling him the truth. Something was bothering her. But what could he do if she refused to share her problems with him? "Sure, let's go."

They walked out to his truck, their breath mingling in the cool night air. Once they pulled out of the lot, he turned on a soulful CD, and during the short stretch to their houses, they remained silent. Oddly enough, it was a comfortable silence, yet awareness of each other was never far from the surface. Out of the corner of his eye, Duane watched her with discreet concern. Destiny sat with her hands folded in her lap, staring out the side window.

What had happened to change her mood? They had been having a wonderful evening, at least he had thought so, and he thought she had, too. Now he wasn't so sure.

Scowling inwardly, he again warned himself to be careful. He was getting in way over his head, because he cared too much about what she was feeling, thinking. Each choice he made that concerned her was only drawing him farther into the disarming web that Destiny had unknowingly spun.

As he turned at the next light, he scolded himself. He never should have invited her to Freddy's. He knew better than to spend the evening with a woman he couldn't get off his mind. It was a dangerous decision that was now going to cost him. All he had planned to do was take her to Freddy's and then back home. But the feel of her arms wrapped tightly around his body had been too much.

Destiny had to be as aware of the growing attraction as he was. The more he avoided even the slightest accidental touch, the more he found himself aching to touch her. Their dancing hadn't helped matters at all. In fact, it made things even worse. The feel of her nipples against his chest was going to be forever imbedded in his memory.

He could still feel her in his arms. He still remembered the soft texture of her skin beneath his callused fingers. Already, he wanted to touch her again, and because of it, he knew he was getting in way over his head. Unfortunately, he wasn't willing to do anything to prevent things from progressing so rapidly.

Fifteen minutes later, Duane pulled up in front of his house. He climbed out, then moved around to the passenger door and opened it. Destiny placed her hand in his, permitting him to pull her to her feet. He held her hand; his callused fingers were rough and rasped her skin. Tingles spread up her arm and across her chest, making her nipples tighten against the lace of her bra. He didn't release her hand as he walked with her to her door. She handed him her keys. He unlocked the door, then pushed it open.

Duane studied her intently for a moment, letting his large, dark eyes examine her face before his gaze softened and strayed to her mouth, to linger there before returning to her eyes again.

"Well, good night," she whispered.

"Is that the best you can offer?"

Destiny licked her dry lips as she tried to come up with a response. "What else do you have in mind?"

He noted the curiosity in her gaze and the caress

of her tongue across her lips, which gave her away. Duane knew at that instant he needed to taste her. He slowly lowered his head in case he'd read her wrong, but she didn't pull away. Instead, she rested her hands against his chest and rose on her tiptoes to meet him.

The kiss began tentatively. Warm, hard lips brushed against soft, moist ones. Within seconds it turned into something altogether different. Something demanding. Something feverish. Her heart banged against her chest. His kiss was almost more than she could bear. It had been months since she'd been kissed, but in the fifteen years since her first date, it had never been this powerful . . . this intense. Her emotions took over, and her body came alive, tingling from the contact in all the right places. As if they had a will of their own, her arms moved around his waist, her hands spreading over the planes of his back, down his hips, and across his buttocks.

Duane angled his head so he could have complete access to her mouth, then drew her so close he could feel the beat of her heart quicken through the layers of their clothes. Heart racing, hands trembling, nothing had ever come close to the taste of her mouth against his. As his hips ground instinctively into hers, he appreciated the mix of passion and innocence he tasted on her lips. He tasted the mystery, the excitement lurking beneath. He felt as if his very existence depended on getting as close to this woman as humanly possible. When he felt her return his kiss, mating her tongue with his, he totally lost it and began feeding in her mouth greedily.

He pulled her farther into the hard wall of his body. His arms trapped her like a cage as they moved around to her back and crushed her to him.

A delicious shudder of desire heated her body. Moaning, she allowed the kiss to deepen. Rising on her toes, she opened her mouth wider, inviting him deeper, taking whatever he had to offer. He thrust his tongue in and out of her mouth with lover's strokes, and she found the feeling invigorating.

Her breasts felt heavy and full. Her head grew light, and her hands curled at his waist. Her nipples started to tighten as his arms slid over her shoulders and pulled her closer, until her breasts were crushed against his chest. She groaned, certain he could feel her nipples hardening like small pebbles.

Duane took his time. As if by staying there long enough, he'd uncover all the secrets there. He kissed her again, his teeth nipping at her tongue. His hand stroked her face, then her throat, where a pulse beat as though her heart had risen from its usual place.

She froze when she felt the hardening of his flesh against her stomach. *What am I doing?* She tore her mouth from his with a groan.

With regret, he opened his eyes, keeping her at arm's length. Staring down at her, he noticed the deep flush of her cheeks. Her breath came fast with deep, ragged pulls of air.

"I, um . . ." She tried to speak; the words apparently wouldn't come.

"Enjoyed it?" He completed her thought, his voice low, coaxing.

She noticed there was a sensual sparkle in his eyes. Her cheeks grew hot, and a smile trembled over her lips. "Yes."

Duane leaned his forehead against her and laughed. "So did I."

She stood very still, her breathing in unison with his. Then slowly he lowered his head and brushed his lips across the corner of her mouth. She shivered as his lips eased across her skin to the other side, where he grazed her earlobe and nibbled a trail down to her neck. He ran his hand down her bare arm, and she had to suppress a shiver.

"I feel as if we have known each other forever." He did. He didn't understand it, but even though he hadn't known her for long, he felt like he had been waiting for her all his life. Ever since the first time they had met, he had felt an inexplicable connection to her. With one hand, he reached out and stroked her cheek. "You feel it, too, don't you, Destiny?" he said softly.

The tender sound of her name coming from his lips made her heart hammer foolishly. Surprisingly, she felt his heart pounding, too. "Yes, I feel it," she murmured unevenly. The connection with Duane had nothing to do with how long they'd been acquainted.

She closed her eyes, caught up in the warm, gentle kisses he planted along her neck and shoulder, conscious of where his warm flesh touched her as he murmured words she couldn't seem to comprehend in her haze of need and desire. Her thoughts spun. It was then that Destiny was hit with the realization that before she returned to St. Louis, she and Duane were going to be lovers. She had seen from the expression in Duane's eyes that he knew it, too. Her emotions whirled and skidded. The realization made her shiver with anticipation. She took a deep breath, trying to pull her thoughts together. She had a lot to think about. She needed a clear head to think things through, and that wouldn't happen with Duane around. She needed to think about where their relationship was heading and what she was willing to offer.

Mentally she shook herself from the spell Duane seemed to cast over her with just one look from his fabulous brown eyes. It took several minutes for Destiny to compose herself.

Stepping out of his embrace, she held her breath, then let it out slowly. "See you tomorrow." She rubbed her arm where goose bumps had risen.

As he stood there watching her, Duane realized he didn't want to go home. He wanted to scoop her up in his arms and carry her off to bed. Holding her so close to his body had only added to his sexual frustrations. The only thing that would satisfy his craving was Destiny.

He wanted to explore the soft curves of her lush body, committing the feel and smell of her skin to memory. He wanted to see beneath her clothes everything he had envisioned—the fullness of her breasts, the distinct indentation of her waist, and the curve of her round, feminine hips.

She waved her left hand in front of his face, drawing his attention again. "Good night, Duane."

He had to force himself to back away a step or two, smiling. "Good night, Destiny."

He took a deep breath, trying not to touch her again. He needed to put some distance between them as soon as possible. He wanted to kiss her again but feared that if he did, he wouldn't be able to let her go. He slipped his hands into the pockets of his jeans to keep from reaching out and clasping her tightly to his body.

Stepping back, he watched her go inside. Once the door was shut and he heard the dead bolt slide firmly in place, he strode across to his house.

Damn! He'd never wanted a woman so much. What was it about Destiny? She had a way of unknowingly seducing him. Duane glimpsed the promise of a passionate woman, a woman he wanted to discover. A woman he sensed could fill the void in his life. Until he had met her, he didn't even know that void existed.

Destiny leaned against the door, nibbling anxiously on her lower lip. With her eyes closed, she took a deep breath and smiled. She felt like a teenager after her first date. She had spent time with Duane, discussing nothing in particular, just enjoying listening to the sound of his voice. She missed that type of relationship. She had dated a few men other than Lucas, but most times she couldn't wait for the night to end so she could go home alone and crawl in her bed and watch Lifetime Television.

And dancing. She hadn't realized how much she liked to dance until she found herself in Duane's arms. He made her feel totally at ease as he held her close. With him, dancing was easy, skillful. He made her feel so comfortable.

Home renovations, dancing, and now kissing, was there anything Duane wasn't good at? She giggled as she draped her arms across her chest and hugged herself. The man's kisses were addictive, making her crave her next taste. His taste was still on her lips; the feel of his skin, hard and smooth, was still under her fingertips.

She opened her eyes and, after setting the security system, made her way to the staircase and her bedroom. Stripping off her clothes, she tossed them across a chair in the corner near the window, then went into the bathroom. While she brushed her teeth and washed her face, she stared at the woman in the mirror and wondered what was happening to her. As she returned to her room and fell across the bed, she thought about it some more. Whatever was happening, Duane Urban was to blame. Staring up at the ceiling fan spinning over her bed, she realized she was falling under a spell. She was growing increasingly afraid of what she felt every time they were together. The thought stuck in her mind even after she had finally managed to drift off to sleep.

Sitting at the kitchen table, Duane clasped his head in his hands and closed his eyes, then took a deep breath to calm the emotions he was feeling. He had totally let things get out of hand. His sole purpose for inviting Destiny out tonight was so she could have a little fun. But her beauty and charm had gotten to him.

Her lips had tasted like everything he had expected and more. Somehow he had known she would be an excellent kisser. Now he had a problem.

Duane reached into his refrigerator and pulled out a beer, then took a seat at the kitchen table again. The problem was that even now he could still taste the sweetness of her lips and feel the heat stirring in his groin.

Had he ever kissed a woman that way before? He doubted it. The kiss was like nothing he had ever experienced before. It had been so intoxicating that he wanted to do it again and anticipated the moment.

He popped the tab on the beer can, then took

a long drink. He had had more than enough to drink tonight. However, after the feeling he had just experienced, his choices were drinking or going back across the street and finishing what they had started. After a couple more swallows, he realized the beer wasn't strong enough to quench his thirst. The only thing that would do that was pulling Destiny into his arms and making love to her.

He had never been this sexually frustrated before. Since they'd met, he found himself in a constant state of arousal. All because of one woman. He knew when they finally made love it, was going to be like nothing he'd ever experienced.

And then what happens?

He didn't have to be a rocket scientist to know he was failing miserably at keeping his emotions intact.

Chapter 6

What was that?

Destiny's pulse jumped and her body tensed. She sat up in bed, staying very still while she waited to see if the noise returned. A moment went by. Nothing. Things were quiet except for a dog barking nearby. The neighborhood was relatively safe, she assured herself firmly.

With a sigh of relief, she sagged against the smothering pillows and willed her muscles to relax. Glancing over at the bedside table, she checked the time. She had only been asleep two hours, yet it was long enough to dream about lying in Duane's arms. A smile curled her lips as she remembered his lips capturing her nipple between his teeth in her dream, and he tweaked it until it became pebble hard. Even now she reveled at the tingling sensation traveling through her breasts.

She had begun to drift off to sleep when she heard the sound again. Lifting her head and listening more intently, it sounded like dishes rattling in the sink. Tension reclaimed her. *What am I gonna do?*

What if it was a prowler? Her throat went dry. *No,* she told herself, *it's all in your mind.*

Destiny pulled the covers over her head, then hugged her knees to her chest. *Please,* she prayed silently, *don't let it be one of Lucas's goons.*

Creak!

She bolted upright in her bed, her gaze darting to her bedroom door. Someone was walking across the kitchen floor. She could push the panic button on her security alarm keypad. Unfortunately, that would require going down into the foyer. Besides, she didn't want to call the police, because they asked too many questions. It wouldn't be long before they discovered who she really was.

Wait a minute, she thought. Just because she heard a noise didn't mean a prowler was in the house. Old houses were known to creak. In fact, some of the floorboards creaked when she moved through the house, especially in the kitchen. She was fine. It was all in her mind.

Ignoring the persistent whispers inside her head, she turned onto her stomach and closed her eyes again. The next sound rattled her bones and sent all hope that she was mistaken straight down the drain. It sounded like glass breaking.

Dashing out of bed, she reached for the phone and moved toward the window. Down below there were no unusual cars on the street. She cast her eyes in front of her, and when she spotted Duane's light on in his living room, with a thumping heart, she quickly moved over to her dresser and found his business card. With her hands shaking, she dialed. It took several mistakes before she was successful at dialing his number.

Hearing it ring, she silently prayed he wasn't a hard sleeper.

"Hello," said a drowsy voice.

She braced her back against the wall and slid down beside the door, drawing her knees up close to her body. "Duane!"

"Destiny." His voice now sounded like he was wide awake. "What's wrong?"

She kept her voice low, barely above a whisper. "I think someone is in the house."

"I can hardly hear you. You have to speak louder."

Blood pounded in her ears. "Someone's in my house."

"What! Where are you?"

"I'm in my bedroom," she replied in a shaky voice.

"Stay there. Don't move! I'll be right over."

He hung up before she had a chance to thank him. Less than a minute later, she heard a knock at the front door.

Destiny panicked. Did Duane expect her to come down and open it? What if it wasn't him, or if the burglar was downstairs waiting for her to appear?

Another knock came, this one harder, more insistent.

She contemplated what to do next since she simply did not have a clue. She reached for an eight-pound dumbbell and carried it with her as she quietly slipped down the stairs.

"Destiny, if you don't open this door by the count of five, I am breaking the door in!" she heard Duane yell from the other side.

Oh boy, now what? She swallowed a lump of bitter fear as she prayed his voice had scared the bad guy off.

Her heart was doing a feverish tap dance in her

chest. She made her decision quickly. Hoping the bad guy had indeed been scared off, she raced down the rest of the stairs. As she unlatched the two locks and slid the dead bolt on the door, she caught a shadow moving to her left and screamed.

Duane pushed the door open. She ran right smack into him and dropped the dumbbell to the floor. She jumped at the sound, glancing down, then up at Duane as if she just realized he was standing there.

She reached out and held on for dear life. "Duane!" she screamed. "Someone is in there!" With a tilt of her head, she gestured toward the kitchen.

His protective instincts took over. He was anxious to find the person who had brought the panic to her eyes. Duane tried to release the hold she had on him, but she gripped his shirt even tighter.

"No, please don't go!" she begged, clinging to him, unwilling to let go.

"Destiny," he whispered sharply. "You have to let me go so I can make sure there's no one in the house."

"No!" she cried. "Please don't go in there."

He had to pry her fingers loose. Then he took both her hands and held them firmly in his. "Destiny, listen to me."

Her tears increased as she trembled. He had to reassure her everything was going to be okay. "Destiny, I'll be right back. You are to stay here." He looked down at her as she sobbed out of control. He gripped her shoulders and shook her. "You have to stay calm. Nothing is going to happen to you. I promise." He cupped her chin and forced her to look at him. "Do you trust me?"

She didn't answer.

"Destiny, do you trust me?!" Although firm, he kept his voice low, just above a whisper.

Her eyelids closed. Then finally with a sad, defeated look, she nodded.

There was a loud crash, and just as he dashed into the kitchen, Destiny collapsed onto the floor.

Lying on the pillow beside her, Duane played the bizarre scene over and over in his head. He could still see the panic filling Destiny's eyes when she thought there was an intruder in her home.

He remembered once when his sister, Chelsea, had called with the same sound in her voice. She had been certain someone was in her apartment. He had rushed over and discovered the noise was a closet door she had left ajar next to an open window. The evening breeze had caused the door to swing and the hinges to squeak. She had laughed it off and gone immediately back to bed.

But this time was different. The fear he had witnessed was like that on the day he had startled Destiny in the kitchen. She looked terrified of something or someone.

Duane stared down at her sleeping face. She looked vulnerably sweet. His hold on her tightened as he considered the possibility that maybe she was afraid of someone. Had someone hit her? She reminded him of a younger cousin of his who had been a victim of domestic abuse. The idea of someone putting their hands on her angered him.

Would she tell him? He doubted it. The last time he asked, she had brushed it off as a reaction she experienced often in her life. He would wait until she felt comfortable enough with him to bear her soul. He wanted her to trust him because until she did, there was no way their relationship could ever go a step further.

He hadn't even known her long, yet his protective and possessive instincts were in high gear. The feeling was so intense it stunned him. *Why her? Why now? Because you're falling for her*, an inner voice warned.

"Please don't leave me," she murmured. Her eyelids drooped as she snuggled closely against him.

"I'll be right here when you wake up." He kissed her ear. That was the last thing he said before she drifted off to sleep. He held her to his heart while she slept. No force on earth could have kept him from stretching out on the bed beside her. Holding her soft curves, stroking her back in a soothing manner, his body had no choice but to react to the warmth of her body.

She had fallen asleep clinging to him, leaning against him while he lay in the darkness staring out at the stars above. Sleep was the farthest thing from his mind. It was a good thing he had on clothes, even though his loose-fitting sweatpants had grown tighter. Her hair tickled his chin. Her invigorating scent teased his senses, like the blast of a candle shop, so many fabulous scents mingling together.

There was something warm and almost adorable in her eyes that made him want to protect her. And that warmth called to everything that was masculine in him. It made his muscles flex. It made him want to defend and protect her from everything but him.

He held her because he wanted to give her comfort and because he wanted to hold her. She felt wonderful in his arms. The feeling of her breasts pressed up against his chest was torture in itself.

He told himself there was nothing wrong with comforting her. But, comfort didn't begin to describe the feeling coursing through his body. His body had already decided that there was no way Destiny was going to be easy to resist. She called to parts of him that he had tucked away a long time ago.

Before she had called, he'd spent a restless two hours tossing and turning in bed until he had finally gotten up and gone to sit out on the deck, watching the stars while wrapped in a blanket.

All he could do was think about her. He wanted to finish what they had started earlier. He wanted to make love to her, finish what was brewing between them. However, he knew once he stepped over that line, there was no turning back. He also knew that there was no way he could have her just once. He had hoped that by pushing forward with their relationship, he would figure out what it was about her that aroused his emotions. Instead things had gotten increasingly worse. She consumed his every thought, his every breath, and there was nothing he could do about it. Last night he'd had another erotic dream that left him hard and throbbing. He woke up and was unable to go back to sleep. Even now he wanted to touch her, but even the most casual touch would escalate into full-fledged arousal. Which, under the circumstances, was dangerous.

However, there was no way he was going to be satisfied until he had her hair spread out on his pillow and was buried deep in her sweet body with her legs wrapped around his hips. All he could think about was all the different ways he could make love to her.

One particular position was on his mind now. He felt his body harden.

It had been a long time since a woman affected him deeply. He hoped his reaction to her wasn't visible. His sweatpants weren't made to disguise his arousal. Thank goodness, she was asleep.

She dreamed that she was wrapped in big, strong arms. She felt safe and protected. She nuzzled in deeper and felt her body becoming totally relaxed. This was one dream she was not ready to wake up from.

Shifting slightly, she felt an arm tighten around her waist. Her eyelids flew open, and then she remembered.

Duane was in her bed!

Turning to face him, she stared at Duane, who was lying beside her with his eyes closed.

"Duane?"

Slowly, he opened his eyes. He found her staring at him, face flushed with sleep. Her eyes were glowing with that soft, unfocused look of someone who'd awakened in the last five minutes or so. And she couldn't possibly look sweeter or sexier than right now.

"Good morning, gorgeous," he greeted with a smile.

"What happened?"

He rolled onto his back. "You fainted."

"Fainted? Good Lord, the last thing I remember is hearing you tell me everything was okay."

While stretching his arms above his head, he nodded, then said, "You woke up earlier, then fell into a deep sleep. You were sleeping so soundly that I didn't want to wake you."

Stay? She had asked him to stay? Had he held her in his arms all night? She was too embarrassed to ask.

Glancing at him with her eyelids slightly narrowed, she watched his gorgeous eyes twinkle underneath the streams of sunlight pouring into the room.

Duane folded a bulky arm underneath his head. "Well, I caught your burglar."

She scrambled into a sitting position. "You did?"

He grinned. "Yep. It was a cat."

"A cat?" When his words finally sank in, she gave a sigh of relief. "It was only a cat," she murmured in a faraway voice.

"He must have slipped in when you opened the door." Duane stretched one more time, then yawned. "He was on the counter and knocked over a glass."

That was the sound of broken glass she had heard.

He registered her embarrassment and reached out and touched her chin with his finger. "No harm done. I sent him on his way. It was a good thing he was here. I found mouse droppings. I guess that's why the cat was running around the kitchen. He probably ran Mickey, and Minnie, and the rest of their friends off."

Destiny frowned at him, studying his expression. "Did you say, *friends?*"

Duane tried and failed miserably to suppress a grin. "Well, if there's one, chances are there are more. No need to worry. I'll find the source of entry and seal it off."

He smiled at her, and she realized she liked the way he teased her. "I feel so silly."

Sitting up, he braced his weight against the head-board. Looking down into her upturned face, he grinned. "You shouldn't be. You had every right to feel frightened in this big house all by yourself."

Staring up into Duane's eyes, she felt a slow surge of want rising up inside her. An intoxicating flow of heart-pounding desire that was so thick it nearly choked her.

She couldn't ignore the physical attraction she felt for this man. She felt a strong desire to lie back down and ask him to hold her again, and she knew from the longing in his gaze, he felt it, too, and her heart turned over. Because of it, she needed to get up and step away from the intimate setting.

"I'm going to take a shower."

"How about I fix breakfast?" he suggested.

She smiled shyly up at him. "All right."

Slowly, Destiny climbed off the bed and headed towards the bathroom, all the time aware his eyes were on her. Goodness! She was in way over her head.

A half hour later, dressed in a pair of shorts and a black T-shirt, she descended the stairs. She walked into the kitchen and was met by the smell of crisp maple-cured bacon and the sight of Duane standing in front of the stove, scrambling eggs. She stood in the doorway, listening to him hum along to a rap song coming from a small radio on the counter.

Arms wrapped around her, she lingered in the doorway, one bare foot covering the other, survey-ing his attire. While she was in the shower, he had removed his shirt, and she could see the firm mus-cles on his back flex beneath a white muscle T-shirt.

Her stomach growled, drawing his attention. Duane glanced over his shoulder, smiled, then looked down at the stove again. "How was your shower?"

Her eyes crinkled slightly. "Wonderful."

"Good." Turning around, he flashed a warm smile of approval as his gaze traveled down her body so quickly, it was almost as if he'd touched her. She squirmed a bit against the flow of heat warming her blood.

"Grab some coffee and have a seat."

Glad for the distraction, she moved over to the coffeepot, and after pouring a mug, she glanced at Duane again, who was concentrating on preparing breakfast.

"Duane," she said softly, but loud enough to draw his attention. She inhaled sharply, deeply, then said, "Thank you."

"You don't have to thank me. I'm glad I was able to be there for you."

She met his dimpled smile and found herself staring at his lips. *That kiss.* If she closed her eyes, she could still taste him on her tongue.

Easy girl.

Shaking it off, she carried her mug to the table. Duane came over carrying a plate of eggs and bacon.

"The toast should be out shortly."

She dropped her eyes, flattered that he was making her breakfast. She felt like royalty. "Oh, I could get used to this," she murmured.

So could I, Duane thought, as he poured two glasses of orange juice and moved back toward the table. As he handed her a glass of juice, he took a deep breath. The scent of soap lingered on her skin. The smell elicited an immediate hardness of his loins.

While he was cooking, all he could think about was going back upstairs and joining her underneath the spray of the water. Holding her in his arms had ignited a raw lust within him, which made him want to spend every night in her warm embrace.

He served her, then took a seat opposite her at the table. "How about I come by later and we go shop for tile?"

"Okay."

"And while we're there, I can pick up some mousetraps."

Her eyes widened in alarm. He had made the suggestion before; only this time it registered. "Oh no! I can't kill a mouse."

His eyes twinkled. "Then what would you like for me to do?"

"Isn't there some kind of sticky strips they walk across and get stuck on?"

He nodded as he chewed on a strip of bacon. "Yeah, but that means you have to pick up the strip and carry the mouse outside."

She looked pleased. "Then that's what I want."

His brow rose quizzically. "And who's going to discard the mouse outside?"

She lowered her head, then looked at him from beneath her thick lashes. "I was hoping you would."

Duane tossed his head back and howled with laughter. "It's going to cost you."

She studied him for a long moment before taking a deep breath and asking, "What's the price?"

A slow smile curved his lips. "I'll tell you later."

She could have read that statement in a couple of different ways. Her stomach quivered and her mouth went dry as she stared into his dark eyes. They were deep with the glint of something just a little wicked. There was also a promise in his eyes that sent sparks shooting clear down to her toes.

They finished their food, both comfortable with the silence surrounding them. Afterwards, Duane helped her clear the table.

"I'll see you this afternoon," he said with barely an inch of space between them, his brown eyes boring into hers.

"I'll be here."

She felt a slam of desire, and she didn't have long to wonder if he had felt it, too. Duane curved his arm around her waist and pulled her solidly against him. With his other arm, he tilted her face upward. There was something about the way he stared down at her knowingly that did crazy things to her insides. She was breathless, and there was a dull ache inside her stomach. There was no mistaking the passion in his eyes before he lowered his warm mouth over hers.

At first touch, she began to shudder. He brought her closer, and Destiny closed her eyes and held on tight as he thoroughly savored her mouth. After he kissed her, he didn't let her go, and for some reason, she was in no hurry to break the contact. She stood still, secure in his grasp, enjoying the heat flowing from his body. Their rapid breathing mingled until their heart rates returned to normal.

"Why don't you kick back and relax for the rest of the day?" he suggested with a quick kiss to her forehead, before he turned and walked out the door.

She stood for the longest time in that same spot. Relax? After a kiss like that, how was she supposed to manage that?

* * *

Adrenaline mixed with overheated hormones gave him a quick rush. A woman he had barely known a week had somehow managed to slide over the makeshift wall he had created to keep women at arm's length. That included everyone he had met since his breakup with Veronica.

Already he knew that what he was feeling for Destiny was more than physical, because the emotions stirring inside him ran deeper and were stronger than anything he had ever experienced before. He had barely been home fifteen minutes, and already he was feeling a heart-pounding level of anticipation at seeing her again.

He headed to the bathroom and turned on the hot water in the shower. As he stripped off his clothes, he wished she was there right now, sharing the hot water with him. He wanted her body bare and thrashing under him while he brought them both to sexual pleasure, something he hadn't done in months. He wanted his hands to touch every inch of her silky skin; then he intended to follow the same path with his tongue.

Climbing in the shower, he closed his eyes as his mind raced. He wanted Destiny despite an inner warning not to get too close to her. His need to make love to her overshadowed any doubts that he had. All he cared about was showing her how much he cared. How much she meant to him in such a short period of time. Something or someone had frightened her, and he planned to show her how protective he had become. No one touched what was his. No one.

Chapter 7

As Destiny came out the door, curiosity hit Duane hard. Duane's eyes swept over her large white T-shirt, which fell well below her knees. It was the kind worn by young males between the age of sixteen and twenty-one. She matched it with a pair of loose-fitting jeans. Nevertheless, even in the oversize clothes, she managed to still look feminine. Nothing could hide all those luscious curves.

"What's with the outfit?"

Destiny secured the locks, then slipped her sunglasses from the top of her hat and over her eyes. "I burn easily." She offered no further explanation as she turned and brushed past him.

He knew she was lying but kept his mouth shut. Something he had been doing quite a bit of lately. There was an aura of mystery that surrounded her. There was a part of him that wanted to unravel all of her secrets.

Placing a hand lightly at her waist, he escorted her out to the curb and into his truck. Walking around to the driver's side, he looked forward to spending time together.

Destiny slumped down low in the seat and closed her eyes. She was well aware that Duane was watching her. She couldn't think of a better excuse, so she decided it was better not to say anything at all. She was taking a big risk by coming out on a weekend. But how else was she going to get her tiles if she didn't go herself, she thought as he put the truck in gear. She ignored the annoying voice that told her that was a lame excuse.

As they whizzed down the road in his truck, she curled her fingers around the armrest on the passenger's side door, hoping to squeeze in some confidence. Sneaking a glance at Duane, she felt her heart rate calm. She was certain that as long as Duane was with her, everything was going to be okay this afternoon. She could feel it. As much as she didn't want to lean on another man, she needed his strength. She had a strong feeling he could make everything right. She knew he was going to make everything whole in her life. She closed her eyes. She didn't know how, she just knew. She wasn't sure how she felt about it. Nor did she know what she was going to do when she found out.

Destiny felt someone shaking her. She raised her eyelids to find Duane staring down at her.

"Wake up, sleepyhead."

"Oh my!" she mumbled as she blinked several times. "I can't believe I fell asleep."

He flicked his brow. "I can. You didn't get much sleep last night."

What he didn't know was that last night was the first time she had slept more than four hours in weeks. She was already dreading spending another night alone.

Taking Duane's hand, she climbed out of the truck. She could have gotten out on her own, but he told her that lending a hand was a gesture that was instilled in him by his parents. It might sound strange to someone else, but each time he raced around to assist her, he made her feel special.

As soon as he clasped her hand, shocks of wanting radiated through her. She tilted her head so she could see him beneath the brim of her hat. Lowering his head, he lightly caressed her lips, then increased the pressure until she returned the kiss with equal passion. Sooner than she wanted, he eased back and released her.

Destiny used her hand as a fan. "Boy, it's going to be a hot day," she said, trying to maintain control by blaming the weather for the immediate rush of heat to her cheeks. It wasn't a complete lie. It was already beginning to warm up. She tipped her head back. The sun was shining brightly in the blue sky.

His fingers curved around her forearm, and he led her toward the store entrance. As they walked, Destiny glanced around, pleased to find nothing out of the ordinary. Inhaling slowly, she felt the cool air filling her lungs, easing the apprehension simmering inside her. It was going to be a great day.

The smell of hotdogs and onions wafted to her nostrils. Near the store exit was a mobile hotdog stand and a line of people waiting.

Destiny gazed up at Duane, smiling. "That smell reminds me of going to Cardinals' baseball games with my grandfather."

Duane stopped in his tracks and turned to face

her. "I thought you told me you were from San Antonio?"

Destiny, realizing her mistake, fought for the right words. "Uh . . . I am, but I had a grandfather in St. Louis that I used to visit quite often." She grasped his arm and resumed walking toward the door again. "He passed away when I was ten." She remembered how sad she had been when her grandfather had suffered a massive stroke.

"I'm sorry to hear that. It sounds like the two of you were close."

She pulled in a long breath. "My grandfather meant the world to me. We used to spend hours catching fireflies in jars. Every summer he took me camping. We would lie in sleeping bags on the ground and study the stars. He was so patient with me," she said in a faraway voice, with a dreamy smile.

"He sounds a lot like my grandfather. He's eighty-five and hell on wheels." Duane smiled at the memory.

They entered the store, and it wasn't long before Duane discovered that Destiny loved home improvement stores as much—if not more—than he did. They strolled down each and every aisle. She spoke with excitement as she shared all of the ideas she had for her great-uncle's house.

The last aisle they reached housed ceramic tile. He was amazed at how well she listened when he explained the different usages for the various tiles. She decided on an Aztec blend, which he had to admit would look perfect in the kitchen. They loaded down the cart with mortar, grout, and five boxes of the tile squares. Next they found the mouse strips. The store did not sell security bars for windows, and Duane didn't miss the look of apprehension on

Destiny's face. However, he assured her he would find some by the end of the week.

"That was fun," Destiny said as they left the store.

"Yes, it was. How about a hotdog loaded with onions?" he suggested.

She smiled radiantly and replied, "That sounds wonderful."

Together they got in the relatively short line at the hotdog stand.

"Oh, Duane, look!"

He looked in the direction of her finger. There was a yellow Labrador retriever sniffing around the stand. Destiny reached out her hand and signaled for the dog to come to her.

"Destiny, be careful," Duane warned.

She gave him a dismissive wave. "He's harmless."

Before he could stop her, she approached the dog and patted him on the head.

"You're hungry, aren't you, boy?" He wagged his tail as if he understood. "Yes, Mama knows."

Duane raised a brow. She was obviously a dog lover. "How about I get our furry friend here a hotdog also?"

She nodded, then added, "Make that three. His stomach looks like he hasn't eaten in weeks. I wonder where his owner is?"

"Excuse me, sir," Duane said to the man working inside the stand. "Is this your dog?"

The man shook his head as he handed a woman her change. "No, sir. He's just been hanging around all week."

"Maybe he's lost." Destiny checked his neck for a collar and found he wasn't wearing one.

"I haven't seen anyone, and I'm here every day at this time. He stands there and waits for someone to drop their hotdog, which is one out of every ten people who stop here. Now what can I get you?"

"We'll take five hotdogs. Two with onions and three without."

Destiny smiled up at Duane, and it caused his heart to pitter-patter.

The vender handed him the three plain hotdogs, and Duane immediately tossed them over to the Lab. The dog consumed them in ten seconds flat.

Duane handed Destiny a hotdog, and then they each squirted theirs with ketchup and mustard. Biting into his, Duane saw the dog staring up at him with big, sad eyes. After taking three bites, he tossed the remainder to him. Destiny did the same.

As Duane went to retrieve their cart, Destiny placed a hand on his arm and stopped him. "Duane, we can't leave him here. He'll die of dehydration."

"Why don't we take him with us? Labs make excellent guard dogs." He saw the idea register.

"That's a wonderful idea."

"Let's go." He reached for the cart and pushed it towards his truck.

"Come on, boy," she called. The dog instantly obeyed and trotted along beside her.

"What are we gonna call him?" Duane asked as he reached for his keys. "Killer?"

She frowned. "No, nothing like that."

"How about Champion?"

"Champ . . . I like the sound of that."

He lowered the bed of the truck, and the Lab immediately jumped in. Duane loaded the mortar, grout, and boxes of tiles, then closed the bed.

"Stay, boy," he commanded.

As if he understood, Champ lowered himself on top of the boxes.

Destiny smiled. The dog was smart. She watched him until Duane came around and opened the door for her.

"I think we need to stop at the convenience store and pick up some dog food on the way," she suggested as she climbed in.

"Sounds good." Duane shut the door, walked around to the other side, and got in behind the steering wheel. He started the engine and waited until he pulled out of the lot before he said, "I went by Mannie's house a couple of days ago."

Destiny swung on the seat to face him. "You did? What did he say?"

"He doesn't live there anymore. Apparently, they were evicted a couple of months ago."

Her face sagged. "That is so sad."

"Yeah, I agree. I tried calling the agency, but unfortunately, they can't release any information. However, the lady was sympathetic and said she would pass the message to his caseworker."

"At least that sounds hopeful."

"Yeah," he murmured, even though he wasn't too sure. Mannie and his mother couldn't be too far away. He would just have to try and track them down. If all else failed, he would have to hire his brother to do it. Reyn had a way of finding people who didn't want to be found, which was why he was often asked by the police to assist them on some of their toughest investigations.

Destiny sighed. "I wish there was something I could do."

Duane took his eyes away from the road long enough to note her frustration. He was touched by her kind heart. "I know how you feel. There are kids like Mannie all over the city, looking for foster homes. I've thought about becoming a foster parent."

"You have?"

He smiled. "You sound surprised."

"I am. . . . I mean I've never met a man who was willing to give up his bachelorhood for a child."

"I like kids."

She shook her head, smiling. "I didn't mean it like that," she quickly amended. "What I meant is that most men wait until they are married before wanting to spend their time with kids."

"I used to be a Big Brother."

"Really? I used to be a Big Sister."

Duane came to a complete stop at the light and gave her his full attention. "I guess we've got something else in common."

Destiny nodded. "The last little girl I had was named Anissa. We were together for three years, until her mother remarried and they moved away. I got a lot out of spending time with her. She brought the kid out in me."

"Same here."

Duane could bet she was a lot of fun to be with. He enjoyed her company, so he could only imagine that children felt the same way when they were around her. Destiny was gentle and compassionate. She worried about kids from broken homes and had a soft spot for stray dogs. The more he got to know her, the more she pulled at his heartstrings.

The light changed, and Duane pressed his foot on the gas. As he followed the flow of traffic, he told her about an eight-year-old he used to spend a great deal of time with until the boy's mother remarried. The man had five grown sons. With enough positive role models surrounding him, the boy no longer needed the support of the organization.

Duane stopped at a corner gas station and picked up enough dog food to last until Destiny had a chance to go to the grocery store. When he pulled in front of her house, it was after three o'clock. While he carried the tile in the house, Destiny introduced Champ to his new home. In minutes, he was trotting around like he owned the place.

Destiny moved into the kitchen and searched the top shelf of one of the cabinets until she found two large bowls. She filled one up with water and the other with dog food. Champ dove right in.

"He must have been really hungry," she heard Duane say as he came into the room.

"He was all alone in the world," she murmured as she watched him. Like her, Champ had nobody to call his own. If she didn't have the royalties from her book sales, she wouldn't know what she would have done. She couldn't get a job and risk using her social security number. The fake San Antonio driver's license was the only claim she had to her new identity.

"Destiny?"

She jumped. "What? Did you say something?"

He gave her a concerned look. "I promised a client that I would drop by and give an estimate. The mouse strips are in place."

She tried not to appear disappointed that he was leaving. "Thank you for all of your help."

He crooked a finger under her chin and forced her to meet his direct stare. "Are you sure you're going to be okay?"

She fought for the strength to breathe. "I'm fine. I've got Champion to take care of me."

He put his arms around her and tugged her until her body was pressed against his. He tilted her head back and touched her mouth in a deep, searing kiss. Her hands clutched his shoulders. She moaned deep into his mouth and parted her lips, allowing his tongue to curl around hers.

He lifted his mouth from hers and stared down at her, eyes questioning. Then he released her and headed for the door. He had barely taken four steps when he pivoted on his heels and asked, "How about I cook dinner for you tomorrow night at my place?"

She was pleased to hear that he was finally inviting her over to see his house. Curiosity as to how the bachelor lived had gotten the better of her. "I thought you didn't cook?"

Duane gave her a sheepish grin. "Okay, let me rephrase that. How about you come over tomorrow and I pick up takeout and a movie?"

She shook her head. "You're always doing things for me. It's time I returned the favor. Remember my offer of roller skating?" She almost laughed at the frown on his face. Duane was afraid of falling flat on his face.

"We'll save that for next time. Besides, you haven't seen my place yet."

She ignored the voice that reminded her she was going to maintain her distance. "All right. I'd like that."

"I'll see you tomorrow at six."

"Should I bring anything?" she asked.

He winked. "Just yourself."

He fought the impulse to go to her and hold her once more, to feel her breath against his cheek.

Burying his hands in his pockets, he turned and walked away.

While Champion happily lapped his water, Destiny stood there for the longest time rubbing her burning lips. Why did Duane make her feel so tingly inside?

She gasped as the answer became clear. She knew exactly what was going on. For the first time in months, she felt safe. She was living what she considered a normal life with everyday hopes, dreams, and desires. Even though she knew it would be a mistake that she might later regret, there was no way she was going to be able to keep Duane at arm's length.

From the first moment Duane had looked at her with those dreamy brown eyes, she'd been pulled into a whirlwind of attraction. She responded to him, and for the first time, in a long time she felt the wonderful stir of her heart and singing in her chest. She also felt hope that everything was going to be okay.

She spent the rest of the evening outlining the next three chapters of her novel and proofing the first two, stopping long enough to make herself and Champion a hamburger. Tomorrow she would take him to the groomers, then grab him a larger bag of food and a few doggie treats.

By sunset she had taken a hot shower and had curled up on the couch.

Champion trotted in the room and lay on the floor beside her. She grinned sheepishly. It was good having him around.

While watching a sitcom, she heard a car coming down the road. From the screech of the tires she knew it had stopped right outside of her home. Suddenly, all happiness left her and her apprehensions returned. It wasn't until the car pulled away that she realized she had been holding her breath. She inhaled deeply, then pulled a blanket tightly around her.

How long was it going to take before she felt safe again? she asked herself with a tinge of disappointment. Weeks, months, years? She wasn't sure she could wait that long. After her outing today, she had truly believed that she was safe. With an ache of inner pain, she wondered if she would ever feel that way again. Because even if Lucas was behind bars, who was to say he wouldn't still seek revenge and appoint someone else to do her in?

She squeezed her eyes shut, wishing she could remove the painful memories from her brain. Wishing Duane was still with her. When he was around, she felt as if everything was going to be all right.

She had brought all this anguish on herself, and only she was to blame. It was still hard to believe how gullible she had been. How stupid. Anyone else would have seen the warning signs and been suspicious of Lucas's actions. But not Desiree. Oh no . . . she was too busy trying to find her Prince Charming.

Destiny wrung her hands, putting a stop to her ceaseless persecution. She needed to quit beating herself over the head. What was done was done.

She leaned back against the comfortable cushions and closed her eyes. She tried to shut out the negative thoughts and think about last night. Closing her eyes, memories of Duane's kisses came back. Her lips tingled in remembrance of his touch.

She felt a prickle at the back of her neck and slowly raised her head and glanced over her shoulder into the hallway. She had an eerie feeling that someone was watching her. *Impossible*. Yet as she tried to relax, again she had that feeling.

The alarm was on, and all of the doors and windows were locked. There was no way anybody else was in the house or watching her. Giggling at her foolishness, she returned her gaze to the television screen.

She dozed off but was soon awakened by the sound of Champion barking. She opened her heavy eyelids in time to watch him dash down the hall toward the kitchen. Once there, he barked even louder, and before she lost her nerve, she followed his trail. Champion was standing in front of the basement door growling.

"What is it, boy?"

At the sound of her voice, he turned and, with his tail wagging, headed over to her. With one happy leap, he knocked her to the floor. Destiny burst into laughter when she glanced over at the corner of the room and saw a tiny mouse on the sticky strip.

Chapter 8

Destiny rolled over onto her stomach and caught the scent of Duane on her pillow. It was a definite turn-on.

It was still hard to believe he had lain right beside her and held her in the comfort of his protective arms. Sweeping her hand beneath the pillow, she buried her face against the softness and took a deep breath.

With one sniff of his unique masculine scent, Duane's face became as clear to her as the photo of her uncle on the nightstand beside her. A slight smile curled the corners of her lips. Last night she had seen the desire burning in his eyes when he had pulled her into his embrace and kissed her. The touch was nothing she had ever felt before.

Somehow she needed to find a way to conquer her involuntary reaction to him; otherwise, the next several weeks were going to be difficult, if not unbearable. She would just have to work harder at preventing herself from falling under his spell.

Today she was going to try writing or anything else that would occupy her mind. Somehow she needed to find a way to offset the sexual frustration. It had kept her awake the night before and was bound to recur after they shared dinner together this evening.

Leaning over the edge of her bed, she found Champion lying on the floor. He had quickly claimed a large rug as his bed. Destiny smiled as she glanced down at his beautiful golden brown coat. Her nose flared at his smell. Today she was taking him to a local dog groomer.

She dressed in loose-fitting jeans and a peasant top. On her head, she slipped a fisherman's cap, followed by her phony bifocal frames. One look in the mirror confirmed she looked like a dork. Glancing out the window across the street, she saw that Duane was not at home. She just hoped she didn't run into him before she climbed safely in her car. One look at her attire and he was bound to start asking questions.

Moving into the kitchen, she retrieved a short rope, tied a loose noose, and slipped it around Champion's neck. She didn't want to run the risk of him running off. He happily wagged his tail, trotted out to the car, and immediately jumped in the front seat.

"You are definitely a character," she chuckled as she climbed in the seat beside him. "Gosh, you stink!"

Champion barked in agreement.

Fifteen minutes later, Destiny was staring at a receptionist who had turned up her bulbous nose when she noticed the dog sitting obediently beside his owner.

"Do you have an appointment?" she asked, spacing the words evenly.

Destiny shook her head. "Nope, but the sign said

walk-ins are welcome," she challenged. It was obvious the woman wasn't too happy about her bringing the filthy dog into her establishment. *Well, too bad.*

"I assume his rabies shots are up to date."

Unnerved by the receptionist's disapproving, questioning eyes, she stiffened. "Well . . . I don't know. He's not mine. I mean . . . I just found him."

"Well, we can't see him without it. The last thing we want is for one of our groomers to get bitten."

Great. Destiny glanced down at Champion waiting patiently. She hadn't even considered that possibility, and without knowing who the owners were, there was no way of knowing if his vaccinations were up to date.

"I'm sorry, but you are going to have to bring him back when you have his records." The receptionist's voice was far from apologetic.

Irritated by her sharp tone, Destiny gritted her teeth; then upset by the smug look on the woman's face, she turned on her heels. She knew the woman was just doing her job. However, had she ever heard of customer service?

Destiny would just have to wash him herself.

Together they went down several aisles of the pet shop adjoining the grooming salon. Scanning the items on the shelves, she found shampoo that not only killed fleas, but smelled good, too. By the time she made her way to the register, she had grabbed a collar, leash, some treats, a big bag of dog food, and several toys. With the help of a clerk, she was able to get everything loaded into the car and headed back home.

Finding that Champion like to ride with his head

hanging out the window, she decided to take the scenic route back.

Destiny drove through the historical downtown and found it a quaint little place. Built around 1776, Main Street evoked the true charm of a bygone era. It reminded her of something out of an old movie: vintage mansions, mom-and-pop stores, and several little shops with brown awnings overhead. There was a post office that was so small, she almost missed it; the same was true about the police station and bowling alley. The barbershop had a real candy cane–striped pole just outside, and the fruit market actually had a display near the door so that people driving down Main Street could see how fresh and ripe the fruits and vegetables were. There was a neighborhood diner, which was filled with patrons, and retired couples sitting out on their porches waved as she rolled by. She had to admit she really liked Delaware.

She reached over and rubbed her dog's coat. It was nice having company in the car, and with him, she felt safe.

Riding past a small veterinary clinic, she pressed her lips together thoughtfully. Champion wasn't hers. In fact, his name wasn't even Champion, and she had no idea what it was, because he wasn't her dog. As much as she hated to face it, there was a possibility that someone was out there looking for him. With a sigh, she turned at the next corner and circled the block. Before she had a chance to change her mind, she pulled into the veterinary clinic's parking lot. Reaching behind the seat, she pulled out the collar and leash from the bag and put the collar around Champion's neck.

After the vet was unsuccessful at identifying the

dog, Destiny went down to the Humane Society to report him found. She swore she would never forget the look of relief on the clerk's face when she told the clerk that she'd keep Champion until his owner was located. Apparently, the Humane Society was full to capacity.

Destiny arrived home relieved to have Champion still with her and to discover that Duane was still not at home.

The street was relatively quiet. She suspected that the only people at home were retirees, who were probably peeping out their window, keeping track of her comings and goings, which didn't bother her at all. The good thing was that if there were any strangers lurking around or unusual cars in the area, they would be easy to identify.

She checked the rearview mirror to make sure she hadn't been followed, then took Champion into the house and quickly unloaded the car.

As soon as she emptied the bags from the pet store and put the things away in a cabinet, she tossed Champion a treat and went to get a glass. She was dying for a drink of lemonade.

Glancing in the sink, she noticed a glass there and gasped. *Didn't I wash that before I left?* It was a disturbing thought. She was certain she had washed that glass that morning. Her eyes roamed around the room quickly as she checked to see if there was anything else out of the ordinary. She was relieved to see everything else was just as she had left it. *Maybe you didn't wash it.* She had had a simple breakfast of toast, two hard-boiled eggs, and a glass of orange juice. There was a logical explanation. She had washed the dishes but hadn't finished her juice until they had already been dried and put away. Banishing the thought, she moved to the refrigerator.

With that off of her mind, she reached inside the refrigerator for the ice cold pitcher of lemonade, then poured herself a glass and went upstairs to change. It was time to give Champion a bath.

Duane had spent the morning drywalling a garage. He couldn't understand how a developer could build a new house and not finish the garage. With a spreader, he smoothed joint compound across another seam. Tomorrow he would come back to prep the walls for painting.

As he reached for the drywall tape, Destiny lingered about in the corner of his mind. All through the day he'd tried to stay focused, but he found it quite difficult to concentrate on work. His thoughts had been on her. He could not deny that. In the time since they had met, she had become quite special to him.

The physical attraction he was used to, but the emotional attachment was harder to digest. His heart fluttered. He knew that it didn't matter if he liked it or not, he had no control over his feelings. Destiny had somehow managed to touch him in ways that he hadn't begun to try and understand. Just holding her in his arms had been a memorable experience, one he was having trouble putting behind him.

Destiny had emerged in his life during a time when he wasn't looking for a woman. A time when he thought he was content focusing all his time and energy on establishing his business. It was easy to understand why he enjoyed being around her. She seemed to be everything a man could want in a woman. She was intelligent, compassionate, and feminine. She had a sexy way of nibbling her lower lip. She seemed completely unconscious of how it drove him crazy.

The garage project had been initially scheduled for next weekend, but since he needed to put a little distance between them, to take some time to bring his runaway emotions under control before she arrived at his house that evening, he had decided to start the project a week early.

Lowering the spreader, he sat back on his heels in contemplation. With Destiny, he looked forward to every moment they spent together. Unlike the other women he had dated, whom he always needed to get some distance from after a date or two. At first he had thought his desire was a result of being too long without a woman in his bed. But he had since learned that was not the case. After their time together yesterday afternoon, he knew it had everything to do with Destiny Davis.

Tonight he planned to do everything in his power to impress her.

With that in mind, he glanced down at his watch and found it was almost noon. He planned to leave work after half a day, then head home and tackle the housework. The dinner tonight had to be perfect.

His cell phone rang, and he removed the flip phone from his hip.

"Urban Designs," he bellowed into the mouth-piece.

"Whassup, big brother?" The voice was low, smooth.

He grinned at the sound of his brother. Garrett Urban had spent the last month on tour. He was a comedian. Last week he had appeared on BET Comicview.

"When did you get back?" Duane asked.

"Last night. I'm back now for a couple of weeks; then I'm going on tour next month with Cedric the Entertainer."

Duane whistled at the announcement. "Wow! How'd you land that?"

"My agent is earning his cut."

He didn't miss the hint of pride in Garrett's voice. "No doubt. Congratulations."

"Thanks."

As far back as he could remember, his brother wanted to be a comedian. Their parents thought it was just a phase he was going through until he explained he had no interest in college. He spent years studying the greats, like Richard Pryor, Eddie Murphy, Martin Lawrence, and Chris Rock. As a teenager he used to entertain at school talent shows and even birthday parties. By twenty-one, he was performing at comedy clubs.

"I hear you're seeing someone." Garrett's comment brought him back to the present. Duane groaned at the way he shifted the conversation to his personal life.

He grimaced in good humor. "I guess you've been talking to Mom."

"Oh yeah, and from what I've heard, you're taking yourself off the market."

Garrett could barely keep the laughter from his voice. He and his brothers had a bet as to which one of them would be the first to marry and start a family. So far the three of them had been fighting to keep their bachelor status. Every month for the past five years, they each had deposited one hundred dollars into an account they labeled "the Sprung Fund." There were now several thousand dollars in that account. The money would be used to pay for the wedding of the loser.

"Not quite," Duane finally said. What he didn't tell his brother was that he had thought about it quite a bit since a certain woman had come into his life.

Garrett barked with laughter. "'Not quite' means it's only a matter of weeks before the big announcement. Mark my word."

"How would you even know? You can't even stick around long enough to have a meaningful relationship."

Garrett snorted. "And I plan to keep it that way. I travel too much to be serious. Besides, there ain't a woman around who's going to put up with a man who's never home and is surrounded by beautiful women all the time."

"Do I hear conceit on the other end of this phone?" Duane asked dryly.

"Nah, a brotha's just trying to keep it real."

Duane chuckled and shook his head. He couldn't wait for the day when some woman had his brother's nose wide open.

Destiny peeled off her T-shirt, and immediately a shiver snaked up her spine. She reached for a large bath towel. Bathing Champion had been an experience she was in no rush to repeat.

Water was obviously not one of his favorite things. He had jumped out of the tub several times and raced through half the house before she could get him back in the water. She had washed him three times before he had come clean. Before she could dry him, he shook himself, spraying her and the entire bathroom with water. When he dashed out again, she didn't have the energy to chase him in order to dry him off. Instead, he rolled around on her bed. She then spent the next thirty minutes cleaning the bathroom, her bedroom, and finally, herself.

After she was in clean clothes, Champion curled on the floor at the top of the stairs. Destiny flopped across the freshly changed bed, exhausted. She had a feeling this was what motherhood was like.

Motherhood? The thought froze in her mind. Why did that have such a wonderful ring to it?

Duane clicked on the ceiling fan over the kitchen island, then opened the sliding glass door. Immediately, air flowed through the room, drawing out the heat generated by a large gas oven.

With the back of his hand, he mopped his forehead, then released a sigh of relief. He had spent the last two hours on eggshells all because of his strong determination to impress a special woman.

He had prepared the dinner himself—and only because Destiny had made the comment that he wasn't much of a cook. He had pored over a cookbook he had borrowed from Mrs. Harris next door. He had to answer a million questions before she allowed him to leave. After she had tried to fix him up with one granddaughter after another, he should have expected no less than the third degree.

It took twenty minutes of flipping pages before he settled on salmon, rice pilaf, and a tossed salad. He quickly rushed to the neighborhood grocery store, picked up the ingredients, then raced home and began cooking.

As he removed a saucer of boiled eggs from the stove top, he asked himself why he was going to all this trouble. He had never cooked for a woman before, nor had he ever felt the desire. Yet it was something that he really wanted to do for Destiny. He did it because he wanted to impress her.

Wait until my mother hears about this!

He chuckled as he moved down the hall and up to his room to shower and change. As he removed his clothes, he thought about where the evening would end. He was quite intrigued with Destiny, but part of him was still hesitant about getting too close. There was something about her that was so vulnerable, he wasn't sure how to take her. She came across as innocent, but at the same time he knew there was something going on. Destiny seemed scared of something that she wasn't telling, or maybe she was afraid he might find out something she didn't want him to know. Part of Duane told him to step back while he still could and to keep things between them strictly as friends, while another part of him wanted him to take things to the next level.

It was almost six o'clock when he returned to the kitchen and removed the salmon fillets from the oven. He frowned when he discovered that the bed of spinach beneath was slightly burnt. Moving over to the trash, he slid the fillets to the side, then scooped the green leaves into the trash can.

There's still the salad.

Covering the glass dish, he sat it on the stove and reached for the box of rice. He read the instructions on the box and prepared it in a pot. Noticing that Destiny was expected to arrive at any minute, he turned the fire up a notch. He wanted everything ready and waiting when she arrived.

Swinging around, he reached into the refrigerator, removed a container of brown-and-serve rolls from a bag, and laid four on a cookie sheet, then opened the oven and put them on the top rack. He stood there, arms folded across his chest, beaming with pride. Cooking dinner had been easier than he had thought.

He carried their dishes into the dining room. He hadn't used the room since last spring. His older cousin Brent and his family had come down from New York for a visit. His wife had prepared a feast and invited over the family. It was the first and last time they had all gathered at his house and the last time he had used the dining room. Destiny's visit warranted using it again.

He had just turned off the pot of rice when he heard the doorbell. Duane couldn't help feeling a sense of satisfaction in knowing they were going to spend the evening together on what constituted their second date. He stepped out into the foyer and answered the door.

Destiny stood on his porch dressed in peach. Slowly, he took in the outline of her body in an airy knit dress that stopped at her ankles and displayed her slender shoulders. There were high splits on both sides, which he knew would expose creamy brown thighs when she walked. She had complemented the dress with a simple pair of cream sandals, which proudly displayed manicured toes. Watching her, he felt warmth begin to grow in the middle of his gut.

Duane forced his tongue back in his mouth. "You look lovely," he finally said.

"Thank you." Tilting her chin, Destiny returned the smile, capturing his gaze with hers. Rising on her tiptoes, she pressed a brief yet supple kiss to his lips, then entered the small foyer.

Immediately her eyes traveled up the stairway and back down. Their houses appeared similar from the outside, but on the inside they were unique.

"Wow!" she exclaimed, summing it up in one word.

"Thank you," Duane said as he shut the door.

She stepped into the living room, taking in its size and the rich décor. Arching a questioning eyebrow, she asked, "I thought our houses were the same?"

He nodded. "Originally they were, but a couple of years ago, I gutted this room and extended it into the dining room. Later I built another room, on the other side of my kitchen."

She nodded as she ran her hand across a rich wood coffee table. Two matching burgundy armchairs faced a striped, burgundy-and-cream couch. His was a comfortable home with beautiful oak furniture and gleaming hardwood floors, broken by thick rugs. Light blue colors softened the living room. Heavy tapestry draperies were drawn, allowing streams of the evening sunlight to pour through the room. It had taken a lot of time and expertise to find the right fabric to create such perfect drapes and throw pillows to pull all of the colors in the room together. Destiny was highly impressed. "You're a wonderful decorator."

Duane shrugged. "Actually, I can't take all the credit. My mother has the magic touch when it comes to decorating."

"She did a fabulous job." She focused on several photographs that adorned the walls. Several were of Duane; others she was certain were of his family.

Duane gestured toward the photo in front of her. "That's my sister, Chelsea, and my two younger brothers, Garrett and Reyn."

"You come from a large family." To someone who'd been raised alone, anything more than one was considered large.

"Yeah, and we have quite a large extended family." From the smile on his lips, she could tell he was proud of his family. She felt a slight pang in her chest. Family was something she wanted. Family was also something that at this point in her life, she wasn't sure she'd ever have again.

"Is something wrong?" Duane asked. His voice was soft, comforting.

Unspoken pain was alive and glowing in her eyes, but Destiny shook her head. She wasn't about to spoil the mood. "No," she tossed quickly over her shoulder. "I'm fine. I was just thinking about my grandmother."

Duane dropped a comforting hand on her shoulder and squeezed. "You miss her, don't you?"

Unseeing, she stared past him, lost in her thoughts. "More than I ever thought possible," she replied in a soft, distant voice.

"I know how you feel."

She knew he was referring to his own grandfather. However, what she was feeling he couldn't begin to understand. Her loss ran so much deeper.

Duane wrapped his large arms around her, and instantly Destiny felt comfortable. He lightly pressed his lips to her forehead. When the smile returned to her face, he took her hand. "Come on. Before we eat, let me show you the rest of the house."

She followed him upstairs. Just as in her home, the bathroom was at the top of the staircase. Only

Duane had eliminated the smaller bedroom to the left and had used the space to expand his bathroom. He had a large garden tub with Jacuzzi jets, his and hers sinks, and even a large linen closet. The floor was covered in black-and-white checkerboard tile to match the color scheme of the room.

Down the hall were two bedrooms. The burgundy carpeting in the hall traveled into each. Both had queen-size beds and matching dressers and were tastefully decorated in rich dark green. The smaller room had a desk with a computer on top, set up in the corner.

When they reached the third floor, she gasped. Duane had opened the entire floor into one generously sized suite. There was another bathroom identical to the one on the floor below, except it was decorated in earth tones like the rest of the suite. At the front of the suite was a large sitting area with an overstuffed leather chair that looked like a large beanbag and a matching couch. Both were comfortably positioned in front of a big screen television. Stepping farther into the suite, she saw there was an enormous bed smack dab in the middle. It sat on top of taupe carpeting so plush, Destiny felt like she was walking on a pillow. Other than a chest of drawers, this part of the suite was relatively empty. Large abstract paintings covered the eggshell walls.

"Quite impressive," she finally said.

Following the direction of her eyes, Duane smiled knowingly. "My cousin Robin did them."

She focused on the array of gold and brown symmetrical designs. "He is quite a talented painter."

He nodded in agreement. "Yes, he is." His cousin had struggled for years before a wealthy widow discovered his talent and sponsored a showing for him at an art gallery owned by her niece. Robin's paintings were now in hot demand. The six that covered Duane's walls had been purchased before his cousin had become a well-known artist.

Duane came up behind Destiny and dropped his chin to her shoulder, while his arms found their way around her waist. Lowering her eyelids, she leaned into him, her heart fluttering. Then she opened her eyes again. Glancing at the entertainment system in the corner, the fireplace, and the inviting bed at the center of the room, she found the atmosphere a bit too tempting.

"You have a lovely home," she murmured nervously.

"Thank you," he whispered against her ear.

Tipping her head back, she puckered her lips, preparing for a kiss, when something caught her attention. "Is something burning?" she asked as she wrinkled her nose and sniffed.

Chapter 9

Destiny heard the quick intake of breath only seconds before Duane dashed down two flights of stairs. Curious, she followed him and stepped into the kitchen just as he reached into the oven and removed a pan of burnt brown-and-serve rolls.

Destiny pressed a startled hand to her mouth. "Oh, boy!" Applying slight pressure to her lips, she successfully contained a peal of laughter. "I thought you were ordering takeout?"

Duane groaned as he carried the pan over to the trash and disposed of its contents. "I thought I would impress you and cook instead."

Her head came up slowly, and she met his gaze. His eyes were brimmed with kindness and passion. The gesture made her heart skip a beat. "That's the nicest thing anyone has ever done for me."

"You might want to save that compliment until after we eat." There was a trace of laughter in his voice.

"If the smell of that salmon is any indication, everything is going to taste just fine," she said, feeling the need to reassure him. Smiling, she shook her head in astonishment. It was hard to believe he had gone to all this trouble for her. "You need some help?"

"Sure." He reached into the refrigerator and pulled out a bowl of salad. "Why don't you carry this into the dining room and then have yourself a seat. I'll pop some more rolls in and will be out in a flash."

Hand at the small of her back, Duane gave her a playful push in the right direction. Destiny felt a warmth flow through her as she moved into a room off of the kitchen that could have easily been considered a sunroom. Light beamed in from the sky-light and lit up a large oak table, which comfortably seated six. Two place settings were set with fine china, crystal glasses, and silverware. A bottle of white zinfandel stood at the corner of the table, chilling in a bucket of ice.

Destiny moved over to the floor-to-ceiling window and stared out at a large wraparound deck. The backyard was small. Nevertheless, the scene on the far side was a magnificent portrait of trees and shrubs. She stood there in awe at the beauty of her surroundings. The sun had begun to set beyond the tallest trees, leaving a burst of red and orange in the darkening sky.

Gently pressing her palms against the glass, Destiny wondered if Duane sat out on his deck and appreciated the sunrise in the morning. She wished she were as fortunate. The view from her backyard was into the yard of the house behind her. And the view from the balcony of her condo in St. Louis was of the highway. Never in a million years would she have imagined she'd have such an appreciation for something so rural.

"Madam, dinner is served."

Again, the sound of Duane's masculine voice sent

tingles up her spine at the same time that it startled her. Why did he insist on scaring her? No, that was unfair. Her mind had been absorbed by the scenic view, and she simply had not heard him. She tried to force a smile as her heart returned to normal.

He gave her an apologetic smile. "Sorry. I thought I made enough noise to wake the dead."

"No, it's not your fault. I was so intrigued by the view, I didn't hear a thing." She dropped her gaze to the dishes in his hands. "Boy, that looks good," she said, glad to be able to change the subject. She hated that her fears were constantly springing to the surface.

Duane placed the food on the table, then walked around and helped Destiny into a chair. Once she was pushed comfortably up to the table, he moved to take the seat directly across from her.

"Would you like some salad?" he asked.

Destiny grinned. "I would love some." She handed him her plate and watched as he served her a moderate amount before handing it back to her.

"Thank you." She reached for her napkin and draped it across her lap.

"Do you drink white zinfandel?"

She nodded. "It's my favorite wine."

"Good. Then we have something else in common."

He reached for the bottle and removed the cork, then filled each of their glasses half full. "I also have lemonade and Pepsi if you want something else to drink."

She shook her head. "Water will be just fine."

Duane reached for the pitcher of water and filled her glass, then his.

As soon as he was done, Destiny nodded. "Thank you. Now let's say grace so we can eat."

He couldn't resist a grin before he lowered his eyelids and listened as she gave praise.

"Amen," he repeated before opening his eyes and grabbing his own napkin.

Destiny reached for the salmon, then passed the dish to Duane. "What made you buy a house this size? I mean . . . it's just you."

He fixed his plate as he spoke. "I was spending so much money paying rent that one day I decided it was time to buy something of my own. I know small houses are hard to resell, so I decided to get something that an average-size family would appreciate. I also wanted a fixer-upper, and this house was definitely that."

"Really, I would never have guessed," Destiny commented as she reached for a bottle of ranch dressing.

"Oh yeah, the old woman that lived here hadn't done anything in years. It looked worse than your uncle's."

She arched an eyebrow as she spooned rice onto her plate. "Thanks a lot."

Shaking his head, Duane tried to force back amusement. "Sorry, sweetheart. But it's the truth. The woman had lived here over fifty years. When her husband died, she just gave up. Her children were forced to put her in a nursing home and gave me a really good deal on the house. I kept my apartment for six months while I gutted the place."

Destiny glanced around the room again. "You did a fabulous job."

He flashed a sensual smile. "Thank you." Reaching for his fork, he pierced his salad. He hadn't eaten all day and was starving. Next, he put a forkful of salmon in his mouth and chewed. Immediately, he reached for his glass of water and took several swallows. The fish was dry as cardboard. And what was with the flavor? The recipe had called for yogurt and dill, yet something didn't taste quite right.

Destiny looked up and caught Duane staring. Dropping her gaze, she focused on her plate. She knew he was attracted to her. Duane didn't try to conceal the deep longing in his eyes. Sneaking a glance, she was met by his hypnotic stare again, and her heart pounded wildly. Looking away, she reached for her wineglass and toyed with it, giving her something to do.

His attraction was obvious in his good deed. After all, he had gone out of his way to make her dinner, even if it was a disaster, she thought as she took another forkful. The rice was half done, and the fish tasted like he had basted it in pickle juice. When she glanced at him again, Duane seemed to be enjoying his cooking. She took another bite, then quickly reached for her water and washed it down.

"How's your food?" he finally asked.

Destiny flushed the vinegar taste from her mouth and forced a smile. "Fine."

"You're lying."

Her eyes grew big, but she ignored his challenging gaze and crunched on her salad. It was the only thing edible. "What makes you think I'm not telling the truth?"

"Because this is the worst meal I've ever tasted."

They stared at each other, then dissolved into a fit of laughter.

"The rice is so crunchy, I'm afraid I might break a tooth," he joked.

"It isn't that bad."

He quirked his brow, and Destiny couldn't keep

a straight face. Laughing, the two carried their plates to the sink, and together they scraped three hours of cooking down the garbage disposal.

"How about I return to the original plan and order takeout?" he suggested as they placed their dishes in the dishwasher.

"Sounds good," she agreed while chuckling lightly.

They were standing side by side at the sink when Duane locked his gaze with hers. In one forward motion, Destiny was in his arms, and his mouth was covering hers hungrily. She had been waiting for this all evening. Now that it was happening, she wanted to lose herself in his embrace. Raising her arms, she circled his neck and felt the strong pumping of his heart, which matched her own. She wanted him. Needed this. Even if it was just for the moment. She would worry about where their relationship was heading and what it meant to them later. All that mattered at the moment was right there and then.

An overpowering rumble of desire emerged from his throat just before Duane slipped his tongue between her parted lips and met her tongue with measured strokes. Her pulse raced wildly against her chest as his mouth took complete and thorough control. At first, the kiss was slow and gentle; then it became greedy and passionate. She tightened her hold, loving the feel of his hard body against her, as Duane's large hands slipped across her back and down her spine. His long fingers dipped even lower and caressed the curves of her buttocks. She groaned softly at the back of her throat, realizing that she was never going to be able to keep her guard up around him again.

She was in trouble. Her life was in danger. Lucas

wouldn't stop until he found her. But as Duane slid his hands down her back, cupping her buttocks and leaning her back against a cabinet while his leg rested between her thighs, she realized she didn't care.

Duane made sure she was experiencing the same level of desire that was surging through his blood-stream. Each kiss left him yearning and craving for more. A groan of pleasure escaped her lips, caus-ing a tightening in his groin. If kissing her made him feel this crazed, he could only imagine how ex-plosive actually making love to her would be. He was losing control. His hands seemed to have a mind of their own as one slid around and grasped her breast. He had felt the hardened nipple brush against his shirt only seconds before. Now he was dying to remove her dress and capture the dark pearl between his teeth. Through the material, he lightly caressed it with his thumb until a soft whim-per escaped her lips.

Destiny was on fire, and Duane was to blame. Her reaction to him was swift and powerful. As he con-tinued to take complete and total possession of her mouth, her most intimate area throbbed with need. She wasn't the only one aroused. Arching against him, she felt the hardness of his erection against his belly. She wanted so badly to ask him to take her to bed. For one night she wanted to feel loved. Only what she wanted and needed were two entirely dif-ferent things, and no matter how good Duane made her feel, now was not the time to confuse them. With a sigh of regret, she pressed gently against his shoulders and eased back.

His mouth was still moist from hers, and she reached up, rubbing her thumb over his bottom lip. When she was done, he gathered her in his arms again and held her gently in a way that made her realize there was more between them than friendship and desire.

For the longest time they just stood there, arms wrapped around each other, trying to regain control.

"That almost got out of hand," Duane whispered softly.

Destiny lifted her head and gazed up at him. His mouth said one thing; the look in his eyes told another story. He was still aroused, and she regretted having to end what was happening. Nevertheless, she could no longer pretend the attraction between them didn't exist. Her heart lurched madly, but she kept her emotions from floating to the surface. Being alone with him in his house was not a good idea.

"How about dinner at Boston Market and a movie, my treat?" she suggested in a quiet voice.

He smirked. "Sounds good."

They saw a romantic comedy and laughed between bites of buttered popcorn, chocolate-covered peanuts, and cold fountain sodas. On the drive back, Duane turned on the radio to KISS 101.7's quiet storm.

Destiny gazed out the truck window, battling the warning signs that refused to go away. How was she supposed to enjoy her movie when her inner voice was constantly chanting, "you're making a big mistake." She didn't need to be constantly reminded that she barely knew Duane and that lately she had been taking too many risks. But never in her thirty years had she met a man that made her feel this good so quickly. Duane made her feel comfortable, safe, and special. Maybe she was losing sight of who she was and her true reason for being on the East Coast in the first place. Maybe it was something she wasn't expected to understand. All she did know was that Duane made her feel something she had never experienced before, and she just wasn't sure if it was something she could ignore or easily walk away from.

"What are you thinking about?" Duane asked, breaking into her thoughts.

She dropped her eyes, and a soft blush swept over her cheeks. She was embarrassed that she had gotten caught daydreaming about him. "Nothing."

"Nothing?" he mocked as he turned at the next corner. "You sure know how to hurt a brother."

She glanced over at his amused expression, puzzled. "What do you mean?"

"I mean, you're sitting beside one of the finest brothas in town, listening to some of the hottest slow jams in the country, and you're telling me nothing is on your mind?"

Realizing what he was getting at, Destiny shifted slightly on the seat and caught his lips twitching. He was trying not to laugh. "Since you're so concerned about my thoughts, what were you thinking about?" she asked.

"You."

Destiny was stunned by his blunt response. "Oh," she whispered, still unable to look away. She watched the humor vanish from his face and seriousness take over. A slow tremor started at her chest and worked its way down to her toes.

Recovering quickly, she moistened her dry lips and boldly asked, "What about me?"

He tore his eyes away from the road long enough

to give her a sexy smile before speaking. "I've been thinking about how badly I want to kiss you again."

As he turned at the next corner, Duane reached down and took her hand in his, then brought it up to his mouth. The feel of his soft lips on her sensitive skin rocked her mental equilibrium.

"I'm also thinking about how good you look tonight in that dress. You had that young cat behind the counter spilling popcorn because he was trying to look at you."

She giggled and blushed.

"As I listen to the words of the music, I find myself thinking about that sexy sway you have when you walk. The way your eyes light up when you're excited, and the way you nibble nervously on those sexy lips of yours." With each couple of words, he paused long enough to slip one of her fingers in his mouth and suck slowly and deliberately as if it were a chocolate ice cream cone.

His declaration made heat travel down her arm, through her chest, and settle at the very core of her. *Get a grip!*

Duane stopped at a traffic light, then turned in his seat so they were facing one another. His eyes met hers. The look was intense and thoughtful.

"I like you, Destiny," he stated simply.

A slight smile curved her lips as his words warmed her heart. "I like you, too."

"I like you a lot." Raising his hands, he cradled her face, staring down at her.

Stunned by the power of his eyes, she didn't know what to say. She didn't miss the look of pure masculine appreciation in them. She hoped he couldn't hear her heart thumping loudly against her chest.

"I like you so much that I want you to know, I can't pretend to be interested in just being your friend," he confessed in a husky voice.

"What do you have in mind?" she asked shakily.

Desire blazed in his eyes as he said softly, "I want to see you."

"See me?" she repeated.

"I don't know how they say it now. Go together, make you my woman, kick it." He paused, chuckling softly. Destiny joined in as well. "All I know is I don't want to share you. I want you all to myself."

Listening to him, she felt a warmth begin to grow in the middle of her gut. "Are you saying you want to sleep with me?"

Duane hesitated slightly, as if stunned by her question. Sleep was only a small fraction of what he planned to do to her. "Yes, I'm not going to lie to you; I envision myself making love to you," he answered truthfully. "But not until you are ready. I would never make you do anything you didn't want to do."

Even though she believed him, she was rendered speechless by his confession. He wanted to make love to her! Why did that have a wonderful sound to it? Her heart pounded furiously at the possibility. The way he kissed left no doubt that Duane would be a fantastic lover.

His fingers caressed the sides of her face. "Right now I want to take things slow and see where they lead us."

Destiny couldn't find her voice. She was mesmerized by his words. He wanted to be with her.

Tell him no!

She inhaled deeply, then shifted her gaze down to her hands. For a long moment she didn't say anything. She swallowed the lump in her throat, not knowing what she should say. If she accepted his offer, then she was going against her decision and taking a risk that he would find out the truth. "I'm leaving in a few weeks," she reminded him, watching him, waiting for his reaction.

"How about we cross that bridge when we reach it?" he suggested with a questioning glint in his eyes.

Closing her eyes, she bit down hard on her lips. She was confused by the mixed emotions rushing through her. Duane sought a relationship, and she could not afford one at this juncture in her life. Or could she? She wasn't going to be in Delaware long enough for a full-fledged relationship to develop, yet she still wanted him. That was no secret. As much as she knew it would be a mistake, she couldn't get her heart to understand what would happen once she stepped over the line. Her body wasn't listening to what her mind had to say. Her body didn't care about regrets. It also couldn't care less about the emotional attachment that was already developing. She had never been able to sleep with a man and simply walk away. But if she never experienced what Duane had to offer, she would forever live with *what-ifs*. Deep in her heart, Destiny knew she wanted to be with him at least once. To lie in his arms, embracing the comfort he brought to her life. For the next several weeks, she wanted to experience happiness and pretend Desiree never existed. The consequences would be something she would have to prepare herself to deal with later. And there would definitely be consequences.

She wasn't sure how long she sat there before she opened her eyes again and found him still waiting for a response.

She nodded.

Duane tilted her face and met her halfway. They sealed their decision with a passionate kiss. She breathed a sigh of pleasure when his lips touched hers. He thrust his tongue between her lips, tasting with a force that shook her to the core. The kiss probably would have gone on for some time if someone behind them hadn't blown his car horn and shouted out the window, "Get a room!"

Destiny and Duane eased apart, and she giggled as he shifted the truck in gear and drove away.

Destiny stepped into the house, giggling, with her heart beating a mile a minute.

He had asked to see her exclusively, and she had agreed. Destiny Davis was now dating Duane Urban!

Why am I smiling?

Because it has a wonderful ring to it.

Duane Urban's woman.

She knew she should have resisted, yet she couldn't deny feeling a sense of satisfaction in knowing he wanted her.

Champion was lying on the living room floor, sleeping so soundly he was snoring. She smiled down at her new friend, then headed happily up to her bedroom. She tossed her purse onto the bed and reached in her dresser for something comfortable to slip into. She was feeling good, probably the best she had felt in weeks.

Destiny slipped into her pajamas, then slid her feet in her house shoes and padded downstairs. She suddenly had a craving for strawberry shortcake ice cream. Making her way into the kitchen, she headed to the side-by-side refrigerator and opened the freezer.

"Duane, Duane, what am I gonna do with you?" she murmured as she scanned the shelves. She was in way over her head, and she knew it. All that talk about keeping their relationship at a minimum had gone up in smoke. She wasn't completely disappointed. After all, she had done what she said she was going to do—go on living. Lucas was no longer dictating her life. She was less afraid and suddenly looking forward to the future.

For once she had followed her heart. She desired a life and deserved a chance to be happy. She would just have to be careful and not allow herself to become dependent on Duane. She would give him time, possibly even allow him to make love to her. But, no matter what happened, she would not lose her heart over him.

Destiny frowned and stopped thinking about Duane long enough to concentrate on finding the open box of ice cream. She pushed a bag of chicken breasts to the side and looked beneath the frozen broccoli. After checking each shelf again slowly, she raised a hand to her hip.

Where was that open box?

She remembered finishing the first box, but the second she had just opened, or had she? She found herself second-guessing herself. Could she have already eaten all four bars? It was possible. She always had an ice cream bar as a reward after she accomplished her writing goal for the day. Yesterday she had had two. Maybe Duane ate them? That was also a possibility.

Refusing to open another box, she shut the freezer. *Oh, well, you didn't need it, anyway.* Without

An Important Message From The ARABESQUE Publisher

Dear Arabesque Reader,

I invite you to join the club! The Arabesque book club delivers four novels each month right to your front door! It's easy, and you will never miss a romance by one of our award-winning authors!

With upcoming novels featuring strong, sexy women, and African-American heroes that are charming, loving and true… you won't want to miss a single release. Our authors fill each page with exceptional dialogue, exciting plot twists, and enough sizzling romance to keep you riveted until the satisfying end! To receive novels by bestselling authors such as Gwynne Forster, Janice Sims, Angela Winters and others, I encourage you to join now!

Read about the men we love… in the pages of Arabesque!

Linda Gill
PUBLISHER, ARABESQUE ROMANCE NOVELS

*P.S. Watch out for the next Summer Series **"Ports Of Call"** that will take you to the exotic locales of Venice, Fiji, the Caribbean and Ghana! You won't need a passport to travel, just collect all four novels to enjoy romance around the world! For more details, visit us at www.BET.com.*

A SPECIAL "THANK YOU" FROM ARABESQUE JUST FOR YOU!

Send this card back and you'll receive 4 FREE Arabesque Novels—a $25.96 value—absolutely FREE!

The introductory 4 Arabesque Romance books are yours FREE (plus $1.99 shipping & handling). If you wish to continue to receive 4 books every month, do nothing. Each month, we will send you 4 New Arabesque Romance Novels for your free examination. If you wish to keep them, pay just $18* (plus, $1.99 shipping & handling). If you decide not to continue, you owe nothing!

- Send no money now.
- Never an obligation.
- Books delivered to your door!

We hope that after receiving your FREE books you'll want to remain an Arabesque subscriber, but the choice is yours! So why not take advantage of this Arabesque offer, with no risk of any kind. You'll be glad you did!

In fact, we're so sure you will love your Arabesque novels, that we will send you an Arabesque Tote Bag FREE with your first paid shipment.

* PRICES SUBJECT TO CHANGE.

YOU'LL GET 4 SELECT ROMANCES PLUS THIS FABULOUS TOTE BAG!

ARABESQUE

Visit us at:
www.BET.com

THE "THANK YOU" GIFT INCLUDES:

- 4 books absolutely FREE (plus $1.99 for shipping and handling).
- A FREE newsletter, *Arabesque Romance News*, filled with author interviews, book previews, special offers, and more!
- No risks or obligations. You're free to cancel whenever you wish with no questions asked.

INTRODUCTORY OFFER CERTIFICATE

Yes! Please send me 4 FREE Arabesque novels (plus $1.99 for shipping & handling). I am under no obligation to purchase any books, as explained on the back of this card. Send my free tote bag after my first regular paid shipment.

NAME _____

ADDRESS _____ APT. _____

CITY _____ STATE _____ ZIP _____

TELEPHONE ( ) _____

E-MAIL _____

SIGNATURE _____

Offer limited to one per household and not valid to current subscribers. All orders subject to approval. Terms, offer, & price subject to change. Tote bags available while supplies last.

Thank You!

AN125A

ARABESQUE

Accepting the four introductory books for FREE (plus $1.99 to offset the cost of shipping & handling) places you under no obligation to buy anything. You may keep the books and return the shipping statement marked "cancelled". If you do not cancel, about a month later we will send 4 additional Arabesque novels, and you will be billed the preferred subscriber's price of just $4.50 per title. That's $18.00* for all 4 books for a savings of almost 30% off the cover price (Plus $1.99 for shipping and handling). You may cancel at any time, but if you choose to continue, every month we'll send you 4 more books, which you may either purchase at the preferred discount price. . . or return to us and cancel your subscription.

* PRICES SUBJECT TO CHANGE

THE ARABESQUE ROMANCE CLUB: HERE'S HOW IT WORKS

THE ARABESQUE ROMANCE BOOK CLUB
P.O. BOX 5214
CLIFTON NJ 07015-5214

PLACE
STAMP
HERE

her personal trainer, she hadn't been getting the regular exercise her body had grown accustomed to receiving. And if she wasn't careful, the extra calories were going to catch up with her.

Opening the right side of the side-by-side refrigerator, she removed a bottle of water off the top shelf, then carried it up to her office. She suddenly had the motivation to write. If she reached the end of the scene she was struggling with, she could always get that ice cream bar later.

Duane sat out on his deck. It was only eleven o'clock. Too early for bed. He slid his arms in a windbreaker to counter the cool night breeze.

He still couldn't believe he had told Destiny he intended to make love to her. Not that he was shy. He'd told women that before. But with Destiny, he had expected to keep their relationship simple. Friendly, neighborly, but somehow it had gotten complicated. It had gotten so complicated, he had done exactly what he said he wasn't going to do, get involved again. Especially with another woman who was hiding something.

Folding his arms beneath his chest, he looked up at the star-studded sky. The last couple of days he felt more alive than he had in months. And her secrets no longer seemed to matter as much. Because now he hoped Destiny would learn to trust him and eventually bear her soul.

He tried not to think about the woman across the street but failed miserably. None of it made sense. The only thing he understood was his need to taste her, to touch her. All he knew was how right her feminine curves fit against his body. He considered inviting her to sit out on the deck beside him. But if she came over, there was no way they would have just sat there with his hands off of her.

He released a long breath, already regretting the hours to come. Nighttime for him was torture. His restless mind kept returning to their kisses. Now that he knew how she tasted, he couldn't get the sweet flavor from his mind. Not a second had gone by that he didn't envision what he would do to her when the time was right.

Now that he had stepped over the line, there was no turning back. He wanted her, and he planned to have her.

Chapter 10

The next couple of days Destiny felt as if she were dreaming. Despite her feelings of uncertainty and fear, she decided to throw caution to the wind and live her life the way it was meant to be lived— happy. Duane came over every day. He worked on repairing the boards on her front porch and the bathroom plumbing, while she either cleaned up the trash and debris from the yard or worked on her manuscript.

On Monday Duane took her to a small Mexican restaurant not too far from the house. When he brought her home, he walked her to the door and quickly kissed her good night. With each day she had found herself drawing closer to him with long- ing; her instincts had taken over. Now she was anx- ious to explore her feelings further, but she never got a chance that day. The same thing happened on Tuesday. They engaged in another brief casual conversation as they worked, but not once had he come into her house or invited her to his.

Tuesday night she lay in bed wondering what had gone wrong. He was the one who had defined their relationship, not her. She had begun to think she had imagined the discussion they had had in his truck on Sunday. By 2 A.M. Wednesday morning, she realized it was going to be another restless night and grew angry. If Duane was playing a game, then she wanted no part of it. She would just have to keep reminding herself why she had come to Delaware. And it was not to become involved with a man.

Destiny felt like she had just shut her eyes when the phone rang around six o'clock. The sun had barely risen. With a groan, she rolled over and reached for the phone.

"Good morning, sleepyhead."

Even though Duane had ruined a perfectly good dream, she couldn't resist smiling at the sound of his low, husky voice. "Good morning," she crooned softly.

"Sorry to wake you. I'm going to be installing a subpump in a crawl space beneath a house today and might not have another chance to call you. How about lunch?"

She rolled over onto *his* pillow. "That sounds wonderful."

"I was thinking we could go to the park and have a picnic."

"And who's fixing the basket, you or me?" Before he could answer, her eyes sprung open. "Never mind. I'll fix the basket."

Duane laughed, a soft rumble from his wide chest. Destiny shut her eyes again and grinned. He couldn't possibly think she would allow him to be responsible for a meal again after his dinner fiasco.

"Smart move. I'll be by to pick you up around two."

"I'll be ready." With a smile on her face, she fell back to sleep.

It was such a beautiful day. The sun was shining, and the temperature was warm, yet there was a cool, gentle breeze. They took Duane's truck and decided to take Champ along. He enjoyed the trip, sitting in the bed, seeing everything. Once at the park, Destiny put him on a retractable leash, and he jumped down off the truck.

Smiling, she took in her surroundings. Brandywine Park was beautiful. There was a walking and bike trail, lush green grass, and mature trees. There were several picnic tables and barbecue grills.

The park covered thirteen landscaped acres on high ground above the Brandywine River. At the very heart of it was a zoo that hosted dozens of animals, ranging from tigers to snakes. Since pets weren't allowed on zoo grounds, Destiny strolled around the zoo, while Duane walked Champion.

After she finished looking at the animals, she rejoined them, and they walked to the other end of the park and back. Along the way they watched children flying kites and families bicycling. After an hour of walking, they had worked up a hunger and headed back to the truck to retrieve the picnic basket.

Holding hands, the two strolled to a large oak tree. Duane spread a blanket on the grass, then took the basket from Destiny's hand and set it off to the side, while Destiny gave Champion a bowl of cool water and a couple of treats.

Duane lowered himself onto the blanket and pulled Destiny down to sit between his legs. Leaning into him, Destiny pressed her back against his chest and eased her head on his shoulder.

She closed her eyes and breathed in his essence.

A soft sigh emanated from her lips. She felt relaxed and at peace. "This is a beautiful place."

With his arms draped across her middle, Duane tilted forward and planted a kiss on her hair. "Yeah, it sort of makes up for the pitiful zoo."

Destiny chuckled. She had never seen a zoo of that caliber before, and she had seen plenty. "It is pretty small, but cute."

Still holding her, Duane settled back against the tree. "A couple of years ago, a zoo employee was almost killed."

She turned her head, eyes seeking his. "How so?"

His sober look deepened his penetrating eyes. "The woman who cleaned the big cats' cages would open a door so the cats would climb into a smaller cage while she cleaned the area. Apparently, on this particular day, she didn't count correctly. She had thought all four cats had moved into the smaller cage, when only three had done so. She was already in there cleaning before she realized she wasn't alone."

"Oh no!" Destiny shook loose from his comforting embrace and swung around until she was facing him. "What happened?"

"She froze. Luckily for her, someone was strolling by the cage and realized what was about to happen. They screamed until someone came to help her."

"Did she get out okay?"

He nodded. "Two other employees were able to distract the cat long enough for her to get out safely."

Shaking her head, Destiny glanced over toward the zoo. Remembering the size of the big cats, she could easily imagine how frightened the woman must have been to have her life hanging by a thread.

It appears the two of you have something in common.

"Man, that's a scary thought." Destiny swallowed. She had to admit at times she felt like she was waiting for someone to pounce on her. That someone was lurking in the corners, watching and waiting. She found herself further indulging her own fears; then with a smack of her lips, she tossed them aside. "How about a sandwich?"

Duane smiled and tried to peek into the basket. Destiny slammed the lid down. "No peeking."

"I was just trying to find out what you have inside."

He tried to reach around her, but Destiny pushed the basket out of his reach. "No. It's a surprise."

He gazed down at her. "It must be something special."

"It is. Now eat your sandwich and wait." She handed him a sandwich, then tossed Champion one also.

When he saw the teasing glint in her eyes, he grinned. "Yes, ma'am," he said as he unzipped the plastic bag. Inside he found a ham and provolone cheese sandwich just the way he liked it, with lettuce and mustard on whole wheat.

Destiny handed him an ice cold soda, and he finished half of it in one swallow.

There wasn't much need to talk. Seagulls cried overhead. Ducks were swimming in the river. Kids were whizzing by on their bikes.

Bending her knees, Destiny hugged her legs as she chewed her sandwich. She looked across the grass at the beautiful river. "This would be a perfect place to write. It's so peaceful. I could get lost in my thoughts."

Duane laced his fingers together and watched her

as she appreciated her surroundings with her moist lips parted. The look did something to his insides. The seductive gesture made him hot, and the heat was racing down to his groin.

It was bad enough she was wearing less than he had expected. When he had arrived, she was standing at the door, basket in hand, and his mouth dropped. Gone were the baseball caps and loose-fitting tops. He had a hard time keeping his body in control as she came down the newly repaired porch stairs in a pink miniskirt that sat low on her hips and revealed an adorable belly button. She had matched it with a form-fitting white top. Sitting there, he couldn't help admiring her, from her firm thighs all the way down to her sandal-clad feet.

He was starting to lose control. For the past several days he had been ending their day right before sunset. He refused go into her house for fear of what he would do to her the next time they were alone. He was scared of his own reaction to her: he definitely didn't want to scare her off with the passion burning in his chest. Monday he had found himself dreaming about having babies. The depth of his feelings scared him, which was why he had decided it was best to keep his distance until he could sort his emotions out. Only he couldn't anymore. Rather he didn't want to. He wanted Destiny in every way a man wanted a woman.

"What are you thinking about?" he asked.

"Why have you been avoiding me?"

He shook his head. "I haven't been avoiding you."

"Okay, let me rephrase that. You spend the day with me, but as soon as the sun sets, you run off like a vampire," she said with a frown.

Duane tried to suppress laughter. "Actually, sweetheart, vampires hide out during the day."

A shiver of frustration swept over her. "You know what I mean."

He dissolved into laughter when she playfully swatted at his arm.

Glancing up at him, she watched as the laughter melted away. The muscles at his jaw bunched as if he were pondering what she had said.

"What you've been experiencing is called the horny man fade."

She practically choked on the last bite of her sandwich. "The horny what?"

"The horny man fade. I fade away in the evening because I know that as horny as I am, if I were to spend any more time with you, I wouldn't be able to keep my hands to myself."

Her eyes crinkled as she laughed.

"I want to make love to you."

Her lips formed the shape of an *O*. She didn't know what to say. Her eyelids fluttered closed, and she felt Duane's fingers graze her cheek with a gentleness that caused her to inhale slowly.

"Come here," he commanded softly.

The look caused her to tingle, and suddenly, she wasn't sure if she trusted being touched by him right at that moment. "You ready for dessert?" she asked, trying to shift the focus from her to food.

"I'd rather have you." He reached for her. Leaning against the tree, he guided her onto his lap.

"What about my surprise? I-I baked a chocolate cake," she stuttered.

"It can wait. What I need to do to you cannot," he whispered.

Destiny felt the moist heat of his breath seconds

before he pressed his lips against her smooth forehead. She shuddered as his mouth moved and kissed her ear and cheek; then his lips traveled down to her neck. Duane then brought his mouth to her lips, warm, firm, and tempting. She felt her control slip. As the kisses became more intense, Destiny was afraid if she didn't hold on, she would float away. He slid to the corner of her lips, tasting, nibbling, then to her ears, where he slowly set off little sparks within her.

He gathered her to him, caressing her with slow and seductive strokes. He trailed light kisses across her neck. The heat between them was rising, and Duane groaned. He put aside his need to stay in control. At the moment nothing else mattered except for the feel of her breasts against his chest. The feeling of her lush mouth against his.

Destiny had barely caught her breath when his lips fused with hers again. She felt overwhelmed with the need to taste, to experience him. Reaching up, she pulled him closer to her until their bodies were a tight fit. His hand moved restlessly, caressing her waist, hips, then around to her buttocks with slow deliberate moves. She felt his need spiraling up. A need that matched hers.

She savored the sweet hunger rising within her and opened her mouth to his. The muscles of his back flexed with her palms against them. With each stroke, sensual heat moved from his lips and quickly spread through her body. A sigh slid from her parted lips, one of pleasure and need. He pulled her even closer, allowing her to feel his erection.

His hand slid across, and he caught her breast, kneading, then pleasuring it. Warm and rough, his hand slowly climbed up until a thumb caressed her nipple. She felt a surge of joy as it hardened in the center of his palm.

Her breath caught when his hand then traveled down beneath her skirt. His fingers slipped past the elastic of her panties until he found the area that yearned to be caressed. She trembled as he pushed her legs apart and then began moving his hand between them. She was wet. Her breath caught. She found his fingers to be just as skillful as his mouth. All she could do was relax and enjoy it.

Duane's finger entered her as he was determined to give her pleasure. He then began to stroke her. Within seconds she was trembling and whimpering against his mouth. He felt the moment her body gave in to the feeling. Trailing kisses along her cheek and jaw, his strokes increased. He surged even deeper into her heat, then sent her toppling over the edge.

"Duane," she moaned as the sensation took over. Her body shuddered and jerked as she tumbled on the edge of release.

He returned his mouth to hers, muffling her startling cry, and felt the shudder as an orgasm rocked her body. She dug her nails in his forearm as the shock of release flowed through her. It was so intense, she gasped out her pleasure.

He broke off the kiss and held her in his arms. Duane treasured the pleasure of Destiny snuggling close against him as she lay in his arms. While they waited for their breathing to resume, their hearts to quiet, he stroked her back, with her head resting on his chest. Even then, for the longest moment neither of them moved.

Destiny finally raised her head, and they sat there staring at one another. After a few moments it became obvious that their attraction to each other had turned into something physical, because neither of them had the strength or the desire to take control of the situation.

Why was he prolonging the agony? Already he knew that soon holding and kissing her were not going to be enough. Hopefully, he could hold on to his determination to persevere until she was ready.

"How would you like to have dinner with me in Baltimore next weekend?" He traced her jawline with the tip of his finger.

She took a slow breath, trying to calm her heart. "I'd like that very much."

That evening they drove to China King, where they ordered enough takeout to feed an army, and then went to his house to eat it.

Destiny laughed and flirted with him all through dinner. After the meal they settled in his living room, enjoying each other's company as they listened to the sounds of Alicia Keys from his stereo system. He was enjoying her. He was enjoying her so much, it was hard to stay relaxed.

Destiny was lying on the couch with her back to his chest. Duane's arms were draped across her waist. Champion was on the floor beside them. The heat from Duane's hands radiated through her blouse. As they both listened to the melody, conversation wasn't necessary.

"You're the first person I've shared my music collection with," he said at the close of the song.

She turned her head and looked as if she was considering her next question. "Should I feel special?"

His eyes sparkled. "Yes. I usually do this alone."

She smirked. "Then I guess I do feel special."

"You are special." Duane reached out and felt her cheek. She shivered beneath his touch. He was relieved to see she wasn't the only one affected by their close proximity. "I think it's time we end this evening, before I'm no longer responsible for my actions."

She nodded, understanding exactly what he meant. If he touched her one more time, she was bound to be the one initiating the intimate contact. Right now she needed time to think things through to make sure it was exactly what she wanted to do next. Once she took their relationship to that next level, there was no turning back the clock.

"Okay."

Duane walked her across the street. "Have you ever been to the harbor?"

"The Baltimore Harbor?" When he nodded, she shook her head. "No."

"Then you're in for a treat."

"I can't wait."

He took her key from her hand, then opened the door and let Champion in. When he tried to hand her the key back, she shook her head and said, "Keep it."

Duane gave her a puzzled look.

She reached up and rested a palm against his chest. "You're over here so much that it would be easier if you had a key. Besides, this way the next time a cat invades my kitchen, I don't have to run downstairs to open the door."

He looked pleased as his smile deepened. Lowering his head, he kissed her lightly on her cheek. "Good night, Destiny."

"Good night, Duane."

Destiny went inside. After slipping into her pajamas, she sat down at her computer, hoping to get a little work done. After an hour she realized that trying to work was a big waste of time with Duane on her mind. However, at the rate she was going, if she didn't keep up the pace, she was not going to meet her August deadline.

Destiny nibbled nervously on her lower lip. She hadn't talked to Julia in days. Duane had been around so much, she hadn't had a chance to sneak off and make a call, even to her lawyer. The last call she had made was while at Freddy's. That had been a stupid, uncalculated move. She should have never made a call so close to home. She blamed it on the liquor clouding her judgment. Nevertheless, it was careless mistakes like that that could get her killed. She would wait until their trip to Baltimore before she made any further contact.

After another hour in front of the computer, Destiny decided to call it a night.

She was glad she had given Duane a key. It made her feel safe knowing he could get to her at a moment's notice if need be. And that night, for the first time since Destiny left St. Louis, she had a good night's sleep.

Chapter 11

Destiny rose feeling that something was wrong. Something told her there was something she was supposed to remember, but for the life of her, she couldn't figure out what it was.

She got up and let Champion out back while she completed her morning routine in the bathroom. Slipping into a pair of jeans, a T-shirt, and running shoes, she decided to forgo the treadmill for one morning and instead, go for a walk. She reached for the leash near the back door and took Champion along.

Strolling up the street, she found several neighbors out working in their yards early to avoid the scorching afternoon sun. The weatherman had forecast temperatures in the mid-80s, which was relatively high for this time of the year.

Moving down the sidewalk at a slow trot, Destiny took in her surroundings and experienced a deep appreciation for the place her uncle had called home. Before they had even reached the corner, she felt at peace: What was bothering her earlier had dissipated.

The block was lushly landscaped. Mature evergreens ringed most of the properties and provided privacy while shading the yards. Most of the houses were the same, but there were a few that had two stories instead of three.

Crossing the street at the corner, she could see a cobblestone or two on the ground and frowned with disappointment. Instead of the city replacing the historical stones, they had asphalted over them, probably figuring it was more cost effective, or deciding to use the taxpayers' money for something else.

She found that Champion loved the outdoors as much as he liked riding in the car. A couple of her neighbors stopped what they were doing or rose from their rocking chairs to meet their new neighbor and her furry companion. By the time she and Champion had made it back to her house, Duane's truck had pulled into his driveway.

"What are you doing home?" she asked as he came across the street to greet them.

"I forgot my jigsaw." He had barely stepped foot on the sidewalk when he curled an arm around her waist, clasping her body to his. His head came down, and he pressed his mouth to hers hungrily, leaving her tingling from head to toes.

Pulling back slightly, he stared down at her radiant face. After the cozy evening they had shared together, he had spent the rest of the night fantasizing about the woman he wanted to make love to. After little sleep, he had attempted to take a cold shower to shock him into an alert state and to cool the heat that had settled in his groin. Six cups of java cured the attentiveness problem. The latter wasn't going to be as easy to fix. The only person capable of alleviating that problem was Destiny. He just prayed that he could control his rising desire until she was ready to take their relationship a step further.

His thoughts were interrupted by a warm, wet feeling on his free hand. Glancing down, he realized Champ had decided to give his hand a bath.

"I didn't forget about you." He released Destiny and rubbed Champ's head. "That a boy."

Destiny grinned at her man and noted how handsome he looked, even dressed in old jeans and a T-shirt that was spattered with paint.

"We were just getting ready to go in and have breakfast," she said.

Duane reached out and took the leash from her. "How about we go to IHOP?"

Her brow furrowed. "Don't you have to get back to work?"

Duane's voice was filled with repressed laughter. "I'm the boss. I don't think I'll get in any trouble. Besides, I'm starved. I was just going to grab a breakfast sandwich on the way back, but I'd rather look at you while I eat."

She grinned and realized she had been doing quite a bit of that since he had come into her life.

"I never pass up eating someone else's pancakes. Give me a second, and I'll be right out." She took the leash from him and led Champ in the house. It took her ten minutes to feed him and retrieve her purse. She found herself humming as she headed to Duane's truck, where he was waiting.

Sipping coffee and holding hands across the table, they chatted extensively. Destiny found it easy to talk to him. While they ate pancakes smothered in blueberry syrup, she listened as Duane talked about how he and his brothers had reacted when they first discovered their sister was dating. He had been overly protective and jealous. Destiny laughed so loud, she was surprised the restaurant manager didn't ask her to lower her voice.

They returned to her house an hour later, stuffed with too many carbohydrates. Destiny's eyes had begun to droop, and she was certain she was going to fall asleep in the next half hour if she didn't do something.

Duane went inside with her. She removed two bottles of water from the refrigerator and motioned for Duane to take a seat at the small kitchen table. He lowered himself onto the chair, with his legs stretched out in front of him.

"Tomorrow I'll be gone most of the day. I'm scheduled to replace kitchen cabinets and run new plumbing."

She sighed dramatically. "I guess I'll have to try and survive."

"Let's see . . . today is the eighteenth, so Monday will be the . . ."

She didn't hear anything else. At the mention of his schedule, what she couldn't remember earlier finally registered in Destiny's mind. Today would have been Nana's eighty-fifth birthday. It would also be the first time since Nana's death that she wouldn't be able to put flowers on her grave. She choked back a cry.

"Are you okay?" Duane asked.

She glanced at a spot over his head and nodded. "I'm fine," she said, even though she knew he knew she was lying.

Her words were so soft, Duane barely heard her. Leaning across the table, he cupped her chin with his hand and tilted her head back so she had no choice but to look at him. "I hope you don't expect me to believe you."

She stared up at him while willing her tears to stay back. After a pregnant silence, she said, "Really. It's . . . it's nothing."

Observing her, he found sadness lurking in her eyes, which tore at his heart. "Why don't you let me be the judge of that?"

Tears filled her eyes, and she closed them just as the first tear dropped. "I just have a few things on my mind."

"I don't believe you." Before she could protest, he swept her up into his arms and carried her into the living room. To keep from falling, she curled her arms around his neck. Duane lowered himself onto the couch and draped her across his lap.

"Listen to me. The day you agreed to be my woman was the day I made the decision to be there for you. I don't take my role as your man lightly," he said, his voice soft, soothing. "If you need someone to lean on, to confide in, or just someone to hold you, I am the man for the job."

She took a deep, shaky breath, then lowered her head to his chest. "I'll keep that in mind."

He raised his hand and brushed moisture from the corner of her eye, then curled his arms around her. He squeezed her tightly to his chest, wishing he could take her pain away. He wanted to know every intimate detail about her, and that included not only what made her happy, but also what had caused the sadness in her life.

"Today is . . . was Nana's birthday," she finally said.

He closed his eyes. "I'm so sorry." He didn't know what else to say.

Covering her mouth with the palm of her hand, she struggled to control her emotions. "I've always visited her grave on her birthday." Her voice hitched as though holding back a sob. He waited patiently for her to continue. "This will be the first time I won't be there to put flowers on her grave."

He squeezed her even closer, feeling her pain. If she hurt, he also hurt.

"How about we call the florist and have an arrangement of spring flowers delivered?" he suggested while dropping light kisses on her forehead.

"We can do that?" she asked, staring down at her hands.

He would have suggested a flight down, but he was sure she had already considered that and that it wasn't possible. Otherwise, she would have gone. If he had known, he would have bought the ticket for her and possibly even gone with her. He pressed his lips to her forehead. "Sure, we can. If we call now, we can have them do a rush delivery."

She raised her head, and his stomach ached at the sight of her tear-stained face. There was a brief silence as they sat motionless staring at each other.

Still holding her, his thumb caressed the back of her hand in a soothing motion. "Baby, everything is going to be okay. All it takes is a credit card."

"Of course," she murmured. She swallowed, relieving the dryness of her throat. "Why didn't I think of that?"

He looked down at her tenderly. "That's what I'm here for."

She rose and gave an excited smile. Duane was a wonderful and thoughtful man. Any one of the other men she had dated would have run at the first sign of tears, but not Duane. He held on to her comfortably, assuring her that he was in her corner and was willing to stick around for the long haul. His suggestion was logical and one she would have thought of herself if she was in her right state of mind.

Her smile faltered slightly as she suddenly realized she didn't have a credit card. All the ones she had belonged to Desiree, and since she couldn't use them, she had cut all of them up.

"What's wrong?"

She glanced over at him. "I don't have a credit card."

He rose in one fluid motion. "Don't worry. I have enough for the both of us."

She shook her head stubbornly. "Duane, I c—"

"You can and you will." He reached into his back pocket for his wallet. "We are committed, sweetheart, so you might as well get used to it."

The quivering of Destiny's lips said she was deeply grateful. "Thank you."

Taking her hand in his, Duane lowered his head and kissed her soundly on the lips. When he pulled back, he winked. "Come, let's go order those flowers."

He led her in the direction of the kitchen. While she reached for the phone and dialed, he took a seat.

"How about we drive down to the beach?"

"The beach?" She turned around with the receiver to her ear. The suggestion brought a smile to her face.

He shrugged. "Sure, why not? Percy can handle the job without me." Duane rose, then stood beside her. "I think I'm going to take my first official day off."

Destiny gazed up at him. "Can you do that?"

"Of course. Don't forget. I am the boss." He tickled her chin. "Come on. It'll be fun. Actually today is a good time. By the weekend the beach will be too packed for enjoyment."

Her smile broadened with approval. "I'd love to."

Surprisingly, Destiny dressed in a swimsuit, a big hat, and dark sunglasses. The attire was appropriate for the weather, but considering the way she dressed most of the time, he wasn't sure if it was intentional or not.

They loaded her car and headed south. Turning on the cruise control, Duane relaxed in his seat and pushed in Usher's *Confessions* CD. As they listened to a slow ballad, he smiled, looking forward to the rest of the afternoon.

He had contacted Ms. Young to let her know he was taking the day off and to assure her his assistant was quite capable of handling the project on his own. Percy, who normally worked twenty hours a week, was eager to pick up the extra time.

Duane had been contracted to repaint the first floor of Ms. Young's house in sage, which seemed to be the color of choice this year. Next week he would return and paint the crown molding in the living room and dining room white.

A sigh drew his attention. Destiny's head was deep inside a notebook. The only way he could get her to take the entire day off and play hooky was to agree to let her bring a couple pages of her thesis to edit during the drive. Although Duane was willing to compromise, he made it perfectly clear he intended on having her undivided attention during the rest of the day. Once they arrived at the beach, she had to put the papers away. With a military salute accompanied by a "Yes, sir," she had agreed.

He was amazed that in a few short days, he had found a woman he wanted all to himself. He didn't want to share her with his family, not just yet. At that moment he wanted all the time he could have just so he could continue to get to know her.

He chuckled inwardly as he envisioned the expression on his mother's face if she found out he had taken a day off to hang out on the beach. She would probably begin planning a wedding.

Marriage?

It was something he had found himself thinking about quite a bit. To spend the rest of his life with one woman. It was a shocking discovery, especially for him, because after Veronica, he'd thought he was destined to spend the rest of his life alone. He thought he was comfortable with that. Instead he discovered that he was missing something in his life. Something that he hadn't had before. That something was Destiny.

He loved his job and thought that was all he would ever need. When he was bored or thought he needed someone around him that both loved him and cared about him, Duane would drive up and spend time with his family. Most of the time, he just hung out with his brothers. After a day of their loud voices and numerous disagreements, he was always glad to return home by himself. However, lately, being home alone didn't appeal to him as much as it once had. He even felt uneasiness at the thought of growing old with no one by his side. He found himself considering what it would feel like to return every evening to a beautiful woman with her arms wide open, welcoming him home after a long, hard day. Only it couldn't be just anyone. No, the dreams and his every waking thought were centered around one woman in particular, and that woman was Destiny.

All he wanted was Destiny. In just a short period of time, she had disrupted his way of thinking, jumbled his emotions, and made him hunger for her like a wild animal. With Destiny, he was willing to take whatever he could get.

Even if it was only temporary.

He tried to convince himself that he could deal with her leaving in a few short weeks. His life would return to normal, and he would go back to the way things used to be. He had typically worked until late in the evening. But after meeting Destiny, he didn't think his life would ever be the same again. Somehow, some way, he would have to find a way to convince her to stay. With her, he craved something deeper; he wanted something more substantial because he was falling in love despite his determination not to.

Glancing at her, he took in her beautiful face and the way she pulled her lower lips between her teeth when she was deep in thought. He remembered those same lips trailing feverish kisses along his neck and shoulder. Duane quickly returned his eyes to the road and tried to curb the urge to kiss her lush mouth. That was one activity he didn't think he would ever grow tired of.

As they reached the beach, Destiny found her attention drawn away from chapter seven of her manuscript. The area reminded her of the Lake of the Ozarks. Bright sun. Water for miles. Water parks. People dressed in swimsuits, and boats attached to the backs of SUVs.

As they turned onto a long, touristy street close

to the boardwalk, she peered over the rim of her sunglasses and saw several exquisite local shops she hoped she would have an opportunity to visit.

It was crowded, but luckily, they were able to find parking not too far from the strip.

"It's beautiful." Destiny was totally charmed by her surroundings. It was obvious why so many people migrated to the coast on the weekends.

Duane stared at her beautiful profile, a knowing smile curving his mouth. "Before we unload, how about we check out the shops and then grab lunch?"

She tore her eyes away from the scenic view to smile up at him, eyes sparkling with excitement. "Sounds good to me." She had seen a small sandwich shop right next door to a display of summer shoes.

Closing his car door, Duane went around to the passenger side. Destiny waited for him to help her out of the car; then hand in hand, they walked along the mile-long strip, talking and laughing. The sidewalks were filled with tourists, couples, and families. With the warm temperatures, she was grateful for the light, cool ocean breeze.

Shopping became an exploration of specialty and novelty shops. Destiny found several little trinkets she had to have, including a pair of lime green sling-backs. By the time she was given her last receipt for her purchases, she was famished. They found a small sandwich shop at the end of the strip, where they ordered turkey and provolone sandwiches with chips and sodas.

An hour later, they were on the warm white sandy beach, underneath an umbrella.

Destiny stretched her arms overhead with the lazy reach of a kitten just waking and yawned.

"You enjoying yourself?"

Looking at Duane, Destiny couldn't resist smiling. "This is exactly what I needed. Thank you." Her eyes traveled from his face to his bare chest, which was feathered with dark brown hair. Her gaze lingered on the taut, firm muscles in admiration before she looked away. Resting her weight on her forearms, she admired the beach, from the water all the way up to the boardwalk.

Parents were sunbathing, while little children were building sand castles. There were several sun-baked people, who would pay in the morning, when their skin began to blister and peel.

Her gaze wandered down the beach, past the teenagers on body boards, to where several surfers were paddling towards a big wave. Briefly, she scanned the shore, where white lines of foam marked the bridge between land and sea. Several kids, who looked as if they should have been in school on a Thursday afternoon, were tossing a fris-bee to a small dog that appeared to be a mixed breed of some kind. He trotted ahead of them, tongue lolling out of his mouth. She thought about Champion, who was forced to spend the afternoon in the backyard. A soft giggle escaped her lips.

Duane studied Destiny. The first touches of sun had kissed her skin. He stared at the length of her slender neck, her glistening skin, which he wanted so badly to touch. A wave of heat surged through him.

She was wearing a two-piece yellow bathing suit. Although he considered himself beyond adolescent gawking, other men on the beach weren't nearly as concerned with hiding their approval of women. There was a tightening in his groin as his gaze moved slowly up the length of Destiny's legs. The gentle breeze couldn't cool his feverish body.

He removed his glasses. "I'm going to cool off." His mouth came to rest over hers. "I'll be back." He kicked off his sandals and raced across the warm sand.

Destiny sagged against the beach chair. His kiss had scrambled her concentration. He'd done little more than whisper his lips over her. But that light brush left her with a tingling sensation.

In such a short time he had broken her resolve. Duane had managed to undermine her determination to keep their relationship on a friendship level. As much as she didn't want to admit it, what she felt went beyond the physical. Duane had pursued her quietly, with determination and kindness. In his own charming way, he had managed in a few short days to become an important part of her life.

Suddenly feeling the need to be close to him, she jumped to her feet, kicked off her sandals, and raced to the spot where she had seen him dive in. The sand was warm but quickly forgotten when she stepped into the icy water. She splashed like a child until the water was waist deep; then she dived in, parting the water. Making wide strokes, she swam over to where Duane was. The ocean was fabulous. Beaches were something she wished they had in St. Louis. The man-made ones didn't count.

Destiny bobbed her head above water, with her arms sweeping by her sides. She wasn't the strongest swimmer, but she had the basic strokes down to a science.

"Hey, beautiful."

She turned to find him beside her. His legs scissored beneath him with even strokes. She shivered, and it wasn't from the chilly ocean. "Hi."

"How's the water feel?" he asked, his long lashes spiked with water.

She gloried beneath the warm rays of the sun, kicking her feet. "Wonderful."

Reaching out, he grazed a knuckle over her cheek. "Good."

A light, rolling wave went over her head, and she got a mouthful of water. Gulping and choking, she grabbed his arm.

"Easy."

Reaching for her, he held her gently within his protective grasp as he rubbed her lightly across the back until she was breathing normally again. Then, instead of letting her go, Duane pulled her even closer. Her heart pounded an erratic rhythm at the electricity radiating from his touch.

He leaned in close and kissed her. His soft lips caused tingles of excitement to race through her. Their tongues mated, and she released a sigh of surrender. She opened her mouth for him, and the feel of his tongue gently sliding in and out of her mouth sent heat coursing through her veins. His mouth was wet, gentle, yet challenging. Slowly then faster, hot and demanding, he explored, tasted, and teased her into a thrilling game of advance and retreat. Tongues touched, then played. It was amazing how well their mouths moved together. She put all of her heart and soul in the kiss. Duane made her want; he made her ache. Yet somehow he always managed to make her feel part of him. Her legs began to weaken, and she felt herself sinking beneath the water. She pulled apart and started kicking her legs again.

"I think we better save that for the shore," she teased before she dived underneath.

They swam awhile longer until they reached shallow water and walked out onto the warm sand, shaking off the water.

Duane stood back admiring the way Destiny looked with her hair slick and shining wet, then laced his fingers with hers and headed back to their things.

Destiny found it difficult to fall asleep that night. There was no real mystery as to why she was so restless. Duane Urban had become an important part of her life. She wanted him, adored him every waking minute of her day. He wasn't just stirring her sexually, he had tapped into her need for security—something she had found in his arms again and again. However, whenever she thought about the mess she was in, and the painful fact that it was better for him not to know, she tried to ignore those feelings.

She thought about spending time in front of her computer, working on her next chapter, but knew writing a fictional love story was not the type of relief she needed. She had a slight headache, but the pounding was nothing like that going on inside her chest. Did she truly want more from him?

She felt a slow warmth spread over her face, down past her chest, and pulse between her thighs. She nodded. Yes, she wanted him even if it was a short-term affair. Whatever it was, it ran deep. She could still feel him tightly against her body, and there was an ache that wouldn't go away until she was in his arms again. What she felt for Duane was much deeper than a physical need.

Her blood heated and rushed through her

system, leaving a thin layer of moisture on her face. She moved over to the window and raised it, glad for the cool night breeze.

She closed her eyes and took several deep breaths. She had been seeing Duane every day since they met, and she still had not given her body to him. When the time came, she was going to be ready.

Chapter 12

Destiny glanced at her reflection in the mirror, admiring the dress at all angles. She wasn't one who usually stood in front of mirrors absorbed in her appearance, but her night out with Duane was special. This would be the first time he would see her dressed to the nines.

She smiled at what she saw. The soft, lightweight material clung to every curve, making the hefty price tag well worth it.

The dress had been an impulse buy on the Las Vegas Strip. The weekend had been Lucas's Valentine's Day present. After one look at the dress in a shop window, he insisted on buying it. She hadn't put up too much resistance. That weekend had been special. It had also been the first time they had made love. It was one of the happiest times of her life.

She quickly pushed away feelings of regret and instead focused on Duane and the evening ahead. The past week had been perfect. Duane had updated her bathroom, while she had begun tiling the kitchen floor. They shared breakfast and lunch, and when his work schedule permitted, they also shared dinner. With Champion by her side and Duane only a phone call away, Destiny was beginning to feel safe and at home. She just hoped the feeling continued.

The doorbell rang and Champion barked.

"I know, boy. Here I come." Taking one final look in the mirror, she smiled, then turned on her heels and headed toward the door.

Duane chuckled as he listened to Champion announcing his arrival. The dog was definitely an asset.

Taking a deep breath, he forced himself to relax. But it was hard considering he planned to spend the rest of the evening in the company of an extraordinary woman.

The door opened, and Destiny stood before him. A knot pulled in his stomach while his eyes feasted on her. His gaze moved slowly over her, beginning at the thin spaghetti straps of her mauve dress, all the way down to a matching pair of open-toe sandals. The dress material highlighted every last sensuous curve. Just as he had expected, she looked exceptional. Longing vibrated through his body.

He forced himself to breathe. "Wow! You look fabulous," he finally said. She looked amazing. He never could understand how a woman could manage to walk in high heels. It looked almost as uncomfortable as wearing a pair of tight-fitting pants to a smorgasbord. But as a man, he was extremely grateful. His gaze swept over her legs, pleased at what he saw. The sandals made her legs appear longer and shapelier. His eyes traveled up the length of her legs and ended where the hem of her dress brushed against the middle of her thigh.

Destiny lowered her lashes as she blushed. "Thank you."

"Ready to go?" he asked, eager for the evening to begin.

She nodded. "Let me get my purse."

Duane stared in the direction in which she had disappeared for several seconds before he realized what he was doing. Swearing softly, he glanced down as Champion trotted down the hall.

"Come here, boy." Obeying his orders, Champion dashed up to him, wagging his tail rapidly as Duane rubbed him behind his ears. "You like that, don't you, boy?"

"He loves attention," Destiny said as she descended the stairs.

"Most Labs are loyal and very loving. That's why they make such wonderful family dogs."

She nodded, then turned and activated the burglar alarm. With one minute to leave, Duane exited first, and she stopped long enough to lock the door.

He captured her elbow with his hand, and the heat from his touch made her tremble inside.

Stopping in her path, she stared toward the street. "Wow, I finally get to ride in your fancy car."

"Yeah. I only pull it out on special occasions." He stared proudly at his white Chrysler Crossfire. As soon as the model had come out on the market, he had been one of the first to purchase one.

Duane helped her into the car, then moved around to his side and started the engine. The smell of her engulfed him. As he pulled away, he found himself smiling. Tonight he was going to be in the company of one of the most beautiful women he had ever laid his eyes on.

She savored the butter-soft upholstery and enjoyed

the scenic route as they drove along the highway. She tried to relax but couldn't. She was much too excited. The last time she had taken this route, she was so worried about being seen that she hadn't had a chance to take in the beauty of the East Coast. Everything was green. The sun was just beginning to set, and gold and orange burst across the horizon.

As they neared the first tollbooth, Destiny stole a glance over at Duane. He looked absolutely gorgeous. He was wearing pleated gray slacks and a crisp burgundy shirt that draped perfectly over his broad shoulders. A black jacket lay across the backseat. He was so handsome, a lump rose in her throat. They were having a romantic dinner in Baltimore, and afterwards, anything could happen. Her brain raced with possibilities.

"Have you ever been to the Baltimore?" Duane asked in a deep-timbered voice, breaking into her thoughts.

Oh sure. I was just there last week, when I drove one hundred miles just to place a long distance call to my agent. Other than that, no. She shook her head. "No, but I've always wanted to go."

He clicked on the radio, and for part of the ride, they discussed their common taste in music. She loved Beyoncé and Mary J. Blige, while he was wildly impressed with R&B singers like Jaheim and the newcomer Lyfe Jennings. Duane inserted a compilation CD, and for the next several miles, they rode in silence, each lost in their own thoughts.

When they arrived at their destination, Duane pulled up into a circular drive, and a valet in a white coat rushed out to greet them. Destiny waited for him to come around and open the door. He grabbed her hand, helping her out of the car, then draped a possessive arm around her waist.

"You are going to love this place," he whispered close to her ear.

She glanced up at the white awning, which had SHELTON'S printed in large black lettering. She smiled, then her lips curled downward as she glanced up at the cloudy sky. "It looks like it's going to rain."

Duane's gaze narrowed as he followed the direction of her eyes. "I think you're right." He escorted her into the restaurant. Within minutes they were shown to a cozy table near the window.

When Duane pulled out the seat closest to the window, she knew she was in trouble. He had leaned over, and the scent of his cologne was prominent beneath her nose. The fabulous scent was driving her crazy. Even though they weren't touching, she felt the heat radiating from his body. Destiny was glad when he moved and took his own seat.

Trying to get her emotions in check, she looked around the exquisite restaurant. The room was small and quaint, with large green plants and numerous fresh flowers. It was intimate with a magnificent view of the Baltimore Harbor.

"What do you think?" he asked.

She shifted her gaze to meet his. "This place is fabulous. Thank you so much for bringing me here."

He leaned forward. "I'm glad you like it. This is one of my favorite restaurants."

She glanced out the window at a small boat docked in the harbor. "The view is beautiful."

"Yes, it is."

She met his penetrating gaze and immediately read the double meaning of his words. His eyes flamed with appreciation. The heat radiating from across the table ignited a fire that was smoldering inside her.

She dropped her head slightly and stared at him through lowered lashes. "Thank you." She stared down at her menu, giving Duane a chance to lazily assess her.

He was quite taken by her beauty. He couldn't pull his gaze from her face. The candlelight illuminated the brightness of her eyes, and he consumed every magnificent detail. She had applied a light coat of mauve eye shadow to her eyelids, which only intensified their brilliant color. Then his gaze fastened on her lips. Her lips had been graced with a glossy fuchsia tint. When she puckered them in a tempting smile, he had to take a deep breath to calm the desire brewing inside. Dropping his eyes was an even bigger mistake. He found himself drawn to her bare shoulders and a simple bodice that emphasized her generously rounded breasts.

Light tapping on the windowpane drew her attention outside. "Oh my, it's raining."

Duane studied the rain slashing the window. "I guess that ruins the moonlight walk I was planning."

She gave him a warm smile for just considering such a thing.

He waited until their waiter poured their water and left with their drink orders before speaking again. "I finally figured out how you can repay me."

Her heart thundered with curiosity. "And what's that?"

"Come to my family's Memorial Day barbecue." Reaching over the table, Duane held her hands possessively between his large fingers.

Destiny could tell by the way he was looking at

her, her attendance would mean a lot to him. She also knew that if she agreed, their relationship would move to the next level.

"Where is it being held?" she asked.

"In Delaware. It's an annual event that my parents host. A few friends, but mostly family. It is one of three visits a year that is considered mandatory. If I even think about not showing up, I'll never hear the end of it."

"You sure your mother won't mind?"

"Mind?" he chuckled. "She'll be overjoyed. Besides, I kind of already told her you would be there."

Her brow rose. "How did you kind of do that?"

Duane scrubbed his chin and gave her a sheepish grin. "My mother has a habit of trying to fix me up every chance she gets. She had someone in mind for this event before I convinced her I was already seeing someone."

Destiny felt a flutter in her stomach. Hearing him say it made it sound so much more official. She was preparing to accept his invitation when she felt someone tap her lightly on her shoulder. Glancing up she found a petite, honey-colored woman with short salt-and-pepper hair standing in front of their table.

"Excuse me . . . I don't mean to bother you, but are you Desiree Davidson, the mystery writer?"

Destiny stared up at the woman for several seconds, her mouth moving but no words coming out. *Quick! Say something.*

Destiny finally shook her head. "No, I'm not."

The woman compressed her lips and stood beside Destiny for several seconds, looking unconvinced; the disappointment was clearly apparent. "I would have sworn you were her. The two of you look so much alike. Well, sorry for disturbing your dinner."

"No problem at all."

The woman left to join a man sitting at a small bar to the right side of the dining area. Destiny looked down, unable to look at Duane just yet. She needed time to pull herself together.

"Small world. I guess somewhere you have a twin."

Forcing a smile, Destiny looked up from her plate and murmured, "Yeah, I guess so."

"Well, your twin happens to be a well-known author. Next time I drive past a bookstore, I'm going to have to remember to drop in and check out her photo. I'm curious how close a resemblance there really is."

Lightning speared down from the sky, and she jumped. Her nerves were once again in a frenzy. Why had she come out without her glasses?

Duane reached across and cupped her hand with his. "You okay?"

Yes, I'm fine as long as you stay away from the bookstore. "Yes, I'm fine. I can handle rain. I just never cared much for lightning." Glancing out the window, she saw that the sky had grown gray, and the rain was coming down harder than before.

The waiter arrived to take their orders, and as she listened to Duane talk about his family, she found herself starting to relax again. She brushed off the encounter as being an isolated incident. The chances of it happening again were slim to none.

The rest of dinner was perfect. The meal was fabulous—flavorful prime rib, signature garlic potatoes, and a vegetable medley, followed by cheesecake and coffee, all while they sat by candlelight watching the moon beam down across the water.

By the time their waiter brought the check, it was storming outside. Thunder was booming, while the rain fell in bursts. Duane led Destiny outside and waited for the valet to bring around his car.

"This looks like tornado weather." She had seen many such storms while in the Midwest.

Duane's eyes narrowed as he scowled. "I agree."

Duane looked down at her flushed, rain-splattered face. His fingers itched to touch her. He needed to make love to her—tonight. He wasn't sure how much longer he could battle his desire for her. "Please don't take this the wrong way, but why don't we get a room and spend the night?"

She glanced over at him, surprised by his question.

"I'll even get two rooms if you'll feel more comfortable."

There was something very masculine in his tone that made everything feminine in her stir. After mere seconds, there was a distinctly sexual buzz in the air. She looked at him, taking in his chiseled jaw and sexy lips, and her breathing became irregular. For days she had been battling her growing attraction. She hadn't wanted to care about him or any other man. Then Duane walked into her life and threw a monkey wrench in her carefully laid plan. The more she tried to resist, the more pointless it all seemed. No matter how much she tried to fight it, she was falling hard.

"One room is all we'll need."

He stared into her eyes, reading the meaning of her words. Tonight she belonged to him. Leaning forward, he kissed her with everything he had inside. She breathed a sigh of pleasure when he covered her lips with his and he immediately deepened the kiss, mating relentlessly with her tongue. When the valet pulled into the circular drive with his car, they reluctantly ended the kiss. Duane tipped the valet, and they both raced to the car; however, no amount of hurrying saved either of them from getting soaked.

Once they were inside the car, his hands were on her knees, stroking her tenderly, making her tremor with anticipation. As they drove around the block to a hotel, she struggled for control.

Duane pulled in the hotel driveway, and while she was lost in a daze, he checked in, then guided her into an elevator and up to a suite on the sixth floor. She stood shivering beside him. Her dress was drenched, and the heels of her shoes muddy. All the while she was aware of how close he was standing. His scent, his body's warmth, radiated around her. The heat of him burned through her. He escorted her down the long hall, then slid the key card in the slot and opened the door to their suite.

The desire was so thick she had to force air into her lungs. She glanced up at him. "Ladies first," he whispered.

As she strolled into the suite, Destiny knew that she had taken a step that would change her life forever.

Chapter 13

Destiny hugged herself in an effort to stop her shivering. Rain had plastered her hair to her head. Duane tore away his wet jacket and stared down at her. Her dress was damp and clinging to her.

Teeth chattering, she pushed her fingers through her wet, wavy hair. "I guess I better get out of these wet clothes." She removed her shoes. The plush beige carpeting caressed the soles of her feet as she headed toward the bathroom. As the woman at the front desk had promised, large terry cloth robes had been delivered to the suite by the time she stepped out of the shower.

While Duane took his turn in the bathroom, Destiny opened the sliding glass door. She allowed the smell of the fresh rain into the room as she stepped out onto the balcony. The wind slapped at her, but she welcomed the cool air. The shower had done very little to cool the fire burning in her blood. She wrapped her arms around her waist as a chill raced through her. If tonight was anything like the novels she had written, she knew where the rest of the evening would lead.

As if he knew what she was thinking, she heard the door slide open behind her. A nervous excitement bubbled inside her, and shortly after, she felt Duane's warm body against her back as he pulled her into the circle of his arms.

"You're going to catch a cold," he whispered close to her ear.

She shook her head. "Not if you hold me."

Turning her in his arms, he pulled her even closer. Tilting her head back, he gazed down at her.

His lips hovered above hers, his voice tender but filled with need. "I want you, Destiny. I've never wanted anyone like I want you."

Inevitability burned through her. Eyes wide, lips parted, she whispered breathlessly, "Then take me."

As their lips met, Destiny felt as if the next time she inhaled, it would be the first time she had ever taken a breath in her life. Then, a heartbeat later, her heart pounded as if she had just run up a steep hill. A wave of heat and hunger slammed into her, and any pretenses of her resolve to keep their relationship simple and safe dissolved under the heat of that kiss. Staying away from him was no longer an option. She wanted him. She wanted to be close to him, and at the moment nothing else mattered.

His tongue swept into her mouth, seeking hers, and worked its magic, searching and caressing.

She pressed one hand to his lower back, where the muscles flexed as her fingers spread across them. Her other hand slid up his hard chest and along his broad shoulders to his neck, where she traced his collarbone. While his mouth roamed hers, warm and tempting, she wrapped her arms around him, holding tight, savoring the close contact. And when a groan of pleasure and need escaped him, she exhaled one long, slow, trembling breath.

Destiny knew she should speak up and suggest that they get back in his car and return to Delaware, but she needed him. The rhythm of his touch was so comforting that she knew in her heart, she wasn't going anywhere.

Passion pumped through her veins as he explored her with his gentle touch.

"Duane," she began. She was breathing heavily when she pulled away from their kiss. She looked up at his strong face; his gentle eyes made anything seem possible. Suddenly, it felt important to feel everything that she could with Duane before it was time for her to leave. He was what she needed tonight. She needed to lose her identity in kisses and touches and the beautiful music of making love. "I want to be with you tonight."

There was no mistaking her meaning. His eyes deepened to a rich color filled with passion. When he spoke, his voice was low and intense. "Are you sure, Destiny?" He rubbed her arm as he spoke.

She knew he meant the touch to be comforting, but instead, he was starting a fire throughout her body. Desperate for him to understand how badly she needed him, she fused her mouth firmly with his, melting into his warm, soft lips with burning possession. Then she drew her head back and gazed up at him. The uneven rhythm of her breathing increased and could be heard in the still night around them. "I want to give you what you want," she whispered. "What *we* both want."

Their lips met again in a deep, searing kiss, scorching in its intensity. Crushed against him, she savored the feel of his hard body. She let out a sigh of pleasure and need, which she knew now had been bubbling just under the surface since the first day he'd stepped onto her porch. As his mouth explored her, she gasped, realizing the kiss was more than passion. Their kissing was a discovery. She felt as if she wanted to pull him inside her now, bypassing all of the preliminaries and getting right down to business. She was like a simmering teapot: at any moment she was bound to bubble over with desire. She arched into his body, clinging to him with her arms around his neck.

He abandoned her lips and slid to her cheek, nibbling and tasting. When he reached her ear, he nuzzled, slowly seeking. Her head fell back, granting him greater access, and she let out a sound of pure pleasure as his hands cruised slowly downward, finding her waist, caressing the curves of her hips.

Suddenly, he pulled away and looked at her with a gaze that sent chills rippling through her. His mouth claimed hers again, and his fingers gripped her behind, pulling her against him, holding her firmly in place. Destiny moaned as her legs gave out. Without breaking the kiss, he reached down and swept her into his arms. Sliding open the glass door, he carried her inside.

As they entered the suite, Duane groaned, consumed by the soft feel of her in his arms. He knew there was no turning back, but he couldn't stop what was happening even if he had wanted to. He could feel her desire, feel her breath. The air seemed to compress around them. He wanted her, and nothing else seemed to matter. Funny, smart, sexy, vulnerable, all of her qualities made this something he couldn't control.

With her still in his arms, he was headed for the

bedroom when the couch beckoned him. He was on fire, and his groin tightened. Although he would not rush the first time with her, he decided the couch was definitely closer and changed his course.

He deposited her on the cushions, then lay down, the weight of his body resting between her legs. He covered her mouth again hungrily. His lips trailed from her lips, marking a path of wet kisses as he slipped one hand beneath her robe. Destiny's breath caught when his fingers touched her warm, soft skin. His fingers feathered over the slope of her body, just barely brushing one glorious, firm breast. She made a noise deep in her throat that sounded just like a purr. The need between them was rising, becoming so strong. She arched her body into his hand.

Heat rushed through her, settling low in her body. "Duane," she groaned, breaking their kiss. "What are you do—" she whispered as her words were swallowed up by his lips.

When he broke the kiss and leaned back slightly, Destiny stared up at him, waiting and wondering, stunned at her own emotions.

"You're driving me crazy!" she whispered as his tongue traced the fullness of her lips.

She had been driving him crazy, he thought, with her smile, her touch, her beauty, her sweetness, almost since he'd first laid eyes on her. Her time here might be temporary, but tonight she belonged to him, and he belonged to her.

Duane crushed her closer until he felt the soft molding of her body against his. She mated with his tongue, and a wild, incredible pleasure surged through him, settling solidly, achingly low in his stomach. The sweet, honeyed taste of her, the electrifying feeling of her nipple in the center of his palm, it was simply overwhelming. He knew he wasn't thinking straight, but he knew no other woman had ever made him feel this wild.

He slid his hands down her body, molding every inch of her into every inch of him, pulling into the fullness straining painfully against his boxers. She moaned into his mouth, and the heat rolled down and around and through him again.

Her fingers went to the front of his robe. She was in a hurry, and that knowledge sent a shiver of pure desire echoing through him. He shrugged out of the robe and allowed it to drop to the floor.

Destiny's hand caressed his chest, tracing one flat nipple and then the other, then slid even lower until she reached his boxers.

Duane stopped her and pushed his hand between the opening of her robe again. "Now it's my turn," he said.

She gave him a slow smile that was so intoxicating, his groin contracted further. His hand raked up her thigh, then traveled farther. He forced the terry cloth material apart until his fingers stroked beneath her breasts. He wanted to see all of her. He untied the belt to her robe, and Destiny allowed him to tug her arms free. He tossed the robe on the floor beside them, then pulled away from her to see, at last, what had haunted his dreams.

Perfection. He squeezed his eyes shut for a moment, silently praying for control.

"You're so beautiful," he whispered, mesmerized, eyes glazed with passion.

He watched a wicked smile spread slowly across her features. *Man, what would it feel like to wake up every morning to a smile that made so many sinful promises?*

Destiny pushed him away until he was the one lying on his back on the couch; then she leaned over him. He bit back a groan as her fingernails grazed his abdomen and sent a ripple of excitement through his body. He obliged her by lifting his hips so she could slide his boxers from his body. When she stood before him, his eyes drank in the vision of her perfect breasts.

Destiny's heart pounded furiously as she stood there, her body responding to his gaze, silently struggling, begging to be touched. And then he did touch her, reaching out for her, his rough hands cupping her swollen breasts. His hands kneaded her breasts, and his thumbs made devastatingly arousing circles over each chocolate nipple, drawing them into hard, pebbled peaks. She trembled, unable to hold back her excitement as his hand stroked her most sensitive area. All at once, she hoped the moment would go on, hoped it would end, hoped she could survive the intense pleasure, which she knew was just beginning.

With a muffled oath, he pulled her back down on top of him. Their bodies came together, warm, naked, trembling, skin against skin, and she felt an indescribable desire pour through her in thick, turbulent waves. The tips of her breasts tingled where they touched the silky hair on his chest, and when he moved his hand down her back, a trail of fire blazed in its wake.

She felt his hands slide down and cup her bottom. His hands were strong as he grasped her, pulling her closer. Their lips met in a frantic search for closeness. His tongue traveled deeper, tangling with hers, drawing out hot, feverish cries. His hands began to spread liquid fire over her skin, down her hips and thighs. His fingers brushed through the soft mound of hair, seeking the hidden nub of pleasure within, and found her, wet and ready. She gasped, her need for him slipping out in moans against his mouth.

"Duane," she whispered as he rolled her beneath him. "That feels so good."

Lowering his head, he dropped soft kisses on the globes of her breasts. Duane drew one sensitive bud into his mouth. The sensation of his tongue, hot and wet, caressing her beaded nipple caused her to sigh with pleasure.

Duane was driving her mad, bringing forward feelings she hadn't known existed. She was grateful that he was taking his time so she had a chance to experience each and every pleasurable moment.

Drifting lower, his lips left a heated path as he kissed under her breasts, down along the line of her stomach. His tongue lapped at her navel, drawing a circle around the indentation, then indulging at the deep center, sending delicious shudders down the length of her and making her whimper.

"You are so beautiful." His voice was husky.

Destiny released a sound of sheer frustration. "Duane, please . . ." she whispered as his lips closed over an aching nipple. "I need . . ." The rest of her words were lost to a loud gasp.

Duane shifted his weight and moved between her wobbly legs, caressing her inner thighs. Then with his hand, he drew a straight line right down to her source of desire. He touched the bud and felt her tense with pleasure.

"What?" His voice was a low, thrilling whisper as he slipped one finger into her heated core. "Baby, tell me what you need."

"To feel you," she moaned, pushing her hips up against his hands. "Please . . ."

He inserted another finger then flicked and swirled as he increased the rhythm, drawing agonizing cries from her lungs.

Destiny dug her fingernails into his arms, her hips rising to meet each thrust. "Please, Duane. I need you now!"

He kissed her once more, then rose. Destiny released a frustrated cry at his abrupt departure. He had disappeared in the other room for what felt like hours, when it was just a few excruciating moments. As she lay on the couch, she saw the light flip on in the bedroom. She smiled when he returned. He had sheathed himself. Returning to the couch, he pulled her back into his arms and positioned himself above her.

Something inside her wound up like a watch spring as he kissed her deeply. She wrapped her legs around his hips and felt him pulsing at the opening of her desire. Slanting her hips, he gently penetrated her, inch by glorious inch. Everything tensed in her body, and she moaned. Duane was larger than she'd expected him to be, filling her completely. He paused, giving her time to adjust; then she raised her hips to meet his thrusts, drawing him deeper inside her. He murmured her name against her cheek as he began to move inside her, slowly, and smoothly, until together they found the sweet, deep rhythm of pleasure.

Her breathing came in erotic gasps as they flew higher and higher to the height of passion. She sunk into the couch, holding on as she met every move. Her resolve was shattered. Her body began to vibrate, her legs trembled, her last strand of control slipped further, far beyond her reach. She moved her body with his, encouraging him to take her fully. He reached under and clenched her buttocks, angling her hips for deeper entry, and thrust strongly into her until she shattered into a million tiny fragments, holding on to him, crying out his name as a climax took over. Duane released a deep grunt, spilling into her with a spasm of ecstasy.

As his breathing resumed, he rolled off Destiny and fell onto the floor. Hearing her light giggles, he reached up and gently pulled her down on top of him. Her laughter continued, but she didn't resist when he scooped her into his arms and carried her to bed. He joined her under the covers and held her through the night.

One thing he knew for certain, he was never letting her go.

Destiny woke up in the middle of the night, feeling as if everything was going to be all right in her life. She knew Duane was responsible for that feeling. Somehow she had grown to depend on him. He made her feel safe after he somehow slipped under her guard. And she no longer cared.

Turning her head to see the time, she found that it was almost three o'clock. There was an ache between her thighs, which caused her to sigh against the cool sheets. Lying on her side, she reached out to him, making sure he was still there. Knowing he was there, right behind her, filled her with a sense of peace and safety. It was hard to believe, but she felt complete having him lying next to her. For so long she had felt all alone in the world, and then she met him. Now she had someone she could call a friend.

She had never felt anything close to what she was feeling now with Duane, while she was with Lucas. Sure, she had loved him, or at least believed that she had, but she had never felt as close or even as connected emotionally as she did with Duane.

She felt Duane stir and curl against her back. He draped an arm across her waist and held her with a tenderness that made her hope he cared about her as much as she cared for him. It was a new feeling and one that frightened her.

Is this what true love feels like?

She would soon leave Delaware, and she knew it wasn't going to be easy. Because for the first time in her life, she really felt as if she'd found home.

Duane awoke to find the sky still dark and Destiny curled up against him. Savoring the feel of her lush body, he snuggled against her, pulling her backside closer into the circle of his arms.

As he listened to her breathing, he realized that he could no longer deny that he loved her. In Destiny, he had found everything he could ever want in a woman. She was smart, caring, and independent, with a wonderful sense of humor. She put others' feelings before her own.

How could he have even debated whether she was anything like Veronica? Veronica had never put anyone's feelings above her own. Pets were something she wouldn't have even dreamed of considering, and children were a story all of their own.

At one time he couldn't have even imagined raising a child. Scared of having a child out of wedlock, and having to deal with child support payments like so many of his friends, he had always made it a habit of practicing safe sex. He had brought the topic up to Veronica once, and she made it clear she never wanted children. Because he had loved her so much, he had hoped that in time she would change her mind. But after her husband had discovered that they were having a relationship, he was thankful that a child had never entered the picture. But with Destiny, he could imagine her carrying his seed to term and the two of them raising their child together. They had practiced safe sex, but if they hadn't and she had become pregnant, it wouldn't have mattered, because he realized Destiny was going to be his wife.

Last night she had been everything he'd longed for in a woman. Her sexy curves had called to everything male in him. His feelings for her were possessive. He wanted her to belong to him in every sense of the word. There was a burning need to protect her and keep her close to his heart. Her vulnerability was what had attracted him at first, and it continued to reel him in.

He ran his hand along her waist, then down her hips, mesmerized by each rounded curve. She had a perfect body—round, firm breasts and a waistline indented like an hourglass due to the flare of her feminine hips. He remembered the feeling of sliding inside her, the sweetness of her body, so tight and warm around him. He had felt his sanity dissolve as he took possession of her.

He sighed. He wanted so much to tell her how he felt, yet there was a part of her that was still holding back. And he still hadn't figured out what it was that she wasn't telling him. Until he found out what it was, there was no way he could put his feelings out there just to be crushed again. He could only hope that in time she would share what it was that was bothering her. He found it frustrating because a part of him had a strong feeling that she felt the same way about him. He read it in her eyes, saw it in her facial expressions. Now all he had to do was hear the words from her lips, and he would offer her his heart.

Destiny moaned and shifted slightly in his arms. Duane tightened his hold on her while he rained light kisses across her bare neck and shoulder. She rolled over onto her back. Her eyelids fluttered open, and she stared up at him.

"Hi," she whispered.

Duane couldn't resist a smile as he took in everything about her that he loved so much. "Hi, yourself."

"What are you doing up so early?"

"Staring at you."

She tried to hide a blush as she rolled away from him and said, "Go back to sleep."

He pulled her flush against him again and was quiet for so long, Destiny thought he had fallen back to sleep. Still feeling the magic of the evening, she closed her eyes with a smile curled on the tips of her lips. Lying in his arms against his massive chest was something she didn't think she could ever grow tired of. She shifted her hips back and leaned against him, feeling his deep breathing against her back and shoulder.

"Have you ever been in love before?"

His question burned straight through her heart. "Yes."

"What happened?"

She turned onto her back, and he saw the careful consideration in her eyes as she weighed how much to tell him. Destiny swallowed. "I met him shortly after my grandmother had passed. He wasn't the man I thought him to be. I think it's because I wanted so badly to believe he was something he was not. He broke my heart in the process."

His jaw hardened at the thought of someone breaking her heart. No woman deserved to be happy more than her. If it was up to him, she would never have to want for anything. "I would never intentionally hurt you," he crooned.

"I know."

She nestled back against him, her buttocks cradling his hardening erection. He tried to put out the fire she was building in him. Unable to help himself, he slid one arm across her body and ran a finger across her breasts, circling the nipples until they hardened.

He bent toward her and kissed the side of her face. Then he slid his mouth down to her neck and nipped gently at the flesh there. Goose bumps spread down her arm, and she moaned again.

Her hips rocked against him. It was no use denying it. He wanted her again. She was in his blood. And he was in hers. His hands swept down her body and pulled her more closely to him.

She turned to face him, then stroked his chest and belly. One of her hands slid down to clasp his straining flesh, and a groan rumbled from his tight throat. Duane had to grit his teeth and fight for control. As she explored his length and thickness with her gentle hands, she planted light kisses across his chest. Every stroke, every touch brewed the fire inside him.

When she bathed him with her tongue, he nearly lost it. Fighting for self-control, he clenched his abdominal muscles as he endured the sweet torture of her hot, wet tongue. Each stroke brought him closer to the edge. Before he exploded, he took control.

Flipping her over, he pinned her back against the mattress. He searched for his pants with his free arm, pulled a condom from his back pocket, and moved away from her long enough to roll the latex down the length of his throbbing flesh.

Destiny wrapped her legs around his hard, muscled hips and welcomed him as he slipped inside. He couldn't go deep enough, couldn't get enough of her, of the soft sounds she made as they moved together.

He plunged harder and deeper with each thrust. Tiny explosions flared deep inside, then intensified. He'd never come harder. He exploded inside her, then shuddered under the impact.

Well past lunchtime, Destiny woke up to sunlight skimming through the curtains and the sound of Duane humming off-key in the shower. She smiled to herself as she stretched her body. Her energy was drained, and her mind was full of electrifying sensations. She rolled over onto his pillow and allowed the scent of him to invade her nostrils.

Closing her eyes again, she tried to persuade herself that what she felt with Duane was purely physical. She tried to keep her mind centered only on his masculine body and the caress of his lips on her most sensitive flesh. She wanted to focus only on the feeling of him moving deep inside her. Then emotions began to meddle in her private thoughts. She saw his face as he made love to her, eyes burning with hunger, intense with something more than lust. Caring. Did he love her?

That is ridiculous. He couldn't love her any more than she could love him. She wouldn't allow herself. They had a couple of weeks, more if fate allowed. It was sex. The best sex she'd ever had in her life. But purely sex, nothing more. As long as she kept their relationship in perspective, she would be okay, so she told herself. Yet, she had a funny feeling she had already stepped over the line. She had given too much and had taken even more from the kind of man she'd dreamed about all her life. He was the type of hero she wrote about in all of her novels.

Eager to think of something else, she rolled out of bed and reached for her purse. Digging into her wallet, she removed her calling card, then reached for the phone.

"This had better be important," Julia grumbled through the line.

Destiny giggled. "I guess you must have spent the evening entertaining?"

"How could you tell?"

She giggled again. "Because it's almost lunchtime here. Who were you entertaining this time?"

Julia paused long enough to release a dramatic sigh. "A new client I discovered. He is destined to be the next Stephen King."

"Sounds scary," she groaned. Nevertheless, she didn't miss the excitement in Julia's voice. The one thing that had attracted her to Julia from the start was her passion for books. It wasn't just about the money. Julia staked a personal claim on every manuscript she represented, and every client became a friend. Her dedication was what made her an awesome representative.

"Why has it taken you so long to get in touch with me?"

"I've been busy. Besides, I try to call when I am out of town, just in case someone is screening your calls," Destiny conceded and stifled a yawn.

"Smart move."

Destiny rolled back onto the bed and released a sigh. "I'll e-mail you the first hundred pages of the novel in a couple of days. I found a Kinko's not too far from my house."

"Your house? Sounds to me like you're getting quite comfortable."

She sighed. "I am."

"It also sounds to me like there is something more going on than hiding out until the trial. Is there a new man in your life?"

"Something like that," she murmured.

"Perfect! So tell me, what does he look like?"

Destiny smiled. "He's quite handsome."

"I'm not surprised. You've always had good taste."

Destiny frowned as she thought about Lucas and his pretty features. He had spent more time in front of the mirror than she had.

"This one is different. He's an average guy with an average job. He's a jack-of-all-trades."

"It sounds like he's been laying pipe, if you get my drift."

Destiny snorted a laugh. "You are naughty."

"I know, but I'm glad to hear that you are happy. You deserve it."

She smiled because she knew Julia meant it. "Thanks."

On a sober note, Julia's voice dropped an octave. "This will all be over soon; just hang in there, girl."

"I will, and I'll call you when I send the manuscript."

She hung up the phone just as Duane stepped into the room. A towel was tied loosely around his waist, and his head and shoulders were still wet. Destiny sucked in her breath. Duane just stood there, his gaze locked with hers.

His chest was hard with muscles and lightly covered with hair. His stomach was strong and flat. The area between her legs contracted at the sight of his beautiful body. Last night it had been dark. This morning she had a clear view.

Destiny watched as he came around to her side of the bed. She enjoyed watching the way he walked, the way the muscles of his thighs played beneath the towel. The flow of sexual chemistry passing between them was intense. She could not control it. Memories of them making love consumed her thoughts.

She shifted slightly on her pillow, trying to somehow control the shiver that worked its way up her spine, the intense pounding of her heart, and the flow of heat that radiated from her womanly core. Duane was standing so close and staring down at her, there was no way of missing the scent of soap on his skin, which made her nipples throb with yearning. She couldn't tear her eyes away from the water droplets clinging to the hair on his chest. A force of desire suddenly slammed into her, and she gasped as he leaned forward.

"Good afternoon, sleepyhead," he murmured before taking a quick kiss, the scent of soap and man curling around her.

Her eyes twinkled as she stared up at him. "You should have waited. I would have joined you."

He wagged his eyebrows suggestively. "I can always get back in."

She blushed openly. "But you're already clean."

"And I plan to get dirty again."

She watched as he whipped the towel from around his waist. Evidence of his arousal was quite apparent. Before she could respond, Duane scooped her into his arms and carried her into the bathroom.

Chapter 14

During the longest shower she had ever experienced, Duane showed her things she never imagined could be done standing up. He then ordered room service while she enjoyed a long soak to soothe her sore muscles. He fed her fresh fruit while he sat on the side of the tub.

On the ride home the overwhelming sensations of the last several hours hummed through her body and invaded her mind. Duane slipped in Prince's *Musicology* CD, and she closed her eyes, pretending to be asleep. Instead, she was thinking.

Deep down, she really wished she was Destiny, the heroine from her first romantic mystery, *The Hideout*. The story was about a graduate student hiding from a killer. She found her situation with Lucas so ironic that when she had first gone into hiding, she decided to assume her character's identity. Now she found she envied the life Destiny led. *Very simple*. All day Destiny wrote, and every evening she spent in the arms of a handsome contractor. In her book the hero happened to be a retired military police officer. Duane Urban was far better than any male character she had ever created.

Opening her eyes, she stared out the car window as she returned to reality. In the last hour, she had considered telling Duane the truth. Sharing with him who she really was. She hated lying to him, and now that their relationship had moved to the next level, she wanted so desperately to share with him her secret. However, she knew that Duane would not take the situation lightly. She was already stunned at the depth of his feelings. He had somehow appointed himself as her protector. There was no doubt in her mind, he would feel obligated to protect her. As Duane pulled onto the interstate, an even more terrifying realization washed over her. If she revealed her true identity, not only would she be involving him in her problems, but also endangering his life.

She reminded herself that she had made a vow to keep her identity a secret. *Remember what Jarvis said. Trust no one.* Despite the fact that her throat had become congested with fear and uncertainty choked her, she couldn't tell him the truth. The best thing for her to do was to play it safe and pray that when she finally told him the truth, he would find it in his heart to forgive her for deceiving him.

She sighed and clasped her slender hands together. Duane moved his hand to her knee. She felt the heat of his touch through the fabric of her dress.

She was crazy about him. Her biggest fear was how would he feel when he found out he had been dating a best-selling author with a six-figure annual salary. Part of her felt that Duane would find nothing at all amusing about being deceived. In fact, she knew he would feel she had betrayed one of the most important ingredients in a relationship—trust.

Feeling overwhelmed, she drifted off. The next thing she knew, Duane was tapping her lightly on the shoulder. Her long lashes fluttered open. Focusing on her surroundings, she realized that they were in his driveway.

"I think somebody didn't get much sleep last night," he teased, smiling down at her.

"And I wonder why?" she retorted.

He dropped a kiss to her forehead, then chuckled as he came around and opened the door for her. Destiny climbed out to find a warm breeze flowing around her. She smiled. It was going to be another beautiful day.

Glancing across the street, she noticed a small moving van in the driveway two houses to her left.

Duane had also noticed. "Looks like we have new neighbors."

Curious, Destiny watched the men carry in boxes. "Who lives there?"

"That house belongs to an elderly couple, the Kellys. They've been renting rooms to students for years."

They strolled across the street just as a beautiful, young woman stepped onto the porch of that house. She was tall and statuesque, with an oval face and long auburn hair, which she wore swept up in a ponytail. In blue jeans and a white T-shirt, she looked like a teenager.

She waved and met them as they came onto the sidewalk.

"Welcome to the neighborhood," Duane greeted.

"Thank you." Her almond-shaped, whiskey-colored eyes radiated with her smile. "I'm Simone Taylor." She held out her hand.

"I'm Duane Urban, and this is my girlfriend, Destiny Davis."

"Pleased to meet you both." They each shook hands and exchanged smiles.

"I'll be starting at Delaware State University this summer. This apartment was a steal. I'm a little too old for the dorms, so I was happy to stumble across this place."

"It's a wonderful neighborhood. You're going to like it here," Duane interjected.

Destiny glanced up at the woman, who had to be close to six feet. "He's right. I'm the new kid on the block, and so far my experience has been great."

"I'm glad to hear that," Simone replied with a sigh of relief. "I better get back before the movers break something." She raised a finely plucked eyebrow. "Nice meeting you both," she said as she backed away slowly.

"You, too. Drop by if you need anything," Destiny offered.

She smiled. "Thanks. I will."

That evening Destiny closed her eyes and slid low in the tub, allowing the steam to rise and relax her. As usual Champion lay on the floor outside the ajar door. He loved to be close to her. He acted like such a baby that Destiny figured his original owners had to have spoiled him. Which was why she couldn't understand why no one had come to claim him.

She squirted a dab of face cream in the palm of her hand and rubbed it across her face. She was patting her face dry when Champion began to growl.

She opened her eyes. "What's wrong, boy?"

He rose, and his growling grew louder.

Destiny rose from the tub and quickly reached for her robe. It was almost impossible to keep her hands from shaking long enough to slide her arms in and tie the belt around her waist. As she slipped her feet in her slippers, she heard a glass break.

Champion immediately dashed down the stairs.

"Champ, come back here!" she screamed.

He ignored her command. Panic like she'd never known before welled in her throat. Her heart was beating a mile a minute, and she was unsure what to do next. Champion's barking became louder. Then she heard a muffled voice. She came to an abrupt halt, her heart jumping in her chest.

Someone was in the house!

Destiny dashed into her bedroom, reached for the phone, and quickly dialed.

"Miss me already?" he said after one ring.

"Duane, someone's downstairs!" she exclaimed.

"Don't move! I'm on my way."

He hung up before she could say anything else. Nevertheless, she did as he instructed and quickly moved to the bedroom door, pushed it shut, and locked it. Thank God, she had given him a key.

How could I have been so blind? she thought as she pressed her palm firmly to her chest. She couldn't deny the evidence any longer. The cup in the sink. The missing ice cream. Whoever was downstairs, this was not their first time to her home.

She pressed her ear to the door. She didn't hear a thing. Champion's barking had ceased. All kinds of thoughts raced through her head. In the short time, she had grown to love her pet. His safety was important to her.

She moved to her dresser and removed Jarvis's gun for the first time since her arrival. Her heart banged rapidly against her chest. She had been too afraid to remove it before. Today it wasn't just her life that was in danger. However, as she headed for the door, she lost her nerve. Shakily, she lowered herself onto the bed, feeling helpless as she waited.

She didn't have to wait long. The front door opened, and she heard heavy footsteps. She closed her eyes and silently prayed that everything was okay. A tense silence enveloped the room.

Everything was quiet. Too quiet. She rose, ready to go down and investigate, when she heard someone coming up the stairs. Her heart began to beat even more rapidly against her chest, and her breathing increased.

Please, God, she prayed. *Please let that be Duane coming up the steps.* However, just in case it wasn't, she cupped her hand over her mouth to muffle her breathing. The longer it took for her to be found, the better off she would be.

She reached for the phone with one hand. Without pressing the talk button, she dialed 911. All she had to do was push a single button to reach a 911 dispatcher. Even if she couldn't speak, the dispatcher would immediately send out someone to investigate.

With her other hand, she raised the gun and pointed it at the door. She had never fired a gun in her life, but if she had to, she would.

The footsteps grew closer, and then she heard heavy panting outside the door.

Champion!

She released a sigh of relief. But did that mean all was clear? Where was Duane?

Her question was answered when she heard him calling her name as he reached the top of the stairs.

"Destiny, open the door," he commanded.

Leaving the gun on the bed, she moved to the door, turned the lock, and opened it. Champion raced into the room, tail wagging.

Duane stood behind him.

She gazed up at his sober expression, too afraid to ask what he found.

"Is . . . is everything all right?"

He stepped inside, and his gaze shifted over to the bed, where the gun lay. A shiver raced down his body. What in the world was she doing with a gun? He wanted and needed answers. She was hiding something, and he was determined to get to the bottom of things. But right now he had another issue to address.

"Come. I want to show you something."

Destiny put the phone back on the charger and followed him out of the room. His large fingers curled around hers as he led her down the flight of steps. Champion followed close behind.

"Are you going to tell me what's going on?" she asked impatiently.

He stared straight ahead and said, "I'll explain everything in a minute."

As they moved toward the kitchen, she heard movement. She tightened her grasp on Duane's hand. Champion moved in front of them and trotted into the kitchen. When Destiny stepped into the kitchen, she found someone sitting in a chair, rubbing his head.

"Destiny, I would like you to meet Mannie."

Startled, she glanced up at Duane, then stared across the room at a thin boy. His face, pecan in color, was long, and he had large, haunting eyes that looked as if they had seen more than any boy his age should have witnessed. He was wearing worn blue jeans, a frayed brown shirt, and scuffed gym shoes. He looked so sad, she wanted to pull him in her arms and hold him.

"Hello, Mannie," she said.

He patted Champion's head, then gazed up at her and mumbled a weak "hello."

Duane stepped farther into the kitchen and stopped near the table, where Mannie was sitting. "Destiny, Mannie has something he wants to tell you. Isn't that right, Mannie?" His thunderous voice drew the boy's attention.

He leaned forward, then his shoulders slumped. "Yes, sir."

"Apparently, Mannie's been spending his nights in your basement."

"What!" Her delicate jaw dropped, indicating her disbelief. "How did you get in?"

"Through a trap door in the basement."

Goodness, her security system was worthless if someone could come through a door she didn't even know existed. She looked at the little boy and asked, "Why?"

He hung his head and stared down at his shoes.

Destiny moved closer to the frightened boy. Softening her voice, she asked, "Mannie, why have you been hiding in my house?"

Mannie's eyes widened. He was in big trouble and apparently knew it. "I didn't mean to scare you. I just feel safe here."

"Why aren't you at home with your mother?"

"My mom ain't at home," he mumbled in a troubled voice.

"Where is she?"

She could tell her question hit a sore spot with him. She watched as his eyes narrowed angrily. "She's in rehab . . . again."

Destiny glanced at Duane for answers. He moved and took a seat across from Mannie at the table.

"His mom just entered a thirty-day program. She left Mannie with one of the neighbors, and apparently he doesn't want to stay with her," he explained. His voice was coolly disapproving.

"'Cause she's mean!" Mannie grumbled loudly.

"That's no excuse for sneaking into someone else's house. You had Ms. Davis scared." Duane's voice, although low, was stern.

Mannie hung his head like a little kid who had been scolded.

"What do you have to say for yourself?" Duane continued.

Mannie glanced at Destiny, his expression pleading for understanding. "I'm sorry. I didn't mean it, really I didn't."

Destiny shook her head in disbelief. "You mean all that time I thought someone had broken into the house, it had been you?" He nodded while staring down at his shoes. "Were you the one that ate my ice cream?" He nodded again.

She chuckled softly to herself, then released a deep breath of relief. She was safe after all. Destiny didn't know if she should scold Mannie or kiss him. She had been afraid for nothing.

"Mannie, would you like something to eat?"

He glanced up, surprised that she had asked, yet pleased that she had. "Yes, ma'am."

She ignored Duane's stern expression and

headed toward the refrigerator. "How about a hot ham and cheese sandwich and a cup of hot cocoa?"

His eyes lit up as he nodded.

"Coming right up." She removed the sliced ham and American cheese from the refrigerator, then moved to the bread box at the end of the counter. While she heated the sandwich in the toaster oven, Duane and Mannie talked quietly at the table. Even though she wasn't listening, she could tell from the expression on Mannie's face, he didn't like what he was being told. Destiny left the two of them alone long enough to put a load of clothes in the washing machine. When she returned, the two were munching noisily on a bowl of potato chips, and Mannie was grinning. An amused look made his eyes glimmer and added dimples to his cheeks. He was definitely a cute kid.

"I see the two of you have worked out your differences."

Duane nodded as he leaned back in his chair. "Mannie wants to pay you back for scaring you."

Destiny smiled, waving off his words with her hand. "Oh, that won't be necessary," she said just as the timer on the toaster oven went off. She removed a plate from one of the cabinets.

"Yes, it is necessary."

She looked over at Duane's face. His eyes held steady, sending her a message that said it was important that she agreed.

"All right," she said as she removed the sandwich from the toaster oven, carried it over to the table, and sat it in front of Mannie. "Maybe I can think of something you can do around here." She nibbled on her bottom lip as she stared down at Champion, who was lying beside Mannie's feet, and then an idea came to mind. "How about walking my dog for me?"

"Walking your dog? Me?" Mannie stopped twiddling his thumbs and looked over at Duane for approval.

Duane nodded. "I think that sounds like an excellent idea. How about three days a week for one month?"

"Sounds good to me." Destiny grinned down at Mannie and watched as his lips curled with satisfaction.

"I can do that. I'm good with dogs." Mannie's tone betrayed a hint of boastfulness.

"I can tell. It seems that dogs like you, too. Isn't that right, Champion?"

Champion rose, panting, with his tail wagging. She rubbed his head, then began to make a cup of hot chocolate.

"Can I eat my sandwich now?" Mannie asked.

She grinned. "Yes, you may."

He grabbed his sandwich and took a hungry bite.

She glanced at Duane, who was tapping his fingers lightly on the table. "Duane, I'm sorry. I didn't even think to ask you if you wanted something to eat."

"No, but I wouldn't mind a cup of cocoa."

While they each drank hot chocolate, she took the seat across from them and listened to Mannie answer Duane's questions about school. Destiny was pleased to hear that he was on the honor roll and had been chosen to represent his school at a state spelling bee the coming week.

After they were done, Duane and Mannie went down to the basement to repair the latch on the trap door. When Duane left to take Mannie back to the neighbor's house, Destiny let Champion play out in the backyard while she cleaned up the kitchen. She made herself a cup of Sleepytime tea, removing the tea bag just as she heard scratching on the back door. She reached for Champion's treats and gave him one as he trotted into the house.

"Good boy."

After locking up, she set the alarm and carried her tea up to her bedroom. Climbing under the covers, she sipped her tea slowly and thumbed through the latest copy of *Essence*. If it wasn't too late, Duane was coming over after dropping off Mannie.

By the time she had finished skimming the entire magazine, her eyelids had begun to grow heavy. Glancing over at the clock, she saw that it was almost eleven.

She lowered her cup onto the nightstand, then turned out the lamp and slid beneath the covers. She'd had a long, eventful day that had ended on a pleasant note. She now knew she wasn't going crazy: someone had been in her house. She also was happy to discover it wasn't Lucas's hired help. It had been an eleven-year-old boy.

Closing her eyes, she couldn't help thinking about how good Duane was with Mannie. He was a natural. Duane was patient, yet stern. As she drifted off, she imagined a life with Duane and children of their own.

She was holding their newborn child when the phone rang. Reluctantly, she pulled herself from her dream and reached for the phone. It was Duane. "You're back?"

"Yeah, and Mannie is still with me."

"Why? What happened?"

When he spoke again, she could hear the disgust

in his voice. "Ms. Rochelle had a little too much traffic coming in and out of her house. There was loud music, and several people were out on the porch, drinking beer. A couple of them looked too shady, so I told her Mannie was going to spend the night with me. She was so drunk, she quickly agreed."

"My goodness. That poor boy!" she gasped into the receiver.

Duane chuckled lightly. "Actually Mannie looked quite relieved. He's in the kitchen now stuffing his face with ice cream."

She giggled around a yawn. "It sounds like he's in good hands."

"It sounds like you're in bed."

She shifted comfortably on the pillow. "I am."

"I wish I could join you." His voice was low and purposely seductive.

"So do I," she crooned, clutching the phone closer to her mouth.

"Sleep tight, sweetheart. I'll see you tomorrow."

She hung up, and within minutes she was sound asleep.

Chapter 15

Destiny felt a wave of uneasiness when she opened the front door. Out of respect, Duane had knocked instead of letting himself in. Still dressed in a pajama shirt, she stood in the doorway. The look he gave her caused her smile to fade. There was something in his stance that told her she wouldn't like what he was about to say.

They'd held hands, kissed, gone out on several dates and even made love. She found more comfort with him that she had ever found in her life. Duane was patient and compassionate, and she had grown to care for him, despite her every attempt not to. The only hurdle they had left to jump was the secret that weighed heavily on her heart. She knew it, and the unwavering look radiating from him told her that Duane was beginning to sense it also.

"May I come in so we can talk?" he asked, his face expressionless.

"Oh, sure!" Destiny gave a nervous laugh as she stepped aside, allowing his tense, hard body to enter.

"Where's Mannie?" She could use the boy as a diversion from whatever it was Duane wanted to discuss.

"I dropped him off at school. I promised to pick him up tomorrow evening after he finishes his homework."

"I'm sure he'll like that," she commented, her slender hands unconsciously twisted together.

Glancing up at him again, she found his eyes cold, lacking humor. His presence pulsated around her, and her skin prickled, sensing trouble. Something in his expression warned her she needed to put some distance between them. She moved into the living room and lowered herself into a chair.

Duane continued to stand at the entryway, legs wide apart. As usual, he was dressed casually. Today he wore a gray sweatshirt, which stretched across his broad shoulders, and worn jeans.

The silence swelled. Still watching him, she drew her legs up on the chair, circling them with her arms. "What's wrong?"

His eyes were narrowed, focused, penetrating her face as if he could see inside and read all of her secrets. "I want to know what you're hiding."

She shuddered, then asked quietly, "What are you talking about?"

Duane folded his arms across his chest. "The gun, Destiny. Why do you have a gun?"

She laughed unsteadily, resenting the panic that slipped through. Wasn't the answer obvious? "Why do you think? For protection. I am a single woman in a big house," she countered.

He shook his head slowly. "I think there's more to it than that. I think you're hiding something."

She went completely still as she glared at him. His eyes narrowed dangerously. The gun had belonged to Jarvis. When she'd left, she had taken the gun with her. "Are you calling me a liar?"

Squeezing his eyes briefly shut, he inhaled roughly, then said, "No, I just think there's something you're not telling me. Last night wasn't the first time I have felt that way." He felt like a jealous husband demanding answers. "Occasionally, you're distant. Sometimes I see fear written across your face, and whenever you go out in public, you put on that weird getup. Not to mention I caught you sneaking out of the house once."

Her spine stiffened. "How . . . dare . . . you spy on me!" she hissed in a furious tone she didn't bother to disguise.

He sent her a look from beneath raised eyebrows. "I wasn't spying, but I deserve to hear the truth." His voice was deceptively calm, masking his rage.

She leaned forward, shoulders slumped, then with a sigh replied, "I don't have a reason to lie to you. However, maybe I feel my personal life is none of your business."

Duane's eyes darkened as he struggled to control his temper. He gritted his teeth, and a muscle jumped in his jaw. "As long as we are involved, everything about you is my business, especially your safety. So if there is something I need to know, I would appreciate your honesty."

She tunneled her fingers through her hair. "I resent that," she stated fiercely, then sprung from the chair. Before she managed to brush past him, Duane caught her wrist and swung her around to face him. "Let me go!" she demanded.

His jaw was tense and his nostrils flared as he searched her face for answers. "Not until you look me in the eyes and tell me nothing is wrong. That you aren't hiding anything. Then I will believe you," he demanded roughly, trying to hide his unsteady emotions.

She swallowed. He was standing too close, studying her face with that burning intensity she knew all too well. "I'm not hiding anything," she mumbled, shaking with anger. "If anything, I'm stressed about my thesis. My entire future depends on it."

She was gorgeous when she was mad. Duane fought the need to feel her lips buried beneath his. The need to fill her body with his, while he stroked her and whispered her name, riveted through him.

His eyes shifted downward. Almost immediately, he noticed the dark, hardened peaks of her nipples pressed against her shirt. It gave him pleasure to know she was just as turned on as he was.

He tugged her into his arms and kissed her. Destiny moved willingly against him. Arms locked around her waist, he heard a purr that shot heat through his veins. The kiss deepened, and his hands moved possessively over her body. His lips were hot, devouring, and possessive. He was trying to communicate the message that he loved her and that he was there for her no matter what. Despite what she said, he knew she was hiding something. He hoped that in time she would trust him and give him her heart and soul.

He pulled her closer and, locking her against him, dropped his lips to her neck and shoulders. The stubble on his jaw grazed her skin.

"I'd risk my life to save yours."

His deep, sensual voice curled around her. His breath was rough and uneven against her skin. Closing her eyes, she buried her face against his chest as his words warmed her like a winter blanket. She swallowed hard, her feelings swelling her heart. She needed to find a way for him to understand that in time she would share what was on her mind. As her body stirred, she realized there was only one way to communicate how much he meant to her.

Pulling back, she stared at him and witnessed the desire burning in his eyes. She eased her hand up and pressed it to his cheek. He leaned into her palm.

Without saying a word and without breaking her gaze from his, she took his hand and led him up the stairs.

After Duane left, Destiny dug into her rewrites. She was determined to send the first hundred pages of her novel to her agent to read the day after Memorial Day. The words flowed easily and would require very little revision. Duane was obviously an inspiration.

By noon her head was hurting, probably from lack of food. She saved her changes, then headed down to the kitchen. Craving a tuna sandwich, she reached for a can of tuna on a shelf of the pantry and opened it with a handheld can opener. Moving to the refrigerator, she removed two eggs and put them in a pan of water on the stove. While she waited for the water to boil, she hummed softly as she chopped an onion, green pepper, and celery into tiny pieces.

The doorbell rang. Champion barked, immediately trotted to the front door, and waited.

Drying her hands, she went to the door and

glanced through the peephole. An attractive, deep brown face confronted her.

"Good afternoon," Destiny said as she opened the door, allowing in a beam of warmth and sunshine.

Simone's luminous eyes crinkled in a friendly smile. "Hi. I'm sorry to bother you, but my phone isn't in service yet. Would it be too much trouble for me to use yours?" She had a wonderful, low voice, soft and clear.

"Sure, no problem at all." Destiny stepped aside and allowed Simone to enter the foyer

"Thank you. I really appreciate this." She spotted Champion. "Who do we have here? What a beautiful dog."

Champion growled under his breath.

"Champ, no!" Destiny commanded, surprised at his behavior.

"It's okay; he just doesn't know me." Simone stooped in front of him. "Come here, Champ."

He hesitated, growled some more, then finally came to her with his tail wagging.

"See, that's a good boy. I wouldn't hurt you," she replied.

Destiny gave her a proud smile. "He's very protective of me."

"Is that so? Champion, are you the man of the house?" Simone cooed in a baby voice while she rubbed him behind his ears. Destiny smirked at the way her dog was sucking up to a stranger. He was such a ham.

When Simone rose, Destiny signaled for her to follow her into the kitchen and showed her where the phone was mounted on the wall next to the back door. Allowing her privacy, Destiny stepped into the pantry to find something to fix for dinner.

Duane planned to stop over after completing the installation of new oak kitchen cabinets for a young couple who didn't live too far away.

A slow smile of an unforgettable morning slid across her lips. The two of them were beginning to feel like a couple, like they belonged together. The idea no longer frightened her like it had before. What scared her most was that the more Duane got to know her, the more he was beginning to read her. She just hoped she had a chance to tell him the truth before he discovered it on his own.

She reached for a box of penne pasta and decided on baked ziti and a tossed salad. As soon as Simone left, Destiny would drop by the Wonder Bread store up the street and pick up a loaf of French bread.

While Simone's back was turned, Destiny studied her guest. Simone had to have the longest legs she had ever seen, yet they were proportional to the rest of her body. She made a pair of khaki shorts and a plain yellow T-shirt look good. Destiny remembered that when she was twelve, she had dreams of being a world-famous model. The fantasy ended when everyone in her senior class was taller than her.

Today Simone wore her hair loose. The mass fell way below her shoulders. Destiny shook her head. After years of beauty salons and sleeping "pretty" so her style would last until her next appointment, she didn't feel a tinge of remorse about relieving her head of well over sixteen inches off the sides and top.

She walked over to the kitchen counter just as Simone ended her call with the telephone company. She hung up the phone, her expression sober.

"Anything I can help you with?" Destiny offered.

Simone shook her head with apparent frustration. "No, apparently they never received an order for new service."

"When did you order it?" she asked as she moved over to the stove and removed the boiling pot from the fire.

A slight frown marred Simone's tawny forehead. "I made the request almost two weeks ago . . . I think." She dropped her shoulders with a scowl. "I guess I don't have a choice but to wait. They said they should be able to have a technician out by Thursday."

It was only Monday. "Well, look at the bright side. At least they'll have you functioning before the holiday weekend," Destiny commented, in an attempt to cheer her up.

Simone's radiant smile returned. "You're right. No point in crying over spilled milk."

Destiny carried the pot to the sink and ran the eggs under cold water. "Would you like something to drink?"

"Sure, I would love something." Simone took a seat, crossing her mile-long legs.

Destiny reached into the refrigerator and removed a pitcher of fresh squeezed lemonade and filled two tall glasses. She walked over and placed them both on the table.

"Thanks." Simone brought the glass to her lips.

"Actually, I was just getting ready to make myself a tuna sandwich. Would you care for one?"

She noticed Simone's hesitation. "I really don't want to impose."

Destiny shook her head. "It's no trouble at all. I'm glad for the company."

Simone's eyes sparkled. "In that case, I'd love one.

I haven't had a chance to shop, and I am sick of fast food."

Destiny raised a sweeping brow. "Where are you from?"

"South. I grew up in Birmingham."

That explained the southern drawl. While Destiny prepared the tuna, Simone told her about her large family. She was the youngest of twelve. Destiny laughed at her animated tale of growing up in a small house on a large farm. You would have thought she lived in a little house on the prairie.

Simone had attended state college during her under-graduate years. She had chosen Delaware State University because it was a historically black univesity with a dentistry program and was far away from home. Destiny found her funny and intelligent, with an independent spirit.

Simone folded her hands in front of her and groaned. "I love my family, but you can't imagine how good it feels to be away from those crazy people."

"No, I can't imagine. I don't have any family left," Destiny murmured as she carried over two sandwiches on whole wheat bread.

"Oh!" Simone gasped with her hand over her mouth. "I'm sorry to hear that."

Destiny settled in the seat across from her. While they ate, she found Simone easy to talk to as she told her about Nana and her Uncle Benny.

"How do you like it on the East Coast?" Destiny asked as she took another bite of her sandwich.

Simone reached for a napkin and blotted her mouth. "I love it. The weather is fabulous. I can't wait to drive down to the ocean and sit out on the beach. I heard there are two hundred outlet stores in Rehoboth Beach."

Destiny's brown eyes brightened. "You're kidding?"

"Yep. The lady I'm renting from was telling me." Simone paused long enough to push a strand of hair back behind her ear. "Anyway, I'm going to visit my cousin in New York over the holiday. I need something to wear and was thinking of driving down to the outlets."

Destiny suddenly remembered that she had nothing to wear for the Memorial Day celebration at Duane's parents' house. "How would you like to ride down to the beach together?"

Simone's lips curled. "That would be fabulous. When would you like to go?"

"Is tomorrow too soon?" Destiny asked, growing excited about a shopping trip.

Simone's eyes sparkled with glee. "That would be wonderful."

Destiny reached for her glass and smiled, glad to have found a new friend.

Destiny made a fresh pot of coffee. While it brewed, she went into the living room and turned on the television. As usual, the picture was filled with snow. She tried turning several of the knobs to adjust the picture. What usually worked wasn't cutting it today.

"That's it. I've had it. I need a television."

Duane stepped into the room, chuckling knowingly. "I agree. I tried to buy Benny a new television one year for Christmas. He told me to take it back and fix a leak in the second-floor ceiling instead." He was still laughing when he came up behind Destiny and wrapped her in a warm embrace. "The only person who knew how to make this television work was your uncle. He would apply a fist to the right corner and an arthritis hip to the left, and I swear to you, we had a crystal clear view of the news every time."

Destiny leaned into his chest and giggled. "I tried beating the stupid thing, but it didn't work."

He lowered his lips against the corner of her neck, just below her ear, and murmured, "There's a sale going on at Circuit City this weekend. Why don't we go and see what we can find?"

Closing her eyes, she savored the feel of his warm breath, which tickled her skin. "Okay," she cooed.

His hand smoothed over her belly and climbed up to her sensitive breasts. The first sensual jolt hit her, and within seconds her body heated several degrees. Before she could even voice her needs, Duane swung her into his arms and carried her up to her bedroom, tossing her lightly upon the bed. Mere seconds later, he was buried deep inside of her, driving them both quickly over the edge. Just before he came, he stared down at her with a possessive expression and murmured, "You're mine." Then he thrust deeper.

First in.

Then out.

Again and again.

Whimpering beneath him, Destiny spread her legs, and with her palms firmly on his buttocks, pushed him deeper inside her, wanting everything he had to offer. Within seconds, sparks shot through her body, as it sought release. Shortly after, an explosion rocked his body, and together they came.

Lying beneath Duane, with his arm draped

possessively across her stomach, she said in a lazy whisper, "God, I needed that."

He chuckled and kissed her forehead. "You said that about this morning."

"I needed that, too."

He playfully spanked her buttocks, then rose from the bed and moved down the hall to the bathroom. After he left, Destiny pulled the sheets over her naked body and curled in a ball, with a happy smile on her face as she closed her eyes.

It had taken over four hours for Destiny to find the perfect dress at the Liz Claiborne outlet store. She and Simone carried their bags back to Simone's Honda Civic after they had strolled down the entire strip mall, shopping for bargains. By the time they were tired and hungry, Destiny had found an outfit for the barbecue, two tops with matching shorts, and three pairs of leather sandals.

After shopping, they went to Anne Marie's Seafood & Steak and had crab bisque, house salads, grilled salmon, and broccoli with a rice pilaf. They talked, laughed, and bonded. Destiny found Simone to be an outgoing young woman with a fabulous personality.

When they returned home, Destiny put her things away and decided to take a quick nap. An hour later she rose, feeling well rested, and spent the rest of the afternoon writing her next chapter. Around four, she decided to call it a day and went down to the kitchen. Expecting Duane and Mannie in a few hours, she prepared a meal of fried chicken, homemade rolls, and a crisp spinach salad.

She went upstairs and showered, then changed

into a denim dress that stopped just below her knees. After slipping into a simple pair of flip-flops, she returned to the kitchen.

The sound of a door opening made her heart race with excitement. Champion's bark signaled that Duane and Mannie had arrived. When Duane had called to let her know he was on his way, she'd told him to let himself in.

Turning away from the pitcher of iced tea she was brewing, Destiny saw Duane coming down the hall. Familiar warmth inched its way through her body as a smile curved her lips.

He stepped into the room and sniffed the air. "Something smells wonderful."

Destiny crossed the floor and became enveloped in his strong embrace. He leaned down and kissed her forehead. Pulling back, she smiled up at him. "It's my grandmother's famous fried chicken."

He gazed down at her, eyes dancing. "Yum, I can't wait."

Mannie raced into the kitchen with Champion at his heels.

"Hi, Ms. Davis."

She returned his grin. "Hi, Mannie. I think Champion is ready for his walk. The leash is hanging by the door." She pointed to the hook in the far corner of the room.

Turning back to Duane, she gazed up into his eyes. "How was your day?"

He dropped his lips to her earlobes and whispered between nibbles. "Better, now that I'm here with you."

She released a sigh of contentment. Cradled to his chest, her body sizzled. Already, she anticipated lying in his arms tonight.

Mannie hooked the leash to Champion's collar and followed an excited dog to the door. Duane walked out onto the porch to make sure Mannie had everything under control. Then he returned to the kitchen, came up behind Destiny, and wrapped his arms around her waist. "I've got something for you."

She swung around, eyes burning with curiosity. "What?"

A mysterious smile curved his strong, masculine mouth. "Come out and see."

Destiny quickly checked on the rolls she had just popped in the oven and allowed him to steer her outside and across the street to his truck.

"This is for you." He pointed to the box in the bed of his pickup.

Her mouth dropped open, and then she gave a soft gasp of surprise. "You bought me a television?"

Duane nodded. "I hope you like it," he said with a wink.

"Oh, I do!" She draped her arms around his neck and pressed her lips against his. When she pulled back, Duane growled against her neck.

"Woman, keep that up, and you'll be asking for trouble," he crooned against her nose. He lifted her in his arms and swung her around, then planted his lips on hers again as he slowly lowered her feet back to the ground.

Releasing her, Duane removed the box and carried it across the street to her house. By the time they had it set up and placed the old one in the box to be taken to the Salvation Army, Mannie had returned with Champion.

"How did he do?" Destiny asked as he stepped into the house.

"Piece of cake," he said.

"Good." She ruffled his hair. "Why don't you take him in the kitchen and give him a treat?"

"All right. Come on, boy!" Champion gladly trotted behind his friend.

"Let's eat," Destiny said and signaled for Duane to follow.

Dinner was an amusing affair, with Mannie sharing stories about a fishing trip Uncle Benny had taken him on that ended with the boat tipping over. Destiny laughed so hard when Mannie told her that her uncle was so determined to get a fish, it didn't matter that their food was floating away.

"I must say that was the best-tasting catfish I have ever tasted," Duane commented at the end of the story.

After dinner Destiny rode with Duane to take Mannie back to his neighbor's house. She felt a pinch of sadness as she surveyed the conditions of the neighborhood. She had a lot to be grateful for. In fact, she had more than the average person. However, as Duane held her hand while they returned home, and later as she lay in his arms after he made love to her, she realized that no amount of money could give her what she had found with Duane—love.

Chapter 16

Duane opened the car door for Destiny, offering her a warm smile as she settled herself on the leather seat. He then closed the door, rounded his Chrysler, and took a seat behind the wheel. She pulled the seat belt across her waist and turned on the radio as he pulled out of the driveway.

They were relatively quiet most of the ride, allowing the sounds of Gerald Levert to fill the silence that surrounded them. Duane's hand cradled hers in a strong grasp as he drove. Destiny stared out the window, trying to relieve a wave of nervousness.

She was going to meet Duane's family!

She knew that she might be reading too much into the invitation, but at the back of her mind, she was sure he didn't take just anyone home. Their relationship had reached the point where Duane was ready for his family's approval.

As Duane maneuvered into a beautifully landscaped subdivision, she experienced a brief anxiety attack. The houses in the subdivision were in the same price range as her condominium. She found that unbelievable. She would trade her condo for a big house with a white picket fence any day. It took leaving her condo and all of her prized possessions to realize she never needed them in the first place.

The barbecue was scheduled for 3 P.M., but Duane informed her that his family had been arriving in Wilmington since Thursday. The entire family would be there.

She took a deep breath and tried to reassure herself that everything was going to be fine. Even if she never saw his parents again, she wanted them to like her. Probably because the Blakes—Lucas's parents—never had.

When Lucas wasn't around, his parents, especially his mother, made it clear that they didn't think Destiny was good enough for their son. Mrs. Blake had even offered her money, which Destiny refused, to walk away from the relationship. Later, when Destiny told Lucas about his mother's offer, he blamed it on her for not trying hard enough to please them.

Destiny shut her eyes, willing back tears. She couldn't go through that a second time. No woman wanted to be rejected by her in-laws.

"Are you okay?" Duane asked as he steered the car down the tree-lined street toward his parents' home. He squeezed her hand, and she caught a hint of a smile lift the corners of his mouth.

"Do you think your mom will like me?" she asked.

Duane glanced at her again in time to witness a distressed look. "She's going to love you," he assured her as he brought the car to a stop in front of a large house.

Blinking rapidly, Destiny focused on the magnificent setting in front to her.

"How can you be sure?" she asked as he climbed

out of the car. He didn't answer her until he had rounded the car and opened the door for her.

"Because I know my mother." He reached out his hand and helped her from his car. "Whatever I like, she likes."

He gazed down at Destiny and grinned. Everything about her caused desire to brew, from the way the yellow sundress hugged her narrow waist to the cream sandals displaying her small, delicate feet.

He pulled her into his arms and nibbled at a corner of her lips. "She'll love you. I promise," he whispered against her lush mouth before he touched his lips to hers.

His warm kiss was all the reassurance she needed. When he pulled back, she stared up at him, absorbing everything that made Duane who he was. He smiled, and she felt her lips curling upward. He looped his arm over hers and steered her up the driveway, alongside half a dozen vehicles.

One look at the home, and Destiny knew he came from money. Elegant and striking, those two words barely scratched the surface in describing the exquisite stone and wood house. A stone walkway, etched into lush grass and bushes, led to a grand double front door. The white, two-story colonial with red shutters gave a warm first impression. The front door opened to a spacious center hallway. She found the living space to be sheer luxury both in size and design. It had a two-story foyer, polished hardwood floors, exquisite chandeliers, and an elegant curved staircase. The entire house was bright, airy, and rich, with large windows and a wealth of elegant features. However, the formality of the home did not steal its feeling of warmth and comfort.

Hearing laughter coming from the back of the

house, Duane led her through a door that took them into a spacious kitchen, where white appliances matched the rich white cabinets. Two women sat at the kitchen table chatting. Hazel-colored eyes shifted to the door.

"Hi, Mom."

"Oh, Duane, you're here." His mother wiped her hands on her apron and rose quickly to greet him.

He moved into her open arms and met her lips. Looking over his mother's shoulder, he spotted his Aunt Pearl sitting at the table, sipping lemonade.

"If it isn't my nappy-headed nephew." Tiny lines fanned out at the corners of his aunt's eyes when she laughed.

Joining in her laughter, he stepped away from his mother's embrace and moved to hug his aunt.

"Now who do we have here?" his mother asked, staring at Destiny with a smile.

Turning, Duane followed the direction of his mother's gaze. He placed both hands on his aunt's shoulders. "Mom, Aunt Pearl, I'd like you to meet Destiny Davis."

Mrs. Urban ignored Destiny's extended hand and leaned over and kissed her cheek. "Welcome to our home."

Destiny smiled graciously at the short, beautiful woman with eyes like her son. Her black and gray chignon was perfectly elegant and in place. "Thank you."

Aunt Pearl rose from her chair, greeting Destiny with a warm smile before pulling her close to her large, round body. She stepped back. "Chile, let me take a good look at you." She shook her graying curls. "You must be someone special 'cause my nephew ain't brought a woman home in . . . in I don't know how long." His aunt's soft drawl spoke of a southern influence.

Destiny smiled, trying to hide her embarrassment.

"Hey, Dee. When you get here?" asked a man as tall as Duane as he swept in the room and playfully jabbed his shoulder.

Destiny stared at the man and then at Duane. A knowing smile touched her lips. She knew this was one of his brothers.

"Just now," Duane said as he draped an arm across Destiny's shoulders.

His brother looked past him and let out a long whistle. "Who is this honey, and does she have a sister?"

Before Duane could speak, his mother swatted his brother and gave him a look that said, *behave*.

Chuckling, Duane rested a possessive hand on Destiny's shoulder. "Destiny, this is my little brother and comedian, Garrett Urban."

Her eyes swept over Garret. The resemblance was obvious. He looked to be in his late twenties and was extremely handsome. His long and curly hair was pulled back at the nape with a rubber band. He and Duane shared the same eyes and dimpled smile. Garrett was tall and slender. She tilted her head to meet his dark gaze and extended a hand. "It's nice to meet you."

"The same here," he said, grinning broadly at her. "You still haven't answered my question."

Destiny peered closely at Garrett, her arching eyebrows lifting in a questioning expression.

His voice teased and his dark eyes sparkled when he said, "Do you have a sister?"

The group shared a laugh.

"Sorry, man, but she's an only child," said Duane.

Garrett looked truly disappointed. "That's too bad. She is a beautiful woman."

Destiny blushed. Embarrassed by his compliment, she simply smiled.

"We're going out back with the rest of the group." Duane took Destiny's hand and led her through French doors to where dozens of people were sitting and laughing.

Stepping out on a gorgeous courtyard deck, she was instantly mesmerized by an enchanting garden. A curved brick pathway traveled through a niche of nature. Spectacular plants and shrubs were showcased. Colorful perennials emblazed the grounds. Each rose had bloomed to perfection. A pond was tucked away in one private corner, and a quaint bench was off to the other side. The garden was completely enclosed by mature evergreens, which also ringed the property, providing privacy and shading the yard.

The distinct aroma of barbecue wafted in the air. A man Duane identified as his great-uncle Charlie was tending to steaks and foil-wrapped potatoes on a super-sized grill.

Duane's uncles, aunts, and several dozen cousins were scattered around the yard. Most were sprawled on lawn chairs. With his hand loosely at her waist, he took Destiny around to meet his family. By the time they made it to the other end of the yard, he was certain she was overwhelmed. He was hoping to give her a break from introductions, but then he spotted his sister. Chelsea was sitting at one corner of the deck with her husband. The two rose as soon as they saw Duane coming.

He chuckled inwardly when Chelsea glanced

over at her husband with apparent surprise. Destiny was going to be the talk of the afternoon.

His sister wrapped her arms around him, and gave him a kiss on the lips. Once they pulled apart, she turned to the woman at his side.

"Sis, I'd like you to meet Destiny Davis."

Destiny was amazed at how much the two of them resembled each other. There was no doubt she was an Urban. She was petite and quite attractive. She had inherited her mother's hazel eyes and the Urbans' dimpled smiles. She was dressed casually in white Capri pants and a short-sleeved green top.

"It's a pleasure to meet you," she finally said.

Destiny returned her warm smile. "The same here. Your brother has told me a great deal about you."

"Really?" Chelsea glanced at her brother with an amused look. Her mass of ebony hair brushed her shoulders as she turned. "Well, I wish I could say the same about you."

Duane stepped up and patted the man standing beside his sister on the shoulder. "Destiny, this is my brother-in-law, Andre, the best criminal defender in town."

A tall, lean man with a deep tan and kind eyes took her hand and kissed the back of it. "It's a pleasure to meet you."

Destiny nodded. "Same here."

Curving an arm around his sister's narrow waist, Duane kissed the top of her head. "Have you seen Reyn?"

She shook her head. "Not yet."

"What about Aunt Kathy?" Duane asked.

"She arrived last night." Chelsea wrinkled her nose. "Uncle Greg is here and already as drunk as a skunk." She glanced at Destiny. "It would be wise to stay clear of him. When my uncle has been drinking, he has a tendency to ask a lot of embarrassing questions."

Destiny nodded at the advice.

"Let me go and see if Dad needs any help with that grill." Duane released his sister and took hold of Destiny's hand again. "We'll see you two later."

Duane steered her over to the grill, where his father had replaced his Uncle Charlie.

Ural Urban glanced to his left as his son approached. "Duane, you made it." He removed the mitt from his hand and embraced his oldest son, whose dark eyes mirrored his own, then turned to the beautiful woman by his side.

Destiny smiled at Mr. Urban. "Hello, I'm Destiny."

He gave her a familiar dimpled smile. "It is such a pleasure." Leaning down from his impressive height, Mr. Urban kissed her cheek.

Destiny glanced up at the tall man with handsome features and short, steel gray curls and returned his smile. She was looking forward to spending an afternoon surrounded by so much love. So far everyone had made her feel welcome.

"What do we have here? Don't tell me my big brother has found himself a date?"

Turning in the direction of the deep voice, Destiny caught sight of a man walking across the grass beside Garrett.

Duane tossed his head back with laughter. "Too bad I can't say the same about you."

He had to be Duane's brother, Reyn. The Urban brothers were definitely works of art, Destiny thought as she watched the two embrace. All three were handsome and dripping with masculinity.

Even in shorts and T-shirts they were perfect models for the cover of an Arabesque romance. Like his brothers, Reyn had wide shoulders, muscular arms, washboard abs, and massive thighs. Reyn, however, sported an attractive bald head.

A crooked smile tipped his mouth. "You must be Destiny."

"And you must be Reyn."

He gave her a wide, dimpled smile. "The one and only." His eyes quickly swept over her curves, then shot a quick look of approval in his brother's direction. "Dang, Dee, you got yourself a hottie."

Garrett laughed and added his two cents. "Yo, I already asked her if she had a sister."

Destiny turned and looked at Duane so that her embarrassment wouldn't be obvious to everyone.

"Behave," their father scolded. "Destiny is our guest. I expect both of you to treat her like family." He grinned at Destiny and gave her a quick wink before returning to grilling the meat.

Destiny had to stifle a giggle as both of Duane's brothers stuck out their lips and pretended to act like children who had been reprimanded by their bible school teacher.

"It's a pleasure meeting all of you." She shifted her gaze to Duane. "If you will excuse me, I need to find the ladies' room."

"It's the last door on the left," Duane murmured near her ear before he kissed her cheek and released her hand.

All four men watched her disappear inside the house.

Garrett broke the silence with a hearty chuckle. "Man, you are one lucky man."

Duane smiled. "Yes, I am."

* * *

The barbecue was a robust affair with flowing conversation, laughter, and enough food to feed an army. Stuffed with food, Destiny had collapsed in a lounge chair under a red dogwood tree. Duane watched her with a tingling at the pit of his stomach. After a large meal, she was content relaxing in a shaded corner, enjoying the evening breeze. He was playing a game of chess with Uncle Charlie but preferred watching her instead.

He wanted her in ways he'd never imagined he'd ever feel about a woman again. He not only couldn't wait to get her home so he could make love to her, he also realized he wanted her to be a part of his life forever.

Throughout the afternoon, he found himself watching her, and each time his body responded immediately. Only a man who'd held a woman in his arms while buried deep inside of her, with the scent of their lovemaking surrounding them, would find pleasure in the flush of her cheeks and the heat radiating from her eyes each and every time she noticed him watching her. In her, he had found everything a man could possibly want in a woman. Destiny was caring, intelligent, beautiful, and an incredible lover.

He needed some advice and decided that the best person to talk to was his sister. Looking around, he spotted her sitting at a picnic table, holding his niece, Cherie, while laughing at something his cousin Kenyatta had said. Chelsea looked over at him as he approached. He shook his head. He still hadn't gotten used to how much she had changed since she had gotten married.

A former flight attendant, she'd given up flying the friendly skies to be a full-time wife and mother. At first he had thought it strange that a woman who valued her independence as much as she did, had traded it all in for a man. Andre had wanted a traditional wife—a woman who would have dinner on the table and be content with taking care of him and their children.

There was nothing wrong with that, but Chelsea, he thought, had wanted more. It had taken ten weeks for it to sink into Duane's thick skull that staying home and focusing on her family was what she had always wanted. Duane had to admit that she seemed happier and full of life. The arrangement suited her.

He approached the table with a smirk on his face. "Kenyatta, when are you going to give up your badge and settle down?"

The young, cappuccino-colored woman rolled her eyes. "I'm not quitting my job for anyone. A man will have to accept me as I am or step off."

He threw his head back with laughter. "I imagine you lay down the ground rules before a brotha can even think about kissing you."

A smile captured her lilac painted lips. "You better believe it."

A cop, Kenyatta Urban was not one to mess with. She had a short temper and very little patience. Duane didn't think there was a man alive who was brave enough to mess with his first cousin. "Don't let the size fool you," she always said. She still wore her hair the same as in grammar school: pulled back into a ponytail, which she either knotted or allowed to hang over her left shoulder. Never one for more than lipstick, she didn't look a day over sixteen, which was why she was often assigned to work undercover. She had brought down some of the toughest criminals across the tristate area.

"Can I steal my sister away for a moment?" Duane asked. He needed to talk to Chelsea without his cousin adding her two cents.

Kenyatta folded her arms and rose from the table. "Sure. Chelsea, I'll be in the kitchen, finding something else to eat."

"Thanks, Cuz." Duane dropped a kiss to her cheek. She put on a disgusted look and made a show of wiping it off before she escaped through the sliding glass door.

His sister found it amusing. "You're a mess."

"I can't resist with Kenyatta."

She sobered, then rested her head on the palm of her hand. "What do you need to talk about?"

He straddled the bench beside her. "I need some advice."

She smiled and said, "Dear Chelsea at your service."

He suddenly felt awkward sharing his personal life. "I need some advice on women."

"I think I can help you with that," she said with repressed laughter.

He reached for his sleeping niece and cradled her in his arms before he spoke again. "Why do women keep things so bottled up inside?"

She lifted her sweeping left eyebrow. "What do you mean?"

"I mean why is it when you ask a woman what's wrong, she says nothing, even though it's obvious something is bothering her?"

Chelsea giggled. "It's definitely a woman thing. We like to solve our own problems and not feel like we need a man to do everything for us. It has to do with being independent."

"But why would you want to keep a problem to yourself if a man can make it all better?"

"Not all women like feeling vulnerable or, should I say, needy." He must have looked puzzled because she shifted slightly on the bench to make sure she had his complete attention. "Remember when we were kids and Earl Carter used to pick on me on the way to school every morning?"

Duane nodded. How could he forget? The boy used to send her home crying before he realized she had three older, overprotective brothers. "I remember."

"Well, after the three of you threatened him with bodily damage, Earl saved his badgering for recess only."

He blew out a long breath. "How come you didn't tell me?"

Chelsea held up a dismissive hand. "Because I didn't want any of you fighting my battles."

He looked at her as he began to register what she was saying.

"One day he announced to our entire class that I was a big baby and needed my brothers to hold my hand. I was so mad, and before I realized what I was doing, I swung around and decked him right in the nose."

"You did?"

Her eyes sparkled with memories. "I sure did. I was so afraid he was going to hit me back, but when he saw the blood coming from his nose, he ran to the nurse crying."

He smiled knowingly. "I guess teaching you those self-defense techniques paid off."

She nodded. "They did. So what I'm trying to say is that if something is bothering Destiny, let her try to work it out herself. If she needs your help or wants you to know, then she'll tell you."

"Who said I'm talking about Destiny?"

Chelsea rose. "I'm smarter than you think." She slipped her arms around his neck and gave him an affectionate kiss. Releasing him, she took Cherie from his arms and carried her inside the house.

Duane sat alone on the bench, watching Destiny as she napped peacefully in a chair. He thought about the past several weeks and how important she had become in his life. She had him thinking about love, commitment, and marriage.

Marriage!

The very word sent a shudder racing through his body. Since his disastrous relationship with Veronica, he had banished the word from his vocabulary.

Was he willing to commit to spending the rest of his life waking up beside her? Did he want Destiny to be the mother of his children? Both questions caused his heart to tumble. Dropping his head to his hands, he took a deep breath, then glanced over at Destiny as the answer came to rest so clearly in his mind. Yes, he was ready.

They hung around until the mosquitoes began to bite; then Destiny said her good-byes and followed Duane out to the car.

"Did you enjoy yourself?" he asked as they pulled away from the house.

"Yes. You have a wonderful family." His family had made her feel comfortable and at home.

He squeezed her hand lightly before releasing it. "I'm glad."

Leaning back on the seat with her eyes shut, Destiny tried not to make too much of the day's events. However, she couldn't help imagining what it would be like to be part of such a family. To be surrounded by so much love. She even went as far as to imagine a life as Duane's wife before opening her eyes and shaking off such foolishness. She stared out the window at the beautiful two-story homes as they headed toward the highway and thought about how much she had grown to love living in a house, with no one living above or below her. She was able to plant flowers and had even thought about growing a small vegetable garden. In such a short time she had learned to love all of the things she thought she had not wanted.

What am I going to do?

Destiny was lying on the couch in Duane's sitting room, with her legs draped over his lap, listening to the sounds of Jaheim playing in the background. Duane removed her shoes and massaged first one foot and then the other. Slowly, Duane's fingers moved in a rhythm she associated with making love. His lips then followed the path where his hands had worked their magic. Climbing up her leg, his tongue set off tremors that assaulted her senses.

"Raise up," he commanded in a low voice.

Doing as he asked, Destiny lifted her hips and then felt him slide her white thong down and off completely. He slid his fingers across her abdomen, traveling down to the apex of hair between her thighs.

She watched as he pulled her dress up over her waist, then using his hands, parted her thighs so that he could gaze freely at the feminine folds. Destiny felt like she was going to come apart as he took several long, agonizing seconds to visualize before his skillful fingers caressed and searched for her most sensitive point.

Finally, he inserted one finger, then another. Instantly, her body arched against his hand. Duane moved his fingers in and out with slow, torturous strokes.

"Duane, please," she moaned between panting breaths. Fire roared through her body. Tonight she didn't think she could survive the foreplay.

He raised her trembling legs to his shoulders and slid low onto the floor.

"Not yet, baby," he said. "I've got to taste you first." And then he lowered his mouth into the triangle of curls between her legs. With his fingers still inserted inside her body, his tongue caressed the swollen nub that was the core of her desire. She writhed in sweet ecstasy. He licked and stroked, causing lightning bolts of sensation to rip through her body.

The feeling was so intense, she wanted him to stop; her reaction was so strong, she wanted it to go on forever. She thrashed her head around on the cushion and moaned loudly. Together they established a rhythm. She pushed her hips up to meet each thrust of his finger as he moved in and out. No matter how much she moaned, he didn't stop. What he was doing felt so good, she couldn't hold still. She whimpered uncontrollably. Drowning in sweet agony, she couldn't hold on anymore and finally let go. She screamed as her entire body clenched around him as she exploded.

"You had enough?" he asked as her breathing slowed.

His warm breath tickled her sensitive flesh. She was breathing hard, uncontrollably. She was drained; however, she answered, "No . . . I can never have enough of you."

He lifted his head. Still on his knees, he met her gaze. "That's the answer I was hoping for." He stood and scooped her into his arms. "Let's go to bed."

He placed her in the center of his massive king-size bed. Quickly, he removed his shirt, then with Destiny's help, raised her dress over her head and let it fall onto the floor. With his lips pressed to hers, he pushed her backwards onto a pile of pillows.

His kiss made all of her thoughts disappear. He captured her mouth for a second, and then his lips and tongue trailed down the column of her neck, where he placed light kisses at the base. At the same time his hands drifted over her flesh as gently as a feather. Beneath him, Destiny twisted. Heat continued to build between her thighs.

While he caressed her with his fingertips, his lips traveled across her shoulder and finally stopped at her breasts. Destiny arched her back, trying to feel his lips against her nipples. Duane resisted a moment, barely brushing the tips, prolonging the agony. Finally, when she didn't think she could stand it a moment longer, he curled his tongue around a nipple. Destiny arched farther at the contact. His hot mouth and wet tongue sent sparks shooting through her veins. He suckled first one, then the other while she whimpered with joy. She couldn't hold still. Having to do something with her hands, Destiny rubbed her fingers across his head. Each suckle brought a clenching ache deep in her core.

Reaching down, she clasped his shoulders and dragged him back to her mouth. "Duane," she whispered, "I need you now!"

Duane stood and nearly ripped his clothes from his body, pulling them off faster than he ever had before. Taking a condom from his pocket, he handed it to her, then rejoined her on the bed. He watched as she rolled the condom over his hard length; then he lowered his weight on her. She opened her legs to make a place for him.

"Now?" he asked.

"Now," she said. She wrapped her legs around his hips. Duane cupped her buttocks as he slid deep into her.

Destiny gasped with joy. They moved together slowly at first. He pulled all the way out then back in again. She gripped his buttocks and pulled him deep inside of her. Bucking and grinding her hips, she forced him to move faster and deeper. Destiny could feel his muscles working as her hands traveled to his hips and back. She arched off the bed and was hit by a muscle contraction that shot to her toes. She cried out, and shortly after he also exploded.

Duane rolled off Destiny and gathered her in his arms. She snuggled against him and fell asleep.

Chapter 17

Duane lay in the drowsy warmth of his bed, watching Destiny sleep. He stroked her hair and listened to her deep breathing. What he wanted to do was wake her and make love to her again.

He feathered his fingers across her neck, then allowed his hand to continue to explore the precious corners of her face. Slowly, his hand glided down her neck and across her bare shoulders. He wanted to touch every area of her body, which he had already basted with his tongue. As his hand reached her breasts, his groin tightened. *Unbelievable.* He couldn't possibly want her again, yet he did. Shutting his eyes, he willed his emotions to behave, but that was impossible. He loved Destiny more than his own life. He felt hot tears burn at the backs of his eyelids. He couldn't let her walk out of his life. Everyone had at least one chance at finding true happiness, and he had found his with her. And now that he had her, he planned to do everything in his power to keep her here beside him.

Duane opened his eyes, determination shining from their depths. A confident smile tilted the

corners of his strong mouth as he made a silent vow.
Destiny was the woman he planned to marry. The
only woman he had ever truly loved. Those were
both reasons worth fighting for.

While Duane showered, Destiny padded down to
the kitchen to make breakfast. She removed a box
of pancake mix and a bowl from a cabinet, then
went to the refrigerator to find a pack of bacon.

It all seemed so quiet and so perfect, as if all was
right with the world. *How deceptive sex makes the
world seem.* She realized that since Duane had
stepped into her life, she had forgotten everything
that didn't involve him. In a way, she was glad that
he had helped to ease her mind. On the other
hand, she was worried that she had gotten too
comfortable and was asking for trouble.

She mixed the pancake batter and poured some
in a skillet. then she popped six slices of bacon in the
microwave. While the food cooked, she closed her
eyes and did something she never did enough of—
pray. She prayed for answers. She prayed for
strength. Lucas was out there looking for her. She
should be running, hiding. Instead, she was spending her days and nights with a man who made her
feel as if everything was right in her life. She had lowered her guard, and leaving was growing harder by
the day. With Duane, she felt fulfilled, complete—
and scared that she was endangering his life as well.

The timer went off on the microwave. She
opened her eyes and reached for the spatula. She
was turning the golden brown pancakes just as
Duane walked into the kitchen. He came up behind

her and rested both hands on the kitchen counter, making her his prisoner.

"That smells good," he murmured close to her ear.

A tender smile softened her face as she felt the light whisper of his breath against the back of her neck. "So do you," she crooned. He smelled clean and masculine.

Duane lightly kissed the side of her neck, traveling to nibble at her earlobe and down again. His lips tasted and teased, causing a deep ache between her legs. She closed her eyes and savored the feathery touch until a moan escaped between her parted lips. He wrapped his arms around her middle, and she leaned back against his bare chest, where heat radiated. She could almost feel him buried inside of her.

How easy it is to love him.

Her eyes flew up, and she froze as she realized what she had finally brought to the forefront. She not only loved Duane, but their souls were linked. The more she tried to resist, the harder it was to ignore. It was more than physical. She wanted Duane in her life longer than the next three weeks. She wanted him to be a permanent part of her life.

How could she leave him? When she did, she would be leaving behind a piece of herself. At that brief moment she was so confused, she froze, terrified beyond her control.

Duane felt her body stiffen. "What's wrong, baby?" he asked, with his chin resting lightly on her shoulder.

She shook her head. "Nothing. Now go have a seat while I get these pancakes off before they burn."

"Yes, ma'am," he said with mock seriousness. He

stepped away, and immediately, Destiny felt her temperature drop several degrees.

With a dramatic exhalation, Duane grumbled playfully, "A brotha can't get no love in his own house."

Destiny snorted. "I've given you plenty of love, all night and morning long. Now this sista needs some nourishment." She put the stack of fluffy pancakes on a plate, then swung around. "Now sit so I can feed you."

Duane's hands moved up and cupped her shoulders, pulling her close once more. His eyes were large and liquid, with desire swimming in their depths. "And when we're done, it will be my turn to feed you."

Destiny waited until mid-afternoon before she ejected the disk containing chapters of her novel *The Last Mile* from her computer and headed to Kinko's. Baseball cap and dark shades on, she turned right at the corner, her heart pounding fiercely.

After the woman had recognized her at the restaurant, Destiny didn't feel comfortable taking too many chances. She released a shaky sigh. She was tired of sneaking around. She was certain it was going to backfire sooner or later. She just prayed that it wasn't until after the trial. Then she could explain everything to Duane.

She loved him, and the sooner she could tell him, the better.

Duane followed Destiny at a far enough distance that she wouldn't spot him. After arriving at the job, he had decided to take the day off and spend it with Destiny. Percy was eager for the responsibility. After making sure the junior worker had the plumbing under control, Duane had headed home. He was just a block away from his house when he spotted Destiny driving down the street in that crazy cap and those bifocal glasses. Determined to find out what was going on, he had followed her.

Destiny pulled into a strip mall. Duane drove past, then made a U-turn at the corner. He scowled when he pulled into the parking lot and discovered she had already parked and gone into one of the stores. Now he would have to figure out which one.

He waited a few minutes, then climbed out his truck and casually walked past the shop windows, peeping in. After two attempts, he spotted her at the Kinko's on the end. Destiny was sitting at a computer in the back. What was she doing?

Destiny set up a free Internet account using the name Marcie London, then inserted her disk in the drive. With a few clicks of the mouse, she sent the finished chapters of her novel to Julia. She sighed. It had been easier to do than she thought it would be. Removing the disk, she strolled over to a pay phone in the corner of the store. Julia answered on the third ring.

"Julia Joyce."

"Julia, it's me."

"It's about time!" she practically screamed through the receiver. "You had me going out of my mind with worry. I thought you were sending me part of your novel over Memorial Day weekend?"

Destiny cleared her throat. "I've been preoccupied."

"Ooh! I can hear it in your voice. You are in love with that pipe layer."

Destiny chuckled. "His name is Duane Urban."

"Whatever, whomever, you've got it bad," Julia chuckled merrily.

Destiny sighed audibly. "Is it that obvious?"

"Yep. So tell all."

"Well, there isn't much to tell."

"Girl, who are you trying to fool?"

"You," she admitted.

They shared a laugh; then Destiny told her about the last couple of weeks.

"Joyce, I love him," she whispered at the close of her story. "I love him so much, it scares me. I know Lucas plays for keeps, and I don't want Duane involved in this at all. I would die before I allowed anything bad to happen to him."

"Does Duane know who you really are?"

Destiny drew in a quick breath. "No, and I prefer to keep it that way . . . for now. As soon as this is all over, I'll tell him everything."

"I hope you know what you're doing."

"I hope so, too." They chitchatted a little longer then Destiny got down to business and told Julia she had e-mailed her several chapters of *The Last Mile*. Shortly after, she ended the call.

Duane didn't even bother to wait to follow her back home. He had already seen enough. He drove around for a while trying to clear his head. When he finally pulled into his driveway, Destiny still hadn't returned home.

Feeling frustrated and needing something to occupy his mind until her return, he went to the garage, slipped on his work boots, and cranked up the lawn mower.

The grass had grown considerably since his last attempt at cutting it. The job would be perfect for Mannie, who had always enjoyed cutting Benny's grass. However, right now he had to do something to occupy his mind.

For the umpteenth time, he asked himself, what was she hiding?

As he completed half the yard, he spotted Destiny's car coming up the street. Watching her, he released the lever on the lawn mower, and the motor stopped. The only thing he heard was the pounding of his heart. Destiny climbed out of her car and waved.

"Hey, honey," she grinned. Gone were the cap and glasses, as if he had imagined it all.

Throwing her purse strap over her arm, she shut the car door and sashayed his way. Love heated the blood in his veins as he watched the provocative sway of her hips. Why couldn't she love him enough to be honest?

He stood in the middle of the yard, and she came to him, rested a hand on his chest, and leaned forward. Tilting his head, he met her sweet mouth.

"Can you do my yard next?"

"Where have you been?"

She met his direct stare. "I thought I'd hang out at the mall, but I didn't find anything."

Duane frowned. "I thought I saw you heading in the opposite direction."

Destiny blinked. Her smile flickered like a fading

lightbulb. "What are you doing? Spying on me again?"

"No, I just thought it was you."

She knew a quaver in her voice would betray her, so she tried to sound in control. "Well, it wasn't," she lied smoothly. An awkward moment of silence floated between them. "I need to go and let Champ out back. Are you coming by later?"

He stared down at the woman he loved, trying to understand why it was so easy for her to lie to him. "Maybe later. I'm going to go shoot some pool with Reyn this evening."

Her voice was terse as she turned on her heels and headed home. "All right. Well, call me when you get back."

Duane stood and watched her walk away, more confused than ever. He had given his heart to a woman who didn't trust him.

Destiny barely made it in the house. Shutting the front door, she collapsed on the floor. Duane knew she was up to something. She had lied to him, and he knew it. A quick shot of panic raced through her. Now what was she going to do?

Leaning back against the cool steel door, she closed her eyes and took a deep breath, trying to compose her shaky insides. Maybe betraying him had been a bad idea. Maybe it was time for her to take a chance on love and bear her soul. She shook her head of the scattered thoughts. She just didn't know what to do. She had thought it better to keep the truth from him, but now she wasn't so sure that was a smart move.

Champion came down the hall. She didn't open

her eyes until she felt his wet pink tongue on her nose.

"Stop!" Chuckling, she pushed him away. She then moved toward the back door so she could let him out.

While her dog dashed out into the yard, she stood inside the door, lost in her thoughts again. She would have to do some serious soul-searching. Nevertheless, when Duane arrived that evening, she was going to find a way to finally tell him the truth.

"You better not be wasting my time," the Hispanic man sneered impatiently.

"Not at all," the other man said to his boss as he nervously twirled the phone cord around his index finger. "She made a call today to her agent. Apparently, she sent her an e-mail."

"Did she say where she was?"

"N-no, but I'm sure it won't take much to get her agent to talk. However, she did mention a man."

"What man?" his boss barked.

"Someone named Duane Urban." He paused, unsure if he should mention the rest. "She's . . . in love."

There was a brief hesitation before his boss barked, "You find that bitch, and when you do, I want you to bring her to me!"

When his boss slammed the phone down, the man threw his head back and chuckled.

Chapter 18

After a near sleepless night, filled with the endless replaying of Chief Cook's death and haunted images of Jarvis, Destiny woke to find herself cold and alone. Moving her pillows against the headboard, she sank back against them and swallowed tightly as the myriad of painful memories swept over her.

She had never truly known what lonely was until Duane came into her life. He had made such an impression on her world. She found she no longer could sleep without him lying beside her.

Last night had been long. She ached for his touch, was haunted by his scent. Her bed had been cold without him snuggled behind her. Why hadn't he come to her? She pondered that question again as she rested her hands on her stomach. She had waited until midnight. Then angry and upset, she let her pride get in the way and refused to call him. As she drifted off to sleep, Destiny had tried to convince herself it was for the best. But it wasn't. She needed him. She needed Duane in her life.

Tired of lying there feeling sorry for herself,

Destiny climbed out of bed, took care of her dog, then completed a two-mile run on the treadmill. After a shower, she fixed a light breakfast of coffee and fruit. As she sipped her last cup of coffee, she heard Duane pull out of his driveway.

Destiny reached for the white clothes basket in the corner of her bedroom and carried it down to the small room behind the kitchen, with Champion following at her heels. Dumping the contents on the floor, she quickly sorted her dirty laundry into whites, darks, colors, and delicates. She then set the dial on the washing machine to COLD and START. Reaching for a bottle of Woolite, she poured a capful into the washing machine, then tossed in the yellow linen sundress she had worn to the barbecue.

She let Champion out in the backyard, and for the rest of the morning she tried to keep Duane off of her mind as she busied herself around the house vacuuming, dusting, and polishing furniture.

After lunch she moved to her office to work on the next chapter of her book. Instead, she found herself staring at the computer screen. She had no idea what she was typing. All of the words seemed to run together. Logging off the computer, she pushed her chair back. The house was clean, her laundry was done, and she had no motivation to write. At that moment she didn't have anything to do except sit and think about Duane.

Rising from her chair, she walked over to the window and stared across the street. His truck was still gone. She pressed her lips firmly together, trying to hold back the tears that threatened to fall. What happened to him last night? She thought that possibly he drank too much or had stayed out later than intended and didn't want to disturb her. But if that was so, why hadn't he come by this morning?

Folding her arms across her chest, she took a deep breath as the only real possibility came to mind. He was avoiding her. The million-dollar question was why?

Don't play dumb; you know why. He saw you yesterday, and you lied to him.

Destiny nibbled nervously on the inside of her lip as she contemplated her next move. What else could she do but tell him the truth, but after giving it more thought, she decided she wasn't ready to do that just yet. She would in time. *Please, Lord, let Duane be patient with me just a little bit longer. I promise to reveal everything to him when the time is right.*

As if her prayers had been heard, Duane's truck pulled into his driveway. She expelled a quick breath, composed her trembling body, and headed for the front door.

Duane slipped his muddy boots off his feet and stepped inside his house.

He had spent the morning fixing a crack in the foundation of a newly constructed home. In less than three years, the house had begun to settle, which caused a seven-foot crack to spread across a wall of its finished basement. The house had extensive damage, and its owner was unable to locate the builder for repairs and reimbursement. As he moved into the kitchen, he shook his head. He hated to hear about builders that skipped town after building less than standard housing.

He reached into the refrigerator and removed a can of iced tea. As he popped the tab, he heard the doorbell ring. He left the can on the counter, strolled through the house, and opened the front door to find Destiny standing on his porch.

She smiled. "I was wondering if I could borrow your lawn mower?"

He took in her T-shirt and spandex pants, which fit her like a glove. He stared at her running shoes, then reversed the journey up to her mouth. "I can cut your grass this evening."

Destiny shook her head as if she didn't want to impose. "No, I'll do it."

He lifted her off her feet, holding her so that their eyes were level. "I said, I'll do it."

Unable to resist, she curled her arms around his neck. "I missed you," she crooned. "My bed was lonely without you."

"So was mine."

Duane tugged her against him and in his frustration took her lips in hunger. He had given in. She didn't trust him and had lied to him as he had been lied to before. He was still angry about her lies. However, staying mad was difficult to do when Destiny stood before him looking vulnerable, and so damn enticing. She looked so gorgeous and appealing, how could he resist?

When he finished sampling her mouth, he lowered her back to the porch.

"How about I change and come over in a few minutes?"

Rising on tiptoes, she kissed his cheek. "I'll be waiting."

She turned and made her way across his driveway, feeling the heat of his gaze on her back. Glancing over her shoulder, she spotted Duane coming up behind her with a silly smirk on his face.

"Changed your mind?"

"No. I forgot to get my mail out of the box."

Destiny slowed and fell into step beside him. At the mailbox, she kissed him once more, then waved and stepped out into the street. The look she gave him promised something, and he couldn't wait to find out what it was.

As she stepped off the curb, something out the corner of Duane's eye caught his attention. Racing down the street was a black, late-model car.

Duane reacted on impulse. He dropped the mail in his hand and raced across the grass toward Destiny as he yelled, "Watch out!"

At the sound of his voice, Destiny froze in the street. The car was speeding toward her, and her eyes grew large, like those of a deer in front of headlights.

With a burst of speed, Duane dashed forward, grabbed her waist, and pushed her out of the way. The impact caused him to stumble forward, taking her with him. She screamed as she hit the grass just as the car whizzed by, leaving a gust of wind in its wake.

Destiny looked dazed as Duane rolled over and met her gaze. She was shaky and pale; her heart was pounding rapidly in her ears. The car was long gone. All she remembered was a racing black blur.

"Are you all right?" he asked.

Her shoulder throbbed, as it had taken the brunt of her fall, but otherwise she was fine. She nodded, unable to speak. Her lips trembled. The tremor began in her fingers but then traveled through her entire body. Soon she was shaking so hard that her teeth chattered.

Duane lifted her in his arms and carried her across the yard and up to her front door.

"I can walk," she insisted, pushing against his chest.

He slowly lowered her onto the porch. "Give me your key," he ordered.

Without any resistance, she handed him her key ring, then waited for him to open the door.

The door swung open. Champion was waiting anxiously on the other side. Duane rubbed his head, then ordered him to sit. He then gripped Destiny's shoulders and steered her toward the couch.

"Let me go grab my mail out of the street and lock my door; then I'll be right back."

She was saying something, at least her mouth was moving, but she had no idea if anything came out, so she simply nodded.

When he left, Destiny leaned against an armrest of the couch. Her head was spinning, and she had a sinking sensation in the pit of her stomach. Had Lucas found her? She glanced at the front door, which separated her from his goons. How in the world had she imagined she would be safe in this house? Two locks and a dead bolt were the only thing keeping them from getting to her. The burglar alarm would be useless. In the time it would take for the dispatcher to send out a patrol car, she would already be dead.

Duane returned and took a seat beside her. Destiny sat up and folded her legs beneath her.

"You're shaking."

All she wanted was for him to take her in his arms and hold her close to his chest until it was all over.

Duane tucked a knuckle under her chin and tilted her face toward him. "Can I do or get you anything?"

"Can you please hold me?" she whispered desperately.

Lowering his head, Duane brushed his mouth over hers. "I'll take care of you," he crooned, "I would give my life to keep you safe." He pulled her into his protective embrace.

A shiver ran across Duane's spine, and he held Destiny tighter until he had a leash on his anger at the person behind the wheel of that car. He pulled her over to his lap and cradled her close. He could feel the rapid beat of her heart. The near fatal accident had scared her, and she had every right to be scared. It had frightened him also. He closed his eyes. He didn't even want to think about what would have happened if he hadn't reacted as quickly as he had. He said a silent prayer of thanks.

"I don't know what I would have done if I lost you," he murmured as a soft strand of her hair brushed his lips.

Destiny pulled away to look in his eyes and saw something she had never noticed there before.

"I love you, Destiny." His brown eyes darkened.

"You love . . ." Her voice trembled, and the words trailed off. She stopped breathing for a second, stunned by his admission.

"I was prepared to die for you today if it had come to that," he confessed.

Tears of both love and guilt streamed from her eyes. She had finally found a man whom she truly loved and who loved her back, and yet it was all a lie.

Duane was in love with Destiny Davis, the graduate student. He knew nothing about Desiree Davidson, the author who just last year signed a million-dollar three-book deal.

She shook her head, finding it difficult to believe

that he cared so much about her. Duane was a simple man with simple pursuits and enjoyed a comfortable and simple lifestyle. What would he think of Desiree and her flamboyant style of living?

"Baby, what's wrong?" he asked, pulling her from her thoughts.

She looked down nervously in her lap, then back up at him. "I was just thinking about what you said about loving me." She narrowed her eyes against the sudden sting of tears, willing them not to fall.

"I do love you." Duane lowered his mouth and kissed her gently on the forehead, then added, "I feel like I have waited all my life for you. It seems that my past doesn't exist, and all I see is a future with you."

Her heart bubbled over with joy. She wanted so much to tell him that she loved him, too, but she couldn't, not yet. Not as long as he thought she was someone else.

Sadness lurked in her face as her fingers smoothed his cheek, her eyes searching his face. Duane looked disappointed that she hadn't said "I love you" back, but she couldn't think about that right now. She had bigger problems. Someone had tried to run her over. In the back of her mind, she didn't believe it had been an accident. Had they found her? God, she hoped not. She was too close to finally having everything she had always wanted in her life to have to watch someone else take that away. And if they had found her, then Duane's life was also in danger. She couldn't involve him, no matter how much she loved him.

She leaned forward kissing him hungrily, trying to let him know, the only way she could, how she felt. She finally eased away and sighed, suddenly feeling very tired.

"I want to lie down."

"How about I run you a hot bubble bath?" he suggested.

His kindness brought tears to her eyes. She looked down quickly and nodded.

Duane placed a finger beneath her chin and forced her to look at him. "Baby, everything is going to be okay. A hot bath will help you feel a world of good."

"I guess you're right."

"Lie here and watch television while I run your bath." He slipped from beneath her. Reaching for the remote, Duane clicked on the television and turned to the local news, then raced upstairs. He returned with a small flannel blanket and a pillow. He tossed the blanket across her feet, then put the pillow behind her back.

"Anything else I can get you?"

She met his piercing gaze, and she recognized the protective look in a flash. "How about a hug?"

He knelt beside her and put his arm around her and pulled her close. Destiny held on for dear life. In his arms she felt safe. All of her fears seemed to disappear. She nestled so trustingly in his arms. When she tilted her head back, he brought his mouth down over hers. He cradled her head in his arms and dropped light kisses on her mouth and cheek. Then he pulled back and gazed down at her with so much compassion, her heart jumped.

"Now relax."

He released her, then ascended the stairs again. A few seconds later she heard the water running. She was certain Duane had found the bottle of bubbles she kept on the side of the tub.

The television drew her attention. A woman had

been found murdered in an apartment not too far from her house from a single gunshot wound to the head at close range. At the time there were no suspects in custody. The possibility of the same thing happening to her made Destiny's head spin.

She wanted so badly to tell Duane the truth, but she couldn't take the risk of him knowing more than he needed to know. Destiny closed her eyes tightly. Too many thoughts racing through her head at once had given her a headache.

While she soaked in the tub, Duane tried to watch a new sitcom, but he was too pissed off at someone attempting to run over Destiny to focus.

After turning the television off, Duane rose from the couch, then went upstairs to make sure Destiny was okay. Moving toward the bathroom door, he found Destiny lying in the tub with her eyes closed. He decided not to disturb her and instead meandered down the hall to prepare her bed so she could lie down after she was done bathing. For the rest of the evening, he planned to wait on her hand and foot.

As he stepped into her room, something on the end of her dresser caught his attention. He reached down, picked up the sheet of paper, and discovered it was a fax cover sheet from Desiree Davidson to her agent, Julia Joyce.

"Who is Desiree Davidson, and why does that name ring a bell?" Then it hit him. The lady in the restaurant. His breathing stopped as he remembered her question.

Are you Desiree Davidson?

He expelled a long breath, hoping what he was thinking wasn't true. Destiny had betrayed him.

Duane set the paper back on the end of the dresser, then removed his cell phone from his waist and hit number four on his speed dial list.

"This had better be important," a voice grumbled.

"When did you start going to bed this early?"

Reyn yawned. "I did surveillance last night."

"Oh." Duane remembered the last case his brother had that entailed working around the clock with little to no sleep. "I need a favor," he finally said.

"I'm listening."

"This is strictly between you and me. I need you to check out someone for me."

Reyn hesitated. "This doesn't have anything to do with that gorgeous woman you brought home?"

Duane ran a hand across his head and sighed. "It has a lot to do with her." He shared his suspicions.

"Are you sure you want to do this?"

Duane hated that he had to take such measures, but he had a right to know the truth. "Yes, more sure than I've been about anything in a long time." His heart was on the line, and he needed to know which direction to go in from here. "I also want you to check on a Desiree Davidson and a Julia Joyce."

"Got it."

Shortly after, Duane ended the call and went downstairs to the living room.

He loved Destiny, but he didn't really know her, and that was only because there was a part of her that she was keeping from him. And he hadn't figured out why.

He knew how her body welcomed him deep inside her warmth and the sounds she made just before she released. But other than the time they had spent together and the things she had shared, he didn't really know her.

Taking a seat on the couch, he reached for the television remote and shook his head in disbelief. This was the second time he'd found himself in love with a woman only to discover she was hiding something.

The following morning, after Duane left for work, Destiny drove to Philadelphia and called her lawyer. Even though the location was too close for comfort, she used her prepaid calling card, hoping the caller ID would once again show a 708 area code. As soon as his secretary transferred her, she could hear the irritation in Chuck's voice.

"When are you returning?"

Destiny released an exasperated sigh. "I already told you . . . the day before the hearing."

"I think you should come back before the trial," he suggested, clearly unhappy about the whole thing.

"Don't worry; I'll be there," she reassured him. "Any new developments?"

"Nothing more than I've already told you. They still haven't found Hector." At her silence, he continued. "I'm sorry about your friend."

Destiny's response was instantaneous. "What friend?"

"You haven't heard?"

The hairs on the back of her neck stood at attention. "Heard what?"

There was a long pause.

"Chuck, tell me who you are referring to," she demanded.

There was another pause before she heard Chuck's strained voice. "Desiree, I really don't feel—"

"Dammit! I have a right to know what you're talking about," she snapped over the line.

"Julia Joyce is dead."

His words dropped Destiny to her knees.

Chapter 19

Her breathing stopped, then started again. *Oh no! Not Julia.* Tears pushed to the surface.

"Desiree? Desiree, are you still there?"

Hand shaking, she returned the receiver to her ear. "I'm here. What happened?"

"She drowned in her tub."

Drowned. Her head was spinning. Stifling a cry, she whispered, "I've got to go."

"Desiree, wait—"

Destiny hung up before she heard any more and dialed Julia's office. She just couldn't believe it. She didn't want to believe it. There was still a chance that Chuck was wrong. *Please let her be there*, her mind screamed as the phone rang . . . once . . . twice.

"Julia Joyce Literary Agency."

She covered her mouth with her hand, trying to think past her shock. "Yes, is . . . is Julia available?"

"I'm sorry. This is the answering service. The office is closed today."

She closed her eyes as her world tilted on its axis. "When will she be back?"

"I'm not sure. As of right now—"

She didn't hear any more. Her hand loosened its grip, and the phone dropped, the cord swinging back and forth. She was shaking. Her vision was blurred. She closed her eyes, trying to stop the sudden spill of tears, but it was useless.

By the time Destiny reached her car, the dam had burst, and she fell against the hood weeping. This couldn't be happening!

Clutching her stomach, she groaned, "Oh, God! I'm going to be sick."

She stood by the side of her car, and with loud retching sounds, emptied the contents of her stomach.

Duane picked up a pink toilet and vanity that had been special-ordered and headed home. He was scheduled to install them tomorrow.

Destiny's car was in front of her house. Anxious to see her, he strolled across the street and knocked on the front door. When she answered the door, she stood behind it, so Duane wasn't able to see her.

He stepped into the foyer and leaned over to pat Champion on top of his head, while Destiny headed down the hall.

"Have you already eaten?" he asked her retreating back.

She shook her head without turning around.

Duane followed her into the kitchen. "I was thinking about going to this barbecue joint not too far from here and picking up some—" He stopped talking when he suddenly noticed her eyes were red and swollen. "Baby, what's wrong?"

Destiny tried to pull herself together. Her eyes burned and her nose itched. Choking back a sob, she spun away before Duane could witness her humiliating tears.

"Nothing. I've got a lot on my mind and just need to be by myself."

Duane looked at her as she wiped the tears away from her eyes. He knew he should do as she asked but couldn't. "I'm a good listener," he offered.

She wished she could tell him everything, who she really was, what had happened to her good friend, but she couldn't. She just could not. "I know and I appreciate it. Right now I'm just hurt . . . hurting too much to talk." Her voice cracked. She quickly moved down the hall toward the living room and took a seat on the couch.

Duane refused to leave her that way. He had to find out what was bothering her, what was going on with her. Hopefully, Reyn would call soon with the information he had requested. In the meantime, he would have to find a way to get her to open up to him.

He followed her into the living room and knelt down on the floor in front of her. "There's no reason why you have to go through this alone." He then raised his hand to stroke her cheek, his eyes glowing with kindness. "Talking about it does help."

Destiny looked down, shook her head, and tried to hold her voice steady. "I'm okay. Really I am." She leaned into his rough palm while warm tears ran down her cheeks.

"No, you're not okay." He rose and took a seat beside her. "Don't you know people always look away when they're lying?"

She continued to look down.

"Destiny, honey," he said. The intimacy of his tone made her heart skip a beat. "How about I hold you?"

Her throat was tight with tension. "Okay."

He gathered her in his arms, and he held her close, patting her back in a comforting manner. When she felt Duane's fingers close around hers, she grabbed him tightly, holding on because she needed to hold on to something. She rested her head against his chest, shut her eyes, and listened to the steady beat of his heart. She could have stayed there forever, safe and comforted by his strength. Then she wouldn't have to remember anything. For just one moment she wanted to forget Desiree Davidson and all of her problems.

"This is so unreal," she whispered between sobs, her voice smothered against his solid chest.

He held her while she cried soft, painful sobs, which he felt. He held her, feeling helpless, unsure of what to say or how to calm her. So he closed his eyes and said a silent prayer that everything would be okay.

Finally, Destiny's sobs slowed into soft sniffles. With comforting strokes, he rubbed a tense spot at the center of her back. His shirt was damp against her cheek. The steady beat of his heart and the rise and fall of his chest made her aware of his strength. She wished she could stay wrapped in his protective arms until her world returned to the way it once was, but she knew that wasn't possible.

Moving out of his embrace, she hung her head, feeling the weight of Julia's death on her shoulders. Her friend was gone, and she was responsible.

With his index finger, Duane caught the next tear before it could fall and looked at her with so much concern, it sent shivers coursing through her. "Ready to tell me what's wrong?"

Sniffling, she squeezed her eyes shut, asked God

for strength, then opened them and said, "A dear friend of mine drowned."

Duane lifted her onto his lap. "I'm so sorry for your loss. Do you know what happened?"

Destiny closed her eyes tightly, trying to block the fact that she was the reason why Julia Joyce had been murdered.

She should have known Lucas would question her agent about her whereabouts. She just never imagined that it would go this far. He had taken away everything and everyone she had known and loved, which was why she couldn't tell Duane the truth.

Her throat convulsed with a heavy swallow. "No, I was too upset to get all of the details. All I know is she . . . she drowned in her bathtub!" she sobbed.

Duane pulled her against him and pressed his lips against the top of her head. For the longest time he held her, rocking her back and forth while whispering near her ear, "Everything is going to be okay." When her sobs quieted, she heard him say, "If you'd like me to go back with you, I will."

She raised her head to stare at him with a puzzled look.

"Your friend's funeral . . . I'll go with you if you'd like."

She closed her eyes as the tears began again. She was touched by his offer. Truly touched. But it wasn't possible. She wouldn't get a chance to say good-bye.

Destiny pressed her cheek against his chest, "It's too late. The funeral was today," she lied.

"I'm so sorry. Baby, if there is anything I can do, I'm here for you." His warm breath and masculine scent surrounded her.

When his lips brushed her temples with a whispery

soft caress, she felt as if she had awakened from a bad dream. Tilting her head, Destiny kissed him. Tonight she wanted only to feel and to forget about Julia and Jarvis, who had both died because of their involvement with her. She wanted to forget about Lucas and the FBI's case. All she wanted to do was feel.

She pulled Duane closer, and he kissed her. Instinctively, she parted her lips, inviting the mating of his tongue. A primitive passion beat in her blood and drummed in her ears.

Her heart hammered hard. She felt the energy in his hands as they explored her face, her throat, and a powerful shiver passed through her.

"Duane," she said, pulling away from their kiss and looking up into those eyes that made her believe anything was possible. "I need you."

His gaze was intense. "Are you sure?"

She nodded.

Duane carried her up to her bedroom and laid her gently at the center of the bed. Then he removed her clothes. He stared down at her, taking it all in—the creamy smoothness of her skin, the feminine curves of her breasts and hips. Then he kissed her from head to toe and back again. She returned his caresses and clung to him as if she was afraid he'd leave her. He cherished every inch of her with his mouth, and when they both couldn't stand it another second, he slid into her body and made slow, sweet love to her.

Only when he was buried deep inside of her and she was whimpering his name did he let loose the feeling pouring through him. He filled her again and again, with each thrust the tension increasing, until finally the sensual dance ended with an explosion of pure pleasure that left both of them breathing hard and shaking uncontrollably.

Duane held on to her as their breathing returned to normal. Shortly after Destiny fell asleep, he, too, drifted off.

Chapter 20

Destiny spent the next two days in bed, mourning the loss of her friend. Duane left her in the morning but came to her at lunchtime and again in the evening. He even brought Mannie over to spend time with Champion, whom she had unconsciously ignored.

On the third day, Destiny hopped out of bed. Fully dressed, she moved into her office and logged on to her computer. She had a book to finish. She had made a promise to Julia, and the last thing she wanted to do was to break her contract. It had meant as much to her agent as it did to her.

Wiping the tears away, she began her next chapter of *The Last Mile*. The words flowed easily, and before she knew it, half the day had passed.

Glancing over at the clock, Destiny realized it was lunchtime. She logged off the computer and went down to let Champion out and to make a salad. After lunch she was tired, so she lay down on the couch and turned on a soap opera she hadn't watched in a year.

She wasn't sure how long she had been asleep before Duane appeared.

"Wake up sleepyhead. We've got things to do today."

She opened one eye and found him standing beside her, holding a cup of coffee. "What things?" she asked.

He took a seat beside her, and his gaze wandered down her bare legs. Her shorts left little to the imagination. "Mannie's spelling bee is today. Then I want to take you to one of my favorite restaurants."

"Oh, I almost forgot about the spelling bee. I wouldn't dream of disappointing him." With a groan, she sat up on the couch and took the cup from Duane's proffered hand. "Thanks." She took several sips while Duane went to the window and stared out.

"It looks like rain."

"Uh-huh," she murmured against the rim of her cup as she admired the view. She thought he had the nicest behind—narrow waist with just enough curves to look good in a pair of jeans.

After taking another sip, she placed her cup on the end table. "I need to take a shower."

Duane swung around and smirked. "We would save water if we shared a shower."

She grinned. "Is that so?"

He turned and moved toward her. "Yep, that's so."

She felt happy with Duane smiling down at her. "I think that can be arranged."

Duane reached out and took her hand. Destiny rose and leaned against him. "Good," he whispered.

Destiny wasn't sure if they had time to make love with only an hour before the spelling bee, but Duane made time as he carried her upstairs.

After a short, sensuous hot shower, they drove to Drew Elementary. As they were taking their seats, Mannie spotted them, and Destiny noticed his shoulders sag with relief. Tears burned at the corners of her eyes. The poor little boy hadn't expected them to keep their promise. She waved and blew him a kiss just so he would know how happy she was to be there.

Mannie made it to the last round and lost when he missed the word *accelerated*. Even though he hadn't won, he qualified as the first runner-up and would compete in the event that the winner, Tyler Collins, was unable to fulfill his duties.

Destiny and Duane went down to the stage to congratulate him. To her amazement, Mannie wrapped his arms tightly around her waist. She was so touched, there was no way to control the tears that ran down her cheeks. Before he returned to his class, they made plans to pick him up over the weekend.

Duane's favorite restaurant happened to be a small Jamaican establishment on a small side street. As they walked in the door, they were greeted by the sounds of reggae music coming from a stereo in the corner of the room. There were a few other patrons sitting and enjoying their meal. They found a table in the corner.

"What do you suggest?" Destiny asked.

"Definitely the jerk chicken, and rice and beans."

She smiled. "Sounds delicious."

The waitress took their orders and returned shortly with their drinks.

Duane leaned across the table and cupped her hand with his. "How are you feeling today?"

"Better. Much better."

"Good. You look better."

"I know I can't give up living. Julia would haunt me if I did." With a soft chuckle, she closed her lids momentarily as she remembered her friend's enchanting smile. A lump formed in her throat. She was definitely going to miss her.

Destiny descended the stairs and strolled into the kitchen. A bowl of popcorn and she was back to the computer, she promised herself. She went inside the pantry and removed a bag of popcorn and stuck it into the microwave. After pressing the button labeled POPCORN, she turned to the window and stared out. It was so dark out that all she could see was her reflection in the glass. She ran a hand across her hair. It was amazing how she had gotten used to the style in such a short period of time. The new look took years off of her age. In fact, she looked so much younger, she wasn't sure if she was going to change it back when she returned home.

Home.

Her shoulders sagged slightly as she thought of her time in Delaware. She never would have guessed she would fall in love with the East Coast. Yet, it had happened. The beaches, the big old house . . . and Duane.

She was head over heels in love with Duane.

At one time, Destiny had thought Lucas was her soul mate, but after being a part of Duane's life, she realized that she never truly knew what love was until now. Now that she had found it, what was she going to do?

She couldn't continue to hide out in Delaware. She had to prepare for her return home. The trial was only days away. Then what? What would happen after that? Resume her life in St. Louis? Back to living in her condo, where she had a maid? Back to driving her Mercedes SLK? She had a book scheduled for release in September, which meant her publicist would be arranging a twenty-city book tour for her.

Somehow going home and returning to her old life made her feel sad instead of excited, which was how she had once felt. None of it meant anything to her anymore. She would give it up in a heartbeat and spend her life right there with Duane.

Then what's the problem?

She still hadn't told Duane the truth, and she wasn't sure how he was going to react. He had every right to be mad when he discovered he didn't even know her real name.

The microwave beeped, breaking into her thoughts. With a deep sigh, she reached for a bowl and poured the popcorn in. Reaching inside the refrigerator, she removed a can of Diet Pepsi. Normally she brought Champ a nightly snack, but she had learned that he loved popcorn so he would get a few kernels. Glancing around, she was surprised that he hadn't followed her down the stairs. She shut the refrigerator door with her hip.

"Well, Desiree. We finally meet again," said a man with a distinguished Hispanic accent.

Spinning around, she dropped the bowl of popcorn, and it crashed at her feet, along with the soda can.

She should have known Lucas would send Hector to do his dirty work. The Puerto Rican's loyalty made her sick.

Staring up at him, she found his smile was cold and lacking humor.

"What do you want?" She didn't realize she'd asked the ridiculous question until it was already out of her mouth.

He chuckled so loudly that his stomach jiggled like gelatin. As usual, the sound of him gave her the creeps.

"Now why would you ask a stupid question like that, *chica*? You know why I'm here. I've come to take you back."

"Why would you do that?"

"Because Mr. Blake wants to kill you himself." Her breath caught in her throat, and it took her a second before she realized he was holding a gun.

At least I'm not going to die right now.

She spit at his feet.

Drawing back, Hector slapped Destiny, splitting her lip, bloodying her nose, and snapping her head back. "I knew it was just a matter of time before you pissed me off."

Waving the gun, he signaled for her to follow him into the other room.

"Where are we going?"

His dark eyes sliced down upon her. "*¡Callate!* Let me ask all the questions."

He had told her to shut up, and Destiny thought it wise to comply. Hearing whimpering, she glanced up the flight of stairs.

"You have a lovely dog."

"What did you do to him?" she demanded to know.

"Nothing compared to what I am going to do to you." He chuckled again.

He touched her cheek, rubbing one finger down

the length of her face and stopping at her neck. "Mr. Blake always did have good taste in women."

She pushed his hand away. "Don't touch me."

"Then you better do as I say; otherwise I'll kill you myself."

Duane pulled away from Reyn's apartment puzzled and confused. His brother's investigation had revealed that Destiny was, in fact, Desiree Davidson, the mystery writer.

Why had she deceived him?

He had seen the reports, and even her picture. His anger had lessened when he discovered that in her picture she looked exactly the way he thought she should look—with long cinnamon hair that he could curl around his fingers.

He had been willing to accept her betrayal and to hear an explanation until Reyn had handed him her first book, *The Hideout*. After reading the synopsis on the inside jacket, he was hot around the collar. *Destiny Davis*. She was impersonating a character from her book.

He had felt like such a fool. There was more. There was an entire file full of reading, but he had seen and read more than enough. Now he wanted to hear the truth. After that, he planned to walk away before he caused himself any more heartbreak.

Turning onto their street, he felt his mood soften. Shaking his head, he ignored the pounding of his heart. He was not going to fall for tears. He had one mission and one mission only, and that was getting an explanation tonight. Patting the folder on the seat beside him, he vowed to use the information only if necessary.

He pulled his truck in his driveway. Shutting the door, he glanced over at her house and saw the silhouette of two figures in the living room window. His brow bunched with curiosity. As far as he knew, the only other acquaintance Destiny had in the area was Simone.

He had spoken to Simone the day after Destiny discovered her friend had passed and had told their new neighbor that it was not a good time for Destiny to receive visitors. She had commented that she was going away for the weekend but would check in on Destiny when she got back. So it couldn't be her. Besides, the second silhouette was much larger.

A shiver raced through his blood. He had a strange feeling something wasn't right.

Instincts told him to check it out. Duane quietly dashed across the street and rounded the side of the house, listening for voices. He moved closer to the living room window and strained his ears. After several seconds he heard a low voice with a distinguished accent.

"*¡Vamos!*" Hector commanded.

"Go? Where are you taking me?" he heard Destiny ask. Her voice was high and shaky.

"You'll find out soon enough."

Duane clenched his fist in frustration. He had no idea what was going on. All he knew was that Destiny was in trouble. His heart was pounding furiously as he tried to decide what to do. If he made a move for the front door, he might be putting her life in danger. He heard the locks turn and the door open. He quickly dashed into the bushes beneath the living room window and waited. It wasn't long before he saw Destiny come down the stairs, followed by a large, beefy guy. Duane clenched his teeth and waited. As he hoped, Hector tripped over a wide crack in the sidewalk just outside the front door. The moment he lost his grip on Destiny, Duane jumped out of the bushes and tackled the man to the ground. Destiny shrieked, but his focus was on the man who had intended to hurt the woman he loved. Hector cursed and raised his fist and aimed it at Duane. Duane blocked the punch and sent the fat man one, which hit him square in the jaw.

It was dark out so seeing someone dressed in all black was quite difficult. Duane managed to roll on top of Hector. He felt something cold beneath him before he kicked it away. A gun, he'd had a gun on Destiny. Hector struggled beneath him and took a swing at Duane just as he hit him in the stomach. As Duane grabbed him around the neck, Hector caught him off guard and landed one on the side of his jaw.

Ignoring the pain, Duane gripped him tightly around the throat. Before he lost consciousness, Hector picked up a handful of dirt and tossed it into Duane's eyes. Blinded, Duane released his grip and wiped the dirt away.

It was just the opportunity Hector was waiting for. Before Duane had a chance to get the dirt out of his eyes, Hector threw Duane off of him. While black spots danced before Duane's eyes, Hector jabbed a quick knee in his groin. As Duane was beginning to get his bearings, he heard something break, and Hector fell to the ground.

Rubbing his eyes clear, Duane glanced up to find Destiny standing over her attacker with a broken flowerpot in her hand. The other half was lying in the grass beside the motionless man.

"Are you all right?" she asked.

Duane nodded and rose to his feet. "About as good as one can expect. How about yourself?"

"I'm all right," she answered as she dropped the flowerpot on the ground.

Duane glanced again at the lifeless body, then back at Destiny's frightened face. "Who the hell was that?"

"I-I don't know," she answered around a sob.

"I think you do know." He stared at her, pressing the issue because he already knew for a fact she was hiding a great deal about herself.

Duane moved to her. Destiny went to him willingly and seemed to melt against him. Her breasts pressed against him, and her hands cupped his shoulders. He was flooded by emotions. He was mad and angry at Destiny, while at the same time, he was scared for her life. She was in danger, yet she refused to level with him.

"Duane, I'm scared," she wailed as if she could read his mind.

"It's okay, baby. I'm right here, and everything is gonna be okay," he soothed. All he wanted was to hold her and thank God she was alive. He buried his face in her hair and inhaled the familiar scent.

"Duane, I'm so sorry," she sighed.

He tilted her face up and stared down into the depths of her eyes and forgot the reason why a man was laying unconscious in her front yard. The sound of Duane's beating heart drowned out the sound of sirens moving closer. He was oblivious to the neighbors standing out on their porches, curious about what was going on in their relatively quiet neighborhood.

He gathered Destiny closer, then lowered his

mouth against hers. She made a small whimpering sound, which only added to his out-of-control need. He increased the pressure of his lips on hers, urging her to open hers.

"Duane," she gasped into his mouth.

Both desire and fear seemed to flow back and forth between them. Destiny's hands moved restlessly along his back and up to his face. When she felt him flinch, she ended the kiss and stepped away.

"Are you hurt?"

"I'll be fine." He felt himself floating back from heaven and onto his street again. The spell had been broken.

"No, you're not. You're in pain."

Just then two patrol cars rolled onto their street, then stopped in front of her house. Glancing down at the man, Duane draped an arm around Destiny's waist and steered her toward the street.

"We'll worry about me later. Right now, young lady, you've got a lot of explaining to do."

Duane rubbed Champion behind his ear. The dog was still slightly drowsy from the sedative Hector had given him, but there appeared to be no long-term effect.

Glancing over at Destiny, he wanted to press for answers. In fact, he wanted to demand answers, which he was pretty sure he wasn't going to get considering the story she had given to the police.

As far as he was concerned, Destiny had failed to explain the real reason why the man was in her house. According to Destiny, she had never seen the guy before, and it was a case of mistaken identity. She said the man insisted that she was some woman whose name she so conveniently couldn't remember. She had tried to explain, but he refused to listen and had led her from her house at gunpoint.

Tonight Duane was going to demand that she come clean. He glanced down at his watch then over at her as she walked the last two officers to the door. It had been three hours since the attack. Before midnight he expected to know the truth. As far as he was concerned, the sooner the better because all of the lying was starting to make him uneasy.

He loved Destiny and had hoped that before now she would have told him the truth. Only she hadn't, and now he was beginning to wonder what the extent of her feelings were. Did she love him, too? She had never said it, but the way she looked at him at times told him everything that words couldn't.

The front door closed, and he looked up to find her standing in the doorway.

"How about some hot chocolate?" she asked.

He took in the dark circles beneath her eyes. Her lids were red and puffy. "Sounds good."

Without another word, she turned and headed to the kitchen with her four-legged friend close behind. Duane waited until the count of twenty before he rose and followed her.

"Destiny, I want the truth," he demanded the moment he stepped into the room.

She pulled a box of hot chocolate from the top shelf of the pantry, then glanced over her shoulder and gave him a puzzled look. "What truth? I already told you everything I know." Taking out two packages, she tore them open and poured the contents in two mugs.

"So you're saying you don't know who that guy is?"

She shook her head without looking up.

Duane's jaw twitched with anger. She had no intentions of telling him who she really was. How could he have fallen in love with a woman he really didn't know? How could he love a woman he couldn't even trust? She gave him no other choice.

"I know who you are."

She almost dropped the mug she was putting into the microwave. Even with her back to him, he could tell that she was trying to pull herself together. She punched two minutes on the microwave, then turned and faced him.

"What are you talking about?"

He moved forward until he was standing directly in front of her. An inch more and their knees would be touching. "I know that your real name is Desiree Davidson."

She swayed slightly to the right, and he reached his hand out in time to stop her from falling.

"Why don't you take a seat so we can talk?"

She simply nodded as he steered her over to the kitchen table, where he pulled out a chair for her to sit on.

"How do you know—" She stopped abruptly, stunned into silence.

"It doesn't matter. All that matters is why you haven't bothered to tell me the truth."

She lowered her head, shoulders slumped in defeat. She must have left a document lying around, or perhaps he had found one of her pictures lying around the house with her name scribbled across the back. She had gotten careless. How else could he have found out? How had Hector found out where she had been hiding? She had slipped, and tonight it had almost cost her her life.

She took a deep breath and tilted her head and met Duane's intense stare. A burden had been lifted from her chest. She was glad he had discovered the truth. "My life is in danger."

"But why couldn't you share that with me? I told you that I loved you, that I would give my life for you. Doesn't that mean something to you?"

"It's because I love you that I didn't tell you the truth."

He gave a laugh that sent a chill down her spine.

Her shoulders tensed defensively. "It's the truth. I planned on telling you the truth after everything was over. If Lucas found out that I was involved with you, he would've had you killed. Too many people have already died. I couldn't bear for you to be next." Tears stung the corners of her eyes, but she pushed them back. She refused to cry.

Duane silently watched her for a long moment, stroking his chin with his fingers. His look was intense as he waited for her to continue.

She inhaled, and then let her breath out slowly. He had a right to know the truth. "I witnessed the murder of an important public official. The man who did it was my fiancé. I went into police protection and discovered the FBI had been watching Lucas for some time. Apparently, he was the biggest drug dealer in the Midwest." Unable to sit still, she rose from her chair and began to pace the kitchen floor. "I slept and lived with that man for two years and had no idea he was into drugs and guns. He had half the police department on his payroll. I was scared for my life and thought the FBI could protect me, but they couldn't." Her voice trailed off as she thought of Jarvis Jackson's death.

"Did you know the man who was here tonight?"

She leaned against the counter, with her arms folded beneath her breasts, and nodded. "The police have been keeping a tail on all of Lucas's men since the bail hearing, yet somehow Hector managed to slip away."

"We need to tell the police."

She pushed off from the counter. "No! Please don't do that."

Duane felt the pulse of anger quicken inside him. "Why not?"

She threw both arms high in the air and let them land by her sides. "Because I can't." At his silence, she added, "Promise me." She looked up at him, her eyes pleading with him to understand.

Duane saw the silent plea in her eyes and realized he could not deny her anything.

"I promise. But only if you tell me everything."

The hot chocolate was quickly forgotten as Duane took Destiny's hand and led her into the living room. He escorted her over to the couch and took a seat beside her.

She pursed her lips and briefly shut her eyes.

She left nothing out. Her voice was shaky and erratic as she told him every detail. She told him how she and Lucas met. The way she had looked the other way even when she had known something wasn't right. She talked about the first death, then Jarvis. The entire time Duane cradled her in his arms like a newborn baby and murmured words of comfort. Her eyes were red from crying when she finished the last sentence, which lingered in the quiet room like a faded whisper.

"I was so scared and so alone."

"You'll never have to worry about being alone again."

He carried her to bed and held her. Long after she was asleep with her head resting on his chest and his arms tightly around her, Duane thought about Destiny and where they were going from here. He knew that she needed everything he had to offer. She needed someone to stand by her, someone who was willing to hang in for the long haul. She was used to disappointments. And he would rather die than disappoint her.

Duane pressed a kiss at her nape and closed his eyes. As he began to drift off, he wondered if she was staying solely because she was hiding and had no other choice, or because she wanted to be with him. And when it was all said and done, would she stay or would she return to her prior life? Would he play any part in her decision?

Chapter 21

Destiny rose early the next morning. Without waking Duane, she eased out from under him and tiptoed to her office. It was almost nine. A flow of heat surged through her body and warmed her heart. Duane was planning to spend the day with her.

She was glad to have him in her corner. With everything going on, she didn't know how she would get through the next week without him. After that . . . she just wasn't sure what would happen. She couldn't think about that. Right now the only thing she needed to focus on was getting back to St. Louis safely to testify.

Picking up the phone, she dialed her lawyer's office. There was no point in driving across town to place the call. Lucas, obviously, already knew where she lived.

"Law offices."

"Chuck, please."

He immediately picked up the phone. "Desiree, where have you been? I've been waiting for you to call me back."

It felt strange hearing someone refer to her as Desiree. "I'm here now."

"We need to meet before the trial begins."

She pressed her lips together and stared out the window. "I'll be home the day before."

"I need you to come back sooner than that."

Gripping the phone tightly, she took a breath. "I can't. I had a visit from Hector. He tried to bring me back at gunpoint."

"Dear God," he gasped. "Are you okay?"

"I'm fine now," she reassured.

"Thank goodness. Well, it might be a relief to know that Lucas was caught yesterday trying to charter a plane to Mexico."

She released a cry of relief. "Thank God." She wouldn't have to worry about him popping up at her door.

"He will be held without bail until the trial."

"Now I can sleep easy," she murmured as she crossed the room, eyes filling with tears.

"I would really feel better if you were still under police protection."

She forced a laugh. "Chuck, I am happy where I am and probably a million times safer than I would be there. Chief Cook was dirty, and there were several other cops who were on his payroll. Someone told Lucas where I was hiding. I just can't afford to have that happen again."

"You're right. Chief Cook was dirty. The DA has turned that precinct upside down. It seems that there were quite a lot of things going on and that Lucas was the icing on the cake."

She wiped her eyes with the back of her hand. "I

knew something was going on. Why else would he have been at Lucas's house."

"Promise me you'll call me in a couple of days."

"I promise," she said soothingly.

Hanging up, Destiny felt a sense of relief hearing that Lucas was back in prison. It would all be over soon. Anxious to share her news, she returned to her bedroom and found Duane sitting up in the bed.

She flopped down beside him and curled one leg beneath her. "Guess what?"

"It must be something good the way you're smiling."

She nodded and told him everything Chuck had told her.

"When are you returning to St. Louis to testify in court?"

"Next Friday." She paused and looked at him, eyes narrowed. "How do you know I'm supposed to testify?" She clearly did not remember telling him that.

Duane hesitated. "When I first suspected something was going on, I asked Reyn to check you out."

Easing back, she glared at him. "Check me out? Y-you had your brother snooping in my personal life?" She looked as if she'd been struck in the face. There was no way she was hearing him right.

Duane forced a smile he wasn't feeling. "What choice did I have? You obviously weren't going to tell me the truth."

She kept her gaze steady. "Then you should have respected my privacy."

"I had every right."

His words stabbed at her. Why was he trying to make her feel like she was the bad guy? Her expression was hard: lines were drawn beside her mouth and between her eyebrows. "It was none of your business."

He reached up and caught her shoulders in his large hands. "I made it my business when I fell in love with you. You knew who you were sleeping with . . . I didn't."

"That's unfair!" she shot back.

"You're right, it is . . . Destiny, or should I start calling you Desiree."

She trembled with fury and swung his pants at him. "Get out of my house," she said with much more venom than she meant to deliver.

"Destiny, this isn't the time to be unreasonable."

Her nostrils flared. "Unreasonable. How dare you snoop in my private life!" She wrapped her arms around herself and dropped her gaze to the floor. "I don't need your protection. Hector's gone, Lucas is in jail awaiting trial, and the police have everything else under control." She threw her arms in the air. "I can't believe this. How can we have a relationship without trust?"

"I don't know. You tell me?"

She stuck her foot in that one. However, she had a legitimate reason for not telling him who she was. He had no right snooping in her life. His curiosity could have jeopardized everything.

Her rage rendered her speechless. When the silence became unbearable, she rose from the bed. Ignoring him, she pulled on a pair of shorts and grabbed her shoes. "I'm taking Champion for a walk. Be gone when I get back." She then signaled for her dog to follow and descended the stairs and went out the front door.

* * *

After a sleepless night, Destiny was still in a foul mood. How dare Duane hire his brother to snoop around in her life? Just knowing that made her feel violated. She felt betrayed.

After rising at six, she had spent the majority of the morning finishing the next scene of her book. All she could think about was Duane. She didn't have much of a choice being that she had molded her hero after him.

Despite what he had done to her, she missed him. She missed him so much, she ached inside. Shaking her head, she brushed her feelings to the back of her mind and resumed her work.

Champion barked, signaling that someone was at the door.

Destiny's heart fluttered; then her anger returned. She dashed down the stairs to the door and swung it open. It couldn't be anybody but Duane.

"I thought I told you—" She stopped abruptly when she saw Simone standing where she had expected to see Duane.

"Told me what?" Simone asked.

Destiny dropped her shoulders and opened the door wide so that Simone could enter. "Oh, I'm sorry. I thought you were someone else."

"A handsome contractor by any chance?" Her lips twitched with amusement.

She signaled for Simone to follow her into the kitchen, where Champion was drinking from his dish. Noticing her, he began to growl.

"Champion, no!"

Simone waved her hand. "It's okay. I guess he isn't

used to me." She reached into her purse. "Here, I brought something." Reaching into her purse she removed a small bone.

Champion walked up to her and stopped at her feet.

"Does that mean I get to rub you?"

His tail wagged, and she reached down, rubbed him behind the ear, then handed him the bone.

"That was nice of you," Destiny said as she moved toward the back door and let Champion out with his bone.

Simone smiled triumphantly. "I am determined to get him to like me."

Destiny shook her head. "They say food is the way to a man's heart. I believe that also works with dogs." Laughing, she strolled over to the refrigerator. "Would you like some iced tea?"

"That would be great." Simone took a seat. Clad in jeans, she crossed her legs out in front of her. "What happened here this weekend? The whole house has been buzzing about two men who tried to rob your house and tied you up at gunpoint. Mrs. Kelly said Duane shot one, and the other he caught in a headlock and broke his neck just as the cops arrived."

Destiny rolled her eyes heavenward. She laughed as she carried two glasses of tea over to the kitchen table. "Oh, brother!" she chuckled. "That old woman obviously watches too much television." Without revealing anything about her true identity, she told Simone what had happened.

Over the rim of her glass, Simone looked at Destiny. "Are you okay?"

She nodded. "I'm fine."

"I can't believe it. I drive down to Norfolk for the weekend, and I miss all the excitement."

Grabbing a bag of potato chips from the cabinet, Destiny tore it open and took a seat at the table. "I wouldn't call it excitement."

Simone gave her a look of disbelief. "Are you kidding? Duane rescued you just like in one of those romance novels. You should feel special."

Taking another sip, Destiny gave an audible sigh. "We're not speaking right now."

"How come?"

"We had a little disagreement." While chewing a chip, she stared out in front of her and wondered if maybe she might have been a little extreme.

"Anything I can help you with?" Simone asked after a comfortable silence.

Destiny returned her gaze to her new friend and shook her head. "No. I'll be fine."

While munching on potato chips, Simone told her about her weekend visiting her boyfriend, who was a sergeant in the army.

"I'm hoping he will ask me to marry him soon."

They had been dating for less than a year, yet Simone was confident she had met the man of her dreams. Based on her own personal experience, Destiny wasn't so sure.

Leaning across the table, she offered Simone advice. "Don't rush it. You'd be surprised how long it takes to truly know someone."

"What took you so long?" Duane barked as he swung open the front door.

Garrett and Reyn stepped into the house, ignor-

ing their brother's deep frown. They knew him well
enough to know his urgent call was far from urgent.

Reyn headed to the kitchen, chuckling. "You
just called me less than an hour ago."

"You got any beer in this joint?" Garrett asked.
Not waiting for an answer, he reached in the refrigerator and removed three cans.

Duane followed them into the kitchen and took
a seat at the island.

Reyn took a can from Garrett's proffered hand.
"Thanks," he said as he popped the top. "Ahhh,
ain't nothing better than a cold beer on a scorching hot day."

Duane took the other can of beer, then nodded.
Already the mercury had hit the low nineties. "Did
the two of you morons come over to drink my imported beer or to help me out?" he asked.

Reyn took a thirsty drink, swallowed, then wiped
his mouth with the back of his hand. "Don't get
your underwear in a bind. Why else would I give up
an afternoon at the shooting range?"

"What's going on around here, anyway?" Garrett
asked. "I've never seen so many nosy people in
my life. I swear every window on this block had
some old lady peering out the corner at me as I
pulled up."

Despite his frustration, Duane had to chuckle at
his brother's keen observation. After yesterday's
fiasco, every person on the street was going to be
watched like a hawk. He shrugged. "They take the
neighborhood watch program pretty seriously
around here."

Reyn's brow arched. "Obviously."

"So tell me what's going on?" Garrett asked.

Using his arms, he raised himself up onto the counter.

Duane gave his youngest brother a hard look. "Don't you know what a chair is used for?"

"Yep, but I prefer the counter. Now tell me, what's the emergency? Otherwise, I am leaving."

Seeing his temper flare, Reyn stepped forward just as Duane leaned toward the island, and he punched Duane playfully in the shoulder. "Hey, come on. Don't let him get you all bent out of shape."

Duane placed his untouched beer on the island, then raked a hand across his head. Even at twenty-eight, Garrett still had a way of getting under his skin. He used to think it was Garrett's way of getting attention from his big brother. Lately, he wasn't sure what the reason was.

Duane paced across the room. "Yesterday all hell hit the fan."

"What do you mean?" Garrett asked, mildly curious.

Taking a deep breath, Duane explained to them what had transpired the previous evening. "And I don't want to hear, 'I told you so.'"

Reyn shook his head. "All right. I won't say it, but I warned you that snooping around in her personal life would backfire on you."

Duane gave an impatient scowl and reached for his beer and popped the top. After taking a swallow, he related everything that had happened, starting with Destiny's strange behavior and ending with her having to testify in court.

"So what're you going to do now that you've gotten yourself put out of her house?" Reyn asked when Duane was finished.

"I was hoping you could help me."

Garrett laughed. "How?"

"Go talk to her."

Garret shook his head. "Oh no, I'm not getting involved."

Duane released a short breath. "I need you to convince Destiny her life is still in danger."

Reyn flicked his brows. "I agree she isn't out of the woods yet. Even if they did catch that guy, there is no telling who else is out there lurking in the corners."

"So will you help me?"

Garrett shrugged, then took another swallow. "Why can't you just walk up to her door and show her who's boss."

Duane quirked a brow. His brother had a lot to learn about women. "It's not that easy. Besides, her friend Simone is over there, and you know how women are when they band together."

Garrett dropped to the floor and sat his beer on the counter. "Come on. Let me show you how it's done."

Duane and Reyn looked at each other, then followed him out the front door.

Destiny's fingers tightened around the doorknob after she peered through the peephole.

Duane! What was he up to? Not only had he come to her house after she had instructed him not to, but he had brought Garrett and Reyn along. Her pulse began racing from excitement and anger.

She took a deep breath, then turned the knob. She looked past Duane and smiled at the other two. "Hey, fellas."

"Hey, Destiny." Garrett leaned forward and

pecked her on the cheek. He stood back grinning with his hands in his pockets.

Reyn looked like he had been roped into doing something he didn't want to do. He shifted uncomfortably from one foot to the other. "Hi, Destiny."

She smiled at him; then her gaze shifted to Duane. She dropped her gaze when she saw the concerned look on his face. He hadn't shaved and had a sexy five o'clock shadow. She wondered how it would feel against her skin. His legs were parted, and his stance was relaxed. She tried not to notice that he was wearing a new pair of black jeans that made his thighs look strong and powerful. He was so sexy, her body responded. She pressed her hand to her stomach, nerves tap-dancing in double time. She could barely manage to stay mad. She cleared her throat and frowned.

"What can I do for you boys?"

Before Duane could answer, Garrett stepped forward. "Can we come in and talk?"

Destiny folded her arms beneath her breasts. "Talk about what?"

"What's going on out here?" Simone asked as she stuck her head out the door.

Duane heard the quick intake of someone's breath. He wasn't sure if it was Garrett or Reyn. Looking from one to the other, he read the attraction. Tension hummed between them that wasn't easy to ignore.

Reyn cleared his throat. "Destiny, aren't you going to introduce us to your friend?"

"Oh, I'm sorry. Reyn, Garrett, meet Simone Taylor."

Garrett stepped forward and grasped her hand. "The pleasure is all mine."

"The same here," Reyn added.

Duane gave both his brothers a hard look and immediately regretted bringing them. He should have known the minute they saw the beautiful young woman that the fight for attention would begin. The vibe generating from Simone was that she wasn't impressed by either of them.

While they each bid for Simone's favor, he focused his attention on Destiny. "We need to talk," he said softly.

"We don't have anything to talk about."

"Yes, we do."

"While the two of you try to hash out your differences, I'm going home." Simone walked out the door.

"How about I walk you home?" Garrett offered.

"I'll join you," said Reyn.

Garrett took one arm, while Reyn took the other. Clearly, both were out to charm. Watching the two of them glare at one another, Destiny couldn't resist a laugh.

"Hopefully, she'll pick one and put them out of their misery."

She and Duane shared in a laugh before she realized what she was doing and stopped.

For a moment, Duane had completely forgotten what he wanted to discuss with her. His concentration had gone to her mouth and his desire to taste her again. Now that he had her alone, he wasn't sure what he wanted to say. He only knew he'd missed her.

Destiny took several deep breaths to calm her

racing heart. "Duane, there really isn't anything else for us to discuss."

"That's where you're wrong." He moved until he was standing directly in front of her. Then he pulled her into his arms and swooped down and captured her lips.

He released her, then whispered, "I love you." He took her hand and led a stunned Destiny into the living room, where he lowered her onto his lap.

"Duane, don't," she finally said.

"Destiny, I'm not going to apologize for my actions."

Her body throbbed out of control.

"You should have been honest with me." Pulling out of his grasp, she stepped away and stood on shaky legs.

He was right. She should have.

"You're right," she finally said. "I should have been honest, but you should have done the same."

"I'm sorry." He stepped forward. "Can you forgive me? My bed misses you, and so do I."

Duane pulled her into his arms. She inhaled his scent and felt the comfort of his embrace. Tilting her head back, she stared up into his beautiful eyes and fought her emotions and failed miserably.

A smile curved her lips. She loved him; that much she knew. She had no idea what was going to happen to their relationship, yet at that moment none of that even mattered.

Duane gazed down at her. The smile on her face made it safe to assume her hostility had passed.

"I love you," he heard her say.

He tightened his grip at her waist and lifted her

off the floor until they were eye to eye. "Care to repeat that?"

She snaked her around him and whispered against his nose, "You heard me, silly. I said I love you."

He smiled down at her, desire flickering in his gaze like a lantern. "I thought that's what you said."

His mouth swooped down and captured hers, stealing her breath away in one long, searing kiss.

"It looks like the lovebirds have made up," Garrett commented as he came through the door, followed by Reyn, who groaned when he found the two locked in an embrace.

"Our work is done. I'm going home."

Destiny pulled back and smiled. "You're welcome to stay. I'm making catfish nuggets and baked macaroni and cheese."

"Did you say fish?" Garrett's eyes grew large.

"A brother loves him some homemade macaroni," Reyn said as he flopped down in a chair.

Duane shook his head. "You should have never mentioned food around these two. Now they'll never go home."

Garrett took a seat on the couch. "Oh, we'll leave, but not until after dinner." He reached for the remote and clicked on the television.

"Have a seat. Make yourselves at home," Duane murmured with sarcasm.

"Don't mind if we do." Reyn glanced at Destiny and winked.

Smiling, she slipped from Duane's arms and headed toward the kitchen, then paused and turned around. "How about I invite Simone over for dinner?"

"No!" Reyn and Garrett cried in unison.

Destiny raised her palms. "Okay, forget I asked."

Garrett scowled as he flicked through the channels, trying to find a sports channel. "There's something strange about that girl."

Reyn snorted. "He's just mad because he struck out."

Garrett rolled his eyes. "What about you?"

Reyn shrugged. "That girl is not my type."

Duane turned to Destiny, chuckling as he rose, then took her hand and led her into the kitchen. "See what I have to deal with."

She giggled happily. Nothing felt better than to be surrounded by family.

While preparing dinner, Destiny let Champion back in the house. Unlike Simone, Champion liked the brothers, and they instantly grew attached to her furry friend.

Dinner was fabulous. The brothers complimented her cooking skills and made sure there were no leftovers. After dinner they played several rounds of UNO before Reyn and Garrett decided to call it a night.

Way past midnight, Duane fulfilled her every wish by making love to her over and over again until she lay exhausted. She pleaded for him to stop and give her a chance to regain her energy. Only he didn't stop. He kept going and going. Afterwards, they talked about the case. Before the sun rose, he made love to her again, and then finally together, they drifted off to sleep.

Chapter 22

Propping an elbow on his desk, with his chin resting in the palm of his hand, Reyn stared at his computer monitor, weighing his suspicions. Something wasn't right with Simone. It wasn't because he wasn't used to being rejected, although that played a major part in his decision to investigate the young woman.

His eyes narrowed as he traveled to the recesses of his mind. In his thirty-six years, he had never once been rejected by a woman. Never. In fact, his experience was the complete opposite. Women had a tendency to latch on. Most of them refused to take no as an answer. He shook his head. One would have thought his hand had been dipped in gold the way women were drawn to him. At one time he had thought the attention was quite flattering.

In high school, he had been so full of himself. College was even worse. He had been known as a love 'em and leave 'em kind of guy.

With a sigh, Reyn clicked his mouse and accessed his e-mails. After earning a degree in criminal justice, he had done eight years in the army.

During his tour with the military, he had watched how the marriages or relationships of several members of his squad had fallen apart due to the frequent deployments overseas. Staring out the window, he remembered one soldier in particular.

After a two-year stint in Panama, Tony Morrow, a good friend of his, had returned home to find that his wife had given birth to someone else's son. He had loved her with all his heart, and all he had talked about those past two years was getting home to his wife. The discovery had been more than he could handle. Only forty-eight hours after their return, he was found dead in his car, with a self-inflicted bullet wound to the head.

Reyn raked a hand across his head in frustration. It had taken him months to get over the anger and resentment he had felt. Since then he had vowed to never let that happen to him. He was determined to stay clear of love and the pain it caused.

Unlike his big brother.

He chuckled inwardly as he clicked open his e-mail and began to compose a letter. Duane was destined to lose their bet. He had been bitten by the love bug and was sprung. The fund they had begun five years ago was more than enough to cover a large wedding and a fabulous honeymoon vacation. He was happy for his brother and was going to do everything in his power to make sure nothing happened to him or Destiny.

Pressing his lips firmly together, he thought about the petite beauty. As long as she was a part of Duane's life, then it was his responsibility to help insure her safety. Destiny was now under the watchful eye and protection of Reyn Urban. Which was why Reyn had been suspicious of Simone.

Not even the sight of her tight-fitting jeans could quell the uneasiness he felt when Simone had come to the door. As soon as he met her piercing amber eyes, he couldn't explain it, but a bitter chill had swept over him. He had stared at her because he was intrigued. He had watched her with distrust. The emotion was similar to what he felt when he was interrogating a suspect. One look in the eyes and he always knew when they were guilty.

What could Simone be hiding?

During the brief walk to her house, she had told him and Garrett that she was a dentistry major at Delaware State University. Garrett was so caught up in her charm that he would have believed anything she said. Reyn, on the other hand, knew the historically black university didn't have a dentistry program. Destiny wasn't from the area, so she wouldn't have known that Simone was lying. But Reyn was and because of Simone's lie, his radar had gone off and his suspicions had been aroused.

With slow careful strokes, he typed a brief note to his friend and former squad leader at the FBI. He needed information, and he needed it yesterday. With one final stroke, he clicked SEND with his mouse, then pushed his chair away from the screen. Simone was lying, and it was his responsibility to find out why.

Later that morning, Destiny opened the front door and found Simone standing on the porch, smiling. "I saw Duane leaving your house. I guess that means the two of you made up?"

Destiny dropped her eyes and blushed. "I guess you can say that."

The two laughed as she stepped into the house.

Champion raced to the door and barked.

"Champ, behave!" Destiny ordered.

Simone stepped back outside the door. "Don't worry about it. I forgot to bring my snacks," she joked. "How about hanging out with me at the mall today? I feel like shopping for shoes."

Spending a day shopping was just what Destiny needed. "Sounds like fun."

Simone's eyes flashed. "Good. I'll be back to scoop you up at one."

Destiny shut the door, and Champion calmed down and trotted into the living room and lay down. "What's gotten into you?" Destiny yelled after him. Her brow bunched in confusion. Champion never barked at anyone but Simone. Why was that?

Shrugging her shoulders, she moved into the dining room and grabbed a bottle of furniture polish she had left there before the doorbell rang. She sprayed polish across the antique cherry dinette table and wiped it off with a rag.

At the back of her mind, Destiny knew she should still play it safe, just in case. Even though the FBI had Lucas and Hector in custody, and had a watchful eye on the others, she didn't want to take too many chances. However, there was no guarantee that hiding would keep her safe. *Maybe it is safer to stay out in the open.* Certainly it would be difficult for someone to kidnap her while she shopped for shoes. Her eyes flickered with uncertainty before she tossed her shoulders back. She waited until Duane returned from across the street and asked him what he thought.

Lines of worry etched across his forehead. "Sweetheart, I'm not letting you out of my sight."

"I'll be fine," she assured him.

He gently cupped her chin. "I'm not taking any chances."

She nibbled on her lower lip, a nervous habit at odds with her bright smile. "Everything is going to be okay. Hector's gone. Lucas is locked up."

Never before had he ever felt so torn. He didn't want her out of his sight, even though he knew he was being overly protective and selfish. "I guess you're right. I can't help it if I feel responsible for you."

She stroked his cheek. "I love you when you do."

"And I love you."

All at once he tasted her mouth in one searing kiss. Savoring the taste, he didn't want it to end. He was aching to prolong the moment and carry her off to bed, where she was safe. When Destiny pushed lightly on his chest, he kissed her one last time, then reluctantly he released her.

"I guess since you have plans for the afternoon, I'm going to go and give Percy a hand. We're putting an addition on a house. Call me on my cell phone if you need me."

She nodded and watched him turn and leave.

"Sorry I had you come all the way over here."

"No trouble at all," Duane said reassuringly to the gray-haired old lady. What Mrs. Douglas thought was a power outage was merely a circuit breaker that had popped. It required only a flick of the switch. She had called him only minutes after he had left Destiny's house.

"How about I give you some cookies for your trouble?"

He could see she wanted to do something for him. "Sure, I would love some." Mrs. Douglas looked pleased as she turned and headed up the stairs to the kitchen.

Duane locked his toolbox and carried it up the stairs and into the kitchen, where Mrs. Douglas had put at least a dozen homemade cookies into a brown sack. When she handed it to him, he dipped his nose inside and inhaled.

"Yum, peanut butter is my favorite."

She clapped her hands together gleefully. "Well, I'm glad I could be of service."

Realizing she was waiting for him to sample her hard work, he reached inside and removed a cookie and bit into it.

"Mmmm, delicious."

She smiled, looking satisfied.

Several seconds later, he waved good-bye as he pulled out of the driveway and turned up the street.

"Ready?" Simone said when Destiny swung open the front door.

"Yep, let me grab my purse."

"Actually, I need to use your bathroom."

"Okay. Let me put Champ in the basement so you can come in."

Grabbing the growling dog by his collar, she dragged him into the kitchen and put him in the basement and shut the door. His behavior was puzzling, and she would have to remember to mention it to Duane.

Stepping back into the hall, she found Simone holding a gun in her hand.

"Simone, wh-what are you doing?" Destiny slowly raised her hands, keeping her elbows close to her sides.

"Sorry, Destiny, but there's a hit out on you for a half of a million dollars, and there's no way I could pass it up."

"How did you know?"

Simone looked pleased by her question. "My brother worked for Mr. Blake. I eavesdropped on one of their conversations. It didn't take a rocket scientist to figure out where you were hiding. Upon reading your grandmother's obituary, I discovered she had a brother in Delaware. It wasn't until I got here that I found that he was dead and you were living in his house. Finding an apartment on the same street was just pure luck."

Destiny had forgotten that that bit of information was in the obituary that she had had printed.

"So now what happens?" she asked.

Simone shrugged. "Now I turn you over and collect my money."

"You're not going to kill me?"

"Actually, I've grown quite fond of you. But don't think I won't if I have to." Her eyes narrowed hatefully as she pointed the gun at Destiny's chest. "The reward is worth twice as much if I bring you in alive rather than dead." Simone gave a haunting laugh. "My brother says you are to be hidden until after the trial, and since you won't be able to testify, Mr. Blake will be released." All laughter was stripped from her voice when she added, "He wants to kill you himself."

Destiny's eyes darted around the room, looking for some way to distract Simone.

"Keep your hands where I can see them, because I will not hesitate to shoot you if you even breathe too hard in my direction. Now sit! You're making me nervous."

Destiny slowly lowered herself onto the couch,

never taking her eyes off Simone. "Simone, I can pay you to just walk away," she replied calmly.

Her eyes sparkled with interest. "How much?"

She cleared her throat and tried again. "N-not nearly as much as Mr. Blake is willing to pay you, but I assure you that if you let me go, I won't have you arrested."

Simone tossed her head back and chuckled. "What do you take me for, some kind of moron? As soon as I walk out of that door, you'll be on the phone to the police."

"I swear that I won't," she said in an almost pleading voice.

"Sorry, girlie, I'll just take my chances. Now sit before I get mad."

Destiny did as she said and took a seat on the couch while Simone made a call.

As Duane turned onto the main street, he thought about the days ahead. Destiny, or Desiree—he just couldn't get used to using that name—whoever she was, would be leaving soon and returning home. What did that mean for them? So far she hadn't mentioned anything about what would happen after the trial. He had to admit that the simple life of Delaware was probably a bit slow for a big city girl. Destiny probably spent a great deal of time traveling, promoting her books.

So if she returned to the life she was accustomed to, then what would happen to them? He knew nothing would ever be the same between them, but that didn't necessarily mean that it was all bad. In fact, their relationship had been going quite well before the attempt on her life. Since then, everything had been strange. He didn't want her to leave, but how could he convince her to give up the fast life and live a simple life with him in the First State? She would probably break his heart or let him down gently. But his heart couldn't take another heartbreak. Besides, he loved her too much to just allow her to walk away. If he had to fight to keep her in his life, then that was what he was going to do.

Duane's cell phone rang. He reached down and removed it from his waist. Glancing down at the caller ID, he recognized Reyn's cell phone number. "Hey bro, what's up?"

"I just found out something I need to let you know. I ran a search on Simone."

Duane chuckled loudly into the receiver. "Do you always run a background check on a woman before you date her?"

"Yeah, I do. And be glad that I did. That Simone girl is related to one of Lucas Blake's hit men."

"What! Which one?"

"The one Destiny clocked in the head last week."

Several seconds later, Duane dropped the phone. He then pushed the pedal to the limit as he took the next exit and headed down Route 13. He tried calling Destiny but got no answer. He raced up the highway. It was all he could do to keep his fears under control. He was angry at himself for leaving her for even a few minutes. But worse than his anger was his feeling of helplessness. *Please God. Please let her be okay.*

He would never forgive himself if anything happened to her.

Reyn said he would meet him there, but he was all the way in Wilmington. By the time his brother arrived, it would be too late.

Don't think like that. Everything is going to be fine,
Duane told himself as he picked up his cell phone
and dialed Destiny's number again. When she
didn't answer, he began to panic again. Then he remembered she had gone to the mall and made a
quick U-turn at the corner.

"Hector's your brother?" Destiny asked only seconds after Simone ended the call.

Simone didn't appear to mind that she had
eavesdropped on her conversation. "We have the
same father, different mothers, but he's still my
brother," she said, sitting across from Destiny with
her legs crossed, waving the gun in the air. "He can't
wait to get his hands on you. Unfortunately, he was
extradited back to Missouri. Nevertheless, Pablo,
Greg, and John-John are on their way."

Destiny swallowed. She knew all of them firsthand
and never liked the way any of them looked at
her. There was no telling what they would do once
they got her alone.

"Why did you pretend to be my friend?" Destiny
hoped that if she kept Simone talking, maybe she
could think of a way to get away.

"My brother asked me to keep an eye on you."

Champion was barking uncontrollably and
scratching on the basement door.

Simone's temper flared. "You better shut that
mutt up or I'm going to shoot him."

Destiny panicked. "No, please! Let me give him
something to occupy his time."

"Hurry up!"

Destiny rose from the couch and walked into the
kitchen, with Simone right behind her. She

grabbed a large soup bone she was planning to use in a pot of pinto beans and carried it over to the basement door. She was grateful Champion's barking had suddenly ceased. Cracking the basement door open slightly, her eyes locked with Mannie's.

Startled, she looked over her shoulder at Simone, who was leaning against the kitchen counter, then back at Mannie. She mouthed the words "go get help."

"Champion, you've got to keep it down. Simone has a gun and won't hesitate to use it."

"Why are you talking to that dog like he's human?" Simone gave a harsh laugh. "Toss him that bone so we can go back in front."

Destiny mouthed the word "go," then tossed the bone down to Champion. Shutting the door, she turned and headed back into the living room. Now all she had to do was stall for time and wait for the cavalry to arrive.

After a quick sweep of the mall for either of their cars, Duane headed home. Once on their street he spotted both of their cars and sighed with relief. Everything was okay. He would get Destiny, and together the two of them would confront Simone and find out what she was up to. Her brother had probably assigned her to watch Destiny's every move.

He pulled in front of his house, then dashed across the street. He was about to knock on the door when he spotted Mannie running from behind the house.

"Mannie," he called, startling the boy.

Mannie's eyes grew wide as he signaled for Duane to follow him to the back of the house.

"Ms. Davis is in trouble. Some woman has a gun on her."

Duane's heart pounded. "How do you know?"

"I was in the basement."

"How did you . . . never mind." He ruffled his hair. "I'm glad you were there. Here, take my keys and go and call the police."

Mannie nodded, took the key ring, and raced across the street.

Duane made his way to the basement trap door, which was beneath a shed in the yard, grateful that Mannie had broken the lock again. Cautiously, he climbed down into the basement. The light was on, and the first thing he spotted was Champion in the corner chewing on a bone. The dog bounced over to Duane the moment he spotted him.

"Good boy." Duane rubbed his head, then slowly ascended the steps. At the top stair, he heard muffled voices coming from the front of the house. He cracked the door just barely and listened.

"My brother's flunkies should have been here by now."

"Simone, there's still time for you to walk away from this. I promise I won't press charges," he heard Destiny say.

Simone gave a haunting laugh. "Are you out of your mind? That's more money than I will ever see in my life. Now be quiet and go in the kitchen and make me something to drink."

Reyn parked his Navigator and climbed out only seconds after a black Lincoln Town Car pulled in front of Destiny's house. Two men climbed out.

Reyn came up behind them. "Looking for someone?"

Reyn caught the first fist sailing at him. Before the guy could react, he landed a punch to his chest, knocking the air from his lungs. The second man tried to reach for his gun, but Reyn, who was trained in martial arts, landed a roundhouse kick to his chin. He heard the man's neck snap as he fell to the ground.

Hearing a noise from behind, Reyn turned in time to find another man had gotten out of the Town Car and was coming up behind him, holding a knife. In one quick motion, Reyn grabbed his cell phone from his hip and slammed it into the side of the beefy guy's head, rendering him unconscious as he fell to the ground.

The first man had the nerve to come at him again. Before his attacker saw it coming, Reyn's fist connected solidly with his jaw. Staggering, he fell from the force of the blow.

Reyn shook his fist, easing the sting on his knuckles, and headed up the sidewalk. "My work is never done." He sighed dramatically. "It's always up to me to save the day."

Duane cracked the basement door open ever so slightly. Destiny stood near the sink, while Simone stood against the wall, holding a gun.

Duane contemplated his next move. He had to find a way to distract Simone long enough to get Destiny out of the range of her gun. Champion came up the stairs and began to growl just as an idea came to Duane.

He waited until Simone turned her back to sit in

a chair, and then he opened the basement door. Champion bounded through the kitchen and startled both women, giving Duane just enough time to come charging through the basement door directly toward the gun.

Mannie came running up the sidewalk just as Reyn reached the porch. "There's a lady in there with a gun," he said.

"Stay back," Reyn ordered. Just as he kicked in the door, a gun went off. He removed his gun from its holster, cautiously entered the house, and moved briskly into the hallway. Hearing screaming coming from the kitchen, he eased his way down the hall. Champion came trotting down the hall with his tail wagging. Reyn breathed a sigh of relief.

"Dee! You all right?" he called.

"Yeah, Reyn. We're fine."

He returned his gun to his side and moved into the kitchen, where Duane had Simone's arm twisted behind her back. Destiny was holding the gun.

"What are you doing here?" Simone spat.

"Sweetheart, you made such an impression, I was dying to see you again." Reyn chuckled at the frown on her face, then approached Destiny and draped an arm around her waist. "You okay?"

Destiny looked up at him, eyes flooded with unshed tears. "I am now." He dropped a kiss to her cheek. He then took the gun from her and put on the safety.

Laying the gun on the table, Reyn then approached his brother and shook his free hand. "Good job. I'll take over from here." In one quick motion, he swung Simone over his shoulder and carried her screaming and kicking outside just as the police pulled up.

Duane ran to Destiny and pulled her shaking body into his arms.

"Duane, I was so scared!"

"Everything is going to be fine. I'm not letting you out of my sight again."

She tilted her head and gave him a sad smile. "Good." He kissed her.

Mannie raced into the house. "Are you okay?"

Destiny held out her arms. "Yes, we are."

"I'm sorry for sneaking in your house again." Mannie looked prepared to be scolded.

"I'm glad you did. You probably saved my life." Tears streamed from her eyes. It was almost over. "Come on, you two, I think this moment deserves a group hug."

Chapter 23

Lucas Blake was sentenced to two life terms in prison. One of his employees turned in state evidence against him, and he was found guilty of killing Chief Cook and Officer Jackson, drug trafficking, and selling and distributing illegal weapons. At the trial Duane was by Destiny's side until the verdict was read. Then, when he thought everything was going to be okay, she told him she needed some time away from him and the media to think. Reluctantly, he had returned to Delaware alone.

Upon his return, he began the renovations at Murphy's Restaurant. The days were long, and he was grateful. He was too tired when he got home to do anything more than grab a shower and crawl into bed alone. It had been two weeks since the trial, and he hadn't heard from Destiny. However, her lawyer, Chuck, had called to assure him she was okay.

She had returned to her life as Desiree Davidson. Destiny was gone, and so was the woman he had loved.

Duane pulled into his driveway and went in the house, where Champion was waiting. When Destiny had left, he decided to keep Champion until her return.

On Saturday he had received a visit from the son of Champion's previous owner. Apparently Champion, aka Hunter, had belonged to his father, who had been to put into a nursing home due to his poor health. The son had been trying to find Champion a new home when the dog ran off. He was pleased to find that Champion had found a home on his own.

Duane fed the dog, then pulled off his shoes, grabbed a beer out the refrigerator, and took a seat. Champion lay on the floor before him and whined.

"I know, boy, I miss her, too."

Yesterday, Mannie had dropped by after school and had taken the dog for a walk. Champion seemed to forget about Destiny when he was around. Mannie's mom had completed the thirty-day treatment program and so far had been clean for two weeks. Mannie was finally back home with his mother. Duane had his fingers crossed that things would work out for them this time.

You're gonna lose her. He would give Destiny until Friday and if he didn't hear from her, he was going to go see her.

Desiree pulled her Mercedes into the driveway. She was finally home.

After the trial she needed some distance away from the media so she could think. She had booked herself on a fourteen-day cruise.

By day ten, in an instant of clarity, she realized how little meaning her life would have without Duane. After more than a week of waking up alone, she couldn't imagine never waking to the sight of his face each morning. She couldn't imagine carrying anyone else's child or spending her years growing old with anyone but him.

As soon as she got off the ship, she drove the sixteen-hour trip east to her uncle's house. A hint of panic touched her heart as she pushed her foot to the pedal. She needed to talk to Duane right away, to let him know that she loved him enough to share the rest of her life with him.

After driving the last mile, she found his truck in his driveway, and a wave of intense relief flooded her. *Please, Lord, don't let it be too late.*

Pulling her shoulders back, she climbed up the steps leading to his house and rang the bell.

The door opened, with the chain lock still firmly in place. "Can I help you?" he said.

She was caught off guard by his question. Was she already too late? A sudden spear of uncertainty shot through her.

"Duane," she began.

"Who's asking?"

Staring at his sober expression, she took a deep breath and said, "The woman that loves you."

"Do you have some ID?"

She spotted the corners of his lips twitch, and her heart flipped. He was teasing her! Relief nearly made her knees buckle.

"Yes, I do." She reached into her purse and pulled out her driver's license.

Duane glanced down at it, then back up at her. "A man can never be too careful."

She nodded knowingly. "Neither can a woman." Following a brief silence, she whispered, "I love you."

"How do I know this is real?" He appeared to have trouble getting the words out.

A tear rolled down her cheek, and she swiped at it with her right hand. "Because I have never felt this way about a man before. You are my life. Without you, my life has no meaning. I am empty inside. I don't want to wake up another morning without you beside me."

He stared into her eyes as he said, "I can't leave Delaware."

"I don't want you to. My place is here with you." He opened the door. Champion was sitting obediently on the floor. She stepped forward. He stopped her.

"Before I kiss you, I need you to answer one question."

She swallowed. "Okay."

"Will you marry me?" His deep voice vibrated with passion.

Tears welled in her eyes. She closed them, drew in a deep breath, and let it out slowly. Eyelids fluttering open, she finally said, "It depends on who you're asking. Destiny or Desiree?"

"I'm asking *you*. I fell in love with you. It doesn't matter what your name is."

She jumped into his arms, wrapping her arms around his neck. "Yes, baby, I'll marry you."

He kissed her with all the tenderness he was feeling, then swung her in his arms, carried her inside the house, and shut the door behind him.

"I missed you," he whispered against her lips.

"Show me how much," she murmured.

When they finally made it up to his bedroom, they demonstrated silently how much they missed each other. Their desires had been heightened by the long, unbearable separation. Much later they lay in bed, holding hands while discussing the future. When she finally fell asleep in his arms, Duane vowed they would never be apart again. She was his life. He had found the woman he would love for eternity.

It wasn't fate. It wasn't luck.

It was destiny.

Dear Readers and Friends,

I truly hope you enjoyed *Destiny in Disguise,* because this story was indeed a joy to write. Finding love is such a wonderful experience. Hopefully, you found Destiny Davis and Duane Urban to be a very passionate and loving couple. And for those of you who are wondering—yes, I plan to write Reyn and Garrett's stories.

Thanks so much for your encouraging words following the release of *Endless Enchantment.* Your feedback meant the world to me. I look forward to creating more compelling love stories in the years to come. When you have a few minutes, please visit my Web site, www.angiedaniels.com, or you can simply send me an e-mail at angie@angiedaniels.com.

Much love,

Angie Daniels

ABOUT THE AUTHOR

Angie Daniels is a chronic daydreamer who loves a page-turner. Already an avid reader by age seven, she knew early on that someday she wanted to create stories of love and adventure. During the fifth grade, she began her journey by writing comical short stories. As her talent evolved, she found herself writing full-length novels that offered her readers a full dose of romantic suspense. "I enjoy writing whodunits because they allow me to use my imagination to the fullest extent. When I combine suspense with a love story, it's like spreading icing on a cake."

Angie was born in Chicago, but after spending more than half her life in Missouri, she considers it her home. She holds a Master's degree in Human Resource Management. You can visit her Web site at www.angiedaniels.com.

BOOK YOUR PLACE ON OUR WEBSITE AND MAKE THE ARABESQUE ROMANCE CONNECTION!

We've created a customized website just for our very special Arabesque readers, where you can get the inside scoop on everything that's going on with Arabesque romance novels.

When you come online, you'll have the exciting opportunity to:

- View covers of upcoming books

- Learn about our future publishing schedule (listed by publication month and author)

- Find out when your favorite authors will be visiting a city near you

- Search for and order backlist books

- Check out author bios and background information

- Send e-mail to your favorite authors

- Join us in weekly chats with authors, readers and other guests

- Get writing guidelines

- AND MUCH MORE!

Visit our website at
http://www.arabesquebooks.com